Praise for *I'm Sorry You Feel That Way*

'A deep dive into a dysfunctional family and its intergenerational trauma that somehow manages to be both desperately sad and extremely funny . . . Its exquisitely detailed examination of interpersonal relationships allows it to become furtively compassionate, generous even to the worst offenders and one of the richest explorations of family dysfunction I've read'
i News

'Toxic mothers, absent fathers, angry sisters and enraging brothers – this sharp, wise comedy explores difficult family dynamics, from all-too-relatable emotional patterns to the inexplicable agonies of mental illness; yet it's also one of the funniest novels you'll read this year'
Guardian

'You'll struggle to find a better opening sentence in fiction this year . . . I loved the deadpan one-liners . . . The dialogue is excellent and captures the way families try to support one another and end up being accidentally horrible instead . . . But even better than the witty observations are the pure comedy set pieces . . . But it's more than just a farce. Things happen, big dramatic things, and there's love and anguish and good people making terrible mistakes . . . It's a warm book and a touching one. And did I mention it's funny? Just read it. You'll see'
The Times

'Perceptive, compelling and dryly funny, this unmissable story of a dysfunctional family . . . is a masterful novel, Wait's piercing wit and laser-sharp insight showing how easily family dynamics can spiral out of control'
Daily Express

I'M SORRY YOU FEEL THAT WAY

Rebecca Wait

riverrun

First published in Great Britain in 2022 by riverrun
This paperback edition published in 2023 by

riverrun

An imprint of

Quercus Editions Limited
Carmelite House
50 Victoria Embankment
London EC4Y 0DZ

An Hachette UK company

A CIP catalogue record for this book is available
from the British Library

Paperback ISBN 978 1 52942 046 3
Ebook ISBN 978 1 52942 047 0

10 9 8 7 6 5 4 3 2

Typeset in Monotype Fournier by CC Book Production
Printed and bound in Great Britain by Clays Ltd, Elcograf S.p.A.

Papers used by Quercus are from well-managed forests and other responsible sources.

For Chris and Iris

2018

ON THE WHOLE, THEY enjoy a funeral. Michael, because it appeals to his sense of ceremony, Hanna because she likes the drama, and Alice because it brings people together. Their mother, because it gives her a sense of achievement.

Alice is early today, waiting at the entrance of the crematorium to greet people. It is her role in life to be early for things, just as it is Hanna's to be late (or else not there at all, or else there when she shouldn't be).

'It would be friendlier to wait outside,' her mother says.

'But it's raining.'

'This is a *funeral*, Alice,' her mother says, as if this requires people to be wet.

But since her mother has shown no sign of volunteering to wait in the rain with her, and has in fact now vanished, Alice stays where she is, loitering in the overheated entrance corridor that smells of disinfectant and damp wool and something else more cloying and elusive that Alice fervently hopes is not the scent of death.

She has helped her mother to organize the funeral, or at least that seems to be the party line. In fact, Alice has done most of it alone, quietly liaising with the funeral directors, finalizing the order of service with the celebrant (a slightly odd title in the circumstances, Alice thinks) and booking the nearby Working Men's Club for the wake. The refreshments have caused her the most worry, since she has very little idea who will be attending. She spent a Saturday a couple of weeks ago going through her aunt's papers in the old house, finding a few addresses here and there (some without accompanying names), to which she sent out notes about the funeral. There were some telephone numbers too, so Alice was able to leave a couple of voicemails, spoke to one very nice man who denied all knowledge of her aunt, and a less nice woman who shouted at her and slammed the phone down. A few of her aunt's neighbours have said they'll come, mostly elderly people who have lived on the street since long before Alice's grandparents died.

Her aunt's coffin is already in place at the front of the chapel. Alice's mother didn't want it being carried in ceremoniously in front of everyone. 'Such an unnecessary fuss,' she said. 'And what if they drop it?'

'They won't drop it,' Alice said.

'They may do. Your aunt was not a light woman.'

Alice, who had always tried to love her aunt, let this pass.

The first few cars are pulling into the car park now. Through the rain-streaked panel of the door, Alice watches people emerge, and feels an anxious pang on their behalf: her old problem with arrivals. She has had difficulty arriving her whole life. As a child, being taken to a friend's house to play (or worse still, for a party), or even to her grandparents' house, she would feel the prickling, restless build of anxiety as the car pulled up, then the horrible plummet in her stomach as the engine was turned off (Hanna, meanwhile, would be striding ahead down the path, never looking back). The occasions themselves would usually be fine, and sometimes even enjoyable. But the chasm that exists between not being at a social gathering and being at a social gathering has always seemed vast to Alice, and yet must somehow be traversed in a few seconds.

Alice can't see Hanna among the arrivals. She heaves open the thick wooden door to welcome in a pair of elderly women she recognizes as her aunt's neighbours, Mrs Linden and Mrs Jackson, the names coming back to her just in time. They exchange some remarks about the miserable weather, then Alice turns to greet the man who has come in after them. He is very thin, with a sparse comb-over, and is dressed in a light brown suede waistcoat, now speckled with darker spots of rain.

'I was an intimate friend of hers,' he says, shaking Alice's hand. Alice is slightly unsettled by the special emphasis he places on 'intimate'.

'That's lovely,' she says. 'Where did you meet?'

He glances round him, as if afraid of being overheard. 'Here and there,' he says.

This response does not seem to invite follow-up questions. 'Did you know each other for a long time?' Alice tries.

'Well. In a manner of speaking.'

Alice is starting to find this exchange rather challenging, so she is relieved when her attention is claimed by a large woman she doesn't recognize in a sparkly navy blazer, who comes through the door and presses her hand and says, 'Hello love!'

Alice says, 'Hello. Thanks so much for coming.'

'Oh, not at all. Good to see you again after all this time.'

This alarms Alice, since this new arrival doesn't look familiar to her. But the woman is staring at her expectantly and Alice doesn't want to hurt her feelings, so she says feebly, 'You too. Lovely to see you.'

'A sad day, this,' the woman says.

Alice agrees that it is. Mrs Linden and Mrs Jackson have moved on down the corridor now, but the intimate friend still hovers at Alice's elbow. Alice hopes he won't ask to be introduced. It strikes her suddenly that she doesn't know his name either.

She hazards to the woman, hoping for useful information, 'How was your journey?'

'It was easy, love,' the woman says. 'You know we only live round the corner.' One of the neighbours, Alice thinks triumphantly.

Then the woman smiles. 'Funny, you look just like him. God, but we'll miss him, won't we?'

Now it dawns on Alice that there has been some kind of mistake, but she can't think how best to address it.

'It's uncanny actually,' the woman says, peering at Alice more closely. 'It's like seeing him again, living in you. You have his eyes. And his nose – his famous nose! – and even his jawline.'

Alice, beginning to feel this comparison does not flatter her, says, 'Actually, I think—'

But the woman cuts her off with, 'Well, I must go and find Marjorie. She texted me saying she's saved me a seat, and you know what she's like.'

Alice is left alone with her aunt's friend in the waistcoat. She feels her humiliation has been compounded by being witnessed by him and tries to come up with a suitably casual, amused comment to carry the situation off, but before she can speak, the man says, 'She seems nice. If you don't mind, I'll go in and sit down now.'

Alice watches him go. She has been thrown into one of her spirals of self-recrimination and spends the next few minutes trying to retrace her conversational steps with the woman in the blazer to decide what she should have done differently. It seems likely that this will become one of those shame memories that haunt her in the middle of the night.

She becomes aware now of being too hot, of the sweat that is already gathering at her armpits, dampening the thick material of her dress. The dress itself was a mistake, a panic buy from a few days ago. It had looked so elegant on the website, but when Alice studied herself in the mirror this morning, she seemed to be wearing a dark sack, the kind she imagines she might wear if performing penance in biblical times. And the material, so voluminous overall, is somehow too tight at the armpits, absorbing Alice's sweat whilst also restricting the movement of her arms.

She is too distracted by this cumulation of small disasters to notice Hanna sidling up behind her.

'I came in through the other door,' Hanna says, when Alice turns and sees her. 'Did you know there's another chapel at the back? I almost ended up at the wrong funeral.' She lowers her voice. 'So . . . Where is she?'

Alice says, 'In the coffin at the front. They already brought her in.'

Hanna gives a sharp laugh. 'I meant our mother. Don't get my hopes up.'

'I don't know. We came together, but then I lost her.'

'How has she been today?'

'Quite cheerful.'

'God in heaven.'

Alice puts her hands in the pockets of her dress, curling her fingers around the clump of tissues she placed in each one before setting off this morning. She says, 'Was your journey OK?'

'Yes. You know. Long.'

They are both silent for a moment.

Hanna says, 'Did you know this is our ninth funeral? As a family.'

'Can't be.'

'It is. Look. Two sets of grandparents. Great Aunt May. Old Mrs Mulligan from across the road, who did not like us. Then Mr Mulligan the following year. Because we'd been such a success at Mrs Mulligan's.'

Alice says the last one, so Hanna doesn't have to. 'Dad.'

'So you see,' Hanna says. 'Quite an extensive list. People will start to ask questions.'

Then she spots their mother coming out of the loos.

'Catch you later,' she says, melting away down the corridor.

'See you,' Alice says.

It is their first conversation in four years.

MICHAEL IS THE LAST to arrive, coming through the main entrance with the air of an important man who has been unavoidably detained. Most people have taken their seats in the chapel by this point, but Alice has lingered by the main door a while longer, waiting for last-minute arrivals. In total, there are four people from her aunt's street, all elderly neighbours who had known Alice's grandparents and still remember her aunt as a child. In addition to the neighbours, there are four friends of Alice's aunt – one other man, apart from the intimate friend in the waist-coat, and two women (not including the woman in the blazer, who has presumably now found the correct chapel). None of them seem to know each other. Counting Alice herself, her mother, Michael and Hanna, this makes twelve mourners, and Alice can see she has ordered more sand-wiches than they can possibly eat. Far too much wine, too; she doesn't drink much herself, and found it impossible to estimate how much other people would get through. And she was so afraid of there not being enough.

'Hanna's here,' she says as Michael leans down to kiss her cheek. He looks smart in his dark suit. He's only thirty-six, but his hair is greying around the temples. It suits him, Alice thinks.

'Well.' Michael shrugs. 'She said she would be.' And Alice sees that he is unwilling to concede anything to their sister.

6

He appears to have come alone, though Alice knows better than to ask about this. Probably best his wife isn't with him; she's always seemed the kind of person who might throw herself wailing into the grave, whether or not the deceased was known to her. Though of course there is no grave today. Alice wonders if anyone has ever tried to throw themselves into the furnace at a cremation. She thinks it would be quite difficult to manage, involving some undignified crawling to get along the metal tunnel. Then she interrupts herself, since this train of thought feels both unkind towards her sister-in-law and unsuitable for a funeral.

'Eight people have come,' she tells Michael, so the silence won't go on longer. 'Apart from us. It's nice that they wanted to, isn't it?'

'I can't imagine why.'

'But I'm afraid I've bought too much wine.'

'How much did you get?'

'Twenty-four bottles,' Alice says.

'Jesus Christ, Alice. It's a funeral, not the Bacchanalia.'

'I know,' Alice says, chastened. She's long been aware that Michael thinks her frivolous, though she doesn't know what she's done to gain this reputation. If anything, other people find her too serious. She often worries she's a bit of a drag.

'Where's Mum?' Michael says.

'At the front. She seems all right. In good spirits.'

'I doubt she's in good spirits,' Michael says. 'It is a funeral, after all.'

'Of course,' Alice says. 'I meant, in the circumstances.' She adds, trying to sound sufficiently sombre, 'It'll be a great comfort to her to know you've arrived.'

Michael nods. 'I'd better go in.' He consults his watch. 'So we'll be starting in seven minutes. You won't come in late, will you?'

'I'll come in with you now,' Alice says.

7

'Good.' He looks at her a moment. 'Is that a new dress?'

'Yes,' Alice says defiantly.

But Michael only says, 'It's nice. I don't like this modern trend for not wearing black at funerals.'

Alice agrees with him, enjoying his approval, and smoothes down her sack dress.

Just then the woman in the navy blazer comes out of the toilet. She sees Alice and waves. 'Catch you in a bit, Jeanie,' she says.

'Alice,' Michael says sternly. 'Have you given yourself a *nickname*?'

AFTER THE SERVICE, THEY spill out into the weak, post-rain sunshine and Alice looks around for Hanna, who did not sit with them during the service, instead choosing a seat on her own at the back. She has not, so far as Alice can tell, spoken to their mother or Michael yet. And now Alice is worried – irrationally, perhaps – that Hanna will have vanished by the time the rest of them make it outside, slipping through their fingers once again. But the next moment she sees her sister, standing by herself a little way away from the clusters of people. Alice quickly wipes her face to get rid of any obvious sign of tears.

She touches Hanna's arm. Says diffidently, 'Hello.'

'Hi,' Hanna says, turning towards her and folding her arms. 'Service was nice, I thought.'

'Yes,' Alice says.

'I'm sure she would have liked it,' Hanna says. Then she catches herself. 'Actually, I have no idea what she would have liked.'

They are silent, thinking of their aunt.

Hanna says, 'Do you remember when she pulled a knife on you?'

'Yes,' Alice says. 'Quite vividly.'

'I was always jealous that happened to you, not me.'

Alice says, 'Did you drive, or would you like a lift? Mum and I are going on ahead to get everything ready.'

'Thanks, but I'll go with Michael.'

This saddens Alice. If there has been one reassuring constant in her life, it is the knowledge that Hanna at least finds her marginally preferable to Michael. But it's her own fault for ruining things.

She nods and watches Hanna go over to where Michael is standing, tapping furiously at the screen of his phone.

'You've turned up in *jeans*?' she hears Michael say.

And Hanna replies, 'Actually, contrary to appearances, I'm in a ceremonial black robe. Can I have a lift to the wake?'

Alice goes to find her mother.

IN THE CAR, GRIPPING the steering wheel tightly, her mother says, 'Of course your sister hasn't come over to speak to me. Of course that would be too much to ask.'

Alice looks at the suburbs sliding greyly past outside the window. She is thankful it is only a short drive to the Working Men's Club. The car feels small and airless, even though there are only the two of them in it. She says, 'But it's tricky at a funeral, isn't it? She probably feels awkward.' She tries to imagine Hanna feeling awkward. Can't.

'Pretends to be a stranger. Sits at the back and pretends not to know me.'

Alice can sense her mother working herself up. She says gently, 'She probably just needs some time.'

'*Time*? She's had time. But this is so like her.'

Was it like her? Alice isn't sure. It seems to her now that they are a

9

family who do not know each other well at all. They spent years and years living alongside one another in the same house and yet somehow managed never to have met. What they have instead are the stories they tell about each other.

At the club, Alice's mother goes to inspect the function room whilst Alice heads into the small kitchen where the caterer is setting up.

'Ah,' he says, greeting her like an old friend. They have spoken twice on the phone. 'You must be Alice.'

Alice smiles gratefully at him. 'Those look lovely,' she says, indicating the platters of sandwiches on the counter.

'They're just sandwiches, love. I've already set up the urns for tea and coffee next door.'

He is incongruously cheerful for a wake, and Alice appreciates this. His name on the website is James, but he asks her to call him Jimmy, which touches Alice, whilst also making her too shy to call him anything at all.

She busies herself going back and forth to the car to fetch the wine and orange juice whilst Jimmy carries the platters through to the function room, along with wine glasses, crockery and napkins.

Her mother comes into the kitchen. She eyes the boxes of wine Alice has placed on the counter. 'Why on earth have you bought so much alcohol?'

'I overestimated,' Alice says.

'Well, for goodness' sake don't put it all out in the next room.' She leaves.

Jimmy, who has returned in time to catch the end of this exchange, winks at Alice. 'You can't have too much alcohol,' he says. 'Lesson for life. Anything else you need?'

'No. Thank you,' Alice says. 'You've been so helpful.'

'All right. Well, good luck.'

He bustles out, leaving Alice feeling faintly bereft, as though she has lost her only ally.

BUT WHERE ARE HANNA and Michael?

The others have started to arrive, and Alice goes to the entrance to welcome people in, pointing them towards the function room, where her mother waits like a monarch in state. The neighbours arrive in pairs, and then the four friends of her aunt separately, at short intervals, with what seems to Alice a slight furtiveness. But there is no sign of Hanna or Michael, and Alice starts to feel anxious. She lingers in the doorway a few moments longer, and then returns to the function room.

The guests have now formed small clumps. The intimate friend in the waistcoat is talking to another friend of Alice's aunt, a woman in red lipstick who introduced herself as Nicky. The elderly neighbours are in one group, Alice's mother among them. There's no sign of the second male friend of her aunt, whose name is Harry or Henry (Alice sent out notes to one of each and although he did introduce himself, she can't now remember which he was), but the other female friend is standing on her own in the corner with a glass of white wine, so Alice goes up to talk to her.

She didn't give her name when shaking hands with Alice at the crematorium, and Alice didn't manage to ask. She looks around Alice's mother's age, early sixties perhaps. She has quite a hard face, Alice thinks. But then, people can't help their faces.

'How are you getting on?' she says to the woman.

'Getting on with what?' the woman says, rather impatiently it seems to Alice.

'With the funeral,' Alice says, feeling foolish.

'I've seen worse.'

There is a silence in which the woman sips her wine and Alice wishes, uncharacteristically, that she had a drink of her own.

'Where did you meet my aunt?' she tries.

'A life-drawing class.'

'Really?' Alice says. 'That's so interesting. I didn't know she took art classes.'

'She was the model.'

'Oh!'

'You're not going to be prudish about it, are you?' the woman says.

'No, of course not.'

'It's a good way to earn some extra cash.'

'I'm sure it is.'

'It's not like it's sex work, is it?'

'No!' Alice says. 'Of course not.' Then she adds, not wanting to sound prudish about that either, 'Not that there's anything wrong with sex work!'

A longer silence follows this pronouncement. Alice is not sure how they have got here in the space of a minute.

'You have kids?' the woman says abruptly.

Alice shakes her head. 'No.'

'Married?'

'No.'

'How old are you?'

'Thirty-two,' Alice says, feeling interrogated.

'Thirty-two? My God, what I wouldn't give to be thirty-two again.' She looks at Alice. 'Well. You enjoy it while you can.'

She sounds melancholy now, and Alice wants to tell her she isn't one of those people who can't ever imagine being old, who thinks it will never happen to them. Alice can imagine it very well. Just as the child Alice lives inside her, anxious and rather forlorn, so too does the elderly Alice, pushing her way a little closer to the surface each day. In any case, it is not as though she is deriving much benefit from her youth. She wonders if it would reassure the woman to know this.

'Still, don't make the mistake of putting it all off for too long,' her companion says. 'Your generation, you think you can have it all, but one day you wake up and find you're old, and it's already too late.'

Alice nods. Her anxiety about Hanna is growing, and now she makes another covert survey of the room.

'Boring you, am I?' the woman says.

'No,' Alice says, shocked at her confrontational tone. 'No, I'm just looking for my sister. She was meant to be here, but she doesn't seem to have arrived.'

'Done a runner, eh?' the woman says, seeming to enjoy this idea.

'I hope not,' Alice says. A new thought occurs to her: What if Hanna and Michael have been in an accident?

A burst of raucous laughter from nearby, and Alice and the woman reflexively glance round: it is the waistcoat man, who seems to be getting on very well with the woman called Nicky. He is topping up their glasses, Alice sees, with a bottle he's taken from the trestle table.

'Flirting at a funeral,' Alice's companion says. 'That's just pathetic.'

Alice spots the missing second man, Harry-or-Henry, returning from the toilets and intercepts him rather desperately.

'Have you two met?' she says. 'I believe you were both friends of my aunt.'

'Lydia,' Alice's companion says, not putting out her hand.

'Hugh,' he says.

He is in his late sixties, and has a gentle, timid manner. Alice feels guilty as she leaves them alone together. She isn't sure he'll be any match for Lydia. However, she can't worry about this for long, because at last she spots Michael, across the room talking to her mother. Hanna is not with them.

Alice approaches, but before she can ask if they have seen Hanna, Michael says, 'Alice, did you know the meat and vegetarian sandwiches are on the same platter?'

'Oh dear,' Alice says. 'Well, as long as people look first at what they're eating, I think they'll be all right.'

'Besides which, didn't you know that when you put egg sandwiches right next to all the other ones, everything ends up tasting of egg?'

'But you like egg sandwiches,' Alice says. 'You're eating one right now.'

'That's not the point. I also like ham sandwiches, and I like my ham sandwiches to taste of ham, not egg.'

'Well, maybe I could move the egg sandwiches on to a separate plate.'

'It's too late now.'

'Where's Hanna?'

'*I* don't know,' he says irritably. 'Am I my sister's keeper?'

'She did come in the car with you, didn't she?' Alice says anxiously.

'Oh. Yes, she did. But she slipped away to "clear her head" when we arrived and I haven't seen her since.'

The dry emphasis he puts on 'clear her head' makes it sound like he thinks Hanna is up to something nefarious.

'I'm fine, by the way,' her mother says. 'Thank you for asking.'

'Sorry, Mum,' Alice says. 'I'm just distracted. Are you all right?'

'So-so. It's been a difficult day. The last thing we need now is Hanna attention-seeking.'

'She isn't,' Alice says. In fact, Hanna seems to be doing the opposite. She has effaced herself so far as to have disappeared entirely.

More uproarious laughter from the waistcoat man, and when Alice looks around she sees that he is coming towards them, followed by Nicky.

'Beautiful ceremony,' he says as he joins their group, raising his glass as if in a toast.

'Yes, you really gave her a good send-off,' Nicky says. She has lipstick on her front tooth, Alice notices. Both of them seem a little the worse for wear.

She glances over at the trestle table and sees to her alarm that of the eight bottles of wine she laid out originally, six are now empty. She assumes this can't be solely down to the man and woman in front of her, and is relieved to see, after a quick look around the room, that a few other people are holding wine glasses too.

Alice's mother says, to no one in particular, 'The sandwiches are a little dry, I'm afraid.'

'Oh *no*,' the waistcoat man says. 'No, not at all. They're *delicious*. Really exceptional.'

'I hope the caterer didn't leave them sitting out too long,' her mother says. 'He did seem rather casual.'

'I thought he was very professional,' Alice says.

'Oh Alice, you always think everyone's professional.'

Alice says, 'I must just go to the kitchen to get some more drinks.' What she really means is that she must go and look for Hanna.

And in the kitchen, there Hanna is at last, sitting on the counter, swinging her legs and drinking a glass of wine.

'Hello!' Alice says, a little more enthusiastically than she intends.

'I needed a drink after the drive here,' Hanna says. 'Michael has not improved with age.'

'He has been annoying today,' Alice says disloyally. But the brief smile Hanna gives her makes the betrayal worthwhile. She goes to the corner to pick up a box of wine. She is wondering if there might be a chance for them to meet up in London before Hanna leaves again, if Hanna will agree to coffee or a drink, to see if they can finally put things right between them. On her worst days, she is terrified Hanna will never forgive her, that she will have to get through her whole life without her.

Aiming for a casual tone, she says, 'So how long are you staying?'

'What do you mean?' Hanna says.

'When are you flying back?'

Not looking at Alice, Hanna says, 'I'm not.' When Alice doesn't answer, she adds, 'You didn't think I came back just for this?'

Alice shakes her head, but this is exactly what she'd thought.

Hanna laughs. 'I haven't travelled over six thousand miles just for the funeral of a woman I barely knew. Come on, Alice. That's the sort of thing *you* would do.'

Perhaps this is true, but Alice isn't sure: she can't imagine how she would ever have ended up six thousand miles away in the first place.

She says, because she still does not dare believe it, 'You're home? For good?'

'I'm back in England,' Hanna corrects her gently. 'For now.'

'What about your job?'

'I'll be working for the Foreign Office in London.'

'That's fantastic,' Alice says. 'Really great news. Where will you be living?'

'Not sure yet. I need to find a place—'

'You could stay with me if you like,' Alice says. 'My flatmates won't mind. You could sleep on the sofa. Or you could have my bed and I could sleep on the sofa. I'm in Clapham, remember? So very well connected. You could get the Northern Line to Embankment or Waterloo and then walk.'

'Thanks,' Hanna says shortly. 'But I'll be fine.'

Alice is silent. She has gone too far, too soon, and she knows it.

Hanna springs gracefully down from the counter without spilling her wine. 'I suppose I'd better go and speak to Mum. Can't put it off forever.'

'She's a bit . . . today.'

'She's always a bit. I'll have to brave it.'

'Your funeral,' Alice says drolly.

She waits a few moments after Hanna has gone, feeling the need to gather herself. Then she picks up the box of wine and carries it through to the function room, where she lays out new bottles on the trestle table and packs the empty ones into the box in their place. Hanna has joined the group that includes her mother, Nicky and the man in the waistcoat. As Alice watches, old Mrs Linden goes up to join them. Sensible of Hanna to greet her mother in this setting, Alice thinks. Witnesses.

'Steady on,' Michael says, suddenly appearing at her elbow. 'Do we really need another six bottles out? That man over there has certainly had enough.'

Alice follows the direction of Michael's gaze. The man in the waistcoat is saying something to Hanna while gesticulating with his wine glass. Hanna is nodding in response, and has the appearance of someone trying not to laugh. Watching her sister, Alice feels a great rush of joy.

'But it's nice that people feel able to relax,' she says to Michael. Hanna is home, she wants to say to him. Hanna is back at last. But the information is still too new and too precious to discuss.

'He's relaxing a little too much for my liking,' Michael says.

'Oh, he's all right.'

'He told me just now I look like a lawyer.'

'Well, you are a lawyer,' Alice says reasonably.

'He didn't say it in a *nice* way, Alice.'

Alice returns the box to the kitchen, where she collects a plate of chocolate biscuits to bring out. There are still a lot of sandwiches left, but she thinks people might be ready for something sweet now.

Then she does a circuit of the room, making sure the guests have got what they need, especially the elderly neighbours. The irritable woman called Lydia is still in conversation with the softly spoken Hugh.

Alice joins neighbours Mrs Jackson and Mr Blight, who are drinking cups of tea together and chatting gently.

'It was so good of you to come,' she tells them.

'It's our pleasure, dear,' Mrs Jackson says. 'We wouldn't have missed it. You know, she was a lovely girl once.'

Alice, remembering her aunt, finds this difficult to imagine. It makes her sad.

'A tragedy, what happened,' Mr Blight agrees. 'A tragedy for the whole family.'

Alice nods. She sees in her mind's eye her nervous, faded grandparents. Her mother's cold, set expression. Then she thinks of Hanna, whose life has been more difficult than it should have.

'Hanna looks just like her, you know,' Mrs Jackson says. 'All that lovely blonde hair. Katy was beautiful when she was young. Hanna's inherited that.'

'But it's funny,' Mr Blight says. 'You look remarkably different to Hanna, don't you? You're very dark. Even though you're twins.'

'Hanna is strikingly pretty, just like Katy was,' Mrs Jackson says.

'You're very different,' Mr Blight says again. 'Polar opposites, really.'

Alice reflects that this has not been a good day for her self-esteem. She says, 'Can I get you anything? More sandwiches, perhaps, or a biscuit?'

When she has brought them a couple of chocolate digestives each on a plate, she feels ready at last to join Hanna and her mother. Mrs Linden and the waistcoat man are still with them, although Nicky has moved on.

'I was just saying to your mother what a gift it must be to have her children with her on a day like today,' the waistcoat man says as Alice joins their small group. He seems almost tearful at the idea.

Alice smiles and nods, noting that her mother hasn't leapt in to agree how lovely it is. Briefly, Hanna catches her eye. Looks away, but not before Alice has seen her gleam of amusement. She feels a thrill, that they should for once be thinking the same thing.

'I don't have any children myself,' the man in the waistcoat says.

'No?' Mrs Linden says. 'What a shame.'

'It's not for everyone,' Alice's mother says.

'Never could, you see,' he says.

'Oh, I'm sorry,' Alice says. She is distracted, because Hanna has just given a murmured excuse and drifted away from the group. Where is she going?

'It wasn't to be,' the man in the waistcoat says.

'I suppose sometimes it isn't,' Alice says. Not wanting to be rude, she forces herself to give him her full attention. He seems drunker than earlier. He is starting to slur his words.

'Not for want of trying, sadly,' he says.

'Oh dear,' Alice says. 'I'm sorry.'

'A common story,' Mrs Linden says. 'A shame.'

The man sighs. 'The spirit was willing.'

A pause, as nobody can think of a reply to this.

'It was the flesh, you see,' he adds, leaning confidingly towards Alice, who he seems to have decided is his most sympathetic listener. 'The flesh was weak.'

Alice can feel her face getting hot. She doesn't dare look at her mother or Mrs Linden. 'I'm sorry about that,' she says.

He takes another swig of wine. 'Well, it is what it is. You do your best.'

'Yes, you do.'

There is a silence, and Alice feels relieved that he seems to have finished with the subject, but then he adds, 'Sometimes your best isn't good enough. That's the thing. When it comes down to it, you just can't rise to the occasion.'

Alice is frozen, unable to come up with a response.

'Alice,' her mother says sharply. 'Why don't you tell Mrs Linden about the sponsored walk you did with work?'

'We did this sponsored walk—' Alice begins.

'They don't understand how *nervous* they make you, that's the thing,' the man cuts across her. 'That look they get in their eyes.' He drains his wine glass and stares off into the distance. 'It's easy for them. All they have to do is lie there.'

'Would you like a cup of tea?' Alice bursts out.

He turns back to her, startled. After a short pause in which he seems to be mulling it over, he says, 'That would be nice. Thank you.' And docile as a child, he follows her over to the refreshments table and waits whilst she takes his wine glass gently off him, pours him a cup of tea instead, adds the milk and hands it to him on a saucer.

'There,' she says.

He takes a slow sip.

'Have a biscuit,' Alice says soothingly, offering him the plate.

Michael is standing at the other end of the refreshments table, morosely eating a ham sandwich. His eyes fix on the man in the waistcoat, and then he gives Alice a hard stare, which clearly conveys the message, *I told you so*.

'I'm going to get some air,' the man in the waistcoat says. With his cup of tea, he heads unsteadily towards the door.

'Why have you let him get so drunk?' Michael says, coming to stand beside her.

'I didn't let him. And anyway, he's not so bad.'

'He can hardly walk in a straight line,' Michael says, watching the man's progress across the room. He takes another bite of his sandwich, chews, then shakes his head. He says, more in sorrow than in anger, 'Tastes of egg.'

'It's so nice that Hanna's here,' Alice says. 'Isn't it? I didn't believe she was going to show up until I actually saw her.'

Michael shrugs. 'Hanna pleases herself. Always has.'

'And she's *back*,' Alice says, unable to contain herself any longer. 'Back to live here, she told me.'

'At least we'll be able to keep a proper eye on her now. Make sure she doesn't go off the rails.'

'She won't,' Alice says impatiently.

He doesn't look convinced.

'The important thing,' Alice says, 'is that we're all together again. At last.'

'Except for Dad,' Michael says succinctly. 'Who is dead.' He expresses this fact without any discernible sentiment, so that Alice, whose instinct is always to offer comfort, doesn't know how to reply.

They are interrupted by the *ding-ding* of a fork against a wine glass. The murmur of voices in the room ceases, and Alice looks around for the source of the noise. To her horror, she sees it is the man in the waistcoat, who has not made it outside after all, but has instead climbed on to a chair which he has moved into the middle of the room. He is once again holding a full wine glass.

'Time to say a few words,' he says, with the exaggerated enunciation of the extremely drunk. 'In honour of the deceased.'

'*What* is he doing?' Michael hisses to Alice.

'He's making a speech,' she whispers back.

'Yes, I can see that, Alice.'

Now he has everyone's attention, the man appears unsure how to continue. Alice sees a brief, panicked look pass across his face. She hopes that he will be able to fall back on a few comfortable clichés, that her aunt lived life to the full and would be sorely missed and so on, and then bring his remarks to a swift conclusion. Then at least everybody's embarrassment will be short-lived.

Unfortunately, in his stage fright the man settles upon a different approach. After a pause, he says, 'Friends, Romans, countrymen, lend me your ears.' This opening appears to renew his confidence. 'I come to bury Caesar, not to praise him,' he goes on, swaying slightly on the chair.

'Alice, you need to stop him,' Michael whispers.

'I don't know how,' Alice says. She risks a glance around the room. The other guests' expressions mostly show confusion, but her mother's face is drawn tight.

Michael, taking matters into his own hands, clears his throat. 'Thank you, but there's no call for speeches,' he says.

The waistcoat man holds up a hand to silence him. 'The evil that men do lives on,' he says.

'This really isn't the time or the place,' Michael says. Alice sees him glance over to their mother.

'The good is oft interrèd with their bones.'

'That's quite enough now.'

'So let it be with *Caesar*!' At this, the man makes a sweeping gesture with his arm, sloshing wine over Hugh, who unfortunately is standing within range.

'Right,' Michael says peremptorily, taking a step forward. 'That's enough. Please get down from that chair.'

Alice wonders for a moment if he is about to perform a citizen's arrest.

The waistcoat man turns on him. 'You, sir, are a very rude person. Hecklers will not be tolerated. Kindly desist, or I will have you thrown out on your ear.'

'Oh for goodness' sake,' Michael says, but he remains where he is, clearly unsure how to proceed. Alice can see he isn't prepared to forcibly tackle the man to the ground. She knows she should help Michael somehow – his cheeks have turned an angry red – but she is paralysed. None of the other guests seem willing to intervene either. Everyone is avoiding everybody else's eye, except for Lydia, who seems to have cheered up considerably and is watching the orator with interest. Alice's mother is staring out of the window as if this ridiculous scene is nothing to do with her. Her expression is one of quiet forbearance, but Alice knows her too well to trust this.

The waistcoat man woozily redirects his attention away from Michael and back to the rest of his audience. 'Where was I?' he says.

'So let it be with Caesar,' Lydia supplies.

'Ah, yes. *So let it be with Caesar.*'

He pauses and Alice dares to hope he has finished, but he is only drawing breath.

'The noble Brutus hath told you Caesar was *ambitious*!' He gestures extravagantly again, and this time the wine glass flies out of his hand, narrowly misses Hugh's head, and smashes on the floor. The waistcoat man pauses, seemingly surprised by this interruption.

Alice sees Hanna appear in the doorway from the kitchen. Her expression, as so often, is inscrutable, but when Alice catches her eye, she winks. Alice isn't sure how to interpret this.

The waistcoat man directs a slow, censorious shake of his head at Hugh, apparently believing it was he who launched the projectile, before continuing, 'If it were so, it were a grievous fault, and grievously hath Caesar answered it. Here, under leave of Brutus and the rest –' at this he leaves a meaningful pause, then goes on with heavy sarcasm – 'for Brutus is an *honourable man*.' Upon pronouncing these words, he gives Michael a particularly long and pointed look.

'I blame you for this, Alice,' Michael mutters.

'So are they all, all *honourable men*,' the waistcoat man continues derisively, now including the whole room in his gesture. His mood seems to have soured since his speech began, perhaps as a result of Michael's interruption. After another pause for effect, he addresses the room in a stage whisper: 'Come I to speak in Caesar's funeral.'

Oh my God, Alice thinks. Was that only the introduction?

'You're embarrassing yourself, and everyone else,' Michael says, recovering himself. 'Please get down.'

'I will not be silenced!' The man rounds on Michael, animated now. '*You*, sir, are a very dishonourable man. The first thing we do, let's kill all the lawyers. Ha! Watch out for him, ladies and gentlemen.' He appears to be working himself up into a fury. 'He'll have you put away for life, because he's got the judge in his pocket. That's right. He's judge, jury and executioner!'

'As a matter of fact, I don't practise criminal law,' Michael says with dignity. 'I'm a corporate tax lawyer.'

Unfortunately, this admission seems to tip the speaker over the edge. 'The height of dishonour!' he shouts. 'This is a den of iniquity! You walk into a room thinking you're safe, and the next thing you know, you find it's *riddled* with tax lawyers! I'll wager the whole *family* are tax lawyers. And their associates, too. Even that lady over there –' he points at the elderly Mrs Linden – 'is probably a tax lawyer. A retired tax lawyer, maybe,' he amends. 'But that is scarcely better. That gentleman, too.' (Pointing at Mr Blight, who shakes his head in bewilderment.) He looks around the room, searching for further inspiration. 'That man,' he continues, lighting upon Hugh, 'may not be a tax lawyer. But also he may be. It's difficult to tell. He may even be an accountant.'

Hugh is staring fixedly down into his glass of wine as if he wishes he could climb into it and hide.

'And *she*,' the waistcoat man says, and suddenly he is pointing at Alice, who freezes in terror. But the man breaks off. 'Well, actually, she's all right. She gave me a biscuit. She's a rose amongst thorns.'

Alice feels quite flattered by this, though she knows she shouldn't.

'No, we must keep our wits about us in a place like this,' the man says. 'It is a nest of vipers. And another thing!' He sways on the spot. 'Be careful about the sandwiches. To be completely honest, although I denied it earlier, they are actually quite dry.' He pauses for effect. 'Truth be told, I think they may not even have been made with *today's bread*.'

Just as he seems about to go on, Hanna breaks into rapturous applause from her position in the doorway. 'Bravo!' she shouts. 'Wonderful.'

Alice watches as her sister steps up to the man's chair and holds out her hand. 'A fine performance,' she says. 'A privilege to watch.'

After a moment's dazed hesitation, the man takes her hand. Hanna raises their joined hands to the room, and together they take a bow. Then Hanna helps him down from the chair.

'Let's get you a glass of water,' she says. 'To soothe those vocal chords.' And the two of them go into the kitchen.

A long silence follows their departure.

It is Mrs Jackson who eventually breaks it. 'I'm afraid he's had a bit too much to drink, hasn't he?'

'I thought he was quite good,' Lydia says.

THE WAKE WRAPS UP quickly after this. The elderly neighbours discover the time, and make their goodbyes. Hugh and Nicky head out the door together, and the man in the waistcoat is led to a taxi by Lydia, who says to Alice, 'I'll make sure he gets home.' She pauses, then adds, 'Do you know, I'm not sure he actually knew your aunt. I asked him what her name was and he said it had temporarily slipped his mind, but that it *may or may not* begin with an M.'

'Oh God,' Alice says, feeling like she might burst into tears.

'Never mind,' Lydia says. 'This kind of thing always happens at funerals.'

Does it? Alice thinks.

When the other guests have gone, Alice leaves her mother and Michael gathering up the plates and glasses in the function room and goes in search of Hanna. She finds her in the kitchen, washing up wine glasses.

'Just making myself useful,' she says as Alice enters.

'You can leave it. I don't mind doing it.'

Some people might demur, but Hanna shrugs and takes off the gloves.

'You threw a great funeral, Alice,' she says. 'I thoroughly enjoyed it.'

'That man . . .' Alice says in despair.

'He was the best bit. Make sure you get him back for my funeral, won't you?'

'Do you want a lift back to London?' Alice says. 'Mum and I will be ready to go in about twenty minutes.'

26

'It's OK – Michael's driving me.'

'He'll go on at you about getting on the property ladder.'

'I'll put my headphones on.'

They look at each other. Alice is about to speak again when Hanna says, 'Right, I'm going to take my life in my hands and go and say goodbye to Mum. Wish me luck.' She heads towards the door. 'I'll see you around.' And over her shoulder: 'You know – if I make it.'

'Good luck,' Alice says, but Hanna has already gone.

ALICE AND HER MOTHER finish the last of the clearing-up in silence. Alice is familiar with the different qualities of her mother's silences, adept at recognizing which ones are best not interrupted.

'I hope you've learned your lesson,' her mother says eventually. 'This is what comes of peddling alcohol.'

'I didn't peddle it,' Alice says.

'This has been a total fiasco.'

'I'm sorry,' Alice says. 'I didn't mean for him to drink so much.'

'You never mean anything, do you, Alice?' her mother says. 'Things just happen to you.'

Alice considers this. It does feel like a bleakly accurate summation of her life.

'People said the service was nice,' she says. 'And the refreshments went down well. Apart – apart from the wine.'

Her mother sighs.

'The service is the important bit, isn't it?' Alice says.

'I suppose so.'

'And Hanna came. Hanna's home.'

To this, her mother makes no reply.

When they have packed up the last of the sandwiches and put away the cups and glasses, Alice locks up behind them and posts the key through the letter box.

In the car, they sit quietly for a few moments. Alice feels the weight of the day settle on her.

'So that's done then,' her mother says. It is what she used to say on Christmas Day, often quite early in the afternoon: *So that's done then. Over for another year.* Alice still remembers the rush of sorrow she would feel at these words.

Alice looks at her mother, who continues to stare ahead. Her mother is grieving, she reminds herself, even if it is not obvious. She has always been a difficult person to comfort.

'I think she would have liked it,' Alice says. 'I hope so, anyway.' She realizes that she has hardly thought of her aunt throughout the last few hours; there was so much else going on. She makes a conscious effort to think of her now. 'Such a sad story,' she says at last.

'What was?'

'All of it. How things turned out for her.'

'That's life,' her mother says shortly.

'But she didn't have the life she should have had.'

'Well, maybe,' her mother says. She reaches out briskly to turn on the engine. 'But tell me, who does?'

2

Sallow and unprepossessing. Here is Celia at eight, unloved and unlovely. Her nose is beaky and her eyes are a touch too deep-set, though their colour – a bright clear green – is admittedly striking. Her skin has an unhealthy, yellowish tinge. Some people grow into their looks, Celia's mother tells her, which perplexes Celia because at eight she still has not worked out that she is not pretty.

It is true that people often comment on the beauty of Celia's older sister Katy and never seem to mention Celia's looks, but somehow Celia has never inferred anything from this. It helps that Katy is pretty in a very obvious way, with golden hair and blue eyes, a golden lustre to her skin too, like the statue of a goddess. People, Celia has observed, are not very imaginative and will in almost every case say what is obvious, not what is interesting.

Celia is a quiet and watchful child, and teachers find her unsettling. She rarely laughs.

'She's rather intense,' her form teacher writes in her report.

Celia believes this is a compliment.

The penny still does not drop when they are discussing in the playground what their husbands will do, and Celia says hers will be a doctor. 'You won't have a husband,' another girl says, and the others giggle.

Celia thinks this is a reference to her intellect. 'It's all right,' she reassures them. 'Most men don't want silly wives these days.' Celia has learned this from her mother, who takes a keen interest in societal trends. It is the sixties: the world is changing.

But the others still giggle at her, and Celia is annoyed; she can't bear that way they have of laughing. She tries to follow them when they move away from her.

It is Katy, aged eleven, who breaks the news to Celia shortly before Celia's ninth birthday.

'You're ugly,' she tells her flatly. 'Everybody knows it. I heard Mummy saying it to Daddy. But she didn't say "ugly". She said "unprepossessing". I looked it up in the dictionary and it means "ugly".'

Katy does not speak with malice, but in that expressionless manner characteristic of her. If she had seemed to intend it cruelly, Celia might not have taken it so much to heart.

In her bedroom, she studies her own tear-stained face in the mirror. Unprepossessing. Yes, she can see it now.

CELIA'S MOTHER SEEMS TO find many things wearisome, chief among them Celia. 'Not *now*,' she will say when Celia goes to her with one of her questions or observations.

Her mother likes to do embroidery, but always of the same thing: daffodils on a white background. Celia will often come across her at work in the living room, her hand moving rhythmically with the needle, her eyes fixed on the window, though there is little to see outside it except a small, neat patch of lawn.

A daffodil embroidery hangs on the wall above the mantelpiece for much of Celia's childhood. Celia devotes many idle hours to trying to work out if it is the same unchanging specimen or if there is a rotation system in place. Somehow she knows better than to broach this with her mother. She studies the picture covertly but every time she thinks she has noticed a change, she almost immediately begins to doubt herself: perhaps the trumpet of that middle daffodil was the same darker shade of yellow all along; perhaps that leaf always had an extra stitch at the edge.

When Celia is little, she goes through a phase of producing her own daffodil artworks. Katy is already learning embroidery but Celia is deemed too young, so has to make do with her felt-tip pens and water-colour set. She herself has no particular passion for daffodils; she has just assumed that this is what people are meant to reproduce in art form.

When her father comes home, Celia proffers her latest daffodil picture to him. Her father, standing in the doorway of the living room, looks at the painting in her hand for a few moments. Then his gaze travels to the embroidered daffodils above the mantelpiece, and thence to the sofa, where Celia's mother and Katy sit side by side embroidering their own daffodils. Finally his eyes return to the painting in Celia's hand. He seems to be lost for words.

Eventually he says, 'I need a drink,' and leaves the room without saying anything about Celia's painting.

Celia asks her mother one day why she does so much embroidery, and her mother says, 'I like having something to do with my hands.'

'Why daffodils?' Celia says. She is older now. She knows there are other flowers one can embroider.

Her mother says, 'The pattern's easy, so I don't have to concentrate.'

To Celia this seems an unsatisfactory answer, but she can't articulate why.

CELIA'S FATHER, MEANWHILE, HAS a penchant for riddles, a source of bewilderment for Celia.

'Hey girls,' he'll say roguishly across the dinner table. 'What goes up but never comes down?'

Celia gives it careful thought. This is true of lots of things, she thinks. A helium balloon when you let go of the string and it floats up into the sky until it's a tiny dot, and then it vanishes altogether. A rocket sent into space. A ball that gets stuck up a tree.

'Well?' her father prompts them. 'What goes up but never comes down?'

Celia agonizes over all the different choices, and finally says, 'That man who climbed Everest and died at the top.'

There is a short silence. Her father is looking unsettled. 'What?' he says. 'No. That isn't the right answer. That's not it.'

'Your age,' Katy supplies calmly.

He seems to relax again. 'Yes, darling. Well done. Your age.'

'But why is that the answer?' Celia says.

'Because it is.'

'But what about all the other answers you could say?'

'They're wrong,' her father says.

'But who decides what the right answer is?'

'That's enough, Celia,' her father says, looking harried.

'You're thinking about it in the wrong way,' Katy tells her. 'It's a word game, not a fact game.'

Celia tries to remember this, but she remains distrustful of the air of superiority riddles have, the way they exist only to catch you out.

EAGER FOR FRIENDSHIP, CELIA does not realize that she engenders a kind of repulsion in other children. She is too forceful, and she wants too much from other people. She ruins their games by trying to take charge, and then crying when nobody will do as she says, when they mess it up by being silly or changing the rules, by shrugging her off or laughing at her. They instinctively turn away from her, from all her need, her intensity.

There is a moment of hope during her last year of primary school, when a new girl arrives in her class. Mary is small and timid, and Celia annexes her with single-minded determination. Mary submits, perhaps grateful to have a friend so early on. For two terms, they are best friends. Celia guards Mary jealously. They sit together in every lesson, and play together at break and lunch. Celia also insists that they wear the same colour gingham dresses (the girls are allowed to choose between green, pink and blue, and Celia decides she and Mary will always wear green). Mary is not allowed to play with other girls, and when she does join in with a skipping game one break, Celia gives her the silent treatment for two days afterwards – she has an iron will – until Mary weeps and begs Celia to be her friend again. They go round to each other's houses and write a shared diary in a special leather-bound notebook Mary received for Christmas. Then, in the summer term, disaster strikes. Celia goes down with a nasty virus and is off school for a week. When she returns, Mary avoids her, whispering in corners with Helen Wilson, the two of them running away when Celia comes near. When Celia tries to speak to Mary in lessons, Mary says to Helen, 'Can you hear that buzzing noise? Is there a fly in the room?' Celia cries out with rage and tries to thump Mary, who moves quickly out of the way. Mary and Helen stare at Celia wide-eyed.

'We haven't seen Mary recently,' Celia's mother says a few weeks later. 'Have you girls had a falling-out?'

Celia shrugs, feeling the hotness of tears rising. 'I hate her.'

'It's not nice to say you hate people,' her mother says.

Then her father comes in and says, 'Hey Cee, you see a boat filled with people in front of you, but there isn't a single person on board. How come?' so Celia has to flee upstairs.

KATY IS SOLITARY TOO, but without any of Celia's desperate efforts to change this. At school, Katy is shy and avoids other children, spending her breaks in the library, or even, sometimes, the toilet. Occasionally, Celia goes to find Katy at lunchtime. But Katy tells her to go away, or even ignores her entirely. Celia has heard that sisters are often best friends. She is not *completely* sure, but she does not think that she and Katy are best friends. At home, she has tried to get Katy to play with her, but Katy prefers to play alone, often seeming to be lost in a world of her own. She adores the family cat Rhubarb, and spends a lot of time stroking him and talking to him. Despite Katy's oddness, she has a gentleness about her which, added to her beauty, makes people tender towards her.

'Away with the fairies,' their father says fondly. 'She has her head in the clouds, that one.'

It is an early indication to Celia that prepossessing girls get away with more than unprepossessing girls.

Given that Katy is the pretty one, it seems only fair for Celia to be the clever one. However, life, as she is fast learning, is not fair. Until secondary school, she believes herself to be an intellectual. She's been collecting Latin phrases for years, which she tries to work into everyday conversation. 'It's not the broccoli *per se* that I don't like,' she tells everyone at dinner. 'It's the mushiness. But mushiness is not a *sine qua non* of broccoli.'

'God, you're a cretin,' Katy says.

Although both Celia and Katy pass the eleven-plus and get into the local girls' grammar school, once there neither really distinguishes

34

herself. They never make it near the top of the class, and in more than one subject they are close to the bottom.

Despite the similar mediocrity of their report cards, it is only with Celia that their mother brings up the prospect of university.

'You could get a degree,' she tells her. 'Lots of girls go to university these days. Then you might become a teacher at a nice girls' school.'

Celia, thirteen now, is suspicious. She has not found girls' schools to be particularly nice places. 'Will Katy go to university?' she asks. Katy is currently studying, in a desultory fashion, for her O-levels.

Her mother is evasive. 'She might, I suppose. We'll see.'

It does not matter whether or not Katy goes to university, Celia realizes. Katy will get married.

There have been a few boyfriends already, but no one has lasted long. Katy accuses each boyfriend in turn of being unfaithful, as though these gawky adolescents are irresistible Lotharios besieged by hordes of women. Nonetheless, it is only after the dispatch of boyfriend number three – the calm, adoring Robbie – that it occurs to Celia that the problem might lie with Katy herself.

'You can't trust them,' Katy tells her. 'You can't trust any of them.'

Celia nods, as she always does, but she looks at Katy with new eyes.

By sixteen Katy, so biddable in early childhood, has become quarrelsome and angry. Having had a fluid, transparent quality to her when she was younger, so that she might enter and leave rooms without anyone noticing, now she makes her presence felt in the slamming of doors. She accuses her parents of upsetting her when they ask her to do the washing-up, or tidy away her things – 'Leave me alone! You're always getting at me, *upsetting* me!' – so that in the end they give up, and cease asking much of her at all. (Celia is still expected to do the washing-up, regardless of whether or not she is upset.)

It is Celia who Katy dislikes most of all. 'You're always looking at me,' Katy tells her. 'Stop *watching* me. Creep.'

Celia, it is true, does have a habit of looking at people too intently. But she can hardly help it. Katy has become an interesting study.

'You're all against me,' Katy tells them flatly at breakfast one day. 'Celia has always been jealous of me, and you,' this, to her parents, 'have encouraged her.'

'Darling, no we haven't,' their mother says.

'You've indulged her moods,' Katy says.

'What moods?' Celia says, but everyone ignores her.

'Oh, we haven't indulged them,' their mother says.

'You've always taken her side,' Katy says. 'Indulged her jealousy.'

'We've never taken anyone's side.'

'But I'm not even jealous!' Celia protests, though nobody is listening.

Her sister's volatility makes the house tremble. Celia wakes in the night to find Katy sitting on the edge of her bed, staring at her. Celia only just stops herself from screaming, and manages to say, 'What are you doing?'

'Keeping an eye on you,' Katy says darkly. After glowering at Celia a moment longer, she gets up and goes back to her own room.

IT IS ALSO AROUND this time that Celia begins to be aware of her surroundings. This makes her restless and unhappy. Nobody can live a romantic life in the Peterborough suburbs (Celia knows; Celia has tried). Their street looks the same as every street around it, and their house is the same as all the others on the street. Celia becomes bitterly aware that she has never travelled anywhere (except to Wales on holiday, which hardly counts), though in some ways perhaps she can say she has: she has a feeling that one suburb looks much the same as another, so maybe she can claim to have been all over the country. This thought is not encouraging.

Beyond the monotony of the city outskirts, there is nothing better waiting. When the houses run out, the fens take over, stretching out in a relentless flat expanse until their edges blur into the horizon. The dispiriting blankness of it all – Celia feels it seeping inside her, dulling her senses, flattening her corners.

She tries to imagine what kind of life she will live as an adult, but can never picture it.

She says to Katy, 'Where do you want to live when you're older?'

And Katy replies, 'What? So you can follow me? Leave me alone. Stupid bitch. I've got my eye on you.'

It worries Celia that she is unable to imagine anything that doesn't look like this.

KATY'S O-LEVEL RESULTS, WHEN they come, are far from spectacular, but their parents take her out for a special dinner nonetheless. Celia is not invited, though she has only been to a restaurant twice in her life and is desperate to go. Her parents say it is because this is Katy's moment and Celia will get her own turn, but Celia knows it is because Katy is less likely to have one of her strange explosions if her sister is not present. (By the time Celia gets her own O-level results, her parents are distracted and nobody mentions going for a meal.)

Then, a couple of months after Katy starts sixth form, Jonathan arrives on the scene, and Katy appears to get over her difficult teenage phase. She no longer torments Celia; now she mostly ignores her. It is like they are children again. Celia is fond of Jonathan, who is nineteen and very sensible. He eats Sunday lunch with them every week, and he and Katy smile at each other across the gravy boat. If Katy ever makes a comment about people being against her, Jonathan says, 'No, honey, don't be silly.'

Celia is not sure where this 'honey' business came from, but she is grateful for the calming effect Jonathan has on her sister. She begins to think of him as her future brother-in-law, and imagines the engagement will be announced sometime after Katy turns eighteen and has her A-levels out of the way.

Neither Celia nor her parents ever discover the cause of the rupture. It is only that one Saturday Katy comes home mid-morning when she was supposed to be out for the whole day with Jonathan, throws down her bag in the middle of the living-room floor and announces, 'He's a bastard. A *bastard*.'

Celia and her mother are on the sofa, Celia reading a book and her mother embroidering. Her mother says, 'Darling, what's happened?' and Katy begins to sob, and then, as her mother goes to embrace her, to wail. It is a terrible, frightening, disconsolate sound, and Celia gets up after a moment and leaves the room.

Katy goes into her bedroom and does not re-emerge for the rest of the day, even for supper. Celia is sent up with a tray for her, but Katy will not open the door.

'Go away,' she hisses from the other side. 'You must be very happy now.'

Then the ragged sound of sobbing starts up again.

'She'll come out the other side of this,' Celia's parents tell each other (and tell Celia, in response to her latest complaint about Katy's vitriol towards her). 'It's a difficult age.'

Celia comes home from school the next day to find her favourite Laura Ashley tea dress cut up into ribbons, which are now strewn across her bed. Katy denies having anything to do with it – which is of course absurd – but to Celia's outrage her parents do nothing beyond promising, discreetly, to replace the dress.

CELIA HAS A MEMORY of Katy as a child, cutting off the heads of flowers in the garden in a way that appears fascinatingly destructive to Celia until she sees the end result: the flower heads bobbing on water in a ceramic bowl which Katy presents to her mother for her birthday. Their mother exclaims over how thoughtful and artistic Katy is. Katy has bought the bowl in an antique shop. It is painted in exquisite pinks and greens. Celia looks at the delicate rim and imagines snapping a piece off, like it's made of chocolate.

Celia's own present is a beautiful teal-coloured scarf that her mother admired several months before in a department store when Katy and Celia were with her. Celia filed this moment away in her memory and determinedly saved her pocket money for it. But when her mother opens the gift, she merely smiles – rather vaguely, it seems to Celia – and says, 'It's lovely, darling, though not quite my colour,' and Celia realizes her mother has no recollection of admiring the scarf, that Celia might as well have gone ahead and picked out something at random like Katy, for no other reason than that she herself liked it. She thinks, too, that she would not have got away with cutting off the flower heads.

The bowl isn't really her mother's colour either, but it sits in pride of place on the coffee table in the lounge, clashing with the room's various shades of orange and brown. It remains there for many years, giving Celia a jealous pang every time she looks at it, until one day Katy herself breaks it to get at the listening device inside.

*

OVER BREAKFAST ONE MORNING, not long after the incident with the tea dress, Katy rises suddenly to her feet and tips her whole bowl of cereal and milk over Celia, placing the upended bowl on Celia's head.

Celia cries out and then splutters as milk runs down her face and into her mouth; their mother cries, 'Katy!' and their father says, 'My goodness!'

Katy sits back in her seat with a satisfied look on her face. 'Stupid bitch tried it on,' she says.

Celia, still wearing the bowl on her head like a ceramic helmet, is too shocked to defend herself.

Moments like this are alarming, just as the cutting up of the dress was, but they do not occur regularly, so it is easy to play them down between incidents, for Celia's parents to convince themselves that Katy is overtired, overwrought, that it is her time of the month, that she is being metaphorical when she talks about Celia wanting to poison her.

'She's not being normal,' Celia tells her parents. 'This isn't *normal*.'

'You mustn't wind her up,' her father says, and all Celia can say in response is, 'I don't!' whilst wondering what they think she is doing to Katy when their backs are turned.

Katy stops going to school mere months before she is due to take her A-levels and nothing can persuade her to return, not even the promise of a second-hand car if she sits her exams ('sits', not 'passes'; her parents' hopes are more modest these days).

When Katy speaks now, it is often hard to follow what she is saying. At times she talks so quickly as to be unintelligible, making rapid leaps from one subject to another. But then, just as the stream of words is in full flow, she seems to lose her thread and falls suddenly silent. Sometimes the ends of her sentences seem to bear little relation to the beginnings.

'I need to go to the seaside,' she tells her parents one evening. 'The sand is being chased and spaced.'

Nobody knows what this means, but they take her to Skegness for the day. Katy refuses to go on to the beach itself – something about the sand again – but she does accept an ice cream, which she eats messily and with evident satisfaction. Celia is surprised to feel an ache in her throat as she watches her sister. Katy, ice cream all around her mouth, greedily intent on her treat, reminds her of a child. And then Celia tries to remember what Katy was like as a child: not like this. Katy has lost her attractiveness too. Her hair is greasy and unwashed, and she has dark shadows under her eyes, spots on her forehead and chin.

Katy stops eating abruptly and fixes Celia with her stare. She says, 'I know what you're doing. We know. They know. No, no. No wise. No room at the inn.'

Once they are home again and Katy has locked herself in her bedroom, Celia says to her mother, 'I think Katy needs to see a doctor.'

She waits to be accused again of jealousy, but her mother nods defeatedly, just once. 'Yes,' she says. 'I know.'

THE GP PRESCRIBES KATY tranquillizers for her nerves, and refers her to a psychiatrist. Celia never finds out how this second appointment goes; all she can ascertain from her mother is that the psychiatrist gave Katy some more pills. Celia looks in the bathroom cabinet but does not find them.

Whatever the pills were, it seems likely that Katy does not take them. Why would she? She has decided by this point that Celia is not the only one trying to poison her. She remains in her bedroom for most of each day, but ventures out at night, prowling the house and muttering to herself. Celia becomes nervous about leaving her bedroom during the night, and takes to peeing in a pint glass in her room if she is caught short, carrying it carefully to the bathroom each morning to empty.

Her parents seem tired and distracted. Celia meets her mother on the landing one morning whilst on her glass-emptying mission.

'What's that?' her mother says, nodding at the full glass.

'My urine,' Celia says.

'Right,' her mother says vaguely, and continues past her.

Apparently the doctor has said Katy needs to rest, but Katy has other ideas. It is not clear if she ever sleeps. She certainly does not have the appearance of someone who sleeps. They can hear her during the day through her bedroom door, talking in a low voice – but talking to whom?

'I think she's reading lines from a play,' Celia's father says, sounding hopeful. 'She was doing Shakespeare at school, wasn't she? The one with the mad king and the inclement weather.'

'She's not reading Shakespeare,' Celia says. 'She doesn't understand Shakespeare.'

'That's enough of your sourness, Celia,' her mother says.

One Saturday the doorbell rings in the afternoon. It's their neighbour Mrs Clarke, returning a casserole dish. Celia is in the hallway at the time, passing between the living room and the kitchen, and therefore witnesses Katy's sudden dash down the stairs and out of the front door – pushing violently past Mrs Clarke – into the street. Celia, her mother and Mrs Clarke watch in shocked silence as her small figure, moving at great speed, vanishes around the corner. Katy is wearing only her nightdress, and her feet are bare.

Celia's mother recovers herself enough to call for Celia's father, who comes running.

They go out to look for her in the car – Celia in the back seat scouring the streets; her father driving slowly, his knuckles white on the wheel. From time to time, her mother makes dire pronouncements, and Celia does her best to reassure her: they are deep in the suburbs of Peterborough, the likelihood of Katy running into a murderous gang or being savaged by wild animals is low.

When they still haven't found Katy three hours later, Celia's father gives in and calls the police. As it turns out, Katy has already been apprehended. It seems she made it a couple of miles on foot before being caught trying to climb into the freezer at a supermarket. By the evening, she has been transferred to a psychiatric hospital, where she will remain for the next three months. She turns nineteen during the first week of her stay.

WHEN KATY FINALLY COMES home, Celia is appalled. Unlike her parents, she hasn't visited Katy in the hospital; to Celia's relief, nobody suggested it. The change in Katy, therefore, comes as a particular shock. Katy is no longer vicious and unpredictable, but she is oddly vacant. She makes strange chewing motions with her jaw even when she is not eating. She sits motionless for long periods, staring absently without seeming to focus on anything, and then her body will suddenly jerk as though she is receiving an electric shock.

Celia's mother sits with Katy for most of each day, completing the housework around her when she can. She reads to her, chats to her (sometimes Katy even replies, and sometimes her replies almost make sense), and they watch *Coronation Street* together, although 'watch' is perhaps too active a verb for whatever it is Katy is doing. Celia's father tells Katy riddles, but he has to supply the answers himself now. At the weekends, Celia's parents take Katy out for day trips, but Celia excuses herself from these outings whenever she can, saying she has schoolwork to do. She is studying for her A-levels now, although nobody asks her how her work is going.

The thing to do, Celia knows, is to find a way to leave home as soon as possible. She sees no immediate possibility of getting married – she doesn't even know any boys, let alone have a boyfriend, and there is also the lingering problem of her unattractiveness – but fortunately there is the prospect of university as an escape.

All her focus over the next few months is on her exams (it is not as though she has much else to do besides schoolwork anyway). Her grades in the end are respectable: Bs in English and French, and an A in Geography, which she has selected as her university subject, not because she particularly likes it but because she seems to be marginally better at it than her other subjects. She is delighted, and somewhat surprised, to win a place at the University of London. It is her first choice, because London sounds glamorous, and is sufficiently far away as to rule out frequent visits home.

She assumes her parents will finally take her out for the celebratory dinner she is owed. She has already decided on an Italian restaurant because she has never had pizza and believes she will like it. It seems grand to her, to be able to go to university having already eaten pizza. *Oh, pizza?* she will say offhandedly to her new friends. *Yes, it's very nice.*

But when she raises the subject, her mother says impatiently, 'There isn't time, and it wouldn't be fair on Katy. Surely you can understand that?'

Celia sees the pizza vanish. But it doesn't matter, she tells herself. She is on her way.

*

UNFORTUNATELY, UNIVERSITY DOES NOT suit her. It reminds her of school as she watches the other students band together during the early weeks, form small clusters around her, but never with her included. How is it that other people have this knack for speaking to each other, for knowing what to say? And more importantly, how to say it, because Celia has tried asking the requisite questions – barking at people, 'What are you studying? Where in the country are you from? Would you like to hear a riddle?' – but others seem to give her the bare minimum in the way of response. It occurs to Celia that she has simply swapped the people who didn't like her at school for the people who don't like her at university.

The lectures are all right, although not especially interesting, and Celia spends most evenings alone, cooking herself large tasteless casseroles in the communal kitchen of her hall of residence, or assiduously completing her reading and note-taking in her bedroom. She goes through a phase of lingering in the kitchen for long periods – she brings her books and her notes in there and sits at the small table with a cup of tea – in the hope of engaging one of the other girls in conversation as they come in and out, but again she finds she can never get beyond the most basic small talk, and no one invites her out to the pub with them as she had hoped.

In lectures, she tries to befriend the other people on her course, though with little success. For a while, her favourite opening gambit is to pretend she has forgotten a pen and to ask to borrow one from the person next to her. Unfortunately, once she has obtained the pen, it is a challenge to proceed further. Celia might compliment the owner on the pen's lovely glide on paper, its useful clip, the pleasant hue of the ink; or if it's a ballpoint, she might share her interesting fact about the Biro brothers. But she has yet to convert one of these interactions into a more prolonged exchange, never mind a friendship.

She phones home once a week, on Sunday evenings, and is always surprised at how homesick this makes her feel. Sometimes her mother will insist on fetching Katy to speak to her, and sometimes Katy agrees, so that Celia has to endure a stilted, excruciating conversation with her sister.

'How are you?' Celia will say.

'All right.'

'Watched anything good on television?'

Pause. Then, 'No.'

'What did you have for lunch today?'

Pause. 'Roast chicken.'

'And for pudding?'

Pause. 'Spotted Dick.'

Katy asks nothing in return. Always so slim in the past, she has put on several stone over the last year, and Celia pictures her sitting on the sofa between their parents, overweight, dead-eyed.

Do you still think I'm jealous of you now? she wants to say.

DURING HER SECOND TERM, Celia decides drastic action is called for. She has seen a poster advertising Christian Union meetings and though she does not believe in God, she decides to attend on the basis that Christian students will at least have a spiritual obligation to be friends with her.

The first meeting she attends is held in a conference room in one of the university buildings on Gower Street. Chairs are set up in rows for the talk, and there are nibbles laid out on tables along the sides, and paper cups of apple juice. Celia had intended to arrive early and sit in the front row, perhaps make the most of the moments before the talk starts to try out her pen gambit on some Christians, but unfortunately she goes to the wrong building first, realizing her mistake only when she finds the room locked and in darkness, and then having to sprint along Gower Street to the correct building, arriving sweaty and only just in time to slip into a seat in the back row as the talk is beginning.

A boy with a bowl cut like Henry V stands at the front, flanked by committee members in a semicircle behind him, and talks for nearly thirty-five minutes about the nature of 'mission'. He has a pedantic, nasal voice and cannot say his 'r's, which strikes Celia as unfortunate given how often the word 'resurrection' seems to crop up in his speech. He tells the audience to remember that the Christian Union exists for the benefit of non-members, that it is the duty of members to bring the Good News to all their friends and classmates. ('Friends', Celia thinks, would have been another word for him to avoid.)

As the talk goes on and on, Celia's thoughts wander. She watches the speaker, taking in his thin face, his haircut, his overly precise enunciation, and then she studies the other committee members behind him. She is disappointed to note how unappealing they are: one boy is wearing a tasselled leather jacket and bolo tie as though he is in a Western; another wears a formal suit that looks several sizes too large for him. A girl at the end of the row has a long plait that reaches past her waist, the final third of the braid so thin and wispy it looks fascinatingly like the tail of an animal; she strokes it tenderly as the boy with the bowl cut speaks. Another girl is wearing what appears to be a ruff. It does not seem to Celia that unleashing these people on the world would be the best strategy for conversion.

Nonetheless, as friendship material she thinks they might suffice, and in the wider audience there seem to be plenty of normal-looking people, so Celia's hopes are still intact when the talk ends and it is time to mingle.

She expects people to approach her, since she is a 'new face', but nobody comes up to speak to her. Celia is dismayed to watch those small groups forming again, she herself on the outside as she always is. She thinks some of the members need to be reminded of what the boy with the bowl cut said, that the CU exists for the benefit of its non-members who require saving. So she sidles over to the nibbles table, takes a cocktail stick with cheese and pineapple on it, and says to the nearest person, a boy in a blue shirt, 'You know, I've never really believed in God. It all seems a bit far-fetched.'

But instead of embracing his mission, the boy merely looks alarmed. He smiles faintly, but moves away at the same time.

Celia finishes her cheese and pineapple as she watches him retreat. She feels the beginnings of angry tears now. She rakes her eyes belligerently over the small groups around her, but nobody meets her eye, and nobody gives her an encouraging smile. It is as though she is being deliberately ignored. Celia takes a sausage roll and tries to transfer it elegantly to her mouth, but in her self-consciousness she fumbles and drops it. Panicked, she attempts to save the situation by catching it before it hits the floor, only somehow her body misinterprets its instructions and tries to catch the falling roll with her foot rather than her hand. The result of this is that Celia drop-kicks the sausage roll across the room, watching in horror as it arcs over the heads of the people nearest and hits the retreating young man in the blue shirt on the back of the head. Celia just barely has time to turn quickly back to the nibbles table as he swings round in surprise. She pretends to be studying the array of snacks carefully, feeling his eyes on her. But he has no way of proving it was her, she thinks, and why would anyone conclude that she'd thrown a sausage roll at his head? If questioned, she will simply deny it.

At last she deems it safe to turn around again, and sees that he has disappeared into the crowd.

'Gosh, that was a good shot,' a voice says next to Celia. 'Have you ever played rugby?'

And that is how Celia meets Anne.

IT IS TRUE, CELIA will reflect later, that at first glance Anne does not appear promising. She has bright orange hair which is cut to her shoulders and is rather bushy in the way it hangs, giving her head a triangular shape like a cartoon character. Her fringe is a little too short and does not lie flat, and her face has a mousy quality to it, with a large nose, small eyes and pale eyebrows and eyelashes. Celia notes all of this in her first quick appraisal. Since she became aware of her own status as unprepossessing, she has been sensitive to other people's looks.

Celia says cautiously, 'It was an accident.'

'Oh, of course,' Anne says smiling. Then she winks at Celia.

'No, it really was an accident,' Celia says.

'I know,' Anne says. And winks again.

'I was trying to stop it hitting the floor,' Celia says, irritated now.

'Well,' Anne says, 'he probably had it coming anyway. Is this your first CU meeting?'

'Yes,' Celia says.

'Great! Welcome. Are you a new Christian or an old one?'

'A . . . new one, I suppose.'

'Great,' Anne says again. 'I always think that sounds more interesting. I've always been a Christian. Went to church every Sunday since I was little, and so on. It would be more exciting to have had a sudden Damascene conversion instead. And imagine all the things you could have been getting up to beforehand. You'd have much more conversation at parties.'

Celia nods, though in fact she very rarely finds herself at parties, so it is a moot point. She looks again at her companion, who smiles back ingenuously. Anne has a very slight burr to her voice, Celia notices; you hear the 'r' in 'conversion' and 'parties' when Anne says them.

'What subject do you do?' she asks Anne.

'Physics.'

'Isn't that mainly men?'

'Yes,' Anne says. 'There are only five of us in our year. Five women, I mean. Eighty-nine men. So women account for 6 per cent. There are three hundred and thirty-nine undergrad physicists in total, and only twenty women. So it's 6 per cent across the board.'

'How do you know all this?' Celia says. She fears this girl might be eccentric.

'I went to the admissions office,' Anne says. 'They were reluctant to tell me at first. Maybe they thought I was an undercover reporter. I'd already counted our year group in lectures, but that's not completely reliable because not everyone attends lectures.'

'Why did you want to find out?'

Anne shrugs. 'It's good to know the lay of the land, isn't it? Have a sense of what you might be up against.'

'It's quite even in Geography,' Celia says warily. 'The balance of men and women.'

'That must be nice.'

'Yes.' When Anne continues to watch her, smiling, Celia finds herself adding, 'Though we have problems of our own. Everyone assumes we spend all our time colouring things in.'

Anne laughs, and Celia is surprised; she can't remember ever making someone laugh before. This might be the first joke she has ever told.

'Where are you from?' Anne says, and Celia explains, attempting to conjure up the drabness of her street, the disquieting emptiness of the fens. Anne, she learns, grew up in Cornwall, in a small fishing village. Perhaps it is this that makes her presence so refreshing; it is as though she carries the sea air with her, bracing and clean. Anne has three brothers, and Celia wonders if she might eventually be able to marry one of them. When Anne asks in return if Celia has any siblings, Celia intends to say no, but says yes.

'My sister isn't well,' she adds after a pause.

'Oh dear,' Anne says. 'What's wrong with her?'

'Just . . . nerves,' Celia says.

'That must be difficult,' Anne says. 'I'm sorry.' And she really does sound sorry.

HAVING DECIDED ANNE HAS potential, Celia wastes no time in consolidating the friendship. She arrives half an hour early for the next CU meeting, and loiters outside until Anne finally appears five minutes before the start time (cutting it rather fine, Celia notes, which is surely not in the spirit of things; she has always imagined Jesus to be a punctual person).

Celia catches sight of Anne before Anne sees her, the helmet of bright orange hair bobbing along further down Gower Street. Celia bends down quickly, pretending to be tying her shoelace. She times it perfectly, rearing up again at the precise moment Anne draws level with her (this seems to give Anne something of a shock).

'Hello Anne,' Celia says, as Anne recovers herself.

'Gosh,' Anne says. 'Celia. You made me jump.'

'I was tying my shoelace,' Celia explains. 'And then I stood up.'

'So you did.' Anne smiles at her. 'Are you here for the meeting?'

'Yes,' Celia says, adding as though it's only just occurred to her, 'Shall we sit together?'

'Of course,' Anne says, and they go in.

It is no great challenge after that to find out where Anne's room is (usefully, it is in the same hall of residence as Celia is the floor above), and where and when she attends lectures. Then Celia simply starts bumping into her. She imagines that cementing the friendship will take a while, but this is because she has anticipated resistance. She meets none. Anne, in fact, actually seems pleased to see Celia each time. The friendship flourishes.

With Anne at her side, Celia suddenly becomes a joiner-in. Anne brings her along to the Women's Lib Society and although Celia finds the talks boring, she is proud to be attending them in her capacity as *Anne's friend*. Anne seems to know everyone, and greets people with what seems to Celia an indiscriminate friendliness. But it is Celia she always sits next to. They continue attending Christian Union meetings, where they sit side by side during the talks and chat mainly to each other in the mingling part. They join the Film Society, and doze their way through arty black-and-white films every Thursday evening, and then giggle about them in the pub afterwards. Celia has never giggled in her life before, but now she seems to have got the hang of it. They join Amnesty International, and throw themselves into the letter-writing campaigns, writing to Idi Amin to ask him to end the disappearances of political opponents. Celia is briefly nervous, signing her real name to this letter, with her real address at the top. What if Idi Amin decides that she also counts as a political opponent?

When she shares this thought with Anne, Anne laughs hard. 'Celia,' she says, 'I think you'll be quite far down his list.'

Celia has discovered that she doesn't mind being teased by Anne.

Unlike Celia, Anne does have other friends, but Celia decides she is more than capable of seeing them off. Anne's friendliness makes her likeable, but she is also uncool, unfashionably dressed and unconventional in her behaviour, so the friends she has are mostly quiet, mousy girls from her corridor who have no hope of joining the more popular crowd. Perhaps Anne has been waiting all along for someone with more fire in them. The mousy girls are no match for Celia's intensity, and melt away beneath her glare. When they try to join Celia and Anne for lunch, Celia pointedly ignores them and talks only to Anne until the interlopers become self-conscious and tongue-tied. Anne does not seem to notice this. She is open and welcoming to everyone, but Celia usually manages to draw Anne's focus back to herself soon enough. After a couple of months of slow, patient progress, Celia feels satisfied that the other girls have been demoted and she herself is Anne's main friend.

She and Anne wait for each other after lectures, work side by side in the library, and eat their lunch together every day. But what Celia likes best are the evenings they spend either in Celia's bedroom or in Anne's, drinking cocoa or gin and talking about their lives. It becomes their habit to stay up late into the evening. They have so much to tell each other that sometimes there hardly seems enough time to say it all. Celia even shares the details of Katy's illness. What has always felt impossible to her becomes easy with Anne. The mystery of friendship unrolls itself before her.

THE ONLY LINGERING TROUBLE is Anne's boyfriend. His existence surprises Celia when she first hears of it, since Anne, like Celia herself, is not the kind of girl you would assume has a boyfriend. But Paul turns out to have been on the scene for a long time. They have been together since Anne was fifteen and Paul was seventeen; Paul is a friend of Anne's older brother. One of *those* relationships, Celia concludes: safe and unimaginative, born out of proximity and circumstance rather than any real passion.

She is amazed when Anne tells her it was she, in the beginning, who asked Paul out, and not the other way round.

'I don't think he'd ever have asked me, left to his own devices,' Anne says. 'But fortunately he's very suggestible.' And she bursts out laughing.

Celia thinks there is something unseemly about all this, but she does not say so to Anne.

Thankfully Paul is not around very often. He has a job in Plymouth, in marketing or selling or buying or something like that (to Celia these terms are meaningless anyway). Celia listens carefully to the way Anne speaks about him, which is offhandedly, and not often, until she is convinced Paul poses no real threat.

She does not meet him until the summer term of her first year, when he comes to visit Anne. Celia is surprised at how normal he looks. He is not quite good-looking – his chin is a little too weak, and his eyes a little too closely spaced – but he is proximate to it. It is as if his features have stumbled close to good-looking, and then slightly overshot.

Above all, he is not at all the kind of boyfriend Celia imagined Anne having. She had pictured someone odd, nerdy, awkward, paired with Anne because they occupy the same social rung, because neither can do any better. This boy – or man, perhaps she should say, since he is out in the working world, as he seems eager to remind them – unsettles Celia with his almost-handsomeness, his normality. Unlike Anne, he has no flicker of oddness. It is not that he is exactly cool, nor especially charismatic. But there is a certain ease in his manner that Celia knows she herself lacks, that ability to be with other people in a way that seems untroubled, all of them communicating in some secret language she herself does not understand. Paul has that camouflage that allows him to blend in with all the other normal people. Celia has spent some time since the start of university wondering if this ability is innate, or if it is something she has failed to learn. She had assumed Paul belonged to the same world as her and Anne, and cannot get over her disorientation at discovering he does not.

Not that he is anything special. Their first meeting, which takes place in a pub in Camden, leaves Celia unimpressed.

'So Celia,' he says over their drinks, which he has grandly paid for, 'what are your ambitions in life?'

'Um,' Celia says.

'Come on,' Paul says. 'You must have some. It's a necessity. Did Anne tell you I'm ambitious?'

Celia glances briefly at Anne.

'I told her,' Anne says brightly.

'My chief ambition,' Paul says, 'is to be lead toy-buyer for one of the big companies. Woolworths, even.'

This information, along with the earnest way in which it is delivered, is so unexpected that Celia wants to laugh. She does not, however. She says, 'What is it you do at the moment?'

'Oh, I'm a buyer,' he says. 'For Budgens. I'm on the canned-goods team at the moment, but it looks like I might get promoted to fruit juice and carbonated beverages soon.'

'Celia is going to be a solicitor,' Anne says. 'Or a teacher, or perhaps a circus performer.' She grins at Celia. 'We could have an act together. Acrobats, or lion tamers.'

Celia feels Anne is being a little frivolous about their futures, though she is pleased that Paul has received no mention in this flight of fancy.

Feeling magnanimous, she turns back to him and asks, 'Why toys?'

'They make people happy,' Paul says. 'Don't you think so? Lots of people associate their happiest memories with a particular toy. Don't you remember that rush of excitement when you were given a toy you'd wanted forever? My best ever was an Etch A Sketch. I still remember playing with it all of Christmas Day.'

Celia considers. She cannot remember ever having a favourite toy. 'I was fond of my Sindy doll,' she ventures after a moment.

'Yes,' Paul says, taking this up enthusiastically. 'I bet she was like a best friend to you, wasn't she, or even a sister? And you'd chat to her and tell her your secrets.'

This strikes Celia as an extraordinary suggestion. She studies Paul carefully for a few moments, wondering if he goes round the supermarket confiding in cans of beans and lentils, imagining them to be his friends or cousins.

Paul seems to interpret her silence as emotion.

'Exactly,' he says. 'Memories of our most cherished toys are very precious. Toys are emblems of hope, of possibility. They're our friends in good times, and our companions in bad times.' (He slips into talking like this sometimes, Celia has noticed, like he suddenly believes he is in a play. He did it earlier, when he described Plymouth as a 'city of great possibility'. Success, he informed them, is not only about *the hunger*, but about putting yourself in the right place at the right time. Anne does not seem to find any of this irritating, but then, Celia is coming to realize, Anne is not easily irritated.)

When Paul has left to get the train home, Anne says, 'I'm so glad you two could finally meet. He's heard so much about you.'

Celia is pleased to reflect that she hasn't actually heard all that much about Paul.

*

BUT SHE IS LESS than delighted when, halfway through their second year, he gets a new job in London (apparently Plymouth is no longer the right place, or else it is no longer the right time). Celia tries to appear pleased like Anne. Paul is on the way to achieving his dream: the new job is as an assistant buyer in the toy category for a small stationery and gifts company. London is at the heart of the toy-buying industry, he tells them, and full of opportunities for a man like him (it is a pity in that case, Celia reflects, that he'll actually be working in Hounslow). But his job will also involve substantial travel, he adds. He rents a room in Putney, buys a beaten-up second-hand car and is suddenly around all the time.

Celia watches the interactions between Anne and Paul minutely, weighing them up against her own interactions with Anne, ready to feel furious at being excluded. They do not, however, exclude her. Anne is generous by nature, and during evenings and weekends they are often a trio, going to the cinema, to cafés and pubs, for walks along the river in Putney, or by the canal through Camden, Kings Cross, Angel. It helps as well that Paul has always been around, always in the background; clearly Anne is not one of those girls who thinks she no longer needs friends once she gets a boyfriend. Celia decides that she and Paul fulfil different roles in Anne's life. It need not be a fight to the death.

She is almost sure Paul and Anne are not sleeping together. Anne never stays over at his digs, and he certainly does not visit their all-female hall of residence. All their socializing seems to take place in public spaces. Celia watches them closely, but sees no opportunity for them to engage in the sexual act, and is relieved that she does not have to think less of Anne.

But sometimes, it is true, Anne does disappoint her. During the summer term of their second year, for instance, Celia and Anne go away together with the Christian Union on a weekend trip to Oxford. It is a joint conference with the Oxford University CU. They stay overnight in a dormitory at the youth hostel, and listen to a series of student-led talks in the day, punctuated by a lunchtime picnic in University Parks. Although Anne and Celia sit next to each other on the coach, the rest of the time Anne seems eager to chat to others, both members of their own London group and the Oxford students. What can Anne possibly have to say to them? The Oxford members are even stranger than the London ones, which seems to Celia quite a feat. At the picnic, Anne sits with a big group of girls from Oxford, beckoning Celia over to join them but not marking Celia out by any special attentions as her most important friend, the one above all others. Celia sits in silent fury as Anne talks and laughs and offers around cheese sandwiches. It is as though Celia is just anyone, as though she and Anne simply met on the coach journey.

She reminds herself often that Anne values her friendship; Anne has said this many times, and often refers to Celia as her best friend, making Celia's core turn molten with pleasure. But still Celia worries. She feels sometimes that Anne's affection is too easy-going, that she does not differentiate sufficiently between people. There is something cheerful and open in Anne's nature that Celia does not trust. She can't imagine being like Anne. Sometimes she feels she is burning up from within with all her yearning, her need.

DURING THE CHRISTMAS AND Easter holidays of her first two years at university, Celia returns home to Peterborough, where she gets on quietly with her work and counts down the days until the start of the new term. Katy does not trouble her much; she has grown subdued, no longer given to her strange outbursts. It is easy, most of the time, to pretend she is not there at all.

Summers pose more of a problem. Three months, Celia feels, is far too long to be trapped at home with her parents and sister. During the summer of her first year, she goes with Anne down to Cornwall for a fortnight, and after that returns to London, where she works in a pub until term starts again. She tells her parents she needs to be near the library and they seem to accept this. The arrangement works out well, though the job itself is not a huge success. 'Would it kill you to smile?' the bar manager asks her. 'You look like you're planning to bury the customers under your patio, not give them their change.' Celia gives him a look intended to indicate that if she must be forced to interact with boorish idiots, at the very least she should be allowed to choose her own facial expressions. The bar manager shakes his head and walks off.

The summer of her second year, she is told the pub is not hiring (more specifically, they are not hiring *her*). Celia tries and fails to get a job as a waitress, and in the end has no choice but to go home.

It is a difficult summer. Celia writes long letters to Anne, who is down in Cornwall working in a local café. Celia pours her heart into these letters, and all of her smallest thoughts.

I was sitting at my window reading this morning, she writes, *when a magpie landed on the other side of the glass, right on the windowsill. Magpies are meant to be in pairs, aren't they? One for sorrow. It made me sad to see this one on its own. I thought the magpie had a mournful look about it.*

Reading back over what she has written, she feels pleased with this passage, which strikes her as particularly soulful. Then she wonders if it'll be sufficiently clear to Anne that the magpie is a metaphor. After some further thought, she adds a hint at the end of the paragraph: *The magpie feels somehow symbolic, don't you think?*

Then she reads the whole paragraph again. It is very good. But will Anne work out what the magpie symbolizes? Anne can be quite literal in her thinking sometimes. Celia ponders the matter further. Eventually, she adds a final sentence: *Does it make you think of me?*

This, she thinks, will have to suffice.

Anne replies to her letters, but usually not for a week or more. Her letters give the impression of being written in a great rush.

Paul came down at the weekend, she writes, *and we spent the whole time at the beach! Trying not to get too sunburnt this year. Not easy for a ginger biscuit like me! Mum and Dad being a bit trying. Nice to have some home cooking though! Not sure why you asked if you look like a magpie. I don't think you do, if you're worried. A xx*

Anne's letters tend to be considerably shorter than Celia's, so Celia tries to write less to ensure their correspondence does not look too unbalanced, but she always finds she has so much that she wants to say, and no one else to say it to. She replies to Anne's letters as soon as they arrive, and then waits anxiously for the next one, trying to restrain herself from writing again in the meantime, though she feels the words bubbling up inside her, all of these things she wants to share with Anne. Every time she reads one of Anne's replies, Celia feels a sink of disappointment. There is something so deflating in their breeziness. Oh, the anguish of loving more than you are loved!

IT IS UNFORTUNATE THAT Celia's return that summer coincides with a change in Katy. Although the first few weeks of Celia's visit pass quietly enough, something shifts in July. That month, the IRA detonates a bomb at the Tower of London, killing one person and injuring many more, and this seems to trigger something in Katy, even though a similar bombing at the Houses of Parliament the previous month passed without comment from her. Perhaps the timing is only coincidental, and it is that Katy has stopped taking her medication, or else it is no longer effective. She spends hours scouring the newspaper reports of the Tower bombing, or sitting with her ear pressed up against the radio. She claims the murdered woman was a decoy, but nobody knows what she means by this.

By the end of the month, Katy's enemies are everywhere, listening through walls and following her on her daily walks with her mother.

'She was my double,' she tells them. 'I'm the target.'

Celia can see that her sister is terrified, but no amount of reassurance seems to help.

Given the recent bombings, she imagines her parents might make a fuss about her going back to London in September, so she says to her mother one afternoon, 'I'll be all right, you know.'

'What do you mean?' her mother says, not looking up from her daffodil embroidery.

'Back in London. I'll be fine.'

Her mother pauses irritably in her work. 'Why wouldn't you be fine?'

Celia is thrown by this reaction, but she musters her dignity. 'I just want you to know that I'm not afraid.'

'What on earth is there to be afraid of?'

'The IRA,' Celia says.

'Oh for pity's sake,' her mother says. 'Not now, Celia. I can't be dealing with your histrionics on top of everything else.' She returns to her embroidery, shaking her head.

AUGUST ARRIVES, AND KATY does not improve. At supper one evening she remarks ominously, 'Once upon a time, the world was one. Then there was a sign and the land broke and then there were separate continents. The sea came in between them. It was the work of the gods of old.'

Celia raises her eyebrows. 'Actually, it was continental drift,' she says.

Her mother says, 'Don't show off, Celia.'

Katy says, 'I'm the key. That's it. Lock, turn.'

She gets up and, leaving her own plate, which she hasn't touched, picks up Celia's and walks out of the room with it.

Once she has gone, Celia's mother passes Katy's plate over to Celia and Celia begins to eat again.

'Katy's always been creative,' Celia's father says at last. 'Ever since she was a little girl. It's the same creativity we're seeing now, only a different side of it.'

'She's not creative,' Celia says, mouth full of potato. 'She's doolally.'

Her father gets up quickly and slaps her across the face.

For a few moments, everyone is too shocked to speak. Celia puts her hand up slowly to her cheek and feels the heat in its sting. Tears come to her eyes but she will not allow herself to cry. Carefully, she swallows the mouthful of potato and looks at her mother, but her mother says nothing and doesn't meet her eye, only stares down at her plate. Without a word, Celia's father walks out of the room.

'It won't be long now,' Katy says cryptically, reappearing in the doorway.

WITHIN A FEW DAYS, Katy has smashed up anything breakable in the house looking for listening devices.

'You have to trust me!' she screams at her parents when they try to restrain her. 'I'm trying to keep you safe! I'm trying to keep you safe! You have to trust me!'

Celia has never seen her father cry before, but he weeps now, and Celia feels embarrassed for him.

After Katy smashes the kitchen window and badly cuts her arm, she is sectioned again.

CELIA TRIES TO PUT all of this in a letter to Anne. But somehow Anne's most recent letter, lying on the desk in front of her, has an inhibiting effect. (*We went to a bonfire on the beach yesterday! Lots of people from school there. Great fun!*)

Celia finds she cannot convey what she wishes, and ends up writing only, *Things are difficult with Katy again*.

When Anne does respond, she says, *Sorry to hear about Katy. You'll be back in London in a few weeks though. Just hang on a bit longer. I'm going back a bit early, probably next week – Paul's getting lonely! Men are such delicate creatures, aren't they?*

Celia stares at these words. Anne has not mentioned this new plan before. She rereads the sentence in case Anne has suggested Celia come back early as well so they can be together, but Anne has not suggested it.

BACK IN LONDON, ONCE term starts, Anne does seem pleased to see her. But although on the surface things return to normal, Celia cannot settle. She feels a new distance between herself and Anne, made all the worse by the fact that Anne does not seem to notice it, or perhaps does notice but does not care.

Anne has started to talk about the end of university. She plans to join the civil service, she says, if they'll have her. She likes the idea of wearing a suit, and she needs to be where Paul is.

'Do they have civil servants in Hounslow?' Celia says.

She herself has no idea what job to choose. For some time, she has cherished a secret hope that she and Anne might rent a flat together, but now she sees how absurd the idea is: Anne will of course get married and live with Paul. And in any case, none of Anne's post-university plans seem to involve Celia. Celia feels a growing sense of panic. The future is a blank and terrifying expanse and everybody seems to be moving into it without her.

IN OCTOBER, PAUL ASKS Celia to come with him on a very special shopping trip. He and Anne have been together almost six years now, and he has decided it is time they were engaged. He is going to ask Anne to marry him on her twenty-first birthday, he says, which is in five weeks' time.

'Will you help me choose the ring?' he says. 'Honestly Cee, you're the only girl I could ask.'

Celia is flattered, and annoyed with herself for it.

She bunks off lectures the next day and Paul takes a few hours off work so they can go out together for the whole morning without Anne suspecting anything. They wander round second-hand jewellers looking for a ring that is both pretty and affordable.

They don't find the right one that day, but they go to a pub afterwards to debrief. Paul tells Celia (again) about his plans for his career: to one day be head of toy-buying for Argos or Woolworths or somewhere similar. Then he shares his thoughts on historic trends in toy-buying.

'Fascinating,' Celia says.

He says, 'You know, I wish you'd mention to Anne how interesting you find all this. I sometimes feel . . . well . . .' He stares wistfully into

64

space for a few moments. 'I suppose I feel that Anne doesn't quite grasp all the *nuances* of toy-buying. You know, its finer points. Its subtleties.'

Celia wants to tell him that she knows what 'nuances' means, but she does not. Instead, she says, 'Perhaps it's hard for someone on the outside to fully appreciate the . . . nuances involved. And the level of challenge.'

'Yes. But you do, don't you?'

'Oh, absolutely,' Celia says.

The next week they go shopping again. This time, they stop for a break in a café and have tea and cake together. Paul confides in Celia his intuitions regarding the 'next big thing' in toys, leaning across the table with the furtive manner of someone sharing atomic secrets. Celia tries to appear sufficiently impressed.

It feels exciting, Paul says, to be off work in the middle of the day, in the middle of the week; it's very freeing. 'But I can't take any more time off after this,' he adds. 'It makes me look unambitious. So we absolutely *must* find the ring today.'

And they do.

'That one,' Paul says at last, pointing at a delicate ruby solitaire on a gold band in the middle of the window display.

Celia looks. He is right: it is perfect.

Still staring at the ring, she says, 'Don't marry Anne.'

She feels his eyes on her and when she turns she meets his gaze levelly. She says, 'She isn't right for you. You should marry me instead.'

He laughs at first, a brief shocked bark.

'Marry me instead,' Celia repeats steadily.

He stops laughing. 'You?'

'Me,' Celia says. 'I'm certain of it.'

She turns all her intensity on him now, while her face remains calm. She will have this, if she never has anything else.

'You're joking,' he says, a note of question in his voice.

'I'm not.' He must know by now that she is not one for jokes. Her heart is beating very fast, but she faces him with the fierceness of her certainty.

'Have you always—?' he begins.

'Yes.'

'What about Anne?'

'Anne will be all right.'

'It would be . . . impossible,' he says.

'It will be easy. Anne will be fine. I know her.'

He is silent, staring at her. But Celia senses a malleability in him that Anne, for all her friendliness, lacks. He will take someone else's stamp.

She says, 'You're supposed to be with me. I can support your career better. I take you seriously.'

'I've been with her so long—'

'Exactly,' Celia says. 'You met her too young and became trapped. You were just children really, when you met. She's not the one you're supposed to marry. She doesn't understand what you need.'

'You do.'

'Yes.'

'But it would be so shocking—'

'Not really,' Celia says. 'This kind of thing happens all the time.'

'She's your friend,' Paul says.

'She'll recover quickly. That's the way she is.'

'She'll marry somebody else,' he says, as though repeating something she has told him.

'Of course. Someone she suits better than you. She isn't right for you. You can't waste your life with the wrong person.'

He is staring at her intently. 'How do you know?' he says. 'How can you be sure?'

'I just know,' Celia tells him. 'You have to trust me.'

'And you're . . .' he falters. 'You are sure, aren't you? You are serious.'

'I am sure,' Celia says. 'I am serious.'

After that it is accomplished easily enough. They go into the jeweller and Paul buys Celia the ring. She puts it on her finger immediately, as soon as they are outside the shop.

'There,' she says.

WHEN IT COMES TO telling Anne, Celia simply cannot picture the conversation. Her imagination, which she tries to force towards this moment, digs its heels in and refuses to proceed any further.

She would like to have Paul be the one who breaks the news, and then the moment with Anne can always remain a blank as far as Celia is concerned. But she knows instinctively that he will not manage it. He will agree, when she suggests it, that yes, of course it should come from him, it's only right. There will be something noble in his insistence, a heroic willingness to face up to a difficult situation. Then, somehow, the conversation will repeatedly fail to happen. It will never quite be the right moment, and the days will slip by, the moment outside the jeweller gradually fading until Celia will no longer even be sure it happened.

So it has to be her.

Anne does not cry immediately, because it takes her some time to believe it.

'What do you mean?' she keeps asking. 'What are you saying?'

Celia, perched on the chair in Anne's bedroom as Anne sits huddled on her bed, is momentarily irritated by her friend's obtuseness.

67

'Paul and I are going to get married,' she says again. Then, because Anne doesn't speak for a while, she adds stiffly, 'I'm sorry. We're both sorry. It's just one of those things, that's all.'

Anne has turned white, which Celia registers vaguely.

'How long?' Anne says at last.

'How long what?'

'How long has this been going on for?'

'Quite some time,' Celia says, since this seems as good an answer as any.

Finally, Anne begins to cry. 'This hurts. God, this hurts,' she says.

'Yes.'

Celia watches Anne cry, and while she does, she has a disorientating realization. It is that Anne is entirely without self-consciousness. None of this crying is for effect, to make herself seem more tragic, to make Celia feel more guilty, and it hasn't occurred to Anne to try to save face. Unlike Celia, whose every act is a strained performance in front of a silent, critical audience, Anne has no imaginary spectators.

This is an important insight for Celia, but it will soon slip away again, like those startling flashes of clarity she occasionally gets after a couple of drinks, which have always lost their power by morning, if they are remembered at all. Any kind of insight is unusual for Celia. Her own self-consciousness rarely translates into self-awareness, and in a year's time she will remember the outline of this scene, but none of its nuances (its finer points, its subtleties). She will remember her own discomfort, and that Anne's reaction was emotional but not hysterical. She will remember that it ended with Anne saying softly, 'I'd like you to leave now.'

Celia doesn't see Anne again after this, or at least not properly. She spots her in passing from time to time, outside halls and once in Tavistock

Square Gardens, where Anne is sitting on a bench with a girl Celia does not recognize.

Celia generally spends her evenings alone now, though occasionally she goes out with Paul. She had always assumed that with a lover you would talk about big things, but she and Paul only ever talk about small things. There are pauses and false starts, and it often feels to Celia as though they are fumbling around the edges of conversation and never getting anywhere near the middle. But men are very different from women, and there is also the subject of Anne to be avoided, which further inhibits their conversations.

CELIA'S MOTHER MAKES HER wedding dress, which surprises Celia. It is a simple floor-length gown in broderie anglaise, with short puffed sleeves and an empire waistline. Celia's mother follows a pattern she has selected (she gave Celia a choice of two) and runs up the seams with frowning efficiency on her sewing machine.

'I didn't know you made clothes,' Celia says, as her mother kneels in front of her pinning the hem.

'Of course I do,' her mother says, sounding irritated. Then she adds, 'You can wear a crown of flowers with your veil. You'd probably better have your hair loose. We can put curlers in it the night before.' She moves round behind Celia to pin the hem at the back. After a few minutes, she says, 'I suppose you'll be happy.'

It is not clear to Celia from her tone whether this is a question or a statement. Unable to see her mother, she has little to go on. She says, 'Yes.' She hesitates, feeling she should add something else, but there is nothing else to add.

Her parents have met Paul, but only once: a brief, rather stilted dinner during the Christmas break. Her mother serves a chicken casserole and her father asks Paul about his work. Katy does not eat with them; this seems to have been agreed between Celia's parents beforehand and is never mentioned to Celia. Unfortunately, Katy does come down from her room towards the end of the meal, and therefore has to be introduced. She greets Paul politely and Celia dares to hope the meeting might pass without incident, until it becomes apparent Katy is convinced Paul is in the army. His denials only seem to make her more insistent, and she asks him a series of increasingly technical questions about tank manoeuvres.

Eventually, Celia's mother says to Katy, 'Darling, shall we have some ice cream and watch *Coronation Street*?' and Katy is enticed next door.

When Paul excuses himself to go to the loo shortly after this, Celia asks her father, 'Where did she learn so much about tanks?'

'I don't know,' he says. 'I thought it was quite impressive.'

Celia has to admit that it was.

Paul leaves straight after supper to get back to London. Celia sees him to his car, bracing herself for the inevitable questions about Katy's behaviour, but all he says is, 'I think that went well, didn't it?'

When Celia goes back inside, her parents say nothing about Paul, beyond her father remarking, 'Seems like a courteous young man,' and her mother saying, 'He finds his job rather thrilling, doesn't he?'

THE WEDDING TAKES PLACES in July, not long after Celia has finished her final exams. It is a small ceremony in her parents' local church, followed by a buffet lunch in the pub. The guest list is sparse: Celia's parents and Katy; Mrs Clarke from next door and her husband; two of Celia's mother's friends, Mrs Linden and Mrs Jackson, along with their husbands; Paul's parents, his brother (who takes the role of best man) and his brother's girlfriend; two of Paul's friends from school; two of his colleagues from the toy company, each with a wife in tow. The animals went in two by two, Celia finds herself thinking unaccountably as she walks down the aisle on her father's arm.

Celia has no friends of her own to invite. When Paul asks her who she will have as bridesmaids, she says, 'Katy. Just Katy,' and tries to give the impression she has never needed anyone else. Her parents, she reflects later, would no doubt have insisted she ask Katy anyway. Her mother makes Katy a dress in a cream and orange floral fabric from Laura Ashley, but the dress is not becoming on Katy, emphasizing her bulk and the unhealthy pallor of her complexion. Celia watches her sister trying on the dress. Katy touches the material gently and then smoothes it down over her stomach. She stares at herself in the mirror. Celia sees with embarrassment that her sister's eyes have filled with tears.

'There, darling,' their mother says. 'You look like a picture.'

At the wedding buffet, which consists of cold meats, potato salad, sausage rolls and an array of damp lettuce, Celia's father makes a brief speech in which he thanks everyone for coming, and then thanks Paul in particular for taking Celia off their hands (dutiful laughter), and then Paul makes a long speech in which he stresses the importance of trusting your instincts, being true to yourself and seizing the day.

Celia's mother murmurs to no one in particular, 'Does he think he's a groom or a motivational speaker?'

Finally, Paul's brother makes a speech in which he tells some faintly off-colour anecdotes about Paul's teenage years, and ends by saying, 'We'd like to welcome Celia to the family. Admittedly we don't know her very well. But I'm sure that will be remedied.'

Celia is certain all this is a veiled reference to Anne, the ghost at her feast, who Paul's family knew very well indeed. Celia only met Paul's family for the first time the previous day, after they arrived in Peterborough for the wedding and had dinner with Celia and her parents at an Italian restaurant. Celia has been evasive over the past few months whenever Paul suggested they should go down to Cornwall for the weekend. 'I have too much work on,' she would say, relieved to be able to cite her approaching finals. In reality, she knows she can never go back there, where Anne's family lives. Paul's parents have been polite to her, but not warm.

Katy behaves impeccably throughout the ceremony and the buffet lunch, but Celia is on edge all the same, waiting for an outburst. When she and Paul get up to leave in the late afternoon – they are catching the train to Great Yarmouth that evening for a week-long honeymoon – Katy rises too, and Celia knows as her sister approaches that the eruption is imminent. And what will Katy say? Perhaps that Celia has betrayed her, that she has stolen her life.

But Katy only leans forward to kiss her on the cheek, and says, 'You look pretty, Cee.' Then she gives Paul an enthusiastic military salute and returns to her parents.

CELIA AND PAUL RENT for a few months and then buy a small house in Wimbledon.

Celia is somewhat dismayed to discover Paul still expects her to get a job, despite being married. Ambition is an important quality, he says, even in a woman. Plus they need the money. So Celia reluctantly undertakes teacher training, seeing the long-threatened nice girls' school taking shape on the horizon after all. It occurs to her that a better option might be to get pregnant as quickly as possible, but she finds she does not particularly enjoy the process by which this is to be accomplished. And besides, Paul says they are very young and there is no rush for children just yet.

'I know you're prey to your biological impulses,' he says. 'But you can hold out a bit longer, can't you?'

Celia reflects. In fact, she does not think her biological impulses have preyed upon her yet. She does not find babies particularly appealing when she sees them out in public. She agrees with Paul that she can hold out a little longer, and resigns herself to teaching for a year or two.

Without the distraction of a baby, she focuses on the house. She paints the walls of the living room cream, and then paints the bedroom a more daring lilac. She tries to feel excited as she chooses fabrics to make curtains and cushion covers, but she can't help imagining how nice it would be to have someone to give a second opinion: a friend, or even a sister. Paul does not take much interest, although he does comment that the house is looking smart.

So, a home of her own, and a husband. Celia knows her younger self would be impressed with how successfully she has organized her life.

But sometimes in the evenings when Paul is still at work, she feels uncomfortably restless. She roams through the neat, clean rooms of the house, which somehow retain their impersonal quality, even after Celia's decorating spree. She tries to sprawl on the sofa in the sitting room, tries to relax at the kitchen table with her magazine, but she can never quite shake the feeling of being a guest in somebody else's house. Not Paul's, who barely seems to be there after the first few months of marriage, but someone else's, someone stern and unseen. At night, Celia lies awake beside her sleeping husband – he snores, as it turns out, which is not an attractive quality – and reflects on everything she has achieved. But the feeling of detachment remains. Perhaps this, she thinks at last, is why people really have children: not a biological urge after all, but because children provide a necessary weight, like an anchor, so that you might at last stop wondering what you are missing, so that you might at last feel you belong in your own life.

3

Y OU KNOW WHEN YOU are the least loved child. From a young
age, Hanna is familiar with the sequence of her mother's affections.
First comes Michael, the favourite, the blessed one, and then, not far
behind, the noble Alice. Then a strained interlude, some tumbleweed,
birdsong, before finally Hanna herself trudges into view, trailing clouds
of nuisance.

Even as a young child, her reputation precedes her.

'This one's the wild child,' she will hear her mother announcing as
she enters a room, in the manner of a medieval herald. Hanna is the
difficult one, Alice is the quiet one. Michael doesn't have a label; he's a
boy, which seems to be a category all of its own.

'She's fiery,' their father says during one of Hanna's rages. 'That's no
bad thing.'

'You don't have to deal with her,' Hanna's mother says in reply.

'Temper tantrum! Temper tantrum!' Michael will chant the moment
Hanna shows any flicker of a reaction, and Hanna will struggle to keep
control of herself.

'The most important thing you'll ever learn,' her mother tells her, 'is
how to regulate your emotions.'

Hanna's mother has a lot to say on the subject of regulating one's
emotions. Apparently Hanna's emotional incontinence will land her in
trouble one day. What kind of trouble, Hanna's mother does not specify.

The adventurer, the troublemaker, the (*whisper it*) attention-seeker, Hanna runs away from home at frequent intervals throughout her child-hood. Each time she really means it, but each time she ends up back home soon enough. She doesn't realize that all of this is a cliché, and she feels faintly humiliated later on to discover it's a well-worn trope. To Hanna, the greatest fault of all is to be unoriginal.

During one of her escape attempts, her father catches up with her before she has made it to the end of the road (no doubt tipped off by Alice, who can be relied upon for betrayal). He persuades Hanna back with the promise of pancakes for tea, which he will make himself *with his own fair hands*. Hanna is so surprised and delighted by his attention that she returns home willingly.

'You're not cross, Daddy?' she says as they walk back together hand in hand. She can see he isn't.

'No, love.'

Pressing her advantage, she says, 'Next time you go away, can I come with you?'

He glances briefly at her. 'What would you do? Come to my meetings with me?'

'I could help,' Hanna says.

He laughs. 'Sure. OK.'

But Hanna is surprised the following Monday when she comes down for breakfast to find he is gone again. He'll be in Hong Kong all week, her mother says.

'But I was supposed to go too,' Hanna says. 'He said so.'

Her mother frowns. 'Don't be silly, Hanna. He must have been teasing you.'

Michael, eating his cereal at the table, snorts. Milk dribbles unat-tractively out of the corner of his mouth. 'Why would he take you?

God, you're such a moron.' He is twelve and has recently started to get spots.

'Shut up!' Hanna says.

'Moron.'

'*Shut up!*' she shouts.

'Now look what you've done,' her mother says to Michael. 'She's going to have another tantrum.'

HANNA'S FATHER WORKS IN the buying department of a large toy company. He is in charge of girls' toys and pocket money, which are two of the company's most valuable categories, he says. He brings home samples for Hanna and Alice and Michael to play with, and at school they are popular because they are always first with the latest craze. They have the first Tamagotchis, the first light-up yo-yos, the first Game Boy Color with *Pokémon Blue*, and they also get the special editions nobody else can get hold of, like the rainbow Furby that sells out everywhere within days, and even, best of all, prototypes that were never released, which allows them to look pityingly at their classmates when asked where they could get one too.

They don't see their father much because he either works late or is away travelling, and when he is at home at the weekends, he usually remains shut away in his study for long hours, working hard, their mother says – although when Alice and Hanna spy on him one time he turns out to be playing solitaire on his computer.

'He's a rising star of the toy-buying world,' Hanna's mother says, though her voice has that strange note in it that it only seems to get when she talks about Hanna's father.

Hanna tries to make the most of the times when her father is home.

The highlight of her childhood is Research Sundays. Sometimes – not every week, but enough for these meetings to take on a feeling of regularity – her father will invite the children into his study on a Sunday afternoon, and they will sit in a solemn semicircle on the floor whilst he asks them questions about the most recent toys he's brought home.

Alice and Michael are limited and unimaginative in their answers, saying things like, 'I liked that it made a funny noise,' and then Alice will squirm with shyness and smile foolishly, and Michael will scowl as if this is the stupidest task in the world. Sometimes they are unable to say anything at all unless prompted by their father: 'And do you like the fact that it lights up, or do you not mind about that? And would you prefer it if it came in more colours?'

Hanna might feel ashamed of her siblings were it not for the chance it gives her to outshine them. Unlike the others, she comes prepared to these Sunday conferences, bustling up the stairs with fresh ideas at the ready. She devotes a significant amount of time each week to analysing what it is she likes or doesn't like about the toys, making lists in her large, uneven handwriting in one of her special notebooks. Inventive and resourceful, she is a 'blue-sky thinker' (her father says) who always 'goes above and beyond'. She even takes her notebooks to school with her and interviews her classmates about the toys they like, pushing them irritably when they are too vague in their answers. 'I'm helping my dad in his career,' she tells them. 'He's a rising star of the toy-buying world.'

She delivers these notebooks to her father, who laughs and says he wishes everyone on his team were as committed as she is.

'It's nice of him,' Hanna's mother says to her one Sunday after Hanna has been briefing her father in his study, 'to play along with your little game.'

Hanna looks at her mother narrowly. She wishes, as she has done many times before, that it were her father who was home all the time instead of her mother. He seems to like her so much more than her mother does. Why can't it be her mother who is sent off to Hong Kong for a week? She could lecture the people of Hong Kong about regulating their emotions instead.

Her mother's emotions, even regulated, are a frightening thing. There is the year, for instance, they forget Mother's Day. Hanna and Alice are six years old, Michael ten. Usually their father reminds them, and takes them to buy a card and a present, but this year he is away, and it must have slipped his mind. The children do not know, at first, why their mother won't speak to them at breakfast, why she bangs the milk bottle down on the table and snatches their bowls away for the dishwasher before they've finished eating. Even when she retires to her room later that morning with a headache and leaves them to their own devices, they do not realize what they have done. They do know, of course, that something is wrong. Hanna and Alice go to knock timidly on their mother's bedroom door after a while, and ask if there's anything they can get her. She snaps at them to go away. 'Can't I have a second's peace? Do I not even deserve that?'

At lunchtime, they agree it's best not to disturb her again and Michael makes the three of them jam sandwiches. They eat standing up in the kitchen, which feels strange to Hanna, and clean up carefully after themselves. Then they sit in the living room watching television, and don't even squabble over what to put on. They are not usually allowed to watch television in the daytime; they are expected to be out on a wholesome walk, or riding their bikes, or playing a board game with their mother, or reading. But today they are too unsettled even to enjoy this treat. They keep the volume down, and talk in hushed voices as though there has been a death in the family, tiptoeing about and closing doors softly.

'She's just ill,' Michael says. 'She'll feel better this evening.'

'What if she doesn't?' Alice says. 'What will we have for tea?'

'I'll take care of it,' Michael says, and Hanna sighs at the thought of more jam sandwiches.

But their mother does emerge in the evening, and, despite their best efforts to be quiet and helpful, the explosion comes.

'Is this how little I matter to you?' she hisses at them, as they stand in an abashed line in the kitchen. 'After everything I've done for you, is this how you treat me, with such *utter contempt*?'

'Mummy, we're sorry,' Alice says, immediately in tears.

Beneath her own fear, Hanna thinks scornfully that Alice doesn't even know what she's apologizing for.

Michael is braver. He says, 'What did we do, Mum?'

A mistake. She rounds on him. 'You really don't know? You're really so disgustingly selfish that you have no idea at all? I don't know how I've brought you up to be so uninterested in others, so utterly selfish and self-absorbed. You really have no idea what day it is today?'

'Your birthday!' Alice blurts in a panic, but Hanna knows this isn't it; their mother's birthday was months ago.

'Mother's Day,' Michael says softly, and the shock of it goes through Hanna at once, turning her cold. Of course.

Their mother gives a bitter laugh. 'Yes. Mother's Day. Which clearly doesn't mean much to you. Never mind that I run around after you every other day of the year. I suppose a cup of tea in bed, maybe even a card, is too much to ask. I suppose I don't matter enough even for that. Even my own children don't love me.' Her voice shakes.

'We do love you,' Michael says. He seems like he is about to cry as well, and Hanna looks away, embarrassed for him.

'I really don't know why I bother,' their mother says. She stalks out of the kitchen.

They spend the evening making her a special dinner tray and a home-made card using Alice's craft set. They only manage beans on toast and a cup of tea for the meal, with a Mars bar Michael's been saving in his room, but Michael writes a message in the card on behalf of all of them, saying how sorry they are and that they will get her a present as soon as they can. They all sign their names at the bottom.

'We should have remembered,' Michael says.

'It moves though,' Hanna says, starting to feel the first stirrings of outrage. 'Every year. It's like a trick!'

'Dad should have reminded us,' Michael says. 'This is his fault.'

'It isn't,' Hanna says.

'I hate him.'

'Shut up!'

Then Alice starts to get tearful again, baby that she is, and they have to make up.

When they knock on their mother's bedroom door, she tells them to go away. Her voice sounds thick and shaky, so they know she is crying. They put the tray down carefully outside the door and slink back down-stairs. When they return to check later, the tray is gone. They don't see their mother again that night, but when they come down to breakfast in the morning, there she is, and although she remains cold towards them, she does make their packed lunches for school, and so they are relieved the storm seems to have blown over. After school, they pool all the money they have saved from Christmas, birthdays and pocket money, muster

£23.73 between them, and buy their mother a delicate silver necklace from a boutique in Wimbledon Village.

'My darlings,' she says when they present it. 'It's lovely. I hope you haven't spent too much. You shouldn't have.'

ONE OF GREATEST CATASTROPHES of Hanna's childhood occurs when she is ten. Her father's company promotes him to the preschool category because he has been doing so well (no doubt as a result of Hanna's help, Hanna thinks, in her first taste of the brutality of irony). He will be the only buyer for this category, he tells them, and not part of a team.

'Isn't that great?' he says. 'I'll be my own boss.'

'Your father certainly has a gift for inhabiting a child's mindset,' their mother says.

He travels as much as ever, but it soon becomes clear that he no longer needs any help with his research. The toys he buys now are for babies. When Hanna tries to bring him her latest findings, he says, 'Thanks, love, but that's not part of my job anymore.'

Hanna has her notebook in hand, already open to the right page, with her lists of colour-coded comments on Dentist Barbie. He makes no move to take it from her.

'Well, shall I have a look at the baby toys?' she says.

'Oh Hanna,' he says. 'You're not a baby though, are you? You're much too clever and sensible to play with baby toys.'

'But I can remember being a baby,' Hanna says. 'I can remember it really clearly. As though it was yesterday. So I can just imagine I'm a baby again and tell you what I think of the toys.'

'No, darling, that won't work. It's a hassle for me to bring toys home, anyway.'

'Well, there's lots of things I can remember,' she says. 'I liked Tiny Tears and Timmy, they were really good, and I liked the pram I had for them and—'

'I said no,' he says, more sharply. 'Now be a good girl and go and play with Alice.'

Hanna is always being fobbed off with Alice, who has been sent to earth as a test of Hanna's patience. Everyone says they are 'peas in a pod' but this is only because they are twins (and not even identical ones at that). 'Be nice to Alice,' is the world's refrain; Hanna gets it at school and at home. But why? Hanna never asked to be given Alice. If she could, she would give her back. In school they learn the story of Cain and Abel, and of course Hanna identifies strongly with Cain. She thinks Abel must have had it coming if he drooped about in the stupid way Alice does, if Abel had the same weird craft projects and big tearful eyes. Poor Cain. 'Be nice to Abel,' people probably kept telling him.

'Alice is such a sweet, good-natured girl,' their mother announces, herald-like, to strangers. 'So steady and helpful.'

One of Alice's helpful habits is her passion for tidying. Their mother claims this started even when Alice was a toddler, as if she was fated, from birth, to be a more pleasing child than Hanna (Alice probably even kept her side of the womb tidier).

'Alice's instinct for neatness is extraordinary,' Hanna's mother tells people. 'When the girls were very little, I couldn't work out what was going on. I'd walk into a room that had earlier been in an absolute *state*, and find it suddenly spick and span. Like the elves had been. And eventually I realized it was little Alice, toddling about and putting things away whilst I wasn't looking. The trouble was, she would sometimes put things in strange places and it would take me months to find them again!' She laughs in a way that Hanna thinks sounds most unlike her. And

Hanna reflects that if she had gone round effectively hiding her parents' things, her mother wouldn't be telling everyone how adorable this behaviour was.

Besides tidying, Alice's other hobby is to take old shoeboxes and stick little cardboard partitions in them to create rooms, and cut a small flap into the side as a door. She makes furniture out of cardboard, corks, plastic bobbins, buttons, matchboxes and anything else she can forage, and she uses scraps of fabric to make carpets and rugs and curtains, and old wrapping paper for wallpaper (which she carefully saves at Christmas and birthdays, going '*Ha*-nna' if Hanna dares to crumple it). She even paints tiny pictures to go on the walls, framed with thicker cardboard.

Their father still brings Alice proper doll's-house furniture sometimes; he hasn't noticed that she never uses it, although she thanks him politely every time. It infuriates Hanna that Alice prefers her own stupid homemade furniture to the special sets their father gets her. The houses remain unpeopled, too. Alice has little wooden dolls, but she never allows them inside.

Sometimes (often) Hanna imagines stamping on these cardboard houses. How good it would feel.

'You're my best friend,' Alice tells her, and Hanna replies quickly, 'You're not mine.'

HANNA RUNS AWAY AGAIN a few months after her father starts his job as a preschool buyer. She plans her escape for the weekend so he will definitely be around, but in the event it is only Alice the Unwanted who comes after her, chasing her almost all the way to Wimbledon Common.

'Did they send you?' Hanna says, still striding along.

'No!' Alice says, out of breath as she struggles to keep up. 'I told them you'd gone and they said not to go after you. Mummy said you were doing it for attention.'

'What did Daddy say?' Hanna stops abruptly and turns to face her sister, who is taken by surprise and nearly crashes into her.

Alice screws up her face as she tries to remember. 'He said you'd come back when you got hungry. Hanna, you have to come back with me *now* or we'll both get in trouble.'

Hanna says, 'Go home. I don't want you.'

When she walks on, Alice still tries to follow, so Hanna stops again, gives her a shove and says, 'Go *home*, Alice. I mean it!'

And this time, when she begins to walk on, Alice stays where she is. Hanna can feel her sister's mournful gaze on her back until she finally turns the corner.

Now, Hanna pauses. She hasn't set off with a clear idea of where she is going, only that her father will discover her gone and be worried.

In the end she resorts to the familiar and steps on to the rough grassland at the edge of the Common, heading towards the woodland where the trees create an artificial darkness and the sounds of the road become muffled. Usually when she comes here with her mother they see lots of other people, but it has been raining recently and the path is muddy underfoot, so perhaps everyone has decided to stay at home. She sees nobody except for a bald man coming the other way with his dog; he gives her a brief nod as he passes, and Hanna nods back, pleased with the grown-up nature of this interaction. The thought that she is alone in these woods gives her a shuddery thrill.

Once she leaves the path and walks into the thicket of trees to her right, it doesn't take her long to find a good tree and she scrambles up into it, not pausing until the branches become too spindly for her to climb any further. She is an adventurer, an explorer, a reckless outlaw.

She is just settling herself on a thick branch when she becomes aware of someone else's presence. It gives her a start. At the base of the tree: the bald man from before. His dog, a Labrador, puttering around in the background. The man is looking up at Hanna. From ten feet up, she takes in a general sense of him, his weathered skin, his bulky shape. A blue waterproof coat. She is sure he has pale eyelashes and eyebrows, blond or white, though afterwards she thinks she cannot possibly have been able to see this from her position up in the tree.

The man says, 'You have a good view from up there?' He has a nice, gentle voice, a bit like Hanna's father.

Hanna feels foolish, no longer an adventurer but a child caught in a silly game. She says, 'Yes.'

'I used to like climbing trees,' the man says. 'Don't get much of a chance these days.'

Hanna wonders for an awkward moment if she is supposed to invite him to join her in this tree. She remains silent, watching as the dog wanders over. The man strokes its head gently.

'His name's Branston,' he says. 'Like the pickle. Would you like to say hello to him?'

'Hello Branston,' Hanna says.

The bald man laughs, a low, soft sound. 'I meant down here, where you can stroke him. He'd like that.'

The tree branch is damp and Hanna is beginning to feel the cold seeping through her jeans and even through her pants. Nevertheless, something makes her hesitate.

'No, thank you,' she says, making her voice very polite.

'It must be nearly your teatime,' the man says. 'Won't your parents be worried?'

Hanna nods dumbly.

'Come on,' the man says. 'It can't be very comfortable up there, and it's not very safe, either. Come on down.'

Mechanically, Hanna begins to climb down towards him. Then she stops again. There is a peculiar thrumming beneath the surface of her skin, and some new current in the air that she does not recognize. The man is still staring up at her, and he is just ordinary-looking, and he has a nice dog, and she is in a place she has been hundreds of times before, close to home – but all the same, she has the sense that something beyond normal life is now occurring. She has climbed a tree and somehow found herself in a different place entirely. She is only half aware of herself thinking these things; she doesn't have the language for them. But the shudder within her hardens into an unreflecting resolve to stay in the tree.

She remains where she is, saying nothing.

'Come on,' the man says again.

Hanna won't look at him now. She stays frozen, does not look down, does not acknowledge him. It is some vague approximation of playing dead.

'Don't be silly,' the man says.

But it has no effect on Hanna, because she has absented herself; she has put up a force field around herself. She tells herself he cannot even see her any longer, not through the force field. If she stays still and quiet, he will forget she is there.

The man continues to stand there for a few more minutes, and then without saying a word, he turns and walks away. The dog trots after him.

Even once he has gone, Hanna does not climb down. She waits in the tree and gradually the twilight begins to gather around her. Her limbs are stiff from the uncomfortable position and she is chilled to the bone. She becomes aware, after a while, that she needs the toilet very badly. As more time passes and the pressure in her bladder grows unbearable, she even considers allowing herself to pee just like this, just where she is, but the thought of her mother's disgust if she returns home with soaked pants and trousers is enough to tighten her muscles and prevent the release of a drop.

It is almost dark by the time she finally climbs down. She takes the descent very carefully, pausing for long periods to listen for any sound, any rustle of leaves or snapping of twigs nearby. There is only silence. Her heart is beating very fast. Still, she hesitates for a long time before she makes the final jump to the ground. She lands clumsily and rights herself. Then she runs.

WHEN SHE FINALLY TRAILS back in through the front door, breathless and bedraggled, it is six thirty. She goes to the toilet first – a great relief – and then goes into the living room, where her mother is on the sofa with a book. Hanna assumes she will be in big trouble for staying out for so long, but her mother merely raises her eyebrows and says, 'I thought you'd tire of your silly drama eventually. I would have been very annoyed if I'd had to go looking for you.'

'I met a man with a dog,' Hanna says.

Her mother's eyes are on her book again.

'He wanted me to come down from the tree,' Hanna says. 'To meet his dog.'

'I've told you not to climb trees,' her mother says. She looks at Hanna properly now, taking in her appearance with a critical expression. 'Look at the state of you.'

Hanna searches again for a way to explain, and finally says instead, 'Where's Daddy?'

'In his study. Don't disturb him.' Her mother regards Hanna for a few moments longer. 'Look, darling,' she says more gently. 'It's time you stopped all this silly behaviour. The tantrums, the running away. If you don't correct it now, you'll be in real trouble later on. I'm only trying to help you.'

Hanna nods.

As she turns to go, her mother says with sudden eagerness, 'Supper will be ready in ten minutes. And I've made apple crumble. That will be nice, won't it?'

Hanna agrees that it will be. She leaves the room, closing the door behind her.

Upstairs, she knocks quietly on the door of her father's study.

'What is it?' his voice says.

'It's me,' Hanna says. When there is no answer, she pushes the door open and steps inside the room, hovering just over the threshold. Her father is still typing something at the computer, but after a moment he finishes and swivels his chair towards her.

'What is it, love?' he says again, sounding a little impatient now.

'I'm back,' she says softly.

'Yes, I can see that.' He looks at her for a few moments with a frown. 'Everything OK?'

'Yes.'

'OK, love. Well, was there anything you wanted?'

She shakes her head.

'Well, run along now and play with Alice. I have a lot of work to do.'

He turns back to the computer and resumes typing as he says this. He doesn't look round as Hanna leaves.

On the landing, Alice has appeared.

'You're *back*,' she says. 'I was waiting for you in the garden, but then it started to get dark and Mummy said I had to come inside.' She tries to fling her arms around Hanna, but Hanna shakes her off angrily, saying, 'Don't be an idiot.' When Alice just stands there looking at her in that stupid way of hers, Hanna says, 'You're such a stupid baby, Alice.'

She never tries to tell anyone else about the encounter with the man in the woods, but some years later, when she is a teenager, she thinks she sees his face again. It is a picture in the *Evening Standard*, which lies discarded next to her on a train seat. Hanna looks at the picture and feels a disorientating jolt of recognition. Those pale eyelashes, which she can't possibly have seen, the shape of the bald head. Beside his picture there is another one, of a young girl in school uniform. Hanna doesn't read the story. She knows it can't be the same man.

SOMETIMES AT NIGHT HANNA lies awake and puzzles over the fact that she seems to have the wrong mother. She is sure that your mother is supposed to like you, or at the very least not actually *dislike* you. Hanna can see in many ways the problem is with herself, in being a fundamentally unlikeable person. But all the same, even if you aren't very likeable, your mother is not supposed to realize. Even murderers have mothers who love them and who visit them in prison (Hanna knows this for a fact; she has watched a documentary).

Nonetheless, Hanna is certain – almost certain – that there was a time when her mother liked her more. She remembers the feel of her mother's arms around her when she was very young, and her mother's lovely, comforting smell. She remembers the chest infections she used to get when she was so wheezy every breath was a struggle and she was always frightened the next one would not come; her mother would sit beside her bed all through the night, talking softly to her to keep her calm, and bringing her bowls of hot water so she could inhale the steam.

It all seemed to unravel quite quickly, but Hanna never does work out what went wrong.

'It was like she just went off me one day,' she tells her best friend Kemi when they are seventeen, sitting in the common room of their college. 'I don't know why.'

'Your personality must have emerged,' Kemi says, and Hanna shoves her off the arm of the sofa.

IT IS HANNA'S FATHER, in the end, who runs away from home and does not come back. Hanna is thirteen by this stage. Because he often travels during the week, it takes the children some time to realize he has actually gone for good. The first weekend he doesn't come back, their mother says he has been held up at a conference.

The second weekend, Hanna queries his absence again.

Her mother stares at her for a few moments, wearing that expression she sometimes assumes when Hanna is being particularly difficult. Then she sighs. 'Can you go and get the others?'

Hanna fetches Michael and Alice from upstairs and they sit side by side on the living-room sofa facing their mother. Hanna wonders if something terrible has happened. A plane crash – except she would have seen that on the news. A car crash, then. She feels sick. It would be just like her mother to learn of their father's death and then not tell them for a fortnight.

But he is, as it turns out, alive and well and living in New Malden.

'Your father won't be coming back here,' her mother says. 'He's left us.'

There is a short, shocked silence and then Michael says, *Left* us? What do you mean?'

'He's been having an affair with a woman at work,' their mother says, 'and now he's left to be with her. In New Malden. Of course, we'll be getting a divorce.'

At the shocking word 'divorce', Alice actually gasps, like they're at the denouement of a murder mystery.

'Her name's Susan,' their mother adds, irrelevantly.

Michael, seventeen now and perhaps already feeling the weight of his new role as man of the house, says absurdly, 'No. He can't do that. It's not on. He has *responsibilities*.'

Their mother says nothing.

Alice is looking tearful, and Michael furious. Hanna seems to be the only one who doesn't blame their father for leaving. She would leave herself if she could.

'So where is he now?' Michael says. 'With *her*?'

'Yes, darling. But you'll still see him. He'll come at weekends and . . . take you for days out.' Their mother says this last part rather doubtfully, as though she can't really picture it either.

'I don't want to see him,' Michael says.

'Then you don't have to,' their mother says.

It occurs to Hanna that perhaps she will be able to go and live with her father now. Her heart lifts a little.

'You'll always have us, Mum,' Michael says, and their mother smiles sadly, and reaches across the coffee table to grasp his hand.

'Thank you, my darling,' she says. 'You know that none of this is your fault, don't you?'

Of course it isn't, Hanna thinks. It's yours.

There is a long silence, punctuated only by the sound of Alice's sniffling.

'I suppose it serves me right,' their mother says at last, 'for marrying a man who plays with toys for a living.'

4

T HEY ARE RICH BEFORE the divorce, but Alice doesn't realize until that life is already over.

About a year after her parents separate, they move from the big house in Wimbledon to a small terraced house in Morden (her father has now moved from New Malden to Barnes with Susan, his partner in sin). The Morden house is less than half the size of the Wimbledon house. Life becomes a vista of hardship. They no longer eat Kellogg's cereal but supermarket own brand. Loo roll, in the new life, is rough and scratchy.

The thing about divorce, Alice discovers, is that there is a finite amount of money to go around, and where it used to cover one household, now it has to cover two. The logic is unassailable.

The most shocking change of all is that Alice and Hanna no longer get their own bedrooms, and Hanna is not shy about expressing her disgust at having to share. Adding to the controversy is the fact that Michael gets his own room, which also happens to be slightly larger than the room in which twin beds are installed for Hanna and Alice.

'A *double bed*?' Hanna says in disbelief. 'He gets the biggest room, with a *double bed*, and he's left for university! Meanwhile we're stuck in this weird, tiny cupboard-room. We're fourteen now, for God's sake! We need our own space. We're trying to *blossom into women* here.'

Alice takes in the room again; it does have a depressing feel to it with its tired red carpet and lumpy wallpaper. There is a slight feeling of damp in the air and although the two beds are pushed against opposite walls, they are still close enough that she and Hanna could reach out and hold hands in the night, should they wish to (Alice has a strong suspicion Hanna will not wish to).

'It's a travesty, that's what it is,' Hanna says. 'We have to live in this *cubicle* whilst Michael dwells in palatial splendour next door – on the few occasions he actually deigns to come home, that is.' She pauses for breath. 'Do you think Mum will hang a huge portrait of him above the bed like Chairman Mao?'

'He's the favourite,' Alice says, and Hanna nods.

'I don't know why,' she says. 'He's the worst one.'

Alice laughs in spite of herself, enjoying this moment of unity between them. She is secretly relieved to discover that she is not considered the worst one.

Then Hanna says, 'Well, there's no two ways about it. You'll have to talk to her.'

'Why me?' It hasn't even occurred to Alice that it is within their power to remedy the situation.

'She greatly prefers you,' Hanna says, and Alice tries to argue, though guiltily she knows this is true.

'She'll just say I'm being dramatic,' Hanna says. 'It'll be much better coming from you.'

Predictably, their mother refuses to shift on the bedroom decision, though Alice, for Hanna's sake, tries her best.

'The thing is, I just think we'd benefit from the space a bit more,' she tells her mother. 'Especially now we have more schoolwork.'

'You can work at the table downstairs,' her mother says. 'That way I can supervise you.'

'Can we at least use Michael's room as a study when he isn't here?'

'Of course not,' her mother says. 'That would be a violation of his privacy.'

As a last resort, Alice even tries calling up Michael. They have never before spoken on the phone, and she hears the anxiety in his voice when he picks up, perhaps assuming someone has died.

'Just calling for a chat,' Alice says quickly, though this doesn't seem to reassure him.

'About what?' he says suspiciously. 'I'm in the middle of an important essay on Thatcher's economic reforms.'

When Alice plucks up the courage to ask how he'd feel about a room swap, he says, 'Don't be ridiculous.'

He sounds just like their mother in moments like this, Alice thinks.

'But we need it more,' she says.

'It's already been decided,' Michael says. 'My hands are tied.'

Alice has to return to Hanna and admit defeat. It is the end of the truce Hanna has called between them. Now, Hanna buys duct tape – the silver kind that serial killers use – and makes a line down the middle of the carpet, between the two beds. 'Do not cross this line,' she says to Alice. 'Even if I'm not here, I'll know.'

Alice does not ask how she will know. She promises not to cross the line.

THEIR FATHER IS A distant figure now, though Alice does not particularly miss him. He was a distant figure all along, flimsy and insubstantial in comparison to the fierce immediacy of their mother. In some ways, he takes up more space in her life these days than he did before. Now two weekends every month must be devoted to visiting him in Barnes. (His new house is larger than theirs, Alice can't help noticing; and the loo roll is very soft.)

She and Hanna submit to these visits quietly, though they talked at first of refusing to see him. Alice was surprised that Hanna was on board with the boycott, but it turned out their father had enraged her by saying she couldn't move in with him. However, their mother has always insisted the visits take place, perhaps driven by that peculiar sense of honour that seems to emerge in her from time to time.

Susan, the Other Woman, has proven an unexpectedly matronly figure. She is actually quite nice, as Alice and Hanna admit to each other eventually. She fusses around them, making them their favourite meals. Their father stays in his study a lot of the time, working.

'He's a bit of a workaholic, your dad,' Susan tells them apologetically, and then offers them more chocolate pudding.

When they get home from these visits on Sunday afternoon, their mother is usually silent. It often takes until after supper before she will speak to them properly. In the early days, she would ask them how the visit had gone, and though Alice quickly learned to say, 'It was boring, Mum. We missed you,' Hanna continued to answer with, 'Exceptional, thanks!' until after a while their mother stopped asking.

DESPITE THEIR NEW STRAITENED circumstances, it is decided that Alice and Hanna will stay at their private school until they've sat their GCSEs.

'That woman will have to forgo her lavish lifestyle until you've got your qualifications,' their mother says.

'Oh, brilliant,' Hanna says, but only to Alice. 'Another two years in that prison. What will they reward us with next? A flogging?'

But Alice suspects Hanna of secretly liking their school. Forever the rebel without a cause, Hanna finally, in their all-girls private school, has something to push against. She rolls the waistband of her skirt up so it is indecently short, wears hoop earrings when they are only allowed studs, paints her nails midnight blue when they are not even allowed clear polish, collects multicoloured shag bands on her wrists, which stealthily reappear however many times she is told to remove them. Her work is scrappy; Alice watches her doing her homework in front of the TV – carelessly, with a purple pen (not allowed) – and winces.

'But why get in trouble for no reason?' she asks her sister. 'It's so easy not to.'

She is genuinely trying to be helpful, but she can immediately see from Hanna's expression how she has blundered.

'Easy when you're Miss Fucking Perfect, perhaps,' Hanna says. (Hanna has recently discovered the emphatic properties of swear words, and Alice has to work hard not to show any reaction.)

Hanna forgets her lacrosse stick so often on the days they have PE that Alice starts to suspect she is doing it on purpose. As Alice and her partner – usually a large, stolid girl called Jess Moore who is as miserably clumsy and uncoordinated as Alice herself – attempt to toss the ball back and forth between their nets, Alice watches Hanna jog slowly round the edge of the pitch, completing the punitive laps before she is allowed to borrow a stick.

'Just take mine for today,' Alice offers a couple of times. 'I'll say I forgot, or else I'll say I have my period.' They both know she won't get into anything like the trouble Hanna does, and if the teacher does make Alice run laps – which she might do, so as to appear fair – she will issue the instruction apologetically, and give Alice an encouraging smile every time she jogs past.

But Hanna is not interested. 'I can take care of myself,' she says, which seems unnecessarily dramatic to Alice, since they are only talking about a lacrosse stick after all.

Still, although Hanna exasperates her teachers, she seems to attract other students. At break times and lunchtimes, she always has an admiring throng about her. Alice is never invited to join them, and if she ever tries to sidle up to speak to her sister, Hanna raises her eyebrows in that cold way that makes Alice want to cry, and says, 'Can we help you?'

On home-clothes days, Hanna and her gang wear wide-leg skater jeans with Vans or DCs and cropped T-shirts (flagrantly breaking the no-bare-midriffs rule, and resulting in them all being sent to Lost Property in a giggling gang to receive spare school jumpers to tie round their waists). They line their eyes with kohl pencils and scrape their hair back into folded ponytails with just a few stray wisps around the face. Alice, oblivious to the tides of noughties fashion, wears navy cords from Gap with colourful stripy jumpers and her beloved pair of sparkly blue Mary Janes. She wears her hair in a neat plait. The mere sight of her is enough to send Hanna's eyes heavenwards in despair.

'You dress like a children's TV presenter,' she tells Alice.

Alice doesn't see why this is such a bad thing.

Although they are in the same form until Year 9, Alice soon learns to follow Hanna's lead in avoiding each other. They catch the bus together every morning but Alice knows better than to try to sit with Hanna, who will go to join her friends if they're already on the bus, or if she's in a seat by herself, will put her bag next to her so Alice can't sit there. One time as the bus pulls up, Alice says, 'Would you rather I just waited and got on the next one?' She is aiming for sarcasm, but Hanna turns to her and says expressionlessly, 'That would be great,' and Alice is so thrown (are they both joking, or is neither of them joking?) that she does end up staying where she is on the pavement and catching the next bus, seven minutes later, on her own.

'Do you ever wish you weren't a twin?' she asks Hanna once, masochistically, hoping for the closeness of a shared confidence, however painful.

And without missing a beat, Hanna says, 'Actually, I've never really thought of myself as a twin.'

FOR ALICE, THERE ARE positives and negatives about the school experience. Positives include the smart blue skirt with its crisp pleats, the old wooden desks with lids that open, the different-coloured exercise books for each subject which Alice fills with her neat, precise writing, and the rules that seem to her so clear and consistent (especially compared to the somewhat arbitrary and unpredictable rules at home).

The chief negative is the friendship issue. Alice is not popular like Hanna. She is shy and awkward, and her only friend is Jess Moore, who she sits with in most lessons, except for Maths, because Jess is better at Maths than Alice, so they are in different sets. In Maths, Alice sits alone.

Alice is grateful to have Jess, but she sometimes feels that it is more a friendship of convenience than a meeting of minds. And occasionally it strikes her that Jess is not all that nice to her. She seems to regard Alice as someone who needs taking in hand.

'Hurry *up*, Alice,' she'll say on their way to lessons. 'You're so slow. God, stop *daydreaming*.'

Or she might say, 'God, I'm so embarrassed about my mark in the Biology test. I only got 84 per cent,' when she knows Alice got 62 per cent (knows because she craned her neck to look at Alice's paper when they were being handed back).

And, 'I heard everyone in your Maths set are going to be put in for the intermediate paper, not the higher paper. Did you know that means you can't get higher than a B? I didn't even know our school *offered* anything lower than the higher paper. Do you mind? I'd mind.'

Alice weathers all this patiently, aware that it is the price she must pay for not sitting alone in lessons or at lunch. And Alice does seem to be the kind of person others feel compelled to offer advice to, so perhaps it is not Jess's fault; perhaps Alice simply brings something out in her.

'You shouldn't let her boss you about,' Hanna tells her, bossily.

Jess talks a lot, and has many stories she likes to regale Alice with. The bad luck that has dogged her family is extraordinary. Whenever the need arises, she will dip into her bank of personal tragedy and produce a choice example. Alice will listen, wide-eyed in sympathy. She has heard how two of Jess's grandparents were killed in (separate) car accidents, how her aunt died in the Lockerbie bombing, how her uncle went down with the *Herald of Free Enterprise* and how her younger brother succumbed to an illness so rare it doesn't yet have a name.

Whilst Alice's natural tendency is to believe anything she is told, her classmates are quicker off the mark. In a Classical Civilization lesson in Year 9, when they are learning about the Battle of Thermopylae, Hanna calls out from the back, 'Didn't Jess lose an uncle or two at Thermopylae?' and the class collapses. Alice feels her own face getting hot, as if the humiliation belongs to her as well.

It is shortly after this that the drama of the threatening notes begins. Jess is suddenly receiving anonymous notes several times a day, left in her bag, or on her desk when she's not around, slipped through the gaps in her locker, or even tucked inside one of her exercise books. *STUPID BITCH*, the notes say in jagged capitals. *WHY DON'T U JUST KILL URSELF?* And, *NOBODY LIKES U*. And, *UR A FAT PIG*.

Briefly, the whole year group is outraged. Although Jess is not much liked, everyone agrees that the notes are a step too far. The writer is nasty, and a coward. Alice, distressed on her friend's behalf, can nonetheless see how Jess basks in the collective rallying behind her cause. Even Alice seems to attain a vicarious glamour through her position as Jess's best friend, with well-wishers coming up to her regularly for updates.

Sentries are set up in shifts to monitor Jess's desk and locker, but the note-sender is too fiendishly clever for them, and only strikes when there is no one else close by, which is almost never. The first they know of it, every single time, is when Jess actually finds the note.

Jess's parents threaten to involve the police unless the school unmasks the culprit promptly and takes appropriate action. The police will apparently be coming into school to question everyone if the note-sender isn't found. Jess announces this self-importantly to the form group, who have gathered round to listen to her latest update at break. But the form, on the whole, are less impressed with this development. The general consensus is that the police have better things to do with their time. (The police seem to think so too, since they never make an appearance.) Nonetheless, for at least two weeks of the summer term, the threatening notes and investigation are all anyone in their year talks about.

It is Hanna who says to Alice one day, 'Don't you find it weird that nobody ever sees any of the notes being placed? But Jess always has a new one, every break, every lunch. Without fail. Even when no one has been near her desk except her.'

Alice shakes her head. This is just evidence of the diabolical cunning of the note-sender.

Hanna huffs out a sigh, half amused, half exasperated. 'Never mind,' she says.

The culprit is never found. The notes continue for most of that term, but it is impossible, even at a girls' school, for the same fever pitch of excitement to be maintained for more than three weeks, and gradually interest peters out, aided by the new rumour that Emma Parry let her boyfriend into school after hours and gave him a handjob in the music practice room. Eventually, the notes stop of their own accord.

APART FROM JESS MOORE, Alice's other best friend is her mother. This fact is declared on separate occasions both by Hanna and by their mother.

'It's weird,' Hanna informs Alice, as if she might not have worked this out for herself.

'It's a great gift to be close to your mother,' her mother tells her.

Alice is not sure why she is blessed with this closeness and Hanna is not, unless it is that Alice and her mother are so alike, both in looks and in temperament (her mother says), whereas Hanna has always been so wild.

'My Alice is very reserved,' their mother tells one of their new neighbours in Morden (who has not asked Celia to describe the personalities of her daughters). 'She doesn't relate well to children her own age. But Hanna's the opposite, a real tearaway – always charging about and climbing trees.'

'I haven't climbed a tree in *years*,' Hanna hisses at Alice as they sit at the top of the stairs eavesdropping.

Alice doesn't bother denying the charges against her. It is true, she thinks, that she doesn't fit in well with the other girls at school; she lacks Hanna's instinct for assimilation.

Alice tries to tell her mother everything, because this is what her mother wants, but she finds herself unintentionally letting her down. There are some things Alice can't put into words, like that feeling she gets sometimes at night, that lurch of sadness and terror she can't explain.

She says, 'Jess had early lunch today because of her flute lesson, so I had to go on my own. I was worried about it, but it was OK in the end.' It hadn't been OK; she had eaten quickly, head down, feeling as though everyone was staring at her with pity (though not enough for any of them to join her).

'Poor love,' her mother says. 'Didn't Hanna sit with you?'

'She had early lunch too,' Alice lies. 'For netball club.'

Alice's mother is hungry for her secrets. 'What are you hiding?' she says sometimes, and Alice tries not to hide anything, tries to empty herself out for her mother to inspect, but always there are a few stubborn traces that cling to her insides and won't be brought into the light.

Then there are her mother's moods, which have to be managed. The consequences for letting her mother down are severe, so it is better to be on guard, Alice finds. But sometimes she gets it wrong, despite her best efforts. This seems to happen more and more once Alice is a teenager; it suddenly becomes much harder to please her mother in the way she used to. Perhaps Alice and Hanna don't do the washing-up properly, or they leave a plate out on the side, or their school bags and shoes untidily strewn in the hall; perhaps they do not thank their mother properly for making dinner, or they ignore her for hours at a time (Alice is never aware until afterwards that they had been ignoring her), or they don't show enough enthusiasm when their mother suggests a family outing.

'She's mental,' Hanna says.

'She isn't,' Alice says. 'She's just sensitive. And we're all she's got.'

'Yeah, interesting to consider how that might have come about.'

One weekend in Year 10, Alice is invited out to the cinema with two girls in her form, Holly Pilkington and Margot Jin. Holly and Margot are also in her Maths set, though they don't usually speak to Alice much. But Alice particularly likes Margot, who is tomboyish and funny and plays the violin to Grade 8, which Margot says is basically the law because she's Chinese. Holly is less friendly than Margot, but has a very wide smile that appears occasionally, showing most of her crowded teeth. The two of them often seem to be laughing at a private joke together, but not in an intimidating way like the cooler girls.

The invitation comes only during Friday morning break, for a Saturday afternoon showing, so that Alice suspects someone else has dropped out. There is no mention of Jess, and although Alice fears she might be betraying her friend, she silences her nobler instincts and accepts the invitation. It is thrilling to be asked. They are to see *Cast Away* at 2.30 p.m. They will go for milkshakes afterwards.

Alice is wary about asking her mother but her mother merely shrugs and says, 'Please yourself.'

'But is that OK, Mum?' Alice persists. She never knows when to leave it, Hanna sometimes tells her. She is forever looking inside gift horses' mouths.

'I daresay it'll have to be,' her mother says in the same distant voice. 'We had planned to go for a walk. Had you forgotten?'

'No,' Alice says. 'But I thought we could go on Sunday instead.'

'I may not feel like it on Sunday.'

'Right. OK,' Alice says. 'Well, we can see how you feel on Sunday.'

'I'm surprised you have the money for the cinema,' her mother says. 'Or are you expecting me to reach into my pocket?'

'I have some of my birthday money left,' Alice says. 'From Grandma and Grandpa.'

Her mother makes no reply to this.

'She's being a bit weird about it,' Alice confides in Hanna later that evening.

'Of course she is,' Hanna says. She is sitting on her bed painting her nails, and doesn't look up at Alice.

'I think maybe I shouldn't go,' Alice says. 'I did say I'd go for a walk with Mum.' She is unsure as she says it whether she is hoping Hanna will agree with her or not. She is nervous about the trip — what if they find her boring and wish she hadn't come? — and perhaps she is looking for a way out.

'For God's sake,' Hanna says. 'Of course you should go. Don't be such a freak.'

'I'm just worried Mum will be on her own,' Alice says.

Hanna sighs theatrically. 'Look, go or don't go. I really don't care.'

Alice goes. The film is great, and she manages to chat normally to Holly and Margot. At one point she makes a joke and they laugh. She feels she conducts herself with distinction, and that Margot and Holly aren't regretting inviting her. She gets home just after seven in an excellent mood.

Her mother is in the sitting room, but Alice doesn't realize this immediately because the lights are off. It gives her quite a start when she goes in and switches on the light and sees her mother on the sofa.

'Mum,' she says, 'are you OK? What's wrong?'

'Why should anything be wrong?' her mother snaps, and Alice wants to tell her, but doesn't quite dare, that people don't usually sit in the dark.

When her mother doesn't speak again, Alice says tentatively, 'I had a nice time at the cinema.'

No response.

'The film was really good. We all cried at the end.'

Still her mother does not reply, or even turn her head to look at Alice.

'I had a chocolate milkshake,' Alice says desperately. 'It was really nice.' When her mother doesn't answer, Alice tries the tactic of a direct question. 'Where's Hanna?'

'Out,' her mother says. 'She said she'd be home by seven thirty for supper, but I won't be holding my breath.'

'What's for supper?' Alice asks. Foolishly.

Her mother lets out a sharp breath, and Alice realizes too late that her mother's fury is upon her.

When she speaks, her voice is loud and shaky. 'Am I expected to stay at home all day on my own, cooking for you, when you're so ungrateful, when you're so *selfish*?'

'Sorry, Mum,' Alice begins. 'I'll make supper. I didn't mean—'

'Just be abandoned here on my own, whilst you're out enjoying yourself, and then serve supper for you when you get home, *like a slave*?'

'It was only a few hours,' Alice says. It comes out whiny, as she feels the beginning of tears.

'Never mind that you had a prior engagement with me,' her mother says. 'Never mind that we'd already made plans. I'm only your mother. Just your boring old mother. Of course you should cancel on me. I don't matter, do I?'

'Of course you matter.' Alice is always bewildered at how quickly these confrontations seem to escalate, but even when she goes over each stage carefully in her head afterwards, she can never identify the point at which she might have been able to steer them to safety.

'I've lost you,' her mother says. 'I know I have, I've lost you.'

'No, Mum. You haven't lost me.'

'You're not the daughter I thought you were. I don't recognize this person in front of me.'

Alice looks for the right words, the ones which will placate her mother, but she feels panicked and can't think what to say. Every time she looks back on these arguments afterwards, she tells herself that next time she will remain calm, that *next time* she and her mother will both be reasonable. But the arguments always go on too long, and Alice can't maintain any detachment.

'I didn't bring you up to be so selfish,' her mother tells her.

'But you said I could go.'

'You make your own decisions. Don't put this on me.'

'I wasn't out for long.'

'Of course. It doesn't matter at all, does it? It doesn't matter what you've promised beforehand, you'll always drop me when a better offer comes along.'

'I'm sorry,' Alice says, because it seems to be the only thing she can say.

'You don't love me.'

Alice starts to cry now. Always the crybaby. 'I do!' she says.

When Hanna gets home twenty minutes later, Alice is sobbing on her bed. Downstairs, they can hear their mother crashing about in the kitchen, slamming pans down and banging cupboard doors.

Hanna stands in the doorway of their room.

'I see you went on your outing,' she says.

WHEN THEY MOVE TO the house in Morden, Alice throws out her entire collection of box houses, feeling Hanna's eyes on her as she bundles box after box into a black bin liner.

'What?' Alice says.

'It's just – you don't have to throw them all out,' Hanna says. 'Seems a bit drastic.'

Alice shrugs and continues to gather up the boxes. She thinks she understands Hanna's anxiety though; somehow it feels like the end of childhood.

She rarely thinks of her old hobby again once the boxes are gone, despite the hours she spent working on them. But some years later, after everything has gone wrong for Hanna, Alice will remember her cardboard houses and long for their familiar comfort. She will wish the two of them could shrink themselves down and inhabit those small, neat, quiet rooms.

In Morden, she has tried to get into scrapbooking, but since she rarely goes anywhere or does anything interesting she never has much to stick in them, and anyway Hanna says it's lame.

'Well, what should I do then?' Alice asks, genuinely curious.

Hanna throws up her hands. '*I* don't know. Something normal.'

'What would be a normal hobby?'

'Alice,' Hanna says, 'for the last time, teenagers are supposed to hang out with their friends and drink. They're not supposed to have *hobbies*.'

TAKING HANNA'S ADVICE, ALICE has tried to focus on her friendships instead of her crafts. In the wake of the cinema trip, she seems to be making real progress with Holly and Margot. In Maths, she now sits with them, in one of the rows of three desks down the middle of the room rather than at a two-person desk by herself. It is a considerable sign of status to be able to sit at the three-person desks, and Alice is delighted at the change in her fortunes.

She also sits with Holly and Margot at lunch, when Jess has her flute lesson, and sometimes she sits with them even when Jess is present, though Holly and Margot find Jess annoying (they have said so to Alice).

But Alice, while she can see their point, does not have it in her to abandon Jess completely.

Then in February a new girl joins Alice's form. This causes a stir, both because it is rare for anyone to move schools halfway through the year (and especially halfway through Year 10, when GCSE work is underway), and also because nothing properly exciting has happened to their year group since Jess's threatening-notes saga the previous year.

No one knows exactly why Milli Stephenson left her last school. It was a mixed state school in north London, she informs them, a note of pride in her voice: very rough, lots of drugs and stabbings; you had to be able to handle yourself. She seems to look rather pityingly upon their sheltered existence at a south-west London private school. In fact, her stories make it sound like she went to school in a war zone, though a girl in Margot's drama group attends the same school, which turns out to be located in a particularly leafy part of Hampstead. Margot shares this information with Holly, Alice and Jess, and they all roll their eyes.

'And Sophie's told me for a fact,' Margot adds, 'that there are no metal detectors on the doors, and never have been. And that everyone who goes there is super posh. Even posher than here!'

Joining a new school in the middle of the year strikes Alice as a terrifying prospect; the cliques are intimidating and impenetrable enough even when you've been there since Year 7. For this reason, she overlooks Milli's boasts about her previous school and tries to be extra friendly towards her, asking her if she is finding her way around OK and if she needs any help with anything.

Not that Milli gives the appearance of needing help. She rewards Alice's offer of assistance with a blank look, and is quite happy to approach the cliquiest clique in the form at break time, plonking herself down on the desk at the edge of their huddle and saying, 'So, what's new? Fill me in.'

Alice winces on Milli's behalf at the inevitable snub to follow. But Milli seems oblivious to the other girls' chilly reserve and pointed hesitations, which somehow renders their weapons useless against her; they are not the type who will ever tell her outright to go away. Before long, Milli has been absorbed into their group, and often seems to be at the heart of the laughter and chatter. A natural leader, Alice thinks, with respect. Just like Hanna.

Later, Alice is able to pinpoint the exact moment things start to go wrong. Not that this offers much comfort. Before morning registration one day, Milli is walking down the aisle between desks in the form room when she trips over Alice's bag, which Alice had only partially stowed beneath her desk. Milli gets her foot caught in one of the straps, which is poking out into the aisle, stumbles and then – Alice watches in horror as it unfolds – goes down.

Alice gets up quickly to help her, but it is too late: the other girls are laughing. They are not cruel, but slapstick gets them, and Milli's fall was dramatic.

'I'm sorry!' Alice says, trying to help her up, but Milli shakes her off and says savagely, 'Watch what you're doing, you fucking idiot.'

'Sorry,' Alice repeats, shocked at Milli's tone as much as her words.

'Well, don't fucking cry about it,' Milli says. She goes to rejoin her group, who are no longer laughing.

Alice, who was not crying, but now feels like she is about to, stares after her.

Margot gives her a look that says, *I think you've just made a powerful enemy*.

ALTHOUGH THE INCIDENT WITH the bag is the catalyst, it soon becomes clear that Milli's chief objection is to Alice's personality: her timidity, her irritating meekness, her infuriating, bland *niceness*. Whilst perhaps Milli strived at first to endure it patiently, eventually Alice proves too annoying for her to bear.

One of her chief contentions is that Alice is wet, pathetic, a crybaby. This seems particularly unfair to Alice because although she did use to cry often, even at small things, she has worked very hard to master this failing, developing a range of strategies worthy of the most determined rising business leader, and has in fact only cried a handful of times at school since Year 8.

'What's wrong *now*?' Milli will often say, stopping in front of Alice's desk.

'Nothing,' Alice replies, midway through a conversation with Margot or Holly or Jess.

'I'd better run for the tissues again,' Milli says. *'Je-sus.'*

She takes to calling Alice 'Moaning Myrtle', which eventually catches on amongst the others.

Alice wonders if she just has a very sad-looking face, because now people seem to call her Moaning Myrtle even when she feels quite cheerful. The trouble is, it is hard to remain cheerful when people are calling you Moaning Myrtle, so it becomes a bit of a self-fulfilling prophecy.

'Some people are natural victims,' Jess tells her, one natural victim to another.

'Better get the tissues ready,' Milli will murmur whenever Alice puts her hand up to answer a question in class. Or, 'Here come the waterworks.'

Alice stops putting up her hand.

Margot and Holly, to their credit, do not join in with the Myrtle joke, although they do not defend Alice either. Alice does not blame them for this. Jess does join in before long, with surprising glee. This hurts Alice particularly, because while she cannot be sure she would be brave enough to defend Jess if their situations were reversed (she thinks probably not), she is certain she would not add to her torment.

Holly and Margot never seem to be around now when Alice looks for them to go to lunch with, and she suspects them of deliberately avoiding her. One day she gets to Maths and finds Holly and Margot have arrived early and are sitting together at one of the two-person desks at the edge of the room, just as they used to. Holly carefully avoids Alice's eye, though Margot gives her a quick, apologetic look and makes a microscopic movement that might be a shrug.

Jess, somewhat to Alice's surprise, continues to sit with her in lessons and at lunch, despite joining in with the teasing. Alice suspects that this is less down to loyalty and more due to a lack of other options, but she is grateful nonetheless.

Unfortunately, this only leads to the next stage in Milli's campaign. Alice and Jess, she announces, are lezzers and are always sneaking away to lez off together in the toilets. It is 2001: this is a humiliating insult. Milli likes to point at things either of them have touched, and say to everyone else, 'Don't touch that. Moaning Myrtle and Droopy Tits have lezzed on it.'

So of course it is not long before Jess will not sit with Alice either; she sits alone, as far away from Alice as she can, and ignores her entirely if Alice tries to speak to her. Alice feels sorry for Jess as much as for herself; Jess always looks pale now, and is often red-eyed.

Alice knows from enough books and films that unkindness is often the result of a secret inner suffering. She wonders now if perhaps the reason Milli had to leave her past school was that she was being bullied herself (for some reason it does not occur to her that Milli herself was the bully). Or perhaps her parents are getting divorced. Alice thinks that if she and Milli can only find some common ground, if she can break through Milli's tough exterior to the pain beneath, then perhaps it will all stop. Maybe they will even end up as friends.

So one morning when Milli stops in front of her desk, no doubt gearing up to deliver the first insults of the day, Alice looks up and says simply, 'How was your weekend?'

Milli seems so thrown by this that she does not immediately reply.

Alice feels emboldened. She says, 'I went to visit my dad. My parents are divorced. It was hard at first, but I'm getting used to it now.'

Milli looks at her for another long moment.

We're connecting, Alice thinks.

Then Milli draws a deep breath and shouts to the whole room, 'Oh God, Myrtle's just tried to molest me! Is nobody safe?'

THE BULLYING IS MOSTLY restricted to Alice's own form group, but it is inevitable that Hanna eventually notices.

Alice is coming down the stairs to the girls' locker room when Milli, standing at the bottom, sees her.

'Watch out,' she says to a group of girls passing. 'Don't touch that banister. Myrtle's just touched it. You might catch lezziness.'

Hanna is among the girls addressed. This, to Alice, feels like the greatest humiliation of all.

Hanna says, 'Have you touched it too, Milli? Because I wouldn't want to catch imbecility either.'

Then she continues on through the double doors to her next lesson.

Alice, too frightened to be pleased, makes herself scarce before Milli can take revenge on her.

*

THAT EVENING WHEN HANNA and Alice are in their bedroom after supper, Hanna says, 'Why does she call you Myrtle?'

They are on their beds, Alice sitting with her back to the wall, rereading the *Cazalet Chronicles* for the millionth time, while Hanna lies on her front and flicks through the pages of *Cosmo*.

Alice looks up from her book, but Hanna's eyes remain on her magazine. Do not cry, Alice instructs herself. She draws upon her repertoire of tactics: think of a lovely mountain; you are alone on the mountain; you can see for miles and miles. As casually as she can, she says, 'It's just a silly joke. Like in *Harry Potter*. You know?'

Hanna is frowning. She turns a page. She says, 'Are you . . . in on the joke?'

'I . . .' Alice is trying desperately hard – the mountain, the sky, oh look, a golden eagle! – but the tears are on their way nonetheless. She shakes her head mutely, and after a moment, manages, 'Not really.'

Hanna looks at her. 'You know, there's nothing wrong with being a lesbian,' she says at last.

I'm not, Alice wants to say, but this feels beside the point. 'It's not a big deal,' she says.

'It is a big deal. No one should be horrible to you.'

'You're horrible to me,' Alice points out.

'That's different,' Hanna says, sounding amused. There is a pause, then she says, 'Milli Stephenson's a psycho. She's in my Maths set. Acts like she's from the mean streets.'

'She's from the mean streets of Hampstead,' Alice says shakily, and feels better when Hanna laughs.

Then Hanna goes back to her magazine, and doesn't say anything else about it.

*

BUT BY LUNCHTIME THE next day, it has all stopped. Alice goes into the toilets and is horrified to see Milli and a couple of her friends already in there. She braces herself for the familiar cry of 'Watch out, everyone! Run away unless you want to get molested!' but nothing happens. Milli doesn't say a word. She doesn't even seem to see Alice. Her eyes glide over her and past her.

It is the same for the rest of the day, and for the rest of the week. In fact, Milli actually seems to be avoiding Alice now. Alice doesn't dare believe it is really over until a fortnight has passed without incident. It seems like too anticlimactic an ending to be trusted. But gradually, Jess drifts back, resuming her seat next to Alice in lessons and at lunch. Margot and Holly return too, rather sheepishly. Alice could weep with relief when she arrives in Maths to find they are at a three in the middle and have saved a seat for her (she holds it together: the mountain! The sky! The eagles!).

'Sorry,' Margot mutters when Alice takes the offered seat, and Alice is so happy and relieved she forgives her immediately, forgives Holly too, though Holly has not asked.

The nickname Myrtle drops out of usage. Alice is Alice again. Tentatively, she puts up her hand in Geography to answer a question about overpopulation. No one whispers anything.

Like Lazarus, Alice is reborn.

'WHAT DID YOU DO?' she asks her sister eventually. They are at the breakfast table eating their cereal.

'About what?' Hanna says. She is working her way methodically through a bowl of supermarket own-brand 'Rice Puffs'.

Alice hesitates. 'About Milli Stephenson.'

Hanna's spoon pauses on its way to her mouth. She smiles briefly to herself.

'What?' Alice says.

'I took care of it,' Hanna says, as though she is in the Mafia. She goes back to her cereal and refuses to discuss the matter further, so that it will in fact be many years before Alice finds out what she did.

ONE AFTERNOON IN THE Easter holidays Alice is home alone, revising for her mock exams. Her mother is doing the weekly shop, and Hanna is out with her friends, though she is supposed to be at home revising too. When the doorbell rings, Alice assumes it is Hanna, who must have forgotten her keys again.

She goes to the door to look through the peephole, and is disconcerted to see it is Aunt Katy on the doorstep. Her aunt is standing there hugging her arms across her body, wearing a shapeless navy cardigan, a white blouse and a long black skirt. There is something odd about the outfit though Alice can't put her finger on what, except that the clothes seem too big, as if they were intended for somebody else. Aunt Katy's hair is in a straggly bun from which strands have come loose and are sticking out around her face. Her hair is mostly faded to grey now, though it used to be blonde when Alice was younger. Aunt Katy keeps glancing reflexively over her shoulder, as if she is waiting for someone else to arrive.

Alice is at a loss. She doesn't know her aunt well and has always been a little afraid of her. They rarely go up to Peterborough to see Alice's grandparents, who Aunt Katy still lives with, and her aunt often stays in her room for most of these visits. There is one occasion that stands out in Alice's memory, when she and Hanna and Michael were still quite young: Aunt Katy had come down to eat lunch with them but had seemed in a very bad mood. She had complained repeatedly about the lamb being tough and said the butcher must be trying to get one over on them. Then, when Alice's grandmother served apple crumble for pudding, Aunt Katy had been insistent that nobody should eat it. Alice had thought her aunt was being extremely rude. Eventually, having failed to convince everyone that something was wrong with the crumble, Aunt Katy had stormed out. Afterwards everybody went on eating as if nothing had happened.

On the drive home, Hanna had remarked, with that worldly air she sometimes adopted, that Aunt Katy must have been drunk, but their mother snapped at her, 'She wasn't drunk. She's *difficult*. Always has been.' Then, almost to herself, she added, 'She ruined my childhood.'

'Ruined it how?' Hanna said, immediately interested. (No doubt believing herself to be in possession of a ruined childhood too.)

'You can see how she is,' their mother said. But she would not be drawn any further on the subject.

Their aunt's rudeness is clearly one of the many things in the adult world that must remain unspoken. Hanna and Alice did try questioning their father once, but he only said, 'Oh, she's always been like that. Your mother doesn't like to talk about it.' He never used to come on the Peterborough visits anyway.

Alice is rather alarmed at the prospect of being alone with her aunt now. When Alice doesn't immediately answer the door, Aunt Katy presses the bell again. This time, she keeps her finger there so the shrill buzz goes on and on.

Alice quickly opens the door.

'Hello Aunt Katy,' she says, as brightly as she can.

She wonders if her mother has forgotten to tell them about Aunt Katy's visit, in which case Alice must now cover up this fact to save everyone's embarrassment. But she is unnerved when her aunt just stares at her without returning her greeting. The shadows under Aunt Katy's eyes are so dark they make her eyes look sunken. She doesn't seem to have a travel bag with her.

Alice takes refuge in politeness, stepping aside and saying, 'Won't you come in?'

But even as she says this, her aunt is pushing past her and going down the hall.

'Is she here?' Aunt Katy says.

'Who?' Alice falters, thrown by the abruptness of the question. 'My mum?'

'Yes. Is she here?'

'She's at the supermarket,' Alice says. 'But she'll be back in a bit.'

Aunt Katy stops where she is and looks around her. Her hands seem to be in perpetual motion, swirling and jabbing as if conducting an invisible orchestra. She takes a shuddery breath and says, 'Is anyone else here?'

'No,' Alice says.

She watches as her aunt breathes out again slowly.

'Not yet,' Aunt Katy says. And then she shakes her head quickly as though her ears are full of water. 'Where are they?'

Alice blinks. 'Where are who?'

'*What*, not who. The *recordings*. Where did she put them?'

'I'm sorry,' Alice says helplessly. 'I don't know what you mean.'

Her aunt looks at her for a long moment, and then says, 'So they got to you too. Did you think you'd fool me? Which are you now? Red, dead, or fed?'

Finally, Alice starts to understand what she is seeing: Aunt Katy is not just eccentric, not just difficult, or rude, or drunk. She is mad.

Alice has never seen madness up close before. There was an old man in the street once, when she and her mother and Hanna were out shopping; he'd been dishevelled and incoherent, ranting at the air. Their mother had hurried them on. Alice had felt upset for the rest of the day, though it was difficult to say why.

She did not expect to find madness here, standing in her own hallway.

'You don't fool me,' Aunt Katy says. Then, after giving Alice another long look, she stalks into the dining room.

After a moment, Alice follows.

It is a very small room, and there is no space for anything in it apart from the table and chairs. When the chairs are in use, their wooden backs touch the walls. Aunt Katy is moving round the chairs quickly, feeling the seat cushions.

'Yes,' she says, 'there's something here. Of course.'

She goes out into the hall again, but Alice lingers where she is in the corner of the dining room, wondering whether she should ring her mother, though she is afraid this might upset her aunt further. She can hear Aunt Katy rummaging in the cutlery drawer in the kitchen.

When Aunt Katy reappears, she is holding a large knife.

Alice's knees go weak but she doesn't fall. There's a liquid sensation in her stomach. After a single frozen second she is able to move again, and she slips further into the room so the table is between her and her aunt. Her eyes remain fixed on the knife in her aunt's hand.

But Aunt Katy does not seem interested in Alice. Instead she starts stabbing viciously at the seat cushions, slashing them open and pulling out the stuffing. Alice flinches with each stab, her whole body baulking in fear with every movement her aunt makes. The floor is soon littered with stuffing as one cushion after another is disembowelled.

While Aunt Katy proceeds from cushion to cushion with the knife,

Alice moves slowly around the room in tandem with her, always keeping the table between them, always keeping her eyes on the blade.

'What are you looking for?' she asks eventually. It comes out as little more than a whisper.

'You *know*.' Her aunt's voice is suddenly savage. 'Do you think I don't know who you work for?' When Alice says nothing, Aunt Katy suddenly raises her voice to a shout, making Alice jolt with fright. 'They think I don't know! I've let them think that. She's an evil bitch! An evil *bitch*!' Her voice is shredded with rage.

Alice is too frightened to speak again. By now she has made it almost the whole way round the table, and is close to the door. She wonders if she should bolt, but is afraid to make any sudden movements.

Just as she is agonizing over this decision, Aunt Katy lays the knife down on the table and says heavily, 'They've moved them. How could I be so stupid?' She beats her hand against her forehead. 'I should have realized.'

There is a pause.

'I'm sorry,' Alice says, for want of any other response.

Aunt Katy doesn't seem to hear her. Her hands flicker and dance in front of her. 'What am I going to do now?' she says. And then, 'There's no way out.'

Alice watches as her aunt begins to weep.

AUNT KATY REFUSES A cup of tea on the basis that it's not safe, but does accept a Penguin biscuit, since it comes in a wrapper. She and Alice sit opposite each other at the table, surrounded by white foam. Aunt Katy sniffs and wipes her hand across her face clumsily, like a child.

'I knew Celia was working with them all along because of her red dress,' she says. 'It was how she sent messages to them. I know it all, you see. I've worked it out. It's so obvious when you think about it. Red scare.'

Alice doesn't know what her aunt is talking about, but feels profoundly grateful that she herself is wearing blue today. She says, 'She's your sister.'

Her aunt looks at her, as if to say, *And what of that?*

'She loves you,' Alice says, though she doesn't feel entirely convinced of this.

Aunt Katy shakes her head. 'Celia,' she says, 'has never loved anyone. Not in her whole life. That's the truth.'

Alice is taken aback by this comment. She says, 'Do Grandma and Grandpa know you're here? Shall we call them?'

Aunt Katy looks at her in disbelief. 'They're dead,' she says.

Alice turns cold. Then she realizes. 'I meant your parents,' she says. 'They can't be trusted.'

Alice is silent for a while. She thinks how exhausted her aunt looks. The crying seems to have worn her out further. She says, 'Would you like to have a lie down for a bit? I can keep watch.'

Aunt Katy shakes her head. 'There's no time. It isn't safe. Celia will be here with her communist allies.'

Alice feels the entirety of her aunt's loneliness as though it is her own. 'What can I do to help?' she says.

'I don't trust you,' her aunt tells her, but she says it gently.

BY THE TIME ALICE'S mother gets home, Aunt Katy has finished eating and, apparently reinvigorated, has gone out to warn the neighbours.

'Aunt Katy's here,' Alice says in a rush, meeting her mother at the door. 'We had some Penguin biscuits. Well, I had one and she had three. I didn't think you'd mind. She had a knife for a bit, but she left it here.'

Her mother is staring at her. 'Where is she?'

Alice says, 'She's talking to Mrs Langford next door.' About you being a communist, she does not add.

'You said she has a *knife*?'

'Yes, but she left it in the dining room, and it turned out she only wanted to cut up the cushions.'

She is dismayed when her mother calls the police.

'But she isn't dangerous,' Alice protests. 'She seems really scared.'

Her mother says, 'You don't know what you're talking about.'

'Please, Mum. I think she'll be terrified when the police come. Can't we just take her home?'

'Are you going to drive her up to Peterborough?' her mother snaps. 'Make that two-hour journey with her ranting and raving at you, and trying to open the door to jump out, or else to grab the wheel and kill you both? Don't be such a *child*, Alice. I've had a whole lifetime of this. You've had it for five minutes.'

But Alice is right: Aunt Katy is terrified when the police come. Alice watches her being half-dragged, fighting, out of Mrs Langford's house and bundled into the back of the police car.

Alice's mother is asked to come to the station to make a statement, so Alice is alone in the house once again.

When Hanna gets back, Alice relays the whole story, and for once Hanna really listens. Then she complains bitterly about having missed all the excitement.

'It wasn't exciting,' Alice says. For the first time, she looks at her sister with distaste. 'It was awful.'

Hanna narrows her eyes. 'Exciting experiences are wasted on you.'

When Alice's mother comes home, she will not discuss what has happened except to say that Aunt Katy has been taken to hospital. Alice is relieved to hear she is not in prison.

She hears her mother on the phone in the hall later that evening, speaking to her own parents. Alice is sitting at the top of the stairs, Hanna beside her.

'We shouldn't really be eavesdropping,' Alice whispers.

'You always say that,' Hanna says. 'Shut up. I can't hear.'

'I had no choice,' their mother is saying. 'For God's sake, what did you expect me to do? Wait till you got here? She's schizophrenic, she can't be "reasoned with". She was tearing up my house, threatening my daughter with a knife! I told you she was dangerous. You should have listened.'

There is a long silence after that, until their mother snaps, 'How did she get my address anyway?'

There are no more visits to Peterborough for several years after this.

AFTER THEIR GCSE'S, ALICE and Hanna have to leave their private school and attend a sixth-form college instead, since the school fees have become too much of a strain for their parents ('A strain when you have to keep your *mistress* in *diamonds*,' Alice's mother says, though in truth Alice has never seen Susan wearing diamonds, nor indeed any jewellery at all). So Alice's friendship progress with Holly and Margot is lost.

The college is large and bewildering, a network of long corridors and modern grey seminar rooms, with open-plan computer areas called 'hubs', a coffee lounge and a large canteen. The students, who are many and everywhere, all seem years older than Alice herself. It is exactly how she imagines university will be (terrifying).

She and Hanna get the bus together for the induction morning. But outside the gates, Hanna stops and says to Alice, 'Look, if anyone gives you any trouble, let me know. Otherwise, don't speak to me.'

'OK,' Alice says, distracted by how queasy she feels.

'And whatever you do, don't tell anyone we're twins.'

'You want me to pretend we're not even sisters?' Alice says.

'Yes.'

'Can I at least say we're cousins?'

'No!' Hanna says.

They go in through the gates. Hoisting her rucksack higher on her shoulder, Hanna offers a parting shot: 'You know, this might be a good opportunity for you. You could reinvent yourself.'

'Thanks,' Alice says to her sister's retreating back.

ALICE FINDS IT HARDER than anticipated, reinventing herself. She has only been alive for sixteen and a half years, but it seems in that time her personality has really bedded down. She makes an effort to appear confident and devil-may-care, but it does not come naturally. It helps, though, that hardly anyone at college seems to know each other, a fact that does not change as the year goes on, so Alice is relieved of the claustrophobic pressures of her private school. No one here is aware she was once called Moaning Myrtle, and she is free of Milli Stephenson forever. Nobody is watching her or commenting on her at all. In college, her intense self-consciousness eases a little.

She does eventually make friends with two girls called Salma and Tahira, who are in her History class. They are warm and funny, especially Tahira, who has a very deep, throaty laugh that always seems to set Salma off when she hears it. Salma and Tahira have been best friends since the first day, but they are kind about including Alice. The three of them eat lunch together most days, though Alice does not see them outside of college. It strikes her that it is becoming a bit of a pattern for her to be the third in a two-person friendship. She hopes this won't also be the case in her romantic life. Whenever that finally starts.

At weekends, during which Hanna is never at home, Alice tries to keep busy. She takes her A-level work very seriously and spends hours on it, though this is sometimes counterproductive because she grows more and more anxious about getting it perfect until she wants to scrap it all and start again. At this stage, her mother will usually intervene and make her come out for a walk, or watch something on television. Alice, discounting Hanna's scathing comments, starts to look for new craft activities, ones in which she can lose herself as she once did with her box houses. She never finds a truly satisfying substitute, though she teaches herself to knit from a book she found in the library, and makes her mother and Hanna a slightly uneven scarf each (she can still only knit in straight lines). She also learns origami, and quilling from a special kit her mother buys her, and she strings beads on to wire or delicate elastic to make jewellery. She presents Tahira and Salma with a bracelet of coloured beads each – marine blues and purples for Tahira, and fiery oranges, reds and yellows for Salma. They seem genuinely pleased, and wear them every day. 'Make yourself one too,' Salma says, 'so they can be friendship bracelets.' Alice does, stringing her own bracelet with cool turquoises and greens.

Nonetheless, there is a loneliness she cannot shake. There is a sense too of something being off with her life, though she couldn't say what it is that feels wrong. Sometimes she worries she is destined to become like her aunt, that whatever sickness is in Aunt Katy is in her too. Don't these things run in families? And Alice has always been the one who doesn't fit in, the one whose closest friend is her mother.

She tries not to think about it too much. But she often doesn't sleep well at night. Many nights she lies awake listening to Hanna's breathing across the duct-tape divide and staring at the shadows on the ceiling or the moonlight that falls across her bed in streaks from the blind. Why is it that moonlight always seems so cold? Sometimes she comforts herself by imagining a secret friend coming to her window and climbing through, getting silently into bed beside her. This friend has no name. Alice can never picture her clearly except in brief flashes when she is thinking of other things; it is as though her friend can only be seen indirectly, exists only at the edge of Alice's vision. But they have always known each other. As Alice grows drowsy she imagines she and her friend talking to each other softly in the darkness, whispering their secrets, and eventually lying in peaceful silence beside one another, because no more words are needed, because everything that might pass between them is already understood.

5

WHEN MICHAEL IS FOURTEEN, he is jogging alongside another student during school cross-country practice when the student collapses and dies. There is no one else in sight at this moment. Michael and the boy – his name is Christopher – are the slowest of the pack and have been left far behind by the others. Christopher is not a particular friend of Michael's, but he is nice enough – a shy boy who doesn't get bullied for it. He and Michael often end up jogging side by side during cross-country because they are both slow, and neither feels the need to outshine the other. They are in the midst of the grassland on Wimbledon Common when Christopher drops suddenly to the ground. Michael naturally thinks he is joking at first. It takes him some time to realize Christopher is not breathing. Cold with panic, Michael recalls his basic first-aid training and feels for a pulse. There is none. He tries shouting for help but no one is within earshot, so he attempts some rudimentary CPR. Christopher's lips feel cold when Michael presses his own against them but then it is November. Michael does not know what the right thing to do would be: should he run for help, or stay where he is? It seems too terrible to leave Christopher lying alone out here, so he stays with him, pumping ineffectually at his chest.

After a time, a dog walker comes by, but the man has no mobile phone on him, so he instead runs for help at the Windmill café. Michael's memories after that are more blurry. It seems like a long time before the paramedics arrive, and whilst he waits he continues to pump at Christopher's chest (eleven minutes elapse between the 999 call and the arrival of the paramedics, the inquest is later told, but Michael is not at the inquest). Michael's PE teacher has come looking for them by this point and goes off in the ambulance with Christopher. Meanwhile Michael's form tutor also seems to have materialized out of nowhere, and ushers Michael back to school.

It is late morning, and Michael is allowed to sit quietly in the sick bay during lunch, a blanket round his shoulders. His form tutor sits with him, and Michael tries to eat the ham sandwich they have brought him from the canteen but the bread goes gluey in his mouth and clogs up his throat, which already feels too thick. Michael is supposed to return to lessons as normal that afternoon, but at some point towards the end of the lunch hour the call comes to say that Christopher has died. Michael discovers later that there was a problem with Christopher's heart, and always had been. He could have died as a toddler, or lived to be sixty. His parents had known it. They blamed no one.

When Michael's form tutor breaks the news to him, he gives Michael a hug, which is entirely out of character. Michael stands there stiffly, wanting it to be over. His mother soon arrives, and she and Michael's form tutor speak for a long time as Michael sits beside his mother. He can never remember afterwards what was said because finally the crying has begun. It is as though his insides have turned to liquid and are spilling out of him. He has no control over himself at all.

His mother walks him out of school eventually with her arm around him and drives him home. There she puts him to bed with a hot-water bottle, and brings him up his supper on a tray (chips, egg and beans: a treat tea).

'My poor boy,' she says. 'My poor darling.'

She sits with him until he falls asleep.

In the morning Michael wakes up to find his school uniform laid out as usual on the end of the bed. When he goes downstairs, his mother is in the kitchen. She says, 'Feeling better, darling?' and so he says yes. Christopher is not mentioned.

At school, none of the other boys refer to what happened either (except for Michael's friend Tom, who tells him they've all been instructed *not* to mention it), but Michael feels everyone's eyes upon him. His form tutor speaks to him again in private, to tell him about Christopher's heart, how it could not have been prevented, how it was just one of those things. Michael nods, and nods, and does not speak.

There is a memorial service at school the following week, which Christopher's parents attend. Christopher's mother is introduced to Michael and gives him a long hug, thanking him for trying to save her boy. After that Michael goes to the toilet and stays there for the rest of the service.

In the years that follow, he rarely thinks about Christopher. Eventually he ceases to think of him at all. It is as if the whole thing – the way Christopher suddenly dropped to the ground, the blue of his lips, the resistance of his chest beneath Michael's hands – had happened to somebody else.

When Michael is thirty-seven years old, he goes to the doctor with a visual disturbance, a kind of shadow that he seems to glimpse every now and then at the edge of his sight line. He is referred to a specialist but they find nothing wrong with him – no brain tumour or incipient blindness on the horizon after all. Michael hasn't thought of Christopher for a long time by this point, but for some reason it all comes back to him whilst these investigations are ongoing. He wonders, fleetingly, what kind of life Christopher might have had if he had survived, if he had got the chance to grow up. But this kind of speculation is uncharacteristic for Michael, and he soon abandons it.

AS AN ADULT, MICHAEL will be an upstanding member of society, but as a young child he is a liar and a thief.

The stealing and the lying are actions he finds difficult to explain, since neither as a child nor an adult does he have much insight into his own behaviour. It is not that he wants the things he takes, and it is not that he believes the lies he tells. It is not that these actions ever serve a particular purpose.

Take the Troll doll, for example. Michael is seven when he takes it from his classmate's backpack, which is hanging half open in the cloak-room. The notable point is that Michael does not even like Trolls himself, and even if he did, his dad could get him as many as he wanted, even the rare ones. He simply finds himself alone in the dim cloakroom one afternoon, having been given permission to leave class to go to the toilet (*lavatory*, his mother would correct him), sees the backpack half open, the Troll's lurid blue hair enticingly visible, and standing there in the silence gets a strange feeling in his stomach, almost as though he needs the toilet again (not for a wee this time but for the *other thing*, as his mother would put it).

And so he takes the Troll and puts it in his pocket. Then, because it creates too visible a bulge, he takes it out again and goes to hide it in his own backpack. He will take it out once he gets home and inspect it in the safety of his bedroom. Then he will put it away in the special shoebox in his cupboard (a serial-killer-style box of trophies) and not look at it again.

Unfortunately, he does not manage to get it safely home. It turns out that his classmate Lucy Myerson is extremely fond of this Troll, which was gifted to her by her uncle, who is now up there with the angels. Lucy Myerson makes a huge fuss when she goes to her bag at the end of the day and finds it missing, and because this is not the first item that has gone missing from someone's backpack (not Michael's first rodeo), a bag search is mandated by his teacher Miss Ferguson and the Troll is found in Michael's bag.

'Someone must have put it there,' Michael protests as they all close in on him. He thinks of Joseph's golden cup in Benjamin's sack of wheat — they have been learning the songs this term — and almost believes his own story.

His mother is summoned to attend a meeting with Miss Ferguson before school the next morning. Michael waits mournfully on a chair outside the classroom looking at the pale knobbles of his knees below the hem of his shorts. He has been bracing himself since yesterday for his mother's fury, but she has remained tight-lipped, barely speaking to him at dinner last night or on the drive to school. When she finally emerges from the meeting, she still does not speak but strides past Michael down the corridor. He hovers uncertainly for a moment, unsure whether he is supposed to stay where he is — it is almost eight, his Casio watch tells him, and the other children will be arriving for registration in twenty minutes — or whether he is meant to follow her. He decides that on balance his mother is more frightening than Miss Ferguson, and runs to catch up with her. He puffs along beside her, sneaking anxious glances at her face, but they are out in the car park before she speaks.

'I told her very clearly,' she says, still staring fiercely ahead, 'that *my son does not steal*. I told her that very clearly.'

Michael deems the greatest safety to be in silence.

'My son,' his mother reiterates, 'is not a thief.' And now she does stop and turns those flaming eyes upon him. 'Nobody in this family would do such a disgusting thing. Would they?'

Michael returns her gaze with difficulty. He manages to shake his head minutely.

'There,' his mother says, and her shoulders seem to sag a little. 'That's what I mean. Come on. We'll go round the corner to Sainsbury's and you can have a strawberry milkshake before school.'

Michael strolls back into school just in time for registration, buoyed up by the combination of self-righteousness and sugar. He is now almost embarrassed on Miss Ferguson's behalf at her false accusation, and is prepared to be magnanimous, making his voice extra polite as he answers, 'Yes, Miss Ferguson,' to his name.

But the other children do not seem so willing to let it go. During their first lesson of the day, Matty Jones hisses, '*You stole the Troll*,' at him, and the others nearby hear and apparently find this hysterical (Michael himself has never found rhyming especially amusing), repeating it to one another until Miss Ferguson tells them to be quiet and to get on with their work. But the chant follows Michael around for the rest of the day, and for the days after that too, and it is a full term before they are tired of it. Michael is stunned at the injustice of it.

'I didn't take it,' he tells them over and over again.

But his protests only spur them on, and they are especially delighted when they can get him to lose his temper, to lash out at them or even burst into tears.

'Just ignore them,' his mother tells him when he complains of his treatment. 'Silly little fools. Children can be very cruel, Michael. Especially when they can see you're better than them.'

133

Michael tries to wear his superiority as a protective cloak. At least his mother is on his side.

THOUGH HE IS IN awe of his mother, Michael has never been a big fan of his father. Even as a toddler Michael is a serious soul, but for years his father – who always wanted a son – persists in attempting to play with him, putting on silly voices or zooming brand new toys about in front of Michael's face in an alarming manner, saying, 'Look how high Mr Plane can *fly*! Zoom, zoom, zooooom! Watch him go!' Michael finds all of this rather trying, and doesn't understand why the plastic plane has eyes and a smile painted on it when everyone knows that planes are not alive. He finds his father's performative silliness embarrassing, and is relieved when these attentions gradually cease. But later he is still press-ganged into the stupid sessions with his sisters where they have to give feedback on his father's toys, as though he has nothing better to do (at eleven!) than pretend to be interested in Furbies.

One Christmas when he is still quite young he asks for a book on astronomy, but instead of the sumptuous Dorling Kindersley hardback he longed for, with its glossy colour photos and dense paragraphs of information, he receives a blue plastic telescope, decorated with pictures of cartoon stars and planets (which of course also have smiling faces). When Michael puts it to his eye, in the delusional hope that it might at least be a real telescope he can use to study the constellations, it turns out to be a kaleidoscope, merely revealing a series of colourful patterns when you twist the end.

'Isn't this great?' his father says. 'You could stare into it for hours and never see the same pattern twice!'

Michael looks at the kaleidoscope disconsolately. It does not seem likely that he will be staring into it for hours. As his father talks on and on about the wide appeal of their new 'introduction to learning' range, Michael feels his contempt growing, until he wants to pick up the stupid toy and break it.

When Michael is twelve, his mother has to go unexpectedly to Peterborough because Aunt Katy is in hospital, though his mother will not answer any questions about what is the matter with her. The visit coincides with half term, which means there is no one to look after Michael and his sisters for the two days she is gone. Somehow it is agreed that they will go to their neighbour Mrs Sheldon's on the first day, and then their father will take them into work with him on the second day. Being at Mrs Sheldon's is OK, because she lets them watch loads of TV, but Michael is appalled at the prospect of going to work with his father. His little sisters' excitement only adds to his dismay.

And of course it is as bad as he expects it to be. Michael has never in his short life been pleasantly surprised by a turn of events. His father introduces them to his colleagues with that strained jollity that reminds Michael of the children's entertainers at every party he's ever hated, calling the twins his 'princesses' and Michael 'the squire', whilst ruffling his hair. Other people ruffle his hair too, however much he tries to shrink away from their approach (he can always tell when a hair-ruffle is coming). Later, whilst the girls are borne away by a large, motherly woman to choose a soft toy each, Michael's father leads him up some stairs to another office, where he is taken on a lap of honour around the room and expected to shake hand after hand whilst people say, 'So you're here to show us how it's done, eh?' and, 'Perhaps you can go through these figures for me? Ha ha!' Michael can't bear the silliness of it all, everyone pretending to think he is an adult when they all know he is not. Then his father gets him a chair, makes him a space at the corner of his own desk, hands him some graph paper and an old biro and says, 'Why don't you do some drawing for a while, pal?'

Michael looks stonily at his father, who apparently has forgotten he is twelve, not five.

'Or write a story,' his father adds, faltering a little under Michael's glare.

Michael wishes he had thought to bring one of his books from home; he has a good one on volcanoes that he has been enjoying. Instead he tries to pass the time by writing down every fact he can think of about volcanoes, and then earthquakes, and then tsunamis, which takes him until mid-morning when his dad says, 'So, pal, we've been working hard – fancy a coffee break?'

'I don't drink coffee,' Michael says.

'I know that. I'll get you a milkshake. Or whatever you want.'

Once they are out on the street, Michael says, 'What about the girls?' but his dad says, 'Carla's looking after them for the day. We're having some father–son time, aren't we?'

Michael does not think that writing out facts on volcanoes whilst his father works nearby and ignores him counts as father–son time, but he is concerned about what the alternative might be, so he lets this pass. His father leads him around the corner to a café, where it turns out they do not serve milkshakes, so his father buys him an orange juice and gets himself a cappuccino, saying, 'That's all right, isn't it?' so Michael has to say yes.

Whilst they have their drinks, his father says things like, 'How's school?' and, 'What did you think of the Colour Writer I showed you? It's going to be big this Christmas.'

Michael answers as best he can, but he suddenly notices his father is not listening to him. Instead, he is staring at a woman who has just come in through the door. She has ginger hair and she is wearing a green coat. She goes up to the counter to buy a bottle of water and when she turns at last, Michael's father stands up and she sees him.

He says, 'Anne! Anne, I can't believe it.'

Michael watches as the woman just stares at his father, and he feels embarrassed to realize his father has mistaken a stranger for someone he knows.

'How are you?' his father says, and then gestures towards Michael, saying, 'I'm here with my son. I work nearby.'

The woman looks at Michael, and then back at his father. 'Hi,' she says at last.

'Do you work round here too?' Michael's father says.

She shakes her head. 'No. Just here for the day.'

'It's wonderful to see you,' Michael's father says. 'It's been so long.'

The woman only smiles in return.

'Won't you join us?' Michael's father says, even though they've almost finished their own drinks.

But the woman says, 'Thanks, but I don't think I will. I have to be getting on.' She picks up her bottle of water and leaves with a polite, 'Goodbye,' which is addressed as much to Michael as to his father.

Michael intuits, without being able to articulate it, this woman's contempt. It comes with a sense of recognition. He has always been connected to his mother by a thousand invisible threads, and has long felt, below the surface of conscious thought, his mother's disdain for his father. Now, somewhere in the recesses of his mind, the scorn of this stranger is laid alongside it. It is this final addition more than anything else that cements his own contempt.

*

DURING HIS FIRST YEAR at university, where he is studying Politics, Michael makes two close friends on his corridor in halls. The first is Jed, who lives in the room next door, and is short with a loud laugh and a brash manner and a way of addressing Michael as 'mate' that Michael secretly loves, as though he is being accepted into a fraternity from which he has previously been excluded.

The second is Olivia.

Olivia lives opposite. She has very dark hair that is almost black, offset by her pale skin and red lips. Michael thinks of Snow White when he looks at her, and fantasizes about the moment he will finally tell her this, whilst leaning towards her and fondly tucking a strand of hair behind her ear (Olivia's ears stick out and she usually tries to hide them under her hair; Michael thinks they are adorable and experiences an agreeable frisson on the few occasions he does get to glimpse them).

Olivia seems to recognize in Michael a kindred spirit, and often confides in him late into the night as they sip whisky (Olivia's drink of choice, which Michael has to pretend to like).

Unlike Michael's, Olivia's parents are still together, and are very much in love.

'They only have eyes for each other,' she tells Michael. 'Sometimes it's like being invisible when you're with them.'

'That sounds weird,' Michael says.

'No, it's not weird. They're so in love. They won't let me have a key to the house because they want to keep their privacy.'

'Privacy? Like—'

'Yeah,' Olivia says. 'They want to be able to make love without someone walking in on them.'

'Urgh,' Michael says, expressing the conventional view. 'That's gross.'

Olivia looks at him sternly. 'It's only gross if you're a prude. Sex is an expression of love. They're just expressing their love.'

Michael blushes, both because he is chastened by her disapproval, and because he finds himself vividly imagining what it might be like to express his love with Olivia.

'So do you always have to ring the doorbell at your own house?' he asks to distract himself.

'Well, it's not my house really. It's theirs. And they like things to be just so. Plus they might have left some of their stuff lying around. They don't want just anyone stumbling across their stuff.'

What stuff? Michael thinks, before deciding he doesn't want to know.

'I suppose it's nice that they're still so into each other,' he says.

'It's beautiful.' Olivia smiles at him. 'One day I'll have a love like that, one that transcends time and place.'

Michael sort of understands the 'time' bit, since he supposes Olivia's parents have been together for many years, but he isn't sure about the 'place' bit – don't they live together in Basingstoke? He decides not to pursue this, for fear of looking ignorant of the mysterious workings of love.

Jed is not as big a fan of Olivia as Michael is. 'Too much crazy,' he says. 'I can see it a mile off. She's hot, yes, but it's outweighed by the crazy. Haven't you heard of the hot–crazy matrix?'

Michael has not, and Jed proceeds to explain it to him, but Michael remains unimpressed. 'Basically, Mike,' Jed concludes, 'most women are crazy. You've just got to decide what level of crazy you can put up with. Or how hot they need to be to balance it out.' Then he honks with laughter, and Michael thinks with irritation that Jed has been with the same girlfriend since he was fourteen, and although she is not very attractive, it is unlikely that Jed can do any better, given that he is stocky and pasty-faced and has acne.

It is a source of private pain to Michael that although Olivia values him so highly as a friend, she does not want anything more. Michael knows this because she frequently says things like, 'I've never had a friend as close as you, Michael. Most men just want to sleep with me. It's such a relief to find someone who wants to know me *for me*, and who I can trust completely as a friend. Who has no ulterior motives.'

Michael stores up comments like this to take out and examine in private later. He is flattered, of course, but also disconcerted, because sometimes he suspects he does have ulterior motives. However, he decides he will continue to do the noble thing and keep his feelings to himself so that he can be the friend she needs him to be.

One night she tells him about Plato's theory of soulmates: that originally humans were beings with four legs, four arms, and a single head with two faces. Then we were severed in two by Zeus and must each spend our lives mournfully wandering the earth seeking out our other half, most of us never being reunited with our soulmate. Michael is amazed that a grown man could come up with something so silly.

'I love that idea,' Olivia concludes. 'And don't you think it feels true?'

Michael agrees that it does.

OLIVIA IS POPULAR WITH men and has a string of boyfriends throughout the first two terms, though none of these encounters mean anything, because there is no deeper, soul connection. It is Michael to whom she turns for support on her dark days, which seem to occur quite frequently.

One day, Michael is getting ready to go on a date with a girl called Maya who he met in a seminar on nineteenth-century utilitarianism. It is unusual for him to have a date, and Jed has been teasing him about it all day (Michael acts annoyed, but he secretly enjoys this). He and Maya are going to meet at the student union for a drink, and then maybe watch a film together in her room afterwards. (How much hope Michael invests in that 'maybe'!)

Olivia comes into the corridor just as Jed is trying to shove a strip of condoms into Michael's pocket and Michael is trying to fight him off. She says, 'You've got a date? Who with?'

Michael tells her, and she frowns. 'Oh yes, I think I know who she is. Really tall, right? Sort of gawky?'

Michael shrugs. 'I suppose she's quite tall.'

'I'd love to be as tall as that,' Olivia says. 'It would be so much easier in a crowd. Must be hard to find clothes that fit though. Poor her.'

As Michael is getting ready to leave, Olivia knocks on his door in tears.

'What's wrong?' Michael says. He folds her into a hug and holds her as she cries, feeling pleasingly manly with his arms around her.

'I'm just in such despair,' Olivia says, muffled against his chest. 'Honestly, Michael, I don't really see the point of going on.'

Appalled, he tries to console her, but she says he must come into her room and hide all the paracetamol and knives. Otherwise she doesn't know what she might do.

Michael follows her to her room, wondering if he should call her parents; the situation seems serious enough to merit interrupting one of their sex sessions. As it turns out, there is only an old blunt penknife in Olivia's desk drawer which he has to confiscate, plus a single pack of paracetamol, with four pills remaining. Michael doubts she could do herself much damage with those, but Olivia says she is very sensitive to paracetamol.

'Throw it all away,' she says. 'I know I'll do something terrible tonight if I'm alone.'

Of course Michael says she won't be alone. He will stay with her.

'You're such a good friend,' she says. She starts to cry again. 'Thank you. I just can't be alone tonight.'

He texts Maya to postpone, saying a friend is having a crisis. Maya is very nice about it.

DESPITE THESE OCCASIONAL DRAMAS, Michael is enjoying his first year of university. He likes his course, and especially the way other students now listen to him respectfully when he talks about politics (which is often). In the final term of his first year, he and Maya start seeing each other properly, having reconnected after a lecture on Gladstone. He loses his virginity to her, rather messily but with great satisfaction. Olivia does not take to Maya, however, and makes snide comments about giraffes behind her back. Michael tries to ignore this, reminding himself that Olivia does not trust other girls, because she has been badly hurt in the past. And it is true, as Olivia says, that women can be very bitchy; it is why she has always been more comfortable around men. Michael is sure Olivia will warm to Maya given time.

But one day during the summer term, Olivia comes to him with that intense look on her face that always makes Michael nervous. 'There's something you should know,' she says, sitting down on his bed. 'I'm pregnant.'

'God!' Michael says. 'Oh my God. Wow. *Wow.*' He can see he isn't doing particularly well. 'Whose is it?'

He knows immediately that this is the wrong thing to say, but it is too late to take it back.

Olivia glares at him. 'Does it matter?' There is a pause, then she says, 'It's yours, if you must know.'

Michael is shocked by this, especially since they've never had sex.

'Not yours *literally*,' Olivia says. 'Yours *emotionally*. I'm closer to you than any man I've ever known. My body is infused with you, and this baby is yours. Its soul is part you and part me.'

Michael is touched, and also somewhat confused. But Olivia has begun to weep now, and before long he finds that he is holding her in his arms and promising to stick by her no matter what.

'You mean you'll help me?' Olivia says, her wet face against his chest. 'Oh Michael, thank God. I don't know what I'd do if you abandoned me like everyone else.'

'I'll never abandon you,' Michael says.

'Thank you,' Olivia says. 'Oh, thank you. I'm not afraid to raise this baby anymore, now I know we'll be doing it together.'

Michael isn't sure how he's ended up committing to this, but it certainly seems like he has. However, he doesn't have time to ponder the matter further because the next moment Olivia is turning her beautiful tear-stained face up to his and saying, 'I love you.'

'I love you too.' His heart is beating so fast he feels it might escape from his chest.

'You're my soulmate,' she says.

And finally, he is allowed to kiss her.

THEY START TO MAKE plans. They agree that Olivia will take a break from university to have the baby, but Olivia is not sure yet whether Michael should drop out too or simply move into a student house that she and the baby can share. Michael is horrified at the suggestion that he drop out, and says it would make more sense for him to continue his studies so he can get a better job in a couple of years' time in order to support the three of them.

'But what'll we do about money in the meantime?' Olivia says.

'I'll get a part-time job,' Michael says. 'Evenings and weekends.'

'I'm scared,' she says.

'You don't need to be. I'll look after you.'

It goes without saying that he has to break up with Maya, even though his relationship with Olivia has not yet progressed beyond hugging and the occasional kiss.

('I'm not ready,' Olivia says if Michael tries to initiate anything further. 'Michael, I've been hurt so many times. I want it to be different with you.'

He nods. He understands.)

When Olivia hears that Michael has gone for a coffee with Maya after one of their lectures — though he and Maya are no longer together, they are still friends — she is distraught.

'How am I supposed to do this alone?' she sobs. 'I might as well just give up and abort the baby. Or else kill myself. Kill us both.'

'You're not alone,' Michael says. He tries to hug her but she moves out of his reach.

'I might as well just kill myself,' she repeats.

'Don't talk like that!'

'Why not? I'm terrified, and you're not committed to me.'

Finally, she allows him to put his arms around her again, and as she weeps against him, he promises he will change, he will make her see she is not alone, he is committed.

A pause, as her eyes search his face. She says, 'You know, I feel like I'll be ready soon.'

'For what?' he says.

'To make love. To take our relationship to the next level.'

Michael leans in to kiss her and she allows it, though when he tries to move his hand to her breast she gently pulls away.

*

A WEEK OR SO later, he is coming back from the shower one morning when he sees a boy emerging from Olivia's room.

Michael fumbles with the key outside his door as the boy puts his shoes on.

'Hi,' Michael says after a moment.

'Hey,' the boy says. He is handsome (of course), and is probably on the first team for football.

'I'm Michael,' Michael says insistently.

'Jack.' (Michael only just stops himself reaching out for a handshake.) No further information is proffered, and Jack departs. But Michael sees him around their corridor more and more often after that. Olivia frequently does not answer when Michael crosses the hall to knock on her door, and if he sees her in the corridor she is always in too much of a hurry to stop and chat. She takes longer and longer to reply to his messages. Michael has no one to confide in. He knows instinctively that Jed would not understand, and wants to protect Olivia from his harsh judgement.

A couple of weeks later, when he finally manages to talk to Olivia alone, she tells him she has lost the baby.

'It just wasn't meant to be,' she says, sitting on her bed with her feet tucked neatly beneath her. 'Well, don't *cry* about it, Michael. Jesus.'

HE STARTS TO AVOID her after that, but she probably does not notice, because now she is spending all her time with Jack.

'Poor bloke,' Jed says, when Michael mentions this new relationship to him (aiming for a sufficiently casual tone). 'He obviously doesn't realize she's mental.'

'She isn't,' Michael says, and hates the pitying look Jed gives him.

*

IN HIS SECOND YEAR, Michael moves into a shared house with Jed and two other boys. He loses sight of Olivia. He starts going out with a Chemistry student called Sophie, who is quiet and steady and heavily involved in the Students' Union, which Michael finds impressive. He even introduces her to his mother, who comments that she seems 'nice enough' (high praise, Michael knows. He translates it to Sophie as, 'She said you were lovely').

One day he and Jed return home after lectures to find their street cordoned off with police tape, and police cars and an ambulance parked further down the road, almost directly outside their house. A house only four doors down from theirs has collapsed, one side of it still standing, the rest reduced to rubble. A gas explosion, it turns out. The female occupant was killed, though her husband was out at work, her toddler safely at nursery.

There is a news team already on the scene, and Michael and Jed are interviewed, standing solemnly by the police tape. The segment is shown on the national news that night, as well as local news throughout the day. Michael watches himself, blinking into the camera, saying, 'It's very shocking. I just keep thinking, if we'd been in at the time, if the explosion had been worse, it could have been me.'

This interview has three main outcomes.

The first is his mother's horror at how close he came to death. Michael calls her to describe the incident (he tells her to look out for his interview on the news that evening). She tries to insist at first that Michael return home immediately because clearly university is too dangerous. It takes Michael a while to talk her down.

The second is that his sisters enjoy the interview a little too much and latch on to the phrase 'It could have been me', which they seem to feel was a self-absorbed response to the woman's death. Whenever he is home after this, they find a way to dust it off and bring it out again. Hanna is the ringleader, of course, but even Alice will sometimes join in, though Michael might have expected better from her. 'Oh God,' Hanna says with tragic intensity when they hear that the Serbian Prime Minister has been assassinated in Belgrade. 'This is horror enough, but just imagine, Michael. *It could have been you.*'

The third outcome is the reappearance of Olivia. A few days after the incident, Michael gets a text from a number he doesn't recognize. It says, *My love, I heard what happened. How scary. Are you OK? xxx* She hasn't signed her name, despite apparently having changed her number, but he immediately knows it is her.

Michael agonizes for a long time over how to reply. He types and retypes his response. Finally, exhausted, he settles on not replying at all.

'Who is this girl anyway?' his housemate Ryan asks, seeing him hunched, frowning, over his phone.

Michael sighs. He says, 'Have you heard of the hot–crazy matrix?' Then, because Sophie has told him this is a well-worn misogynist trope, he softens his comment by adding, 'She's someone I used to love.'

'Love? I don't believe in love,' Ryan says, rather surprisingly. He doesn't elaborate on this any further.

A week later, Michael runs into Olivia on one of the university club nights. Sophie is having an evening in, so Michael has no one with him except Jed and Ryan, who are too drunk to provide any useful assistance. Michael tries to pretend he hasn't seen Olivia, but she comes up to him and throws her arms around his neck. Raising her voice above the music, she says, close to his ear, 'It's so good to see you.'

When Michael tries to pull away, she takes his hand and says, 'Come out to the smoking area.'

Michael shakes his head, but she interprets this as him not being able to hear her. She pulls him towards her again and says, her lips so close they brush his ear, 'Come outside with me!'

Then she leads him towards the exit. Michael can't quite bring himself to snatch his hand away.

Outside, leaning against the wall between the clusters of smokers, she says huskily, 'I have to tell you something.'

Michael hopes she isn't pregnant with his child again.

Olivia says, 'You've always been the one for me. Always.'

Michael hesitates a moment. Then he says boldly, 'It didn't seem that way when you were with Jack.'

'Don't you see?' Olivia says. 'That was all because of you.'

Michael does not see.

Olivia says, more slowly, 'I had sex with him because I was in love with you.'

'I'm still not really following—'

'Oh Michael,' she says, placing her hand on his arm and keeping it there. 'It's so simple. I was frightened by the intensity of my feelings for you. I didn't know how to handle it. I was young and afraid, and . . . I suppose I just panicked.' She looks into his eyes. 'It's the greatest regret of my life that I didn't have the courage to tell you how I felt.'

Michael doesn't say anything. All he can think about is the heat of her hand on his upper arm.

Olivia says, 'Somehow I *knew* we'd find each other again. I just knew.'

So perhaps this is all love is, Michael thinks, as she stands on tiptoes to raise her face towards his: inevitability.

6

2018

IMAGINE HAVING A TWIN you haven't spoken to in four years. Or more accurately, Alice thinks, who hasn't spoken to you. She often asks herself how it came to this, especially when she is lying awake at night, though really she knows exactly how it happened. One of the worst parts of this estrangement has been the knowledge that she has only herself to blame. She still revisits it all very often; there were so many moments when she could have done things differently and averted disaster. Of course it is obvious with hindsight, but Alice is still amazed it wasn't obvious to her at the time. She wonders how many of the world's ills are the result of stupidity rather than malice.

Saturday morning, a week on from the funeral, and she waits nervously in a coffee shop near Waterloo. It is an unusually trendy place for her to have chosen, the walls papered with ancient, yellowing newspaper and each table made up of a colourful mosaic of Lego bricks beneath a glass top. Alice had thought it would be the kind of place that Hanna might approve of, but now she is here she has her doubts; eyeing a shelf of sinister children's dolls arranged above the counter, she fears the café might be trying too hard (just like Alice herself). Now that it is too late, she wishes she had suggested somewhere safe and neutral like Costa, which had been her first instinct. At least then any failings of the venue wouldn't seem to reflect on Alice herself. Only she hadn't wanted Hanna to think she was boring.

When the waitress comes over, Alice orders a cappuccino and a pain au chocolat. Table service feels like a novelty to her: like being on holiday in France. The waitress has dyed-pink hair and a nose ring, and Alice thinks what a square she herself must look with her cord skirt and sensible shoes. She gives the waitress a particularly nice smile as she orders, in the hope of ingratiating herself. She always wants waiters and waitresses to like her, which seems to her now to suggest a troubling weakness of character. In any case, the waitress doesn't smile back.

When her coffee and pastry arrive, Alice tries to focus on this treat instead of on her own anxiety. But although the coffee is good, the pain au chocolat is stale and dry. Alice eats it anyway, every bite, and wonders how she can warn Hanna off the pastries when she arrives. It is ridiculous, she thinks, to be this nervous.

She has invited Michael along as a buffer, but now she sees him standing in the doorway of the café, frowning at the décor in a mixture of bewilderment and horror, she wonders if this was a good idea. He is not one of life's natural buffers. Besides, Alice feels suspicious of her own motives. She has been hoping, perhaps, that she and Hanna might regain some of their old unity in the face of Michael's disapproval. Not very kind to use him in this way.

Michael has reached her table now. 'Alice,' he says, by way of greeting, 'what possessed you to choose this place?'

'I thought it seemed fun,' Alice says without much conviction.

'*Fun?*' He gestures to the display of dolls above the counter, some of which, Alice notices now, are missing their eyes. Most are clad in old cotton dresses, but a couple of the eyeless ones are naked. 'It's like a vision of hell,' Michael says. 'And why is there a coffin mounted on the wall?'

Alice hadn't noticed this. 'It's quirky,' she says.

'It's ridiculous.' He takes the seat opposite her and looks around him. 'Next time, just let me choose the venue, will you? I'd prefer to be somewhere more grown up. Is it table service?'

'Yes.' Alice had planned to alert him to the stale-pastry situation, but now she decides to let him take his chances.

The pink-haired waitress comes over and Michael orders a macchiato and a pain au raisin. Alice is relieved to see that the waitress is no warmer towards Michael than she was towards Alice, so presumably it was nothing personal.

'I think you should have invited Mum,' Michael says when the waitress has gone. 'She'll be hurt to have been excluded.'

'I'm not excluding her,' Alice says, as her anxiety spikes. 'I just thought it would be good to meet with only the three of us. Like old times,' she adds, though she can't now remember a single other occasion when they have met up as a three. Their father's funeral, perhaps?

Michael, too, looks doubtful. 'And Hanna's definitely coming?'

'Yes.'

'She actually told you she was coming?'

'Yes,' Alice says again. She feels less convinced every moment.

'Well,' Michael says. 'I'll believe it when I see it.'

'She'll be here,' Alice says.

'I'll give it fifteen minutes,' Michael says. 'Then I'm afraid if she hasn't arrived I'll have to go. I've got a lot on today.'

Alice wonders what he can possibly have on at the weekend, but decides it's safer not to ask. Michael's busyness is legendary. Alice hears about it constantly from her mother, how hard Michael works, how much responsibility he has within his department, how *extremely busy* he is. Alice is often instructed by her mother not to bother him with messages, as he is much too busy and doesn't need any distractions (as if Alice lives her whole life on the cusp of texting Michael). She is sometimes tempted to remind her mother that Michael is a tax associate and not the Prime Minister, but clearly this would not go down well. And she supposes it's true that he works very hard.

'That's fine,' she tells him. 'Fifteen minutes is fine. I'm glad you came.'

He seems mollified at this. 'Well, it's nice to see you.'

Alice smiles at him, suddenly able to remember all the times in the past when he's been kind to her: when she and her flatmates were having difficulty with their landlord and he drafted a devastatingly effective email for them; or when Alice was twelve or thirteen, in tears over something her mother had said, and Michael went to the shop to buy her a Wispa and a can of Pepsi; or when she was in primary school and he taught her, with great patience, how to do long division.

The waitress returns and places in front of Michael a coffee and a croissant. 'Enjoy,' she says, so flatly that it sounds sarcastic.

'I'm sorry,' Michael says, 'this isn't what I ordered.'

'It's a macchiato,' the waitress says. 'That's what a macchiato is. You might have confused it with an Americano. Some people do.'

'No, I mean I didn't order a croissant. I ordered a pain au raisin.'

'Oh,' the waitress says suspiciously. 'All right. Sorry about that.' She picks up the plate and disappears again.

Michael takes a sip of his coffee. 'Coffee's decent,' he says. 'At least there's that.'

There's a pause. Alice sips her own coffee, which she has nearly finished now. She shouldn't have drunk it so quickly; it's made her even more jittery.

Michael says, 'So, are you seeing anyone at the moment?'

Alice shakes her head, both embarrassed at the question and strangely touched that he still thinks it worth asking. She's never been in possession of a successful love life. She has only, if she is completely honest, ever had two proper relationships, which seems tragic at thirty-two. The first was with her friend Max from university. They'd started going out not long after graduating, seeming more to stumble into it than be overcome with desire. But the relationship proved unsatisfactory, and Max called it off after a year, much to Alice's relief. He lives in Kensal Green now, and they meet up occasionally to go for walks around London parks. Alice's only other relationship was with a man she met at work; he was in the IT department. Although he was perfectly nice most of the time, he also put sheets over his furniture whenever Alice was on her period, as though she might suddenly spring a leak, and made her sleep in the guest bedroom on a plastic sheet. When Alice had finally confided this to Hanna, Hanna had said, 'Jesus fucking *Christ*, Alice! No, of course that's not *normal*!' And so Alice had felt emboldened to end it. Shortly afterwards, he changed jobs. They have not kept in touch.

Michael frowns at her. 'Have you tried online dating?'

'Not recently.'

'You won't ever meet anyone if you're not willing to put the effort in.'

Alice feels suitably reproved, the burdensome spinster sister whom it is impossible for the family to marry off. Then she wonders if Michael is being a bit hypocritical. She suspects his own relationship is not entirely straightforward, though it is difficult to judge these things from the outside.

Prompted by this thought, Alice asks, 'How's Olivia?'

'She's fine,' Michael says. 'Well, she's having a stressful time at work at the moment.'

'I'm sorry to hear that.'

'It's all right,' Michael says. 'I daresay it will pass.'

'Is it anything in particular?'

'No,' Michael says. He hesitates. 'You know, she's a very complicated, unusual person.'

'Yes,' Alice says.

'I'm lucky to have her.'

There is something weary in the way Michael says this that makes Alice sad. Impossible to ask him if he is happy; she can see so clearly how he would bridle at the question. She has never before thought of him as lonely.

Then Michael dispels her sympathy by saying, 'But Alice, you really do need to get on and meet someone. You're not getting any younger, especially if you want to have children.'

'I'm not sure I do,' Alice says. 'I don't know if I'd be a good mother, and that seems like quite a big thing to get wrong.'

'I'm sure you'd be fine,' Michael says. 'Have you tried OkCupid?'

A different waitress, with dark hair and a lot of gold jewellery, appears at their table. Without saying anything, she places beside Michael a Chelsea bun.

Alice watches Michael, whose face is a picture of despair.

'Sorry, but I didn't order this,' he says. 'I ordered a pain au raisin.'

'That is a pain au raisin,' the waitress says.

'No, I think it's a Chelsea bun,' Michael says. 'I saw that Chelsea buns were on the menu, but I ordered a pain au raisin. Not a Chelsea bun.'

The waitress is studying the pastry more closely. 'You might be right,' she says. 'It might be a Chelsea bun. They are quite similar.' She looks at Michael for a moment, as if waiting for him to tell her that the Chelsea bun is an acceptable substitute. When he does not, she says, 'Sorry about that,' picks up the plate again and walks away, leaving the vague impression that Michael is being difficult.

'For God's sake,' Michael says under his breath. He is not the type, however, to be rude to waiters, and Alice is grateful for this. She is starting to feel like the whole café is against them. Over Michael's shoulder, she can see their original waitress with pink hair taking another customer's order. The waitress is smiling warmly at him, nodding along as he speaks.

And then, coming towards them: Hanna. She is in black jeans and boots, and an oversized green cardigan. She looks much more at home here than Alice and Michael do. Perhaps Hanna will provide a protective shield, Alice thinks.

'Hello,' Hanna says. 'This is a strange café.'

'Hello!' Alice says, half-rising from her chair, unsure whether she should hug Hanna or not. She doesn't quite dare, and ends up doing an awkward 'welcome' gesture with her open arms and then sitting down again. 'Yes, I know it is. Sorry.'

'No, I quite like it. Sort of absurdist.' Hanna slips her rucksack off her shoulder on to the floor, and slides into the remaining chair. 'Have I kept you waiting?'

'No,' Alice says, at the same time as Michael says, 'Yes.'

'Tube took longer than I remembered,' Hanna says.

'You have to allow extra time for gaps in the service,' Michael says.

'Thanks, Michael. Perhaps later you could explain to me how the ticket barriers work, too. Is the coffee nice here? It looks like the sort of place that makes a big deal about proper coffee.'

It's amazing, Alice thinks, to be here like this with Hanna, doing something as normal and friendly as having coffee. Hanna herself shows no signs of awkwardness, though she has always been able to carry things off well. From her behaviour, it is as if she has never been away, as if the terrible rupture and all the hurt that followed never even happened. So perhaps it really is over, and Alice is forgiven.

'Alice,' Hanna says, 'why are you staring at me?'

'I'm not,' Alice says, quickly looking away.

A new waitress appears at that moment, a third one they haven't met yet. She is carrying a pain au raisin on a plate. Loudly, she says to Michael, 'Are you the man who ordered the pain au raisin?'

'Yes!' he says, turning to her in his relief. 'Yes, thank you, that was me.'

'I hope you enjoy it,' the waitress says. 'The pain au chocolat's on its way.'

'I didn't order a pain au chocolat,' Michael says.

'Just the pain au raisin?'

'Yes.'

'So who ordered the pain au chocolat?'

'No one,' Michael says.

'Actually, I ordered a pain au chocolat earlier,' Alice says, thinking this must be where the confusion stems from.

'Oh, OK,' the waitress says. 'I'll go and get it.'

'No, sorry, it's already arrived,' Alice says.

The waitress casts her eye over the table, looking confused.

'I ate it,' Alice explains.

The waitress is still frowning.

'We have everything we ordered now,' Michael says.

Hanna, who has the look of someone struggling to maintain her composure, asks for a flat white.

'Have you two been causing some kind of *stir*?' she says when the waitress is out of earshot.

'Through no fault of our own,' Michael says.

'So how are you settling in?' Alice asks Hanna, to distract attention from their blunders. 'Does it feel strange to be back in London?'

'A bit,' Hanna says. 'But nice, too.'

'Must be good to be away from all that pollution, at least,' Michael says, taking a large bite of his pain au raisin. He seems intent on eating it quickly, perhaps worried a fourth waitress might arrive to take it away.

'Actually, the air quality in London is worse than Kuala Lumpur,' Hanna says.

'I don't think that can be right,' Michael says.

'It is.'

'And of course the traffic's very bad out there,' Michael says.

'No worse than in London,' Hanna says.

'Oh, I think it *is*.'

'Just to clarify,' Hanna says politely, 'have you ever been to KL?'

'It's well known that traffic's a problem over there,' Michael snaps. 'It's been widely reported.'

Alice says quickly, 'It's so good to have you home, Hanna.' She's worried Michael is about to get out his phone and start quoting traffic statistics at them. Briefly, she meets Hanna's gaze. Hanna rolls her eyes, and Alice is delighted by the conspiratorial look they exchange. Then she feels sorry for Michael.

'How's your pain au raisin?' she asks him solicitously.

'Stale,' he says. 'Though perhaps it was fresh when I first ordered it.'

Hanna's flat white arrives. 'Cheers,' she says, raising her cup. 'To the reunion.'

Alice loves hearing Hanna refer to it in these terms (with only a hint of irony, too); it makes it sound celebratory. They should do something to mark the occasion properly, she thinks. She could even throw Hanna a welcome-home party. For a second or two she is delighted with the idea: Hanna smiling and thanking her, saying it's a wonderful party; the two of them hanging out together as friends. But then almost immediately she starts to have doubts. She isn't the kind of person who knows how to throw a party, and anyway she doesn't want to come on too strong.

'You must be finding the weather quite chilly now you're home,' Michael is saying to Hanna, sounding slightly more conciliatory.

'I'm adjusting,' Hanna says. She pauses, seemingly looking for something else to add. 'I definitely don't miss the humidity.'

'Of course there's plenty of rain in the UK too,' Michael says.

'Yeah,' Hanna says. 'Different kind though.'

A silence follows. It seems to Alice to extend for longer than is comfortable, and she racks her brains for a subject other than the weather. What if after all this they don't have enough to say to each other? She is afraid that the meet-up will turn out to be a failure and Hanna won't want to do it again.

'No snow in Malaysia, I suppose,' Michael says.

'No.'

'I daresay it doesn't get cold enough.'

'No, not really,' Hanna says.

Another silence. In a panic, Alice wonders if she should bring up the party idea after all, if only to divert the conversation. Then she tells herself firmly that this is not the answer, that it would only make things weird. The more she thinks about it, the more clearly she can see that insisting on throwing a party would be seriously overstepping.

'What would you say the average minimum temperature is in KL?' Michael says.

'Well, it's rare for it to fall below twenty-five degrees,' Hanna says dutifully. 'Minimum would be maybe twenty-one or twenty-two?'

'You wouldn't ever have needed a jacket,' Michael says.

'No.'

Another silence.

'What about sleet?' Michael says, sounding a little strained now. 'Did you ever get any of that?'

'Not really.'

A pause. 'Any hail?'

'We should have a party!' Alice bursts out. She isn't sure how it happens. Both Hanna and Michael turn to look at her in surprise. 'A welcome-home party for you, Hanna,' Alice adds.

Hanna seems unsure. 'Well. Maybe.'

'It does seem rather unnecessary,' Michael says. 'It's not like she's been away to war.'

Hanna raises her chin. 'Actually, having considered the matter further, I'd love a welcome-home party. Kemi's mentioned it already. It would be a good opportunity to see my uni friends again. Maybe some of my old colleagues.'

'We could host it at my flat,' Alice says, surprising herself further. 'I can arrange it with Kemi.'

'Sounds good,' Hanna says. 'A party involving minimal effort on my part. Perfect.' She pauses. 'Just people our own age, right?'

'Yes,' Alice says, catching her meaning.

'Well, I'm in,' Hanna says.

Alice beams at her. What a turnaround this is. A couple of weeks ago, Hanna still wasn't even speaking to her; they only found out she'd be attending the funeral through Kemi. And now look at them! Alice is throwing Hanna a welcome-home party. The thing to do now is not to mess everything up again. Alice feels a brief pang as she thinks of her mother, who is clearly not yet forgiven.

'More importantly,' Michael says to Hanna, 'now you're back, you can start thinking seriously about how to establish yourself.'

'As what?' Hanna says.

'I mean, with a steady job and residence, get on the property ladder, make a plan for the future.'

'Michael, you exhaust me,' Hanna says.

'Well, you need to be sensible about it. I'm here to help if you need it.'

'With money?' Hanna says.

'With *advice*.'

'Oh, OK,' Hanna says, sounding distinctly unenthusiastic. 'Thanks.'

'You're in your thirties,' Michael says. 'It's time to take some responsibility.'

'I'm barely in my thirties, and I'm very responsible,' Hanna says.

Michael does not seem convinced. 'Well,' he says. 'There's still time.' Then, after a pause, 'Are you seeing anyone at the moment?'

He should stop asking people this question, Alice thinks.

A glimmer of amusement from Hanna. 'Yes.'

'Is it serious?'

'No.'

'What does he do?'

'He's a photographer specializing in dog portraits, though he occasionally photographs humans too. We met outside the toilets in Regent's Park last Sunday. Kemi and I were coming out of the Ladies, and he was just sort of lurking.'

Michael's eyes widen, but he manages not to comment on any of this. Formally, he says, 'I'd very much like to meet him.'

'Bit soon for that.'

'Well, you could at least introduce him to Alice.'

'Why Alice?'

'She could vet him, if you won't allow me to.'

'He doesn't need vetting.'

'Sometimes people outside the situation can judge it better.'

'Oh for God's sake, Michael,' Hanna says, seeming to lose patience. 'You're hardly in a position to judge, are you?'

'What's that supposed to mean?'

'I might order another pain au chocolat,' Alice says desperately.

'No!' Michael almost shouts. Then, modifying his tone, 'I can't go through all that again.'

'Go on, order another,' Hanna says. 'I dare you.'

'Well, I suppose I'm not really hungry, and it was a bit stale—'

'Have you called Mum yet, Hanna?' Michael says, still visibly annoyed.

Alice sees Hanna bristle at this. 'Why would I have done that?'

'Perhaps I could try one of the famous Chelsea buns instead,' Alice says.

Michael says, 'Because you've been away for four years with minimal contact and now you're back in the same country, and Mum's just lost her sister.'

'I wouldn't mind if I ended up with a pain au raisin by mistake,' Alice says. 'I like both equally.'

'*You* talk to her if you feel so strongly about it,' Hanna says to Michael.

'I talk to her every Sunday,' Michael says. 'At six p.m.'

'Lucky her.'

'Hanna's only just got back,' Alice says, finally deciding direct intervention is necessary. 'Let her find her feet, Michael.'

'I don't need to find my feet,' Hanna says. 'I just don't want to talk to Mum. Jesus, is that so hard to understand?'

'No,' Alice says, feeling rebuffed.

'I do accept that she can be challenging at times,' Michael says. 'But she's still your mother.'

'Michael, just stay out of it,' Hanna says.

'This can't go on forever.'

'It's none of your business.'

'She's right,' Alice says, seizing the opportunity to redeem herself. 'It's her decision.' She is rewarded with a smile from Hanna, and then feels she has been a bit craven.

'Well,' Michael concludes, 'I've said my piece.' He glances at his watch (he must be one of the only people of their generation who still wears a watch, Alice thinks). 'I'd better get going. I told Olivia I'd be back by eleven.'

'Give her my love,' Hanna says unconvincingly. 'I should head off too. I'm meeting Kemi on the South Bank.'

'The South Bank will be horribly busy on a Saturday,' Michael says.

'Yes, I know, but I'm sure we'll cope. I did use to live here, Michael.'

'I'm just surprised that as a Londoner you've chosen to meet there of all places.'

'Well, it's good to have the river close by,' Hanna says, 'in case the memory of one of these conversations gets too much.'

'Hasn't this been great?' Alice says, with what is perhaps excessive brightness. 'The three of us, together again!'

And both her siblings turn to look at her in perplexity.

7

HERE IS CELIA AT forty-nine, divorced, stuck in a job she dislikes, mother to three almost grown-up children who seem less familiar to her every day. This is not what she had once envisaged for herself.

She had assumed when she was young, for instance, that her children would be enough – that this terrible ache would finally ease. But nobody warns you that even your own children lose interest in you in the end, that they press on into their adult lives without a backward glance. Celia still has her daughters at home with her for the time being, but they feel increasingly remote from her. Hanna has been a mystery for years, it is true, but it is too much to lose Alice as well. The girls are in their final year of college now, about to embark on their university applications; before long they will both be gone, and then she will truly be alone.

'You can make some lovely new friends, Mum,' Alice says encouragingly, after Celia expresses her distress at the prospect of being abandoned. 'You'll have a bit more time for yourself, and you can develop new interests.'

'Don't patronize me,' Celia says.

What she really wants is for Alice to promise to attend university nearby and come home to visit every weekend, but this idea has to come from Alice herself so Celia knows she means it. Celia hasn't managed to elicit the promise yet, but she continues to drop heavy hints.

'Next year, perhaps I'd better get a lodger in,' she says to the girls at dinner one evening. 'Just for the company.'

'Oh Mum, I hope you'll be all right,' Alice says. 'We'll be back in the holidays, and they're quite long.'

'There will still be the term time to fill,' Celia says. 'A lodger seems like the best solution. I'll just have to hope he isn't a murderer, I suppose.' She gives a hollow laugh.

'You could always choose a female lodger,' Hanna says. 'Statistically less likely to be murderous.'

'Please don't get a lodger just for the sake of company, Mum,' Alice says. 'Not if it'll make you feel uncomfortable.'

'I think I'd better, or else I'll just be rattling around the house on my own,' Celia says stoically.

'It's quite a small house,' Hanna says. 'Not much room to rattle.'

A FEW DAYS LATER, Alice presents Celia with a list of local activities she has collated from the library bulletin board and various community websites.

'You might enjoy some of these,' she says. 'You could meet people your own age.'

How is it that the young are able to be so condescending without even realizing it? Celia studies the list. There is a walking group, a book club, a knitting circle, volunteering opportunities with the elderly, and even – God help us – a ladies' dance class.

'Not really my cup of tea,' she says.

'No, but there might be people there you get on with,' Alice says.

It is enraging that Alice assumes it would all be so easy. Celia has tried to have friends in the past, but somehow it seems that friends are something other people get to have and Celia does not. Other people, she has noticed, have this way of being easy with each other, of taking things in their stride. Celia used to hope she might acquire this knack with age, but she never has. It is difficult to take things in your stride when you feel so much more than other people.

She tries to imagine turning up at the book group or one of the coffee mornings, full of hope. But she can immediately picture all those faces turning towards her, blank and unwelcoming. Then they turn away again.

'I can see what you're doing,' she says to Alice. 'Trying to palm me off on other people so you don't have to feel guilty for leaving me.' Ignoring Alice's dismayed expression, she screws up the list and drops it on to the kitchen table before leaving the room. When she returns later, the crumpled paper has gone.

THE FACT IS, CELIA has always wanted so much from others, and they have always had so little to give her. It is tiring, being in this constant state of disappointment. It is a kind of lifelong grief. Even her husband's betrayal did not come as a particular shock. Celia discovered when he left her that she had never expected him to stay. Perhaps she had never expected him to marry her in the first place. Sometimes she sees herself at twenty years old again, standing with Paul in front of a jeweller's window. She cannot imagine now how their conversation might have gone, how any of it could possibly have happened. It turns out that all this time she has simply been trying her luck, pretending she can be a person who is chosen, who is actually wanted. It is almost a relief now to stop holding her breath. The only part that surprises her is that Paul found time in his famously busy schedule to have an affair.

Still, both his departure and the manner of it are an acute humiliation, seeming to make clear to the world some secret shame of hers, some inward, ugly blight that she has struggled all this time to conceal. She tried to get away with something – with what, exactly? – and she has been caught out. Sometimes she senses her daughters' eyes on her and feels herself baulk in mortification, imagining Hanna's scorn and Alice's pity.

'I asked you to lay the table,' she spits at them. 'Must I do everything myself? Why are you both so disgustingly selfish?'

THOUGH THE ABANDONMENT IS difficult to bear, she does not miss her husband. He is surely no one's idea of an ideal companion, however low you are setting your sights. And he was hardly ever around. Over the years Celia has grown used to looking elsewhere for the companionship she craves. There have been occasional bursts of hope. The woman at the toddler group she attended with Michael, who seemed to respond so enthusiastically to Celia's overtures at first. Gemma. She had unnaturally dyed blonde hair and more than one silver hoop in each ear. There were a couple of blissful months when they'd sit next to each other in the circle, and then go for coffees and walks afterwards, just the two of them and their children, and they'd complain about their husbands, reminisce about their lives when they were free. They would sometimes meet up on non-group days as well, whenever Gemma had the time (which was not quite as often as Celia did, it seemed, but Gemma had an older child who'd just started school and a mother who was unwell, so Celia understood). They could talk endlessly together. Finally, a relationship that lived up to Celia's grand ideal of friendship. 'You can tell me anything,' she would say to Gemma, when Gemma would confide her marital difficulties (her husband had grown lazy about everything, made no effort to talk to Gemma the way he used to, let alone to help around the house). Sometimes Celia would ring Gemma in the evenings, when Paul was once again working late. There were always more things she'd thought of that she wanted to say to her friend, just small thoughts from her day that she'd saved up.

She was even preparing to tell Gemma about Katy, so great was the trust between them. But then, just as they were nearing this crucial point, disaster. Abruptly, Gemma began to pull away. She turned aloof at the toddler group, sitting in a different place instead of their usual spot together, and became suddenly busy outside of the group too, with no more time for coffee (though Celia *knows* this was a lie, because once — an agony! — she saw Gemma with some of the other women from the group in a coffee shop around the corner, while Celia herself was of course not invited).

If Celia rang Gemma in the evenings now, Gemma's husband would usually answer instead, and Gemma would always be 'out' (but where?). To this day, Celia doesn't understand what changed, but she thinks it may have been the intervention of the husband. Celia went over it all in her mind for a long time afterwards. She was owed some kind of explanation, surely, but Gemma would never speak to her about it, nor even acknowledge the cards Celia sent her. *It's been ages*, Celia would write. *When can we meet?* But she got nothing back.

Soon enough, she began to hate Gemma. She would watch her chatting to the other mothers at the group — all that warmth for everyone else when she only had coldness for Celia, who she avoided now. Her trashy hair and trashy jewellery. Gemma's little girl was ugly, too, with a large doughy face and small eyes. Michael was a good-looking boy from the first, but he cried a lot in those days, was a whiny, weedy child, and Celia wondered sometimes if it was this too that had put Gemma off.

'*Stop* it,' she would say to Michael as they were arriving, Michael grizzling away. There was always something. '*Stop it*. You're embarrassing me.'

THERE HAS ONLY BEEN one other time since then that Celia has felt the same rush of hope, the prospect of finally being understood. This one had been far more unexpected, since she had long given up looking. Of course, her children know nothing of all this, and would no doubt not be interested.

He was a colleague at the FE college, though it has been more than two years now since Celia last laid eyes on him. She doesn't even know for certain that he's still in London; he may have finally given in to his wife and moved out to the Home Counties: not real countryside, as he used to say, no real wildness; a genteel, neat, unimaginative life. The smallness of it, the meanness. How he must hate it.

Celia has never much enjoyed her job at the college, where she teaches Travel and Tourism to sixteen-to-nineteen-year-olds. But somehow she has stayed, and is in her fifth year now. It does at least make use of her Geography degree, to some extent, though many aspects of the job are a trial. For one thing, Celia does not particularly like young people. However, it is the college principal who is the greatest thorn in her side. He is ineffective and overly familiar, whilst also being difficult to avoid; he makes it his business to be a 'presence' around the college, and seems to believe he has a special way with people.

'Working away, Celia?' he'll say roguishly, sticking his head round her classroom door to interrupt her whilst she is trying to get her marking done.

'Yes,' Celia will say. Trying to.

'No rest for the wicked, eh?'

Celia looks at him stonily.

'Look at you, getting through that stack of papers!' he might then remark, as if Celia's fulfilment of her contractual obligations is a strange caprice of hers.

'Yes.'

'Well, carry on, carry on,' he'll say at last, his conversational verve deflated by Celia's refusal to engage (unfortunately he is never deterred for long). Then Celia will often have to return to the start of the assignment she is marking, so thoroughly will she have lost her thread.

The principal has also got the idea from somewhere that Celia has a keen interest in German language and culture, which he now brings up in every conversation with her. Celia suspects him of once reading a book on management that encouraged leaders to identify a particular interest in each member of their staff, so that they could then display the personal touch. Why he thinks Celia is so fascinated by Germany, she does not know. Probably he has confused her with someone else at some point, and now the mistake is fixed. Celia has never visited the country and doesn't speak a word of German. Nor, apparently, does the principal, though it seems he has taught himself a smattering of phrases since unearthing Celia's interest.

'*Guten Morgen!*' he'll greet her with if he runs into her in the corridor. '*Wie geht's?*' Sometimes he accosts her so insistently that Celia has little choice but to reply with a half-hearted, '*Guten Morgen,*' if only so that she can get away, and now other colleagues also associate her with a passion for Germany. As a result, one of them likes to tell her in excessive detail about his annual trips to Munich for Oktoberfest, and another persistently recommends the film *Das Boot* to her. It is all very trying.

Generally, in fact, Celia has not been impressed by the calibre of her colleagues. The staff turnover is high, too – it seems to be just Celia and the principal who are lifers – and the environment is impersonal, despite the principal's best efforts. With all this in mind, there is not much chance of Celia taking notice of a new colleague, and in fact it is a month or so before she becomes fully aware of Mark after he joins at the start of her second year.

Their first encounter is undramatic. Celia is in the staffroom alone one morning, savouring a moment's quiet to have her coffee and pretend she is elsewhere. It is a small, depressing room with a stained grey carpet and a counter in the corner with a sink, a kettle and a very elderly microwave in which Celia's colleagues warm up their revolting-smelling lunches: leftover curry, or tuna pasta, or broccoli and stilton soup, as if they are in some unspoken competition to see who can bring in the most offensive lunch. The room has a single window, but that is narrow and high, and looks out on to the car park. Someone, a long time ago, has hung a bright abstract print on the wall, presumably in an attempt to cheer the place up, but against the drabness of the room, the garish pinks and reds of the print seem unpleasant, like a shout in the midst of silence.

There are two rather hard sofas against opposite walls, and two circular tables in the middle of the room, at one of which Celia is now sitting, idly flicking through a copy of *National Geographic* as she sips her coffee. She would not spend her breaks in this miserable room if she had anywhere else to go, but it is the only place where she is safe from students. Her teaching room has a glass panel in the door, and students have a tendency to drop by (usually to give an unconvincing excuse for late work, but on occasion, to Celia's horror, *simply to chat*). This room, at least, has an impenetrable, bunker-like feel.

When Mark comes in, she is annoyed at the intrusion. She always spends her free period in here, and knows that most of her colleagues are teaching during this time, so she can finally have some peace. Nonetheless, she says a brief, polite hello, and assumes they will ignore each other beyond this, according to established precedent.

But Mark says, 'Taking a coffee break? Much needed, I'm sure.'

Celia is surprised to note that he is Irish (Northern Irish, by his accent, though she is no expert). Fleetingly, she takes in his appearance. He is not, by any objective standards, an attractive man. He is not particularly tall, and although he is not quite overweight, his belly protrudes, straining the lower half of his shirt. He does have his hair still, but it is sparse on top, and his receding hairline emphasizes a forehead that is already overly large and slightly bulging.

Celia observes all of this, but then her interest wanes again. She smiles thinly at him and returns to her magazine.

But Mark is undeterred. He says, 'I'm glad to catch you alone. We haven't had much of a chance to talk so far. You're a woman always in a hurry.'

Celia does not care to be told by this slightly seedy-looking man what kind of a woman she is. She says, 'I have a lot of work to do.'

'I'm sure you do,' he says. 'There's always work to do, if you're looking for it.'

Celia doesn't know what to make of this comment. After a moment, she decides to be irritated. This is clearly another of those men who swan about, cutting every corner they can because clearly hard work is beneath them, whilst their female colleagues are forced to pick up the slack.

She eyes him narrowly. 'Marking needs to be done,' she says. 'Lessons need to be planned. We have a duty to these young people.' She isn't sure why she is suddenly taking such a strong stand on the rights of her students. Many days she feels like a weary Roman general facing an encroaching Celtic horde.

'Oh yes,' he says. 'I'm not denying that.' And then he actually comes over and sits at the table opposite Celia.

Celia decides to ignore him.

Mark says, 'But you must admit, Celia –' so he does know her name, though she has not invited him to use it – 'it can feel a bit thankless, can't it?'

She glances up, briefly. Yes, 'thankless' is one way of putting it. She didn't dream, when she was younger, of this. And what is it all for? Her retirement will be nothing to write home about: a low pension, and all that time on her hands, alone in the small terraced house she hates, rarely visited by her children. She feels depressed. This man has interrupted her break and made her feel depressed. She says, 'Well, we're not in it for the thanks.'

Mark shrugs. 'Just as well.' He is silent for a moment, then adds, 'Sometimes I wonder how I ended up here. I suspect you do too.'

She does not. Celia knows exactly how she ended up here. But she doesn't mind the implication that he views her as above this place. She views herself as above it too.

'I see you're reading *National Geographic*,' he says. 'More highbrow than most of the magazines you see round here.'

'But it's not exactly a demanding read,' Celia says. 'And anyway,' she adds, feeling a compulsion to tell the truth, 'I mainly enjoy looking at the pictures.'

He is watching her. 'Some of them are a work of art,' he says.

'And sometimes it's nice to imagine being elsewhere,' Celia says.

'That is the particular beauty of it. But if you could go anywhere, right now, where would you go?'

This is a difficult question, partly because nobody has ever asked her anything like this before, and partly because Celia has been to so few places. 'I'd like to go to Uganda,' she says at last. 'I'd like to see the mountain gorillas.'

'So why don't you?'

What an absurd question. 'It's too expensive.' And it would be like living somebody else's life.

He watches her thoughtfully. 'I've always wanted to go to Borneo. See the orangutans. I've never done that either. Isn't that just life? I talk and talk, but I very rarely *do*.' He pauses. 'My wife, you see. She doesn't like to travel.'

'You could go without her,' Celia says.

Then she notices the time: there are only seven minutes until her free period ends and the next lesson starts. She likes to arrive in her classroom early to set up; coming in at the same time as the students flusters her, as if she has already lost control. So she drains the last of her coffee and says, 'I'd better go. I'm teaching a lesson on the cruise industry and I need to lay the resources out.'

'You are most conscientious,' he says, which feels like an insult.

Celia takes her magazine and goes.

SHE ASSUMES THIS CONVERSATION will be a one-off, but Mark seems to seek her out after this, both at lunchtime and occasionally during her free periods. It does not happen all the time. Some days she will see him in the staffroom and he will barely acknowledge her. He speaks to no one on these days, but sits alone on one of the hard sofas, reading the paper. But if he is having one of his more gregarious days, it is Celia who he selects as his companion. She starts to like this, she finds – the sense of being the only one he deems worth talking to.

His cynicism also appeals to her. He murmurs dry remarks to her under his breath about their colleagues, and students they share, as if she is the only other person who can see through all the nonsense. He asks her opinion about politics and about current events. He himself is a Marxist and Celia finds his views interesting. The contrast makes her realize how narrow Paul was – though hadn't she always known that? She tells Mark, briefly, about her divorce, and he says it sounds like she got rid of a dead weight. Celia likes this way of looking at it (as if it hadn't been she who was got rid of).

'So he was a toy buyer?' Mark says. 'What does that involve?'

'It involves spending a large portion of your career assessing the merits of different yo-yos,' Celia says.

Mark laughs. He says, 'You know what I like about you, Celia? Your sharpness.'

Celia stares at him. She is not sure anyone has regarded this as a positive character trait in her before.

'You don't suffer fools gladly, do you?' Mark says.

Celia thinks of the principal, who this morning stuck his head round her door and greeted her with a particularly exuberant and guttural, '*Guten Tag, Fräulein!*' just as her students were entering, causing sniggers across the room. Her whole life, she has been beset by fools.

'Not if I can help it,' she says.

Mark smiles at her. 'It's very refreshing,' he says.

HIS ANGER, SHE DOESN'T notice until later. When she does, she is not perturbed by it. She has anger of her own.

He is angry because he should have been a university lecturer in Economics or PPE, and instead he is stuck teaching BTEC Business at an FE college. He is angry because he feels underappreciated, and because his almost-adult son undermines him and his wife does not take his side. He is angry because he is an idealist in an imperfect world, because social injustice is endemic and his wife still votes Tory. He is angry, above all, because he has not been given his due; he was promised things once, and they were not delivered.

Celia intuits the elements of this that she has not been told. She understands him; she knows better than anyone what a disappointing business life can be.

AS THE WEEKS PASS, Celia begins to look forward to coming into work. Most days they will have one of their conspiratorial chats, and if a day passes when they don't have a chance to speak, because Celia is too busy, or because Mark is in one of his silent moods, he will still catch her eye as they pass in the corridor, or across the staffroom at break, and give her one of his looks.

'Christ, this must be the most depressing place on earth,' he remarks as they drink coffee together one morning. They aren't alone in the staffroom, but he does not bother to lower his voice.

'Perhaps not the *most* depressing,' Celia says, because she has noticed he has a tendency towards exaggeration. Also, she is from Peterborough.

'To be honest with you, I'm impressed I've lasted this long,' Mark says. He glances at her, then adds, 'You know, I might have already jumped ship if it weren't for you. I'm not renowned for my staying power.'

Celia feels a flood of warmth at this, and is unable to reply for fear of betraying herself.

When she gets home that evening, she goes to the bathroom and studies her face in the mirror. Is it possible that Mark doesn't mind the way she looks? She has carried with her the knowledge of her unattractiveness for a long time, ever since Katy first pointed it out. Just occasionally it has occurred to her to doubt it. She will go to look at her reflection, wondering if perhaps it is not as bad as she had thought. But there it still is, as always, unsoftened by time: the dull complexion, the eyes pressed too deep into her face, the thin mouth. Celia has done her best with her appearance over the years: she selects her clothes carefully, and ensures that they are always neat and uncreased; she gets her hair cut regularly and keeps a comb in her handbag. But she knows nobody has ever looked at her and been pleased by what they saw.

Now, she wonders if Mark can see beyond this, if perhaps there is hope after all. She has never worn much make-up (the few times she has tried, it has made her feel even more self-conscious, as if she is drawing attention to her plainness rather than disguising it), but now, with Hanna and Alice both out, she goes into their bedroom and rummages through Hanna's make-up bag until she finds a couple of lipsticks. One is a bruised berry colour, and the other a bright coral. Celia takes them both into the bathroom and carefully applies the berry colour to her mouth. But of course it looks ridiculous on her, and she watches her face, clownlike, flush in the mirror. Quickly, she wipes it off. It hardly seems worth trying the coral one as well, but Celia does all the same, masochistically. And suddenly – a miracle. Instead of looking absurd like the berry shade, the coral is far more subtle and elegant on her, and somehow brings warmth to her face.

After noting the brand and shade of the coral lipstick, she replaces both in Hanna's bag. The next day she goes into Boots to buy her own.

'You look different, Celia,' Mark says the first time she wears it. 'Have you done something with your hair?'

Celia shakes her head, deeply gratified. She wonders if perhaps she should do something with her hair, get it coloured perhaps. But the thought of her daughters noticing and commenting is too much.

Though their friendship continues to grow, she and Mark do not see each other outside of work. Perhaps for some people it might be this meeting in the outside world that cements the relationship, brings it fully into reality, but Celia feels that in their case the opposite would be true. Their friendship feels somehow sanctified by its present constraint, and exposing it to the banalities of wider everyday life would be a desecration. In any case, Mark does not suggest it.

TOWARDS THE END OF term, Mark comes to Celia's classroom after school to tell her about a particularly frustrating exchange he's had with a student.

'He's only doing the course because he wants to go on *The Apprentice*,' he says, leaning against her door frame. 'Told me that with a straight face. Give me strength.'

'He could at least have the grace to aim for *Dragons' Den*,' Celia says.

Mark laughs: a short bark like a seal. 'You know, I mentioned it to our glorious leader, and he said it was wonderful that I was encouraging the students' aspirations. Then he started asking me about the sectarian divide again. Christ, I know I'm Irish, but there *are* other subjects he could discuss with me.'

'No,' Celia says. 'It's one per person, and he chooses it. That's his policy.'

'Did you know, during my original interview he asked me if I'm a Catholic or a Protestant?' Mark says. 'How's that for an opening gambit?'

'He asked me last week if I'll be making my annual trip to Nuremberg for the Christmas markets,' Celia says.

This time they both laugh. Celia's conversations with Mark are unlike her conversations with anybody else. They are natural and easy – amusing, even. Postcards from another life. For a moment, briefly, there is the flicker of a memory: a girl with orange hair. Firmly, Celia pushes the thought aside.

'I think we might be the only two sane people in here,' Mark says. 'Do you think?'

'Yes.'

Then the most startling, exhilarating moment of her life: he steps forward, dips his head and kisses her.

It is the briefest of kisses. His lips brush lightly against hers and then it is over almost before Celia has realized it is happening.

He stands and smiles at her.

Celia feels her whole body ablaze. She can't smile back at him. She stares at him instead. Anyone could have passed the classroom door and seen them, but she doesn't care.

'We are comrades in arms,' Mark says. He turns and is gone.

FOR DAYS AFTERWARDS, CELIA can feel the press of his lips on hers. She finds herself smiling at strange times, luxuriating in her secret, so that Alice says at breakfast, 'Mum, are you all right?'

'I'm fine.' She tries to imagine how her girls would react if they knew. They would scarcely believe it, no doubt. And would not understand.

Although she and Mark are often alone after that, the kiss is not repeated, nor even mentioned. Mark's behaviour towards her does not change, except that for a while he is perhaps a little breezier than usual. Celia is puzzled. For a few weeks, she finds she is slightly on edge when they are together, waiting to see what he will do. But of course he is married, and he has his sense of honour. Besides, Celia thinks, he has made his feelings for her clear enough. Maybe she doesn't need any more from him than this.

IN THE SPRING TERM, there is an incident. Celia arrives in the staffroom early for break. It is unlike her to dismiss her class before the bell, but she is only human, and today she has reached the limits of her patience.

When she enters the staffroom, she is surprised to see Mark in there already. She feels the first flicker of pleasure before her brain processes the fact that he is not alone. Standing very close to him is Holly, who teaches hairdressing and is at least ten years younger than Celia and Mark.

Mark and Holly do not notice her presence at first, so Celia is able to study them. They certainly look very cosy together. Holly is giggling, leaning in towards Mark.

Celia clears her throat, and they both jump. It is then that Celia sees, as he removes it, that Mark's arm had been around Holly.

'Celia,' Mark says, seeming to recover himself. 'Here for the requisite caffeine hit?'

'Yes,' Celia says coolly. 'But I've changed my mind.'

It is a relief later, at least, to reflect that she showed great dignity in this response, and in her wordless retreat from the staffroom. But when she is safely alone in her classroom, she discovers she is trembling. There is a throbbing in her ears. She would like a cup of sweet tea to help her with the shock, but of course she can't go to get one because they are still in there. The humiliation is terrible. How could she have imagined he might prefer her to others when she knows so well that she is never preferred? Savagely, she wipes the lipstick off her mouth, leaving a coral smear on the back of her hand that she has to rub at with a tissue. How pathetic it all is, and how tawdry.

AT LUNCHTIME, SHE REMAINS in her classroom and eats her sandwiches at her desk, feeling self-conscious since any of her students passing could see her through the panel in her door.

She wonders if Mark will come to find her, but he does not.

For the next few days, she avoids the staffroom entirely, even bringing her own coffee from home in a thermos. The days seem especially bleak without her conversations with Mark to look forward to, but Celia is afraid that if she sees him she might break down and cry, and then she would never recover from the shame. It seems safest to keep her distance.

However, on the fourth day he thwarts her by turning up at her classroom door during break.

'Oh, Celia,' he says, as if he's just stumbled across her by chance. 'There you are. You've been very elusive recently.'

'I've been busy,' Celia says. She focuses on pouring coffee from her thermos into the small plastic cup, careful not to look at him.

'Is that right?' he says.

'Yes.'

There's a silence, which Celia does not feel it's her responsibility to break.

'Well, what is it you've been so busy with?' Mark says.

Celia wracks her brains, determined not to let him see how much he has affected her. She says, 'I've been teaching a particularly challenging unit on the customer experience.' When he still looks unconvinced, she goes on, 'My students have been taking it in turns to role-play as travel agents and members of a local tourist board.'

'Sounds vivid,' Mark says.

'They've needed extra support. Some of them have struggled with the experience.'

'All got a bit too real for them?' Mark says.

'They haven't been able to grasp the finer points of customer service, which generally don't involve berating the customer for making a poor choice of destination.'

'Certainly does sound like you've been busy,' Mark says. 'You know, I've missed our talks,' he adds, and for a moment Celia almost relents. Then she reminds herself that his actions tell a different story.

'I'm surprised you've had time to notice,' she tells him.

'What do you mean?'

She had not intended to go this far, but now she feels caught. She says, 'What with all your attention being elsewhere.'

'Where?'

'You know where.'

'I truly do not.'

'Well, never mind then. Never mind.'

'You don't mean,' he says slowly, 'because I've been talking to Holly?' When Celia doesn't reply, he goes on, 'Holly! Of course we chat from time to time. She's a friend.'

'*Is* she now?' Celia says. 'Is she.' She can't seem to stop repeating herself.

'What's wrong with that?'

'Oh, nothing at all,' Celia says. She might have got up and left her classroom then, but he is still standing in the doorway.

He says gently, 'A person can have more than one friend, can't they? People need different friends. Surely you do too.'

'I do not,' Celia says, on a wave of emotion. 'I value true friendship.' Sacred friendship, she almost says. 'I don't waste my time elsewhere.'

He is looking at her. 'Celia,' he says, 'aren't you taking all this a bit too seriously?'

So after everything, he has still not understood at all.

THAT EVENING, SHE WRITES him a letter. In it, she explains quite clearly how she views their friendship, what it has meant to her, why it is elevated above other friendships (his other friendships, she means; for her, there are no others). If she can just make him understand, she thinks, perhaps he will see how much is at stake.

She leaves the letter in his pigeonhole the next morning. Throughout the day, she goes back and forth to the staffroom to see if the letter has gone, but Mark is slapdash about checking his post, and Celia worries it may be weeks before he finds it. When it is still in his pigeonhole at the end of the day, she discreetly retrieves it, and, feeling faintly ridiculous, slips into his classroom after she knows he will have gone home and leaves the letter on his desk.

But though she waits patiently throughout the following morning, Mark comes to her classroom at lunchtime and greets her with no change to his normal manner.

'How's the travel-agent role play going?' he says cheerily. 'Any of them come to blows yet?'

'No,' Celia says.

'Coming for a coffee?'

'I have too much to do,' she says.

So he must not have seen the letter. But how can he not have done? It was impossible to miss.

Mark says, 'Celia, just come for a coffee, won't you? I'm lonely without you.' He says it lightly, teasingly, so she is not sure whether to take him seriously.

'Chat to Holly then,' she says.

'I don't want to chat to Holly,' he says. 'I want to chat to you.'

Celia is on the cusp of asking him if he got her letter, but she can't quite bring herself to do it. She studies his face for clues, and finds none.

'Look,' he says, 'are you coming for a coffee or not? I've got a problem with a student I want to run by you.'

And finally, seeing how much he needs her, Celia gives in. They have the staffroom to themselves, and drink their coffee at their usual table. When Holly comes in later with another teacher, Mark does not even seem to notice her. Celia decides that equilibrium has been restored.

IN THE SUMMER TERM, Mark finds himself in conflict with the principal. Apparently some students have complained they never receive feedback on their work. The principal, by the sound of it, has been mild in his conversations with Mark, but Mark is furious nonetheless, and Celia is enraged on his behalf. She greatly enjoys the time they spend huddled in corners discussing his unjust treatment. He barely ever spends time with Holly these days.

Celia says if he walks out, she will walk out too in protest; she is sure others will follow, and the principal will come to regret his behaviour. But before long the matter seems to blow over of its own accord, and there is no need for anyone to walk out.

During these summer months, Mark and Celia sometimes eat their lunch together on the bench at the front of the college, enjoying the sunshine, despite the road noise.

'This is the life,' Mark says.

Celia has to agree. In fact, sitting beside him in the sun one lunchtime, she has an unexpected thought: she has never felt so carefree, not in her whole life. She doesn't even mind her job these days. It is so wonderful to have a friend you can look forward to seeing every day, one who understands you and is on your side.

Mark says, out of nowhere, 'You know, you've been a real ally to me, Celia. God knows I needed one in this place.'

'Yes,' Celia says. 'Me too.'

So this, at last, is happiness.

THE SUMMER HOLIDAYS COME. Celia is glad of the break from planning and marking, but is dismayed at the thought of eight weeks without seeing Mark, only their occasional text exchanges to keep her going. But it seems that even this can't be relied on. The first two weeks go by, and he does not contact her. When Celia at last messages him, she receives no reply. After a couple of weeks, as her further messages go unanswered, she decides there must be something wrong with his phone, so she writes an email to his school account instead, which she knows he will check occasionally over the holidays. She is studiedly casual, simply asking how he is, mentioning some of the reading she has been doing and then adding, offhandedly, that she can't seem to get in touch with him by phone.

She waits for a week, but no reply comes. His wife, she thinks at last. This must surely be his wife's doing: she has discovered their friendship and is jealous. Celia reassures herself that she will soon see Mark in person again, and everything will be as it was.

But when term finally starts there is still no sign of Mark, and Celia discovers that a new man is teaching the Business BTEC. He introduces himself to her in the staffroom: a small, pale man with a damp handshake and a loud tie.

'Business?' Celia says in confusion. 'Will you be teaching alongside Mark?'

'Was that the last guy?' the man says. 'Think he works in north London now, doesn't he?'

The shock is very great. But it can't be as simple as that, Celia thinks, that Mark has taken another job. He wouldn't have done that without telling her. She can't think of any explanation.

The next morning, after a restless, miserable night, she finds herself cornered by the principal ('*Guten Morgen*, Celia!') whilst she is in the staffroom getting a coffee. Although she would usually make a rapid excuse and leave, Celia decides to seize this opportunity.

She says, as casually as she can, 'The new Business teacher seems OK.'

'Oh, Colin?' the principal says. 'Yes, he's very well qualified.'

'We'll miss Mark though,' Celia says, carefully laying her trap.

'Oh yes, absolutely,' the principal says, and then does not expand on this.

'It won't be the same without him,' Celia says more insistently.

'It certainly won't,' the principal says.

'What a shame he left,' Celia says, starting to despair of gleaning any useful information.

'Yes,' the principal says. 'Still, sometimes people need a change of scene, don't they? I'm sure he'll enjoy Finchley. It's a decent enough college.'

So it is true. Finchley! Celia is appalled. But none of it makes any sense.

Fortunately at this moment the kettle comes to a boil, so she is able to turn away and busy herself pouring hot water into her mug, fetching the milk, stirring her coffee.

'Must be getting on,' she says, picking up her mug. Her voice comes out almost normal.

'Of course,' the principal says jovially. 'The devil makes work for idle hands, eh? *Auf Wiedersehen*, Celia.'

SOMETHING MUST HAVE HAPPENED, Celia thinks. Something terrible, for him to leave like this, without saying anything to her.

That night, after her daughters are in bed, she tries ringing his phone. It goes straight to voicemail. She tries again from the landline, and this time the call goes through. She waits, breathless, as it rings.

And then he answers! It is wonderful to hear his voice again, the familiar, gruff, 'Yep, hello?'

Celia says, 'It's Celia.'

There is a fractional pause. Then he says, his voice sounding warmer, 'Oh hi, Celia! It's so nice to hear from you.'

'You didn't tell me you were leaving!' Celia says. It bursts out of her.

'It was all quite last minute,' he says.

'It can't have been that last minute. I've been so worried. I'm your friend!' she almost wails.

He seems to hesitate, and when he speaks again his voice sounds tired. 'To be honest, Celia, I wasn't sure how you'd take it.'

'How I'd take it!'

'And sometimes a clean break is best all round.'

Nothing about this feels very clean to Celia, and she says so.

'Look,' Mark says, 'it would be great to catch up soon. Let's get a coffee sometime, or a bite to eat, shall we? But I'm afraid I can't talk now. Can I call you back later in the week?'

But though she waits patiently, he never does call.

OVER THE FOLLOWING WEEKS, she gathers her grief to herself. Of course, nobody notices anything is wrong. There is nobody to notice. Her daughters are absorbed in their own lives, and Michael rarely comes home to visit. Anyway, it is not from her children that Celia wants comfort. She feels like a child herself, and she wants her mother. Or perhaps not precisely her own mother, who has never been particularly comforting, but *a* mother: some loving, soothing figure who will put her arms around Celia and tell her everything will be all right, that this desolation will not last. But there is nothing like this for Celia and never has been, and she does not know how to comfort herself.

She tries her best to keep busy, losing herself in the small, steady routines of her week. On Mondays, Wednesdays and Fridays, she teaches at the FE college. On Wednesday and Thursday evenings, she does a little private tutoring. On Saturdays and Sundays, she usually goes for a walk with Alice, and sometimes they might go into town to visit a museum or gallery. She likes to read, and to play bridge on her computer; both these activities help to fill up her time. On Tuesdays, she does the shopping for Edith Langford next door, who is ninety-one and frail after a fall, and whose adult sons never seem to visit. Since the time she saw Edith struggling back from the corner shop with a bag of provisions, Celia has volunteered to do Edith's shopping herself. She never begrudges this weekly task, and indeed barely thinks of it beyond the practicalities; she is no more reflective about her acts of kindness than she is about her less generous behaviour.

But it is this small ritual, finally, that trips Celia up. One Tuesday afternoon in Edith's kitchen, as she places the shopping on the table — two pints of milk, a loaf of bread, butter, two fish-pie ready meals, eggs, bananas — and Edith is fussing over counting out the correct change, Celia suddenly finds that she has tears in her eyes. She hopes they might pass unnoticed, but instead of stopping, the tears multiply, and the next moment they are running down her face and dripping on to the table. Celia would not have chosen Edith Langford of all people to cry in front of. Despite appearing so small and fragile, Edith retains a brusqueness that reminds Celia of the headmistress of her girls' grammar school, all those years ago.

'Celia,' Edith says. 'What's wrong?'

And although Celia tries to get herself under control, once she has started crying she cannot stop. She fumbles blindly in her pocket for a tissue.

'Has something happened?' Edith says. 'Is it the girls?'

Celia shakes her head. 'Everything's so unfair,' she says. 'It's always been so unfair.' And she stands weeping in Edith's kitchen.

Edith makes her a cup of tea, which takes a long time, either because Edith's hands shake so much these days, or perhaps because she is trying to give Celia time to compose herself. But Celia cannot compose herself, and continues to cry helplessly, even as she clumsily raises the mug to her lips.

Edith sits at the table with her. She says, 'Why don't you stay for a bite to eat? I was only going to have an egg, but company would be nice.'

Celia is going to refuse — she wants this embarrassing scene to be over now, and besides, it is too early to eat and Alice and Hanna will be home soon — but then Edith adds, 'You'd be doing me a favour. It isn't often I have company for supper.' So Celia feels she has to say yes.

Edith makes them each two boiled eggs, with triangles of toast, and as she prepares the meal she talks inconsequentially, telling Celia about her father, the careful way he used to make boiled eggs, how fanatical he was about getting the yolk just right. Celia has managed to stop crying by the time they start to eat.

'You seem to have had rather a hard time,' Edith says in her brisk way, as she breaks the shell on her second egg.

Celia swallows, feeling dangerously close to tears again. 'Yes,' she says. 'I have.'

'I find that a hot-water bottle and a cup of tea in bed helps all manner of sorrows,' Edith says.

Celia nods. 'Perhaps I'll try that.'

'One has to try something, after all,' Edith says, and Celia feels faintly admonished.

But when she gets home, finding Hanna out and Alice absorbed in her schoolwork, she goes into the kitchen and stares at the kettle. After a moment, she does make herself a cup of tea and a hot-water bottle, which she takes upstairs with her. The evening has been obscurely consoling, even for someone like Celia, who does not really believe in consolation.

THE EXPERIENCE WITH MARK was the hardest lesson, though Celia tries not to think about it much these days. After all, there have been plenty of other reminders since then that you can't depend on other people, not even your own family. It seems as though Celia will have to give up on the idea of finding solace in her children. The latest blow has been Alice's announcement that she is putting Edinburgh University as her first choice. It has broken Celia's heart. And it is just unfathomable when London universities are among the best in the world. 'But I might not end up at Edinburgh,' Alice says. 'I might not get an offer, and even if I do, I might not get my grades.' As if Celia can rely on that!

Maybe she really should get a lodger, she thinks. Michael doesn't use his bedroom anymore; he's back in London after graduating, but has opted to rent a flat with his girlfriend rather than living at home, which makes no financial sense at all whilst he's completing his law conversion course. Unfortunately Celia's counsel has fallen on deaf ears, but she hasn't given up on the possibility of things not working out with the girlfriend, who has always struck her as rather difficult. She doesn't want to scupper the chances of Michael moving back in by giving his room away to a lodger. In fact, it might discourage all three of her children from returning if there is a stranger in the house.

Celia often thinks back to when her children were very young, how they would cling to her, when she was the centre of their world. She does not dwell on the exhaustion and loneliness of those years, the frustration and resentment she often felt towards her children, and towards Paul, who was never there, and if he ever was there, was useless. ('Give her to me,' Celia tells him sharply, as he tries to soothe a crying Alice. 'You're just making her worse.') No. What Celia remembers instead is how her children needed her, how they adored her. They were part of her in those days, and she knew them perfectly, and they knew her perfectly. ('She doesn't *like* that,' she tells Paul, as he jiggles Hanna up and down on his lap. 'You'll make her sick.')

Now, Celia finds herself looking with irritation at pregnant women, and at women with young children. There is a smugness about them, these expectant and new mothers. They have no idea what is to come. They think their children will be theirs forever.

8

H ERE IS HANNA AT eighteen, a student at Cambridge University. It is a surprise to her too.

For one thing there are her GCSE results, which are decent enough, but not exactly glittering. Not Cambridge material, certainly. Hanna comes late to scholarship. It is only at her sixth-form college, where the teachers treat her less like a pupil and more like a distant acquaintance (warm, but non-committal – say, a Canadian second cousin), and the other students aren't so institutionalized that they obsess over each other's smallest actions, that Hanna's rebellion finally runs out of steam. Belatedly, she discovers she enjoys studying, and that she is good at it. She is assisted in this by her new friend Kemi, who unilaterally decides one day that she and Hanna will sit next to each other in their English class. And after that, Hanna simply can't shake her off. Kemi is an enthusiastic student, and under her influence Hanna becomes enthusiastic too. Kemi wears her hair in short box braids, and the gap between her front teeth makes her look winning when she smiles, but her humour is a razor through Hanna's pretensions.

Hanna's English teacher is Ms Howard and she tells Hanna she is talented (news to Hanna).

'You should try for Oxbridge,' Ms Howard says.

Hanna stares at her. It's like being told she should try for the Navy Seals. But the idea takes root. Hanna likes the thought of the tutorial system, and the colleges, and the history. And the prestige, above all. Her father would surely be impressed (in Barnes, in his study, from a distance).

It is only once she's decided she definitely wants to apply that she comes up against the problem of her GCSE results.

'Most people going for Oxbridge have straight A*s,' the university adviser tells her. 'Especially if they've previously had the advantage of going to an independent school.' There is a slight edge to her voice when she says this.

'I didn't realize,' Hanna says, though she would have realized if she'd been paying attention. She hadn't paid enough attention to know that all that time she spent messing around at her girls' school she was squandering an advantage most people never got.

Ms Howard is more optimistic. 'Ace your AS-levels,' she says. 'Then we'll see.'

And Hanna does ace them. She knuckles down and works furiously alongside Kemi, coming out with a strong A in every subject, and full marks in two of her English modules.

'Some people are late bloomers,' Ms Howard says. 'I'd give Oxbridge a go if I were you.'

'A classic underdog story,' Kemi says. 'Privately educated white girl tries for Cambridge after all.'

'Yes,' Hanna says. 'Something in it for everyone.'

They laugh – in those days, they are always laughing. It's annoying for everyone around them.

HANNA THINKS KEMI SHOULD apply to Cambridge too, because Kemi is cleverer than she is, and hasn't had Hanna's embarrassing private-school advantage, but Kemi says, 'No, not for me.' Kemi has her heart set on Bristol.

Hanna says, 'Well, maybe I should make Bristol my first choice too, so then we could go together.'

'You're just saying that,' Kemi says, 'because you're scared.'

This is true. Hanna doesn't like the idea of rejection. (But who does?)

'I do,' Kemi says. 'I find it very bracing. Still, I'm going for Bristol, and if they reject me, I'm going anyway.'

Hanna applies to read English at one of the oldest colleges in the centre of Cambridge. She chooses it because the buildings are beautiful, and because the English fellows look friendly in their pictures.

She imagines her application will be thrown out as soon as they see her shameful, unstarry GCSE results, but to her surprise she is invited to interview.

'You'll be great,' Kemi says. 'You'll come across well at interview.' Then, noting Hanna's expression, she adds, 'Don't overthink it. It's only some questions about books. It's not gladiatorial combat.'

Hanna asks her father if he will drive her up for the day, but he says, 'Sorry darling, I'd love to but I can't get the time off work. Susan could probably take you though.'

This is actually quite appealing to Hanna – Susan is a soothing, undemanding presence – but Alice says when they are alone, 'Han, can you imagine Mum's reaction if you let Susan take you? Is it worth it?'

'Well, Mum's teaching,' Hanna says. 'It's not like she can take me. Not that she's offered. Not that I'd want her to.'

'But she'd never get over it if you let Susan take you.'

'For God's sake,' Hanna says. 'Looks like I'm getting the train.'

But when Hanna delicately raises the issue of the train fare with her mother the next day, her mother says, 'I'll drive you. I've already arranged cover.'

Hanna watches Alice beam, because Alice loves moments of family unity, whether she is involved in them or not.

Hanna says, 'All right. Thanks.'

ON THE MORNING OF her interview day, Hanna is feeling pretty good. For one thing, she is well prepared. Kemi has spent the past fortnight firing questions at her about her personal statement at the most unpredictable moments. In the lunch queue: 'Are you going to have chips with your wrap? And why does Milton make Satan so sexy?' Sometimes these questions are delivered with unexpected verve, startling Hanna. At the bus stop: 'Shit, look, we've just missed the fifty-nine. WOULD YOU SAY DONNE'S VERBAL PLAYFULNESS UNDERMINES HIS RELIGIOUS MESSAGING?' In Boots, browsing the make-up: 'Can I pull off orange lipstick? Can anyone? WAS SHAKESPEARE A HERETIC?' (A woman passing down the aisle behind them starts violently.)

Hanna says, 'Well, I suppose you could argue—'

'SOME OF HIS CHARACTERS SEEM QUITE AMBIVALENT ABOUT THE AFTERLIFE.'

'Kemi, I don't think they're going to shout at me in the interviews.'

'You don't know that,' Kemi says, finally lowering her voice. 'Best to be prepared for all eventualities.'

Having handled Kemi, Hanna feels she will not be thrown by anything the interviewers ask her. Still, she is anxious about the drive with her mother. The train would have been better, or her father, or Susan. What she wants in the time preceding her interviews is peace, not her mother needling her. The journey will take two hours. Hanna wouldn't put it past her mother to have prepared some kind of anti-pep talk for the occasion.

There is a dangerous moment before they set off ('Is that what you're wearing?' 'Yup.' 'You could borrow my brown skirt. And Alice's brown cardigan to match.' 'Thanks Mum, but I'm OK in jeans.' 'The skirt would look smarter. And brown is your colour.' 'My colour is *brown*?'), but actually the drive itself is fine. They listen to Radio 4 for most of the journey, and Hanna's mother stays mercifully quiet, commenting only on the light traffic and the overcast weather. Hanna obediently eats the banana her mother has insisted she bring as a snack.

It is only once they have parked on the outskirts of Cambridge and taken the park-and-ride into town, and have walked almost all the way to the college, that her mother delivers the blow that she may or may not have been planning all along. She says, still striding along, 'Now Hanna, remember to think about how you come across.'

'What do you mean?' Hanna says.

'You don't want to come across as combative or difficult.'

'I'm not difficult!' Hanna protests. 'That's ridiculous.' Ridiculous: one of her mother's words.

Her mother says, 'See, you're already being difficult, when I'm simply trying to give you advice.' She sighs. 'I'm trying to help you. Remember, the interviewers are looking for someone they'll enjoy teaching over the next three years.'

They have reached the college now, and come to a stop outside the arched stone entrance. Around them, nervous-looking candidates are arriving, stepping through the wooden doors and vanishing into the shadowed courtyard within.

Hanna's mother tells her, 'It's very important that you come across as likeable.'

Hanna shifts her bag on her shoulder and looks at her mother's hard, set face. I am likeable, she thinks. But then, in a moment of chilling clarity, she is reminded: My mother doesn't like me. My father is indifferent. And if your own parents don't like you, doesn't that say it all?

But Kemi likes her. Ms Howard likes her. Others have liked her in the past. The girls at school. Alice. Piece by piece, person by person, standing outside this seven-hundred-year-old college, Hanna offers up evidence to the universe, to herself, that she is a person it is possible to like.

Her mother says, 'I want what's best for you.'

'No you don't,' Hanna says, surprising herself.

'Believe what you want,' Celia says coolly. 'You'd better go in.' And belatedly: 'Good luck, Hanna.'

THE INTERVIEWS PROVE NO more challenging than Kemi's practice sessions, and certainly less startling. And yet somehow here, at the eleventh hour, Hanna finds herself falling apart. Her mother's voice is in her head: *It's very important you come across as likeable*. And so Hanna grows self-conscious, second-guesses everything she says or does, even down to the way she introduces herself, her handshake, how she arranges herself in the various chairs she is directed to. She worries her jeans look too informal after all, even though many of the other candidates are also wearing jeans. She fiddles with her bracelet, stops herself, then fiddles with it again. In her first interview, she misdates the unseen passage by several hundred years, and then finds herself admitting that she skipped all the whaling bits in *Moby Dick*, never finished *Sons and Lovers* and doesn't find Dickens funny. She can't seem to help herself; it is as though her brain has mistaken the fellow's office for a confessional and is frantically unburdening itself.

Her second interview goes better, and she and the interviewer have quite a good discussion about Milton, but her third is another disaster. The sofa opposite the interviewer's chair is so old and indented that when Hanna goes to sit on it, she sinks down into it to an absurd degree, her legs coming up off the ground, as if the sofa is trying to swallow her whole. She spends the first few minutes of the interview trying to respond coherently to the interviewer's questions whilst simultaneously struggling to free herself from the sofa.

'Everything all right?' the interviewer says rather belatedly, just as Hanna has finally managed to hoist herself out and perch in relative safety on the very edge of the sofa cushion.

'Yes thanks,' she says, out of breath. She wonders if the sofa was a test. If so, she is sure the other candidates have acquitted themselves with more dignity.

The interviewer turns his questioning to *Othello*, her A-level text, asking her about the symbolism of the wedding sheets in act four, but Hanna, exhausted by her battle with the sofa, just says idiotically that they haven't got to that bit in class yet.

'But it's probably a great bit of symbolism,' she adds, feeling the need to fill the silence that follows. 'I'm sure I'll enjoy it when I get there.'

Then he asks her why Iago wants to destroy Othello, and Hanna quotes Coleridge on Iago's 'motiveless malignity', and the interviewer says, 'Yes, but that's rather an outdated view now,' and Hanna feels crushed. He ends by asking her if it's surprising Desdemona defies her father to marry Othello in the first place, and Hanna, having more or less given up by this point, says that people will go to great lengths to annoy their parents. The interviewer looks at her sombrely and says it was nice to meet her.

'How was it?' her mother asks when Hanna finally emerges,

ashen-faced, from the college in the late afternoon. When Hanna only shakes her head, her mother says bracingly, 'I'm sure it went better than you thought.' She buys Hanna a chocolate muffin to eat on the drive back to London. It occurs to Hanna that she must look pretty harrowed if her mother is being nice to her.

A FEW WEEKS LATER, she receives her rejection letter.

'It's their loss,' Alice says, but Hanna is too busy pretending not to mind to accept any comfort.

The letter says, somewhat surprisingly, that she has been pooled, though Hanna doesn't hold out much hope. It sounds like a random prize draw. But two evenings later, a woman rings to speak to her. Hanna is not used to receiving phone calls from anyone other than Kemi, and takes the phone gingerly from her mother. The voice at the other end introduces herself – an elegant, Spanish-sounding name to match the elegant, Spanish-sounding voice – and offers Hanna a place at an entirely different college, one that she hasn't heard of. They don't even want to interview her; they will take her sight unseen. (Surprising, Hanna thinks, that people aren't queuing up to chat to her about *Othello*.)

Later, when she looks up the college online, Hanna discovers with a strange feeling of having come full circle that it is one of only three remaining all-women's colleges.

Kemi laughs hard at this. She says, 'That sounds right up your street.'

'I suppose it'll be all right,' Hanna says. 'It's not exactly a nunnery.'

'Good. Because you're not exactly a nun.'

Hanna accepts the place. She liked the Spanish woman on the phone, and Cambridge is Cambridge after all. Both her parents seem impressed. Her father even sends her a card to say congratulations (the handwriting,

Hanna can't help but notice, is Susan's). Alice, meanwhile, is going to Edinburgh, and Kemi has got her place at Bristol. Just A-levels to slog through now.

'Sing ho! for the future,' Kemi says.

HANNA ASSUMES SHE WILL thrive at university, as she has thrived everywhere else. But Cambridge is a shock.

She has not looked round her college before arriving for Freshers' Week and is immediately disconcerted. She has seen pictures online of course, but somehow the buildings appear much more brutalist in person, and seem to have been designed by someone with a fetish for concrete. The main roof rises above square columns, culminating in a huge, unexpected dome that might have been intended to lend an exotic air, but actually makes the building look like a great concrete spaceship.

Once inside her accommodation block, Hanna is both amused and dismayed: some of the corridors actually have padded walls like an insane asylum. In her bedroom the floor is covered in squares of old brown linoleum, peeling at the edges, and two of the walls, oddly, are tiled. The room has the feel of an old boarding-house bathroom. It is very cold, even once the ancient radiator has rumbled and gurgled into life.

The other students prove even more unsettling. The girl in the room next door to Hanna's goes by the startling name of Lavinia de Lacy. She is tall and thin, with an exceptionally severe bob haircut and a strange accent that is sometimes cut-glass English and sometimes takes on an American inflection. She lived in the States, she informs Hanna, until she was seven, then attended an international school in Geneva for a while, before moving to London when she was thirteen. She never mentions her parents, and in fact her phrasing makes it sound as if she was travelling alone all this time, a preternaturally self-possessed child who didn't find America to her taste so drifted across the Atlantic and finally settled in London. 'I have an apartment,' she tells Hanna, 'just off the Regent's Park.' (But no one calls it *the* Regent's Park anymore, Hanna thinks. Or do they? Lavinia has the peculiar effect of making her question herself.)

Lavinia dresses exclusively in black and wears a long string of seed pearls every day and a bright tangerine lipstick (it is Chanel, she tells Hanna Frenchly, in the shade 'Excentrique'; the unprompted offering of this information makes Hanna realize she must have been staring). The brightness of the lipstick and the lack of any other make-up make Lavinia seem even paler than she already is. Up close, you can see the delicate blue veins around her eyes and temples, and on the underside of her wrists when she makes gestures, which she does often, sharply. She is studying Modern and Medieval Languages, though this does not seem to play a prominent role in her life. Hanna finds it impossible to place Lavinia in any of the usual categories at her disposal.

The girl who lives on the other side of Hanna is called Santiago, though she is English. She was conceived whilst her parents were on holiday in Chile, she tells Hanna (who has not asked). Santiago has curly brown hair and a wide face, and she wears a violently sweet-smelling perfume she says her father gave her for her eighteenth birthday. Hanna can't tell if it is the scent itself that is particularly heavy, or if Santiago is actually bathing in it; the cloying smell reaches you long before she does. Santiago recently watched a programme on ITV about developing your own signature style, and as a result has an extensive range of wide-striped Breton tops and a black beret she often wears; Hanna thinks she looks a bit like a mime.

'You should watch it too,' Santiago says to Hanna, writing down the programme's name on a Post-it note for her. 'Your style at the moment is quite undefined. My mum and I both watched it, and so did my aunt.'

(Just then Lavinia sweeps past in her flapping black dress and seed pearls, and Hanna wonders if she has watched it too.)

Santiago also has the most detailed skincare regime Hanna has ever encountered; it involves multiple products, most of which Hanna has never heard of, among them a 'glycolic toner' and something called a 'double cleanse'.

'You must wear factor fifty on your face every day,' Santiago tells Hanna. 'Every. Single. Day. Even in winter. You'll thank me when you're forty.'

I won't know you when I'm forty, Hanna thinks.

Further along their corridor is a girl called Yasmin who is studying Maths and has no discernible sense of humour, a girl called Jia whose brother knows Alex Kapranos from Franz Ferdinand (they hear about this a lot), and a girl called Lola who likes to give Hanna unsolicited sex advice. 'Men have a thing about virgins,' she tells Hanna in the college bar at the end of their first week. 'So a good move is to wait till you're starting to, you know, get down to it, and then lean forward and whisper in his ear, "I have never known the touch of a man."'

Hanna, who has known the touch of a man (sexy Tom Li in her first year of sixth-form college, and Joe Phillips in her second year), has no idea how to respond to this. She changes the subject.

There's also Lucy, who lives on the floor above but seems to spend a lot of time in their kitchen. When Hanna asks one day about the state of the kitchen on Lucy's own floor – she is imagining some kind of post-apocalyptic hellscape – Lucy whispers, 'People don't always wash up as they go along.' She has a manner so nervous it has the effect of making the other person nervous as well. Hanna finds herself stumbling through conversations with her, as though shyness is catching. But Lucy's unexpected skill, it turns out, is breathing fire. She volunteers this to them one evening, standing at the hob whilst Hanna and Lavinia sit at the table drinking gin. She has trained in Munich with a real circus troupe. Hanna and Lavinia are so surprised they don't immediately reply. Lucy returns, beatifically, to stirring her casserole.

HANNA SPENDS THE FIRST few weeks of term trying to catalogue the myriad ways in which the other members of her college are odd.

'I've ended up with all the misfits,' she tells Kemi on the phone. 'And did you know, some of these girls weren't even pooled here? They *chose* it. Some of them have the excuse of religion, but loads don't. I can't even imagine how they coped at school. I can't see them fitting in *any*where.'

'Well, you did accept the place,' Kemi says mildly.

'I know, but I didn't realize it would be like this!'

'Come down to Bristol for the weekend,' Kemi suggests. 'It'll be fun.'

'Can't. Too much work.'

After they've hung up, Hanna goes along the corridor to the kitchen to make herself some toast. Passing Lavinia's room, she sees that Santiago and Lola are in there too, the three of them cross-legged on the floor, apparently studying a small array of rocks arranged in a circle, with a mug of some kind of liquid in the middle.

'Come and join us,' Santiago says, looking up and spotting her. 'We're doing a Wiccan spell.'

Lavinia adds in her grave way, 'Lola is Wiccan. She's inducting us into the power of crystals.'

'You're, like, a witch?' Hanna says to Lola.

'Not a witch as we think of them now,' Santiago says, with a quick glance at Lola, suggesting this faux pas has already been made once today. 'It's a common misconception.'

'I used to be more powerful,' Lola says. 'Before I surrendered my virginity.'

'I'm going to make some toast,' Hanna says.

'I can do a spell to purge you of your negativity,' Lola offers.

'I'm not negative!' Hanna says.

Lola smiles at her tenderly.

As Hanna continues along the corridor, it dawns on her at last that she is the only one here who does not fit in.

BUT THOUGH SHE COMPLAINS about her college to Kemi, Hanna can't bring herself to admit the full truth: that it was not her college that was the mistake but Cambridge itself. The work is unlike anything she was expecting. There is just so much of it. Whereas at her sixth-form college she would happily spend a fortnight writing a single essay, here she has to hand in two essays a week, on top of all the reading. She hasn't realized until now what a slow reader she is, how sluggishly her thoughts move. And she seems to be getting slower by the day: sometimes it is as though her brain has turned to sludge.

In her second week she labours over her essay on Thomas Hardy, plodding first through *Tess of the D'Urbervilles* and *Jude the Obscure* before skimming *The Woodlanders* and *The Mayor of Casterbridge* in a blind panic after she realizes she's barely left any time to get through the suggested criticism. She finishes her essay in the early hours of the morning before it is due, fuelled by coffee and anxiety, and feels quite pleased with it when she finally emails it to her supervisor. Ms Howard always praised her essays effusively, and this one is particularly long and detailed: much more detailed than anything she's written before.

'It's rather pedestrian and unfocused,' her supervisor tells her two days later, holding her essay out with what seems to Hanna an air of disdain. 'You need to develop an argument. I mean, there are times here when you're simply describing the plot.'

Hanna is mortified. She nods humbly and takes the essay back, even more assured of her own stupidity. She remembers how her first college rejected her, and knows that they were right. And this second college didn't even interview her, which now seems especially reckless of them. They may even have confused her with somebody else; it is very possible she is here only as a result of administrative error. She wonders when she will be found out.

Each week, she continues to struggle through the reading list, not realizing (because no one has told her) that most people don't actually read the whole thing, but just pick a couple of books and wing it on the rest. It wouldn't have occurred to the old Hanna to try to read everything, but this new Hanna has so much ground to make up that she feels she needs to do everything asked of her and more. She works hard on her essays, often late into the night, but they remain 'imprecise' and 'overly descriptive', her supervisors tell her. It is utterly humiliating. Hanna, who believes she has developed immunity to even the harshest criticisms from her mother, now finds herself crumbling at the gentlest hints from her supervisors. She doesn't understand what's happening to her. It is as if she has suddenly lost her nerve.

It is a relief when the Christmas holidays arrive; Hanna thinks that now, at last, she can return to her normal life, her normal self. But even at home, the equilibrium is disturbed. Alice is having the time of her life in Edinburgh and bounces around talking about her brilliant course (she is studying Archaeology and has developed a passionate interest in Neanderthal burials). Alice has the sense, at least, not to do this in front of their mother, who is still upset that she chose a university so far away and is prone to outbursts of emotion if reminded of it, but Hanna herself is not spared. And why would it occur to Alice to be tactful? She assumes Hanna is having a wonderful time too. She assumes, in fact, that for the first time in their lives they are perfectly aligned.

'I wasn't sure about the people on my corridor at first,' she tells Hanna, 'because they all seemed so confident and cool, but actually they're really nice when you get to know them.'

'That's great,' Hanna says.

'What are the people you live with like?'

Hanna thinks of the evening she spent in the kitchen on the last night of term, Lavinia playing the harmonica whilst Lola showed them how to cast a spell for increased virility. ('In yourself?' Hanna asked. 'In a *sexual partner*,' Lola said witheringly.)

Hanna tells Alice, 'They're fine.'

So there is not even the consolation of knowing she is coping better than Alice. And Kemi is happily living her Bristol dream, in the face of which Hanna feels too embarrassed to admit how much she hated her own first term. Plus she has been given a ton of holiday work to do, so doesn't have much time to see Kemi anyway.

Alice says to her after Christmas, 'Are you OK?'

'Yes. Why wouldn't I be OK?'

Alice says, 'You just seem . . . different.'

'I'm not,' Hanna says. 'I'm exactly the same.'

*

SHE HOPES THINGS WILL improve in her second term, but they do not. In fact, they get worse because suddenly Hanna loses the knack for sleeping.

Sleep has never been a problem before. She has never even thought about it really, just goes to bed, and there: asleep. Alice is the one who struggles to get to sleep, who needs to have a bath and a warm milky drink and a gentle book to read and nothing too exciting on television in the hour beforehand. Hanna has always taken this as evidence of Alice's general incompetence. Sleep is the easiest thing in the world.

Not anymore. Night after night, Hanna lies awake, panicked, turning first on to one side and then the other, lying on her back, staring at the shadowed ceiling, the walls, the glimmer of the street light coming through her curtains. She worries about her work, which will be even harder the next day because now she will be tired on top of everything else. Eventually she starts to worry about sleep itself: why can she no longer do it? Can you simply lose the ability to sleep? It seems to Hanna that she has. Her body won't shut down at night, but fizzes with nervous energy. She starts to follow Alice's old routines: warm milk before bed, making a list of her worries to get them out of her head, reading something soothing. Sometimes she feels quite hopeful when she gets into bed: she really does feel relaxed and sleepy. But as soon as she turns off the light, the thought recurs: what if she can't sleep? And then she can feel the panic rising in her body, and another tortuous, desperate night begins. If she is lucky, she might fall into a shallow, tense doze in the hours before dawn. If she is unlucky, she will still be awake to meet it, wrung out, dry-eyed.

It becomes impossible to concentrate during the daytime. When she tries to read, the words won't keep still on the page, and when she tries to write, it is as though her brain has been taken over and someone else is writing through her, chaotically, in another language. She will look back at the paragraph she has just written and find it has turned into nonsense during the moment she glanced away from her screen. What a failure she has turned out to be. She imagines the humiliation when Cambridge finally throws her out. Her mother's lack of surprise.

'You look unwell,' Lavinia tells her, matter-of-factly.

'I can't sleep,' Hanna admits, her defences stripped away by exhaustion.

Lavinia shakes her head. 'That's a method of torture in many countries.'

Unhelpful, Hanna thinks.

How long, she wonders, can a person go on without sleep before they die or go insane? She is getting two or three hours a night. On a good night, possibly four (but fitful, broken). It is hard not to be obsessed with sleep when you are not getting enough. Throughout the day, Hanna eyes Santiago, Lavinia and the others furiously: these people who are sleeping deeply for eight or nine hours a night, and just taking it for granted, feeling wonderful but barely even aware of it. Santiago usually goes to bed at ten thirty, and doesn't reappear until eight the next morning. Surely that is too much sleep for anyone? Surely that is just greedy. Hanna feels murderous when Santiago stumbles yawning into the kitchen in the morning and says, 'I slept right through my alarm. I guess I was particularly tired.'

Eventually she visits the college GP, a man called Dr Bryan who has the weary air of someone who would have liked to retire long ago. He wears a distant expression on his face whilst Hanna describes her insomnia, as though his body is present whilst his mind roams free across the golf course.

When Hanna has finished, he tells her she needs to build more time for relaxation into her day, and have a consistent bedtime routine. 'That's especially important,' he adds kindly, 'if you're a bit highly strung.'

'I'm not highly strung,' Hanna says.

He gives her a look that seems to suggest he knows a highly strung person when he sees one.

'There's nothing wrong with me,' Hanna says. 'I'm very normal. I've just forgotten how to sleep.'

He offers her an antihistamine with mild soporific effects.

Hanna says, 'I think I need something stronger.' She wonders if haggling with your doctor over medication is some kind of slippery slope.

'Sleeping tablets should only really be considered as a last resort,' Dr Bryan says. 'They can do more harm than good in the long run.'

'But I can't sleep,' Hanna says stupidly. 'I can't sleep *at all*. I can't think, I can't function—' To her humiliation, she bursts into tears, which does admittedly seem like the action of a highly strung person.

But it turns out to be a masterstroke. Hanna leaves Dr Bryan's office with a prescription for temazepam. She only gets six, because apparently they are addictive. For three blissful nights, she sleeps for eight hours at a time.

But on the fourth night the pill doesn't work, and Hanna remains awake, jittery, until two in the morning, when she finally falls into a fitful sleep and jerks awake again at six, groggy from the pill but very much not asleep. The next night, she is awake until three. The final night, she doesn't sleep at all.

There does not seem much point in going back to Dr Bryan after this. She can see she is a lost cause. When she looks at her face in the mirror, it is haggard; she hardly recognizes herself. It is sleep, then, that keeps us human.

There is a strange, shivery feeling in her body much of the time now, an agitation bubbling in her chest so that she finds it difficult to keep still. One day it is so bad that she feels she will go mad if she doesn't do something to distract herself. She decides to head into town to buy a present for Kemi, whose birthday is approaching.

But once she's in the Grand Arcade, she can't remember why she's there. A feeling of dread comes over her. Trying to gather herself, she goes to buy a coffee, but messes up her order and somehow ends up with a white chocolate mocha instead of a normal latte. The aggressive sweetness does help to pull her back to herself. She will go to John Lewis and buy Kemi a cushion, she thinks. Something nice and bright for Kemi's room. She can afford to push the boat out with a nice present; she has saved money over the past two terms through all the fun she is not having.

But – although she successfully circumnavigates the tight maze of perfume and beauty counters on the ground floor, weaves her way around throngs of people to reach the escalators and arrives at last at the correct floor – once she is staring at the array of cushions, she comes apart again. It is as though someone has put a brake on her brain. There are so many options, and she cannot make a decision. The panic beats and beats in her chest and in her face. And there is something off about these cushions. Hanna cannot explain it, but she knows it would be easy to make the wrong decision here, and buy a cushion that is – somehow – amiss. That would do harm.

She feels a sudden need to call someone, and unaccountably the person she chooses is Alice.

Who picks up on the third ring.

'Hi Hanna,' she says. 'Is everything OK?'

Oh, Hanna thinks. Because I never call her. She says, 'Everything's fine.' And her voice, in fact, does sound fine now she is speaking aloud to her sister. A huge relief. She says, 'I need some quick advice.'

'Sure!' Alice says, sounding delighted.

'I'm trying to buy a cushion,' Hanna says. It feels important to break the problem down into its constituent parts. 'For Kemi's birthday. And I don't know which one to pick. I'm in John Lewis and I just . . . can't decide.' How simple the problem sounds now. How simply and easily solved.

There is a pause, then Alice says, 'OK, right. Well, what are the options?'

Hanna talks Alice carefully through the options: patterned, floral, plain; the range of colours; the ranges of textures.

'I'd go for something striking for Kemi,' Alice says. 'What was the swirly one with the different greens? Describe that one to me again.'

Hanna does, and Alice says it sounds perfect.

And so it is accomplished, and Hanna says goodbye to Alice and takes her cushion over to the counter to pay. She is pleased with herself, and greatly reassured to have completed this simple but important task. She is grateful to Alice, too – perhaps more grateful than she has ever been in her life.

But the satisfaction of the purchase doesn't last long, and soon she feels the dread creeping back in. As she leaves the shopping centre, she notices a man by the doors watching her. He is bald, with the invisible eyebrows and eyelashes of someone whose hair was once ginger, or very pale blonde. The fear that comes over Hanna is old, though she doesn't think she has ever seen him before. She has to walk right past him to get out of the doors, and he watches her steadily the whole time. It comes to Hanna that although she does not know him, he knows her. He knows something about her, what she is capable of, what she has done. (What has she done? She is not precisely sure, but she knows it is something terrible.)

When she gets back to college, she joins Lola in the kitchen, feeling an urgent need for company.

'What'cha got?' Lola says, looking at the bag in Hanna's hand.

'It's a cushion,' Hanna says. 'A birthday present for my best friend.' It's a reassuring sentence to speak. She gets the cushion out to show Lola.

'Oh, nice,' Lola says. 'I used to have a cushion like that. Similar shades of green.'

'My sister advised me to pick this one. She said it sounded jaunty.'

'I had to throw mine out in the end,' Lola says. 'It had a semen stain on it.'

There is a pause.

'Who did the semen belong to?' Hanna asks eventually.

'To this day, I don't know.' Lola's eyes take on a faraway look, the haunted resignation of a cold-case detective. 'Never did find out.'

Hanna goes to her room to write a card to Kemi. The exchange with Lola has calmed her.

Hope you like the cushion, she writes. *Lola says she had a similar one that she had to throw out due to semen staining. So I might have accidentally bought you some kind of aphrodisiac sex cushion. Let me know if it really seems to get people going. But you'll be relieved to know I got it new, not from a charity shop, so we can at least be confident it isn't the same one.*

She feels a bit like her old self, writing this to Kemi. The horrible episode, whatever it was, has passed. A panic attack? She's never had one before, so doesn't know if that's what they are like. She seals the card and wraps the cushion, before packaging both up together in brown paper and many layers of Sellotape (she and Kemi take great pleasure in making their parcels to each other as challenging as possible). Across the back of the parcel she writes the words of Julian of Norwich: *all shall be well, and all shall be well, and all manner of things shall be well.*

*

THE NEXT DAY SHE goes to the post office to send the parcel. It has been another night of almost no sleep. She is feeling washed out, and has a headache coming on. The anxiety of the previous day has been replaced by a strange feeling of dislocation. On the walk to the post office, she experiences a sense of distance between herself and the people around her, as though the crowd is parting to let her through. But this is better, at least, than the accusing glare of the man from yesterday.

In the post office, she queues with her parcel. Look how well she is coping, she thinks: although she is exhausted, here she is at the post office, about to send a parcel. It is all reassuringly normal.

As she moves nearer the front of the queue, her eye drifts to the wrapping-paper stand next to the counter. The individual sheets are displayed on rails, and she is particularly drawn to a red one near the bottom of the rack, which has a glossy metallic pattern. There is a breeze coming from somewhere – the weather is still, so perhaps somebody has put a fan on – and as Hanna watches, the draught lifts the bottom of the red sheet so that it rises and falls, rises and falls very gently. None of the other sheets move. It is strangely mesmerizing how the metallic pattern on the red sheet catches the light as it rises and falls. Hanna can't stop watching it. It strikes her again how strange it is that none of the other sheets on the rack are moving. If there is a breeze, why doesn't it stir the other sheets?

Suddenly, she becomes aware that nobody else in the queue can see the red sheet moving. The red sheet is focusing only on her. The numb feeling is back, but now she knows it is because her whole being is concentrated on the red sheet, the light catching its metallic pattern in a way meant only for her.

The person behind her in the queue touches her arm, making Hanna jump, and she realizes it is her turn to approach the counter. She realizes too that it has been done this way deliberately, that they do not want her to receive whatever message the red paper is sending her. Hanna goes forward clutching her parcel, knowing that she must not give them any reaction. She fumbles for the correct money, distracted the whole time by the glint of light on the red paper, which she can no longer see but can still feel. It is very important to act as if nothing has changed.

Then she is out of the post office, her arms feeling empty and light without the parcel. She has got away with it, she thinks.

But terror comes over her again. She understands at once that everyone in the post office knows what she has done. It will not be long before the rest of the world knows it too. The nature of her crime remains hazy. But she knows the red paper was a warning.

She hurries back to college, head down, careful not to meet anyone's eye, and once there she goes straight to her room and locks the door.

It is important that she absorb herself in normal activities to keep the terror at bay, so she sits cross-legged on the floor and opens up her laptop. She has an essay on James Joyce due tomorrow, and has lost time going out to the post office; she must make it up now by being extra efficient and working into the night. But it is difficult to remember where she has got to. She reads and rereads her paragraph of notes, but nothing makes any sense. She wonders if she can pass this off to her supervisor as Joycean. Probably not, she thinks. Then she realizes he will read her wickedness from the essay, if he doesn't know it already. She remembers Milton's Satan, how appealing she has always found him, and now this makes sense at last: it is another test, of course, and she has failed.

She snaps the laptop shut and goes to lie down on her bed. She closes her eyes, but she does not sleep.

Only she must eventually, because now she jolts awake and the room is in darkness. Can it be night-time? No, it is just that she has closed the curtains, which she does not remember doing. When she pulls them open again, the daylight hurts her eyes. She has no idea what time it is, or what day: the same day or the next day or the day before? She pulls the curtains closed again.

The guilt is appalling, and the shame too – and soon the whole world will know what she's done. Every now and then she gets a sense of someone watching her over her shoulder, a black shape that appears in her peripheral vision. She flinches, but each time she turns to catch it, the black shape has vanished. It might already be in the papers, and they are just biding their time until they come for her. Should she hide, or should she give herself up? She's a coward; of course she will hide.

Although she is ravenous now, it is not safe to go to the kitchen. She has a supply of flapjack and oranges in her room. She will have to eke them out. At least she is one of the lucky few with an en-suite toilet, so she doesn't need to leave the safety of her locked room to use the communal bathroom. There is no need to leave this locked room at all. For the time being, she is as safe as it is possible for a person like her to be.

But the dark shape is in the room with her. She keeps catching glimpses of it. She tries to keep her eyes closed so she won't have to see it.

IT IS NOT LONG after this that the voice arrives. It is not saying anything especially unsettling at first, but it bothers Hanna all the same. It likes to narrate what she is doing. It is a male voice, and it makes its observations flatly, without emotion. *Hanna is sitting on the bed. Hanna is crying.*

At some point, a knock on the door jolts her.

A knocking at the gate, the voice observes.

Lavinia's voice, from the other side of the door, says, 'Hanna, are you in there? Are you OK? We haven't seen you for ages.'

Hanna manages to speak. 'Yes. I'm fine. Just . . .' Just what? She searches around for something to say. Don't let them know you know. 'Just a bit hung-over.'

'Oh, right.' She thinks Lavinia sounds relieved. Maybe Lavinia never wanted to be part of the arrest. 'Want me to bring you anything?'

'No thanks,' Hanna says.

Hanna is getting under the covers.

Kemi rings a couple of times, but Hanna can't answer because the phone is bugged.

IT TAKES HER A while to realize Alice is in danger. If they can't get to her, they will get to her twin. Hanna knows she has to warn Alice. She can't say much; everything she writes to Alice they will read too. She types out a message, deletes, retypes, edits it carefully, then sends: *Alice, tell them the truth. Don't try to protect me. They'll make you pay.*

Sometime after she has sent the message, Alice rings. Hanna doesn't pick up. It is too late. It was always too late.

And her room isn't safe anymore. She knows they're on their way. She creeps to the door and listens very carefully. She can't hear anyone moving in the corridor, but she listens for longer, just in case. She holds her breath to see if she can hear anyone else breathing. Nothing. Carefully, she unlocks the door and waits, heart pounding. When a few minutes have passed without anyone bursting in, she eases the door open very slowly. Waits again. Finally, she dares to put her head out and peer around the door. The corridor is empty.

Hanna is running, the voice says.

*

SHE DOESN'T PAUSE UNTIL she is almost a mile away, and then she has to stop because the pain in her side is excruciating and she feels like she can't breathe. But any head start she has won will be surrendered if she stops moving, so she limps on, more slowly now. It is broad daylight and cars are passing on the roads. Then the danger of the pavement strikes her: this is how they will take her, a car or a van pausing beside her, bundling her into the back, screeching off again. It is safer to meet them head on. She steps into the road.

You'd be better off killing yourself, the voice says. It has taken on expression now, speaking with relish. It's also started switching between second and third person, which is confusing.

Hanna is disrupting the traffic.

'Shut up!' Hanna says. She begins to cry again, her hands to her face.

You'll get hit by a car. Good riddance.

'Stop it!' Hanna says.

She doesn't want to die. But how can she live?

She is crying too hard to notice the police officers until they are already quite close. A man and woman in uniform. The woman is approaching Hanna, her arm held up to halt approaching vehicles. A lined face and hair in a sensible bun beneath her police hat. The man is on the other side of the road, pausing the traffic in the other direction.

Hanna doesn't register at first that the policewoman is speaking to her.

The policewoman says it again: 'Let's get you out of the road, love, OK?'

Hanna can't back away from her, because that would only move her towards the male officer.

'Come on, love,' the policewoman says. 'It's not safe here, with all this traffic.'

She has her arms spread, as though she is going to herd Hanna.

They'll throw you in prison, the voice says.

'I don't care,' Hanna says. And perhaps this is true. At least in prison she can rest.

'We don't want you getting hurt,' the policewoman says.

And after a moment, Hanna does allow herself to be ushered to the side of the road.

They are asking for her name and where she lives, and if she's taken anything. It's an effort to recall the information they want. She manages parts of it, jumbled together.

Then she is getting in the back of the police car, because there is nothing else she can do, and she is exhausted from crying, and has decided to do whatever they tell her. They are speaking to her gently, which is a nice change from the malice of the voice. Strangely, once she is in the police car it doesn't go anywhere, which Hanna supposes is another trick, but there's nothing she can do about it now. She is very frightened, but oddly peaceful too; it's such a relief to have given up.

After a while an ambulance pulls up, and now it seems Hanna is supposed to get into the back of that instead. The policewoman goes with her. Hanna wonders how many more vehicles they might try out together today. There are two paramedics, one male and one female, and the male one stays in the back with Hanna and the policewoman whilst the female paramedic gets into the front to drive. They set off without saying goodbye to the male police officer, or perhaps Hanna just misses that bit.

She seems to have lost her shoes and socks at some point, so they give her some thick red socks to put on, and a matching red blanket to wear round her shoulders.

The paramedic asks her some more questions, but she can't concentrate.

'Am I going to prison?' she says.

'No, love,' the policewoman says. 'Like I said before, we're taking you to a place of safety for your own protection.' She sounds like she is reading off a script, but her eyes stay on Hanna. 'Everything will be OK. Try not to worry.'

Weary to her bones, clutching the blanket around her, Hanna says, 'OK.'

THEY REACH THEIR DESTINATION quite soon: a long, low building which has the faintly depressing appearance of a conference centre. In the car park, they are met by a young woman with blonde hair. Her outfit theme seems to be blue: blue jeans and a blue shirt, with a matching blue lanyard. She smiles and introduces herself, though her name and job title slide off Hanna's brain without registering. The woman is not dressed like a police officer, nor like a doctor or nurse, though Hanna is sure someone has mentioned a hospital, and she has arrived in an ambulance after all. They all follow the blonde woman through a side door into the building and down a long corridor – the policewoman, the paramedics and Hanna in a small gang.

Then Hanna is ushered into a room with lilac walls, two chairs and a bed with only a thin plastic mattress and no sheet.

'Have a seat, Hanna,' the blonde woman with the lanyard says, and the voice says, *How does she know your name?* But of course Hanna has told the police officers her name, so it is no great mystery really.

'Sorry?' the woman says, and Hanna realizes she must have said at least part of this out loud.

Hanna shakes her head.

The woman says, 'We're just going to do a search, take your blood pressure and things like that, all right?' She has a northern accent – Lancashire, maybe – and Hanna wonders if she might have zoned out on the journey, if they have travelled further than she realized.

The policewoman says, 'We'll be off then.' To Hanna, she says, 'Take care, love.'

Hanna offers up her red blanket to the paramedics. She hopes they'll say she can keep it, but they take it from her. As she watches the male paramedic bundle it up in his arms, she thinks it might be a signal, the waving of a red flag, but she can't work out what it means, or if she is the one making the signal, or them.

Then she is distracted again by the black shape, which has reappeared. She glimpses it out of the corner of her eye and turns towards it reflexively.

'It's all right,' the blonde woman from the north says.

A young man has appeared now, also wearing a blue lanyard. They get Hanna to stand up and she keeps very still as the blonde woman moves a device near her arms and legs. The man is saying something to her. Hanna nods, because this is what seems to be expected.

Then they leave her alone in the room.

SHE DOES NOT KNOW how much time passes, because there is no time anymore. The door is not locked – she is grateful they haven't locked her in – and there is a toilet opposite her room, which she is allowed to use. The blonde woman comes to check on her once, and brings her a cup of very milky tea and some biscuits. But the doors at either end of the corridor are locked. Hanna works this out quickly from seeing people scanning their lanyards at the doors, which leads to a click and then a beep, before the doors can be pushed open. So there is no escape. And in any case, she has nowhere to go. It is nice not to be responsible for herself any longer, not to have to make any decisions. The lanyard people have taken her on. Good luck to them.

After what feels like hours, they remember her again and she is led through one of the locked doors – click, beep – and into a larger room with four soft chairs placed around a low table. It reminds Hanna a bit of the coffee lounge at her sixth-form college. It doesn't look like an interrogation room.

The blonde northern woman introduces another woman who has just come through the opposite set of doors. Her name is Dr Walsh, and she is young like the blonde woman, but unlike the blonde woman, whose hair is loose, she has her hair tied up in a ponytail. Hanna doesn't know how to interpret this: is it to communicate that they have already found Hanna guilty? Hanna decides she must remember the doctor's name in case it is a test for later.

'Please have a seat,' Dr Walsh says, and so Hanna does. The blonde woman has vanished, but now another woman, not so young, has come in through the other door. She is dressed dowdily in a rumpled linen dress, and her hair is loose, but it is too short to tie up anyway so the information is inconclusive. This woman says she's a social worker, which pleases Hanna because the woman looks like a social worker, and it is reassuring when things match up in this way.

The third person who comes in, to Hanna's great surprise, is her college GP.

'Dr Bryan!' Hanna says.

It is quite the reunion.

After that, there are lots of questions. They ask how things have been going for her recently. They ask what she was doing in the street. They ask about her studies. They ask about her sleep. It is strange, because they seem to know a lot already. The dark shape is still behind Hanna and although she tries to ignore it, they ask her what she is looking at.

Dr Walsh says they are concerned about her safety, that they would like her to stay in hospital for a little while so they can help her properly. They ask her how she feels about that. Dr Walsh has a nice, gentle voice, but people can be deceptive. Hanna herself is deceptive.

Hanna does not want to stay in hospital.

There is more, but she doesn't listen.

Then the three of them go out of the room for a while, and Hanna sits where she is. Everything has become very slow and very quiet. It is like being underwater.

When they come back in, Dr Walsh talks for a while, but Hanna does not take the information in. She is looking out of the window, where she can see the branches of the trees moving sedately. She thinks they might be signalling to her.

'Hanna, do you understand?' Dr Walsh says.

Her eyes still on the trees, Hanna says, 'Yes.'

The social worker says, 'Your mother's here, Hanna. And your brother.'

At the word 'mother', Hanna refocuses. The view beyond the window blurs and she turns back to the people in the room.

'My mother?'

'Yes, and your brother.'

She's in trouble now.

'Are you OK to see them?' the social worker says. 'Is that what you'd like?'

What she'd like? Hanna doesn't know what she'd like. She is not a person with likes or dislikes any longer.

But when the social worker asks again, she nods yes, I'll see them.

They go out through the second door (click, beep) and into another room similar to the last one, with soft chairs and a blue carpet.

And there are Michael and her mother. Although she's been told they are here, Hanna is nonetheless surprised to see them. They do not belong here, in this strange place, this strange reality.

They are sitting, but both rise when they see Hanna. They must have come straight from work; Michael is in a suit, and her mother is wearing navy trousers and a cream blouse. Their faces look empty to Hanna, but she thinks they are angry.

Michael says, 'Hanna, what on earth——?' but all her mother says is, 'Hanna.' Her voice does not sound like her own voice at all.

The social worker says, 'Shall we all have a seat? Hanna's very tired.'

'Had a busy day,' Hanna says.

They sit in silence for a few moments. Hanna is glad the social worker has stayed, though Michael keeps eyeing her warily, as though he fears Hanna might have got them all into trouble.

Hanna waits for her mother's reprimand, but her mother says nothing. She has her hands clasped in her lap, but she doesn't keep them still; they twist and turn, and Hanna watches them. Her mother still does not speak, and is not looking at Hanna but at the hands in her lap. Both of them watch her mother's hands in her lap as they move and turn.

'Hanna, what's all this about?' Michael is saying.

Hanna pulls her eyes away from her mother and tries to concentrate on Michael. 'Are you angry with me?' she says.

'No, of course not,' he says, angrily. 'We're worried about you.'

The black shape is behind Hanna again. She turns her head quickly.

'What is it?' Michael says.

He's in league with them, the voice says.

'I don't think he is,' Hanna says.

'Stop it,' Michael says.

She looks back at the dark shape again.

'Stop it,' Michael says again. 'Please. We're here now.' He turns to their mother, but their mother does not speak. He turns back to Hanna and says, 'Tell us how to help.'

Hanna shakes her head. 'Nobody can help. Events are in motion.'

'Hanna's been having a very difficult time,' the social worker says, apparently feeling the need to apologize for her.

A silence.

'What?' Hanna says to Michael.

Michael, startled: 'I didn't say anything.'

'Hanna will receive excellent care here,' the social worker says. 'So she can get back to her old self.'

Hanna looks at her mother, but her mother's head remains bowed.

'You know there are cameras,' Hanna announces, because somebody needs to say it. 'And bugs in the walls. Be careful what you say.'

She sees Michael flinch at this news. As well he might.

'Alice is on her way,' he says. 'She's still on the train from Edinburgh. She won't be here in time today, but you can see her tomorrow.'

'Alice should stay away,' Hanna says. 'It isn't safe for her here.'

'It is safe,' Michael says. He turns to their mother again. 'Mum, tell her. *Say* something.'

But Hanna's mother is still staring at the hands in her lap, which have stopped moving now. She does not reply. Like the Gorgon, Hanna has turned her to stone.

They are afraid of me, she thinks. All of them are afraid – her mother, her brother, the social worker, even gentle-voiced Dr Walsh with her cryptic ponytail. Hanna is dangerous, and she needs to be locked up.

Somehow, she dredges up from the depths of her memory the fact that her mother saw this coming: her mother always knew.

'I'm sorry,' she says.

The door opens again and the blonde woman appears. She says, 'Let's go and get you settled, Hanna. We've got your room ready, and I'll give you a quick tour, show you where everything is. Mum can come too.'

Hanna's mother stands. She picks up a bag from the floor, which Hanna hadn't noticed. It's Hanna's old rucksack, the one she used for school.

'I brought some things for you,' she says, when she sees Hanna looking at it. The first words she has spoken since her greeting.

What things?

'I'll be off now, Hanna,' the social worker says. 'You'll go with Natalie and your mum, OK?' She nods at them all, or perhaps just at the blonde woman, and leaves the room.

The blonde woman takes the bag from Hanna's mother. Hanna does not carry her own things anymore.

'We'll say goodbye to your brother for now,' the blonde woman says.

'I'll see you soon, Hanna,' Michael says. He reaches out and then Hanna finds he is hugging her. She can't remember him ever hugging her before, though perhaps he did when they were children. She can see now why he doesn't administer hugs very often: he is not very good at it.

'Tell them whatever you want,' Hanna tells him, disentangling herself from his awkward embrace. 'It doesn't matter. They know everything already, so it makes no difference.'

He says, 'You'll be OK. You just need to rest. You'll be fine.'

Because she is not attuned to anything just now except her own exhaustion and fear, Hanna does not notice he is in tears.

She and her mother follow the blonde woman out.

It will not be until several days later, once she has had some sleep, and the olanzapine has started to kick in, the diazepam has dulled her terror, and the voice has quietened, the black shape receded, that she will realize she has been sectioned. She was told this was happening at the time (repeatedly), told which section of the Mental Health Act she was being detained under (the glamorous 136, and then the relatively tame Section 2), but for the time being, all this is unclear.

So it will come as a surprise to her to discover that she is not allowed to leave the hospital. She will not remember, by then, much about her admission or the events leading up to it, but she is willing to concede that she was behaving strangely. When she is given her phone back, she is able to see the messages she sent before she ran from her college room. The first one, to Alice, is the only one she remembers writing, and it is actually rather more coherent than the others that followed. She can hardly believe these lunatic ramblings were written by her, but there they are in her sent folder, to Kemi, to Tom Li (who she hasn't spoken to since school), to Susan, to her mother, to a range of other people she is no longer in touch with, but who unfortunately have lingered in her contacts. Most are apologies for her crimes, along with dire warnings over what is about to happen to her, for which they should not blame themselves. It also seems that after the original message to Alice she had a falling-out with punctuation, and it is quite a challenge now to decipher her own communications. The shame is acute.

People will visit her over the next fortnight, but Hanna, fogged by the medication and her own fear, will not be able to offer much entertainment to her visitors beyond agitated warnings or silent crying. Later still, she will think of her life as falling into two clear halves: before the madness, and after. The before-life is closed off forever; she can never go back.

But now, on the day of her admission, she is still psychotic, and has limited insight into her condition (to use Dr Walsh's terminology). She knows she is in hospital, but she still half-believes the doctors and nurses wish her harm. She has only given up resisting because she knows there is no point.

She and her mother follow the blonde woman through to the inpatient ward. Hanna shuffles along, feeling a thousand years old.

The blonde woman gives them a quick tour: men's and women's toilets, the female-only television room, the laundry room, clinic room, small kitchen, crafts room. Hanna isn't paying much attention. She is looking at the other people on the ward. They pass a girl about her own age, ago-nizingly thin, with what look like sores on her face. Her fragile arms protrude stiffly from the sleeves of her oversized T-shirt, and her hair is pulled back in a wispy ponytail, revealing bald patches on her scalp. There is no flesh on her face, and her eye sockets are wide and sunken: it is like looking at a skull. The girl doesn't meet Hanna's eye, though she must feel Hanna staring. An older woman sits alone in the women's television room, crying quietly. Hanna registers all this without much emotion.

They follow the blonde woman through another door and down another corridor, where they are shown the women's bathroom and then Hanna's bedroom. It is a small room containing a single bed with a white pillow and sheet, a flimsy-looking plywood wardrobe and a sink with a single tap.

The blonde woman says, 'I'll be back in a minute,' and vanishes, leaving Hanna and her mother alone to take in the room.

'Well, this looks comfortable enough,' Hanna's mother says after a moment.

Hanna looks out of the window. A view of the car park. There are no bars on the window, but she knows instinctively that it is locked.

Her mother goes over to the wardrobe and opens it. 'There aren't any hangers,' she says. 'Just shelves. Everything must get very creased.'

Hanna tries out the tap. It operates on a sensor, and seems only to have one temperature, which is very cold. The mirror above the sink is not made of glass but of some kind of plastic; the face looking back at her is distorted.

Behind her, her mother says, 'I never wanted this for you.'

Hanna sees for a single second what she has done, how she has struck at both their hearts, but the knowledge flickers out almost as soon as it appears.

The blonde woman is back. She has Hanna's rucksack, which she hands over, along with a leaflet. Then she explains mealtimes, ward rounds and medication slots. It is like a very clinical boarding school.

'OK, are we ready to go, Mum?' the blonde woman says.

'I'll be back to see you tomorrow, Hanna,' her mother says.

Hanna returns her gaze levelly. She knows her mother is never coming back, but it does not seem necessary to say it.

'You need to rest,' her mother says. 'Try to get some sleep.'

Then her mother steps towards her, and Hanna prepares for her second unwelcome hug of the day. But her mother's arms rise briefly, and then drop without making contact with Hanna.

And now, finally, it seems that her mother is going, and here Hanna will remain in the seventh circle.

'To Alice, my second best bed,' she says, and starts to laugh. It is only now that the absurdity of the situation has struck her.

Her mother says again, 'You need to rest.' But it is Hanna's mother who needs to rest: her face is grey.

And if Hanna weren't so unwell she might reflect on all the time she wasted when she was younger, fruitlessly looking for ways to get at her mother, to wrong-foot her, to wound her – all that wasted effort, when all along the way was this.

9

'D o you think it's overstepping,' Alice says to Kemi, 'for me to be the one throwing the party? It's not too presumptuous?' Now that the day is here, she is paralysed with anxiety.

'Well, we're throwing it together,' Kemi says. 'You just have a bigger place.' They're in the living room of Alice's shared flat, arranging bowls of crisps on the table. 'Anyway, she liked the idea, didn't she?'

'I *think* she did . . .'

'She's not angry with you anymore, Alice. I told you. She's over it.'

Alice nods, and tries to believe it.

They have put the 'Welcome Home' banner up on the wall above the mantelpiece so it's the first thing you see when you come into the room. Alice's two Brazilian flatmates, Vitoria and Gabi, helped Alice make it the day before, which touched Alice, though this does mean the banner features rather more glitter than she had envisaged (Gabi's contribution), and definitely more drawings of the Virgin Mary (Vitoria's).

Alice has put on her favourite dress for the occasion: a vintage shirt dress in blue cotton, with a pattern of pink boats on it. She had hoped it would make her feel more confident but it is only now, noting Kemi's trainers and jeans, that she realizes how wrong her own outfit is. It had felt jaunty and cheerful when she put it on, but now it strikes her as childish, even absurd.

'I like your dress,' Kemi says, uncannily.

'I think I'm going to change,' Alice says.

'What? No, Alice. You look like . . . yourself.'

This feels to Alice like a mixed compliment.

Kemi is now lining up stacks of plastic cups (she's managed to get red ones, like at a frat party; not great for the planet, Alice thinks, but does not say). Kemi asks casually, 'So, you seeing anyone at the moment?'

Alice shakes her head.

'Tried Tinder?' Kemi says.

'No.'

'You should! It's great.'

Alice doesn't want to admit that she's terrified of Tinder, so she says to Kemi, because she's read somewhere that the best tactic is to turn the question back on your interrogator, 'Are you seeing anyone?'

'Yes,' Kemi says serenely, and then doesn't add anything else.

Gabi comes in from the kitchen behind them, carrying a plate of biscuits.

'Oh, brilliant!' Kemi says. 'You got Party Rings.'

'Alice bought them,' Gabi says. 'I've never understood these strange snacks.'

Kemi has already taken one, ruining Gabi's neat display. 'They're great,' she says, her mouth full.

'They're for children,' Gabi says. 'But adults seem to like them more. I don't get it. And also there's a bit missing in the middle?'

'It's not missing,' Kemi says, swallowing her mouthful. 'They're *rings*. There's meant to be a hole.'

'And this is . . . fun for you?' Gabi says.

'Yes,' Kemi says. She takes another.

'Jammie Dodgers have a hole too, don't they?' Alice says.

'That's England for you,' Gabi says morosely. 'Holes in everything. Your roofs leak. Woodworm in all your old furniture. And I've tried Jammie Dodgers. Dis*gust*ing.'

'It's about nostalgia,' Alice says gently. She is used to Gabi's sudden bursts of disapproval. 'I suppose it's about what the biscuits represent, rather than the biscuits themselves. What's your top nostalgia snack in Brazil?'

Gabi says, 'None. In Brazil, we move on.'

The front door slams, and Vitoria comes in from the hall. She goes to her church on Saturday afternoons, often trying to get Alice to accompany her (it seems to involve a lot of talk about angels, and apparently takes place in the church leader's basement, and only has seven members, so Alice is quite worried it's a cult).

Vitoria says, unclipping her beautiful hair and shaking it loose, 'We asked the angels to make your party a wonderful success.'

Alice is moved by this. 'Thank you,' she says.

'Did you know,' Gabi says thoughtfully, 'that in all the time you have lived here, Alice, you have never thrown a party?'

Alice does know this.

'What, never?' Kemi says. 'Even though you have this amazing entertaining space? This huge reception room?' She sounds like an estate agent.

Alice shrugs, trying to appear nonchalant – the sort of person who takes parties so lightly that she can't remember how many she may or may not have thrown.

'No, this is the very first one,' Gabi says decidedly.

'Yes, OK, probably,' Alice says.

'Never a single one before,' Gabi says. 'Not even for your thirtieth birthday.'

'Not even for your thirtieth?' Kemi says.

'Well, I—'

'This is party number one,' Gabi says.

'Actually,' Alice says, 'I did throw a party a few weeks ago.'

'You did?' Gabi looks incredulous.

'Yes, a family party,' Alice says firmly. It seems best not to mention it was a funeral. It also strikes her that three weeks on seems a little early to be making a confident return to party-throwing, given how the last event went.

'Well, this is the perfect place for a party,' Kemi says.

It's true that the flat has a living room ideal for hosting. It's large, light and wooden-floored, the bay window looking out on to the street. Today Alice has pulled up the sash to let in the late September air, and so that they can see any guests approaching. But the living room is the glory of an otherwise unprepossessing flat. Behind it is the narrow kitchen, which can be entered either through the door at the back of the living room or through a separate door off the hall, or from the back door to the garden. The living room also has a second door from the hall, as well as the window at street level, resulting in multiple entrances and exit points for each room, should the occupants ever wish to enact a farce. But it is best, in any case, to stay in the living room and let the other rooms remain an abstraction. If you were to start your tour here, moving into the cramped kitchen, then back into the hall to look in on each of the three small bedrooms in turn, before ending with an inspection of the tiny, ancient bathroom, you could complete the full cycle from hope to disillusionment in a matter of minutes.

'I can see why you've stayed here so long,' says Kemi, who has only experienced the living room.

Alice doesn't want to tell her that the main reason is apathy, though admittedly the flat is convenient for work. She has lived here for seven years now. Gabi has been here the whole time, was here already when Alice moved in, but Vitoria is a more recent addition, replacing Gabi's friend Federica, who had previously replaced Juliana, who previously replaced Alana (a revolving door of Brazilians, all of whom seem to know each other's friends, if not each other; Alice adores the sound of Portuguese, which she thinks is a particularly beautiful language, but she still hasn't quite got over the paranoid fear that sometimes it is her they are discussing).

The doorbell goes, making Alice jump. She looks at the others in panic. It is too early for the first guest; they are not ready.

'That's Steve,' Gabi says. 'He'll help us set up.'

She disappears into the hall, and Alice hears the door opening, the murmur of their voices, and then the sound of Gabi's bedroom door closing.

'He is helping us set up,' Vitoria says, raising an eyebrow, 'in her bedroom.'

Alice has never been particularly fond of Gabi's English boyfriend, who makes odd comments to her when they are alone, or sometimes even in front of Gabi. He once memorably asked her, when she was trying to secure a broken cupboard door with a bungee rope, if she was into bondage.

So it does not shock her now when Vitoria lowers her voice and says, 'Steve, you know he's bad news.'

Alice nods.

'For weeks,' Vitoria says, 'he's been coming on to me.'

'Gabi's boyfriend?' Kemi says. 'What a snake.'

'Yes. Whenever we're alone, he creeps closer, and says he'd like to smell my hair.'

'He sounds gross,' Kemi says.

'And last week he asked what I'd do if he kissed me.'

'What did you say?' Alice asks.

'The truth,' Vitoria says. 'That I'd stab him in the eye.'

Kemi is nodding approvingly.

'But it only seemed to encourage him,' Vitoria says.

'Perhaps he thinks that's how you flirt in Brazil,' Kemi says.

'Are you going to tell Gabi?' Alice says.

'How can I? It would break her heart. And you know how it goes. She would stab the messenger. No,' Vitoria says, 'I will just have to keep avoiding him, and hope he doesn't get too drunk. Alice,' she adds, 'I made the milk pudding for your party.'

'Oh, lovely,' Alice says. 'Thanks so much!' She loves Vitoria's milk pudding, though it does occur to her now that it isn't very normal party fare.

'Hey,' Kemi says in wonder once Vitoria has fetched it. 'This pudding has a hole in the middle.'

'You set it in a tube pan,' Vitoria says.

'I'll be sure to mention this to Gabi.'

HALF AN HOUR LATER, the first guests start to arrive. There is not yet any sign of Hanna, who claimed she would be there early.

'But "early" for Hanna still means late by most people's standards,' Kemi says. She doesn't seem at all worried that Hanna might not turn up, so Alice tries not to be either.

She welcomes in a couple of Hanna's friends from sixth-form college (Alice doesn't recognize them, though Kemi greets them enthusiastically), and then a woman Hanna worked with at the restaurant before she started in the civil service. Alice is very glad Kemi is there. Kemi smoothly handles these awkward early moments as the first guests are shown into the living room (which now seems cavernous, like an empty cathedral), ensuring everyone has a drink and making some quick introductions.

There is a painful early lull when there are still too few guests and they are all standing looking at each other in the too-large, too-quiet room, but after that everyone starts arriving at once. Alice goes back and forth between the front door and living room, never quite finishing introductions or showing people where they can put their jackets before the bell goes again.

Hanna's Cambridge friends arrive together, and Alice is relieved to see them; they are the first guests she actually knows, if only a little. It is odd to find yourself at a party full of strangers when you are the host. Alice, truth be told, is rather frightened of parties, and she keeps being astonished afresh to discover herself in the midst of throwing one. But she is doing this for Hanna, she reminds herself, to show Hanna how pleased she is to have her home, and that she wants things to be different between them from now on.

So here is Lavinia, statuesque in black, and curly-haired Santiago coming in behind her, and the slender, pale Lola in a sequined dress. They are slightly unexpected friends for Hanna, but Alice will always be grateful to them for how kind they were when Hanna finally returned to Cambridge.

She ushers them into the living room, where she has collected quite a few guests now (it is starting to feel like a large holding pen), and tries to emulate Kemi's ease in pointing out the drinks, though she is conscious of sounding less like a suave host and more like an anxious waiter. As she goes through her drinks spiel she is remembering how these girls switched their student house when they heard Hanna was coming back, so that she could live with them instead of alone in halls; and now Alice finds she wants to offer them more than just rum or vodka or gin, though nothing will ever be enough.

She says, 'And there's milk pudding, too. Please do help yourselves.'

'Sorry, what is it?' Santiago says.

'Milk pudding. It's Brazilian. My flatmate Vitoria made it.' She tries to remember what Vitoria has told her. 'It's called *pudim de leite condensado*.'

'It looks very nice,' Lavinia says. 'I like your Portuguese accent.'

'Vitoria made me practise.'

'It'll be full of calcium,' Lola observes.

'Yes,' Alice says. She is on the cusp of listing more of the pudding's merits when the doorbell goes again. 'Excuse me,' she says.

On the doorstep are a couple of young men in a smart-casual uniform of jeans and blue shirts. They introduce themselves as James Symonds and Ye Chen, Hanna's friends from the Foreign Office, each proffering his surname automatically, as if at a networking event.

'I'm Alice, Hanna's twin,' Alice says, since this seems like the most pertinent fact about her.

'Really?' the man called Ye says. 'Hanna never mentioned a twin. You don't look like her.' He sounds both fascinated and suspicious, and Alice has to suppress the urge to go and find a childhood photo as proof.

Ye is holding a bottle of wine, and James is holding a large plastic carry case with a metal grille at the front. Alice glimpses movement, a flash of fur and eyes gleaming in the darkness within.

'Did you bring a cat?' she asks, alarmed.

'No, it's a ferret,' James says.

Alice considers various follow-up questions, but doesn't quite know how to ask them.

They go down the hall, but James hesitates at the sitting-room door. 'Is there somewhere quieter I can put him? He'll go to sleep quite happily if it's quiet.'

'Yes, of course,' Alice says, trying her best to be a good hostess. 'You can put him in my bedroom.'

'Thanks,' he says, following her back across the hall.

'Does he live in that box?' Alice asks.

'Oh no,' James says. 'He's a house ferret. It's just that I've been visiting my parents, and I didn't want to put him on his lead on the Tube. And I don't want anyone stepping on him once the party takes off.'

Alice hopes the party does take off. She opens her bedroom door for James, and he places the carry case carefully down. Momentarily, Alice takes in the unwanted vision of her bedroom through James's eyes: peeling paintwork, a small double bed that takes up most of the floor space, an IKEA chest of drawers wedged in the corner and a narrow built-in wardrobe, the door of which can't open fully because the bed is in the way. She is thirty-two; she shouldn't still be living like a student. But this place was meant to be temporary, sourced quickly from SpareRoom one day when she realized she couldn't possibly live with her mother a moment longer. It was supposed to be a stepping stone to somewhere else, somewhere of her own. To furnish it properly would be an admission of defeat, and yet what is she other than defeated? In another decade, she will no doubt still be here, perhaps with different Brazilians, but still sleeping alone every night in this small, bleak room.

'Nice place you've got here,' James says, and Alice hopes, since he works in diplomacy, that he is capable of lying more convincingly than this.

James adds, 'I'll let him out at some point so he doesn't get too claustrophobic, but only in here, with the door shut. Is that OK?'

'Sure,' Alice says, not feeling very sure.

'He's extremely well trained. And there's not much in your room for him to chew on,' James says.

'No, I suppose not.'

'It's quite minimalist.'

Alice nods.

'Not much in it at all, actually,' James says.

Unwillingly, Alice surveys her room again.

'Just the bed and the chest of drawers, really,' James says.

They return to the sitting room, and amazingly there is Hanna herself, having arrived whilst Alice was dealing with the ferret.

'Hi Alice,' Hanna says when she sees her. And then she actually hugs her. Alice feels overcome by the bounty of Fortune as her sister's arms go round her. Perhaps this is how it will be: she and Hanna will just pick up where they left off. (Although where they left off, it occurs to Alice now, was complicated enough even without a dramatic falling-out.)

'Thanks for the party,' Hanna says.

'Well, Kemi did most of it.'

'She said the same about you. What a modest pair you are.'

'Welcome home,' Alice says. She has decided she no longer wants to be one of those people who are always too afraid to say what they mean. So she adds, 'I'm so glad you're back.'

'Me too, I suppose,' Hanna says. 'All things considered.'

'Kemi says you've found somewhere to live.'

'Yup. Move in next week. It's in Kennington, a house-share with a couple of others. They seem OK. Can't sleep on Kemi's futon forever.'

'If you need help moving, I'm free.' She is always free.

Hanna smiles at her. 'Thanks, Alice.'

And Alice has a brief, out-of-body sensation: here she is, chatting casually to her sister.

Then the doorbell goes again, and Hanna says, 'Well, I'd better mingle,' and the moment is over. But Alice looks forward to the other conversations they might have this evening.

She opens the door to find Michael and Olivia outside. Alice is more relieved to see them than she might have expected, even Olivia. Two more people she knows at this party.

'Thanks so much for coming,' she says as she takes their jackets and hangs them on the crowded rack.

As ever, Michael looks rather ill at ease out of a suit. Tonight he is wearing a crisply ironed blue shirt and jeans that look like they might also have seen the iron. Olivia is strikingly pretty in a green dress and red lipstick. Alice realizes that it has been a long time since she has seen them together. The thought worries her, and is hard to shake once it has arrived. She reminds herself again that it is impossible to judge other people's marriages from the outside. But it has been a surprisingly tumultuous relationship for Michael to be involved in, not at all the kind of thing they might have imagined for him. There was the original engagement straight after university, which was quickly broken off, and then the first wedding nine years ago, in Italy, that was cancelled at the last moment. By the time they got to the second wedding three years after that, in Islington Town Hall, the whole family was on edge in case this ceremony didn't go ahead either, Hanna wondering aloud how many run-ups Michael and Olivia were going to take before they finally managed to complete a wedding. (Hanna hadn't yet had a broken engagement of her own; later on, she might have been more sympathetic.) But then there was Olivia coming in, serene in her huge ivory gown, her waist tiny above the voluminous folds of the skirt, a bouquet of peonies in her hands. In his speech at the reception, Michael described himself as the luckiest man alive. Alice thought he looked exhausted.

'We can't stay long,' Michael tells her now. 'I have a lot of work to do tomorrow.'

'On a Sunday?' Alice says before she can help herself.

'I'm in the middle of drafting a very important memo.'

'Parties aren't really Michael's scene these days,' Olivia says. 'Too much fun. Not enough tax.'

Alice sees Michael's jaw tense, though he doesn't say anything.

'They're not really my scene either,' she says. 'I was so nervous earlier that I felt a bit sick.'

'It does seem like an unnecessary carry-on,' Michael says. 'Why go to all this effort, Alice? I don't think she'll really appreciate it.'

'She will,' Alice says. 'She does.'

'Nobody ever throws parties for me,' Olivia says, with a pointed look at Michael as the three of them move down the hall.

'I held that dinner party for your birthday last year,' Michael says.

'Oh yes! Talking politics over our cappuccinos. It was all very wild.'

'Is Hanna here yet?' Michael says as they enter the living room.

'Yes, she's over there in the corner with Kemi.'

Michael nods. 'I need to have a chat with her.'

'About what?'

'Making sensible choices. Investing in property, not throwing all her money away in rent. Hopefully she'll be more receptive this time.'

He disappears, leaving Alice and Olivia alone.

'He used to have chats with me about investing in property,' Alice says sadly. 'I think he's decided I'm a lost cause now.'

'Owning property is very unimaginative,' Olivia says. 'It ties you down. I miss my freedom desperately.'

Alice doesn't think she'd miss her freedom too much if she owned a half-a-million-pound flat in Kentish Town. She says, 'I suppose renting gives you a bit more flexibility. But security is nice too.'

'Most of the ills of our society can be traced to ownership of one kind or another,' Olivia says.

Alice reminds herself, in a ritual she often seems to carry out in Olivia's presence, that Olivia has a good heart (and if Alice hasn't seen much evidence of this, then perhaps that is because she hasn't been looking hard enough). To pre-empt any more of Olivia's well-rehearsed views on the oppression of ownership, she says, 'Can I get you a drink?'

'I can't drink at the moment,' Olivia says. She gives Alice a meaningful look.

'Oh right,' Alice says. 'Oh dear. Are you feeling unwell?'

Olivia puts her hand to her stomach, still looking at Alice meaningfully.

'Do you have a stomach upset?' Alice says.

'No,' Olivia says, sounding irritable now. 'I'm *pregnant*.'

'Oh!' Alice says. '*Oh*.' Reflexively she thinks, Now he won't ever be free of her. Then she is shocked at herself.

'That's wonderful,' she says to Olivia. 'Wonderful! Wow!' I'm going to be an aunt, she tells herself, not quite believing it.

'Don't tell Michael I told you,' Olivia says. 'He doesn't want to tell his family yet.'

His family. Alice isn't sure if she is imagining the distancing quality of the pronoun. She says, 'Of course, I understand. That makes sense. This is wonderful news! Let me get you a soft drink. Lemonade? Coke?'

Olivia reacts as if Alice has just offered her a puff on a crack pipe. 'Do you have anything less sugary? A lime and soda, perhaps?'

'I'm afraid we don't have any limes,' Alice says. 'Or soda.'

'Sparkling water?'

'No, sorry,' Alice says humbly.

'Just tap water then,' Olivia says. 'Do you have any little canapés that I can nibble on? It tends to help with the nausea. There's not much I can eat at the moment, but I can usually tolerate a bit of flaky pastry or a few olives.'

'I think there are some sausage rolls in the kitchen,' Alice says. She is ready to acknowledge her failure as an adult. Plenty of lemonade and party rings to go around, but no sparkling water or vol-au-vents.

'I'm a vegetarian,' Olivia says. Her tone is reproachful, though Alice is almost certain this is new information.

She says, 'Oh! Sorry. Well . . . I could, sort of, disembowel it for you? Take the sausage bit out and leave you with the pastry?'

'Disembowel it?' Olivia says.

'Or!' Alice says in relief, as she remembers. 'There are some bread-sticks somewhere. I'm sure there are.'

'Fine,' Olivia says magnanimously.

Alice goes to the kitchen to fetch Olivia's water and snacks. She is searching the cupboards for the breadsticks when Vitoria appears at her shoulder. She has a furtive, hunted air. 'Steve is already drunk,' she says. 'I just ran into him in the hall.'

'Oh God,' Alice says. 'I hope he and Gabi don't row.' Their rows are epic, involving screaming, crying, and occasionally objects sailing through the air (launched by Gabi) and smashing against walls. It would be the end of the party, though it does occur to Alice that it is the kind of thing Hanna might enjoy.

'He has already tried to smell my hair once,' Vitoria says. 'As soon as he gets drunk, it becomes an *obsession* with him.'

'I suppose you'd better try to keep out of his way,' Alice says, and then has the uneasy feeling that this is the wrong way round.

When she returns to Olivia, triumphantly bearing a glass of tap water and a whole box of breadsticks, she finds her talking to Hanna's friend Santiago. Olivia receives the water and breadsticks, and then almost immediately says, 'Excuse me,' and melts away, leaving Alice and Santiago staring at each other in mild panic, having been catapulted into an unexpected tête-à-tête.

'How are you?' Alice begins.

'I'm fine, thanks.'

'Sorry,' Alice says, 'because I'm sure Hanna's told me –' she definitely hasn't – 'what is it you're doing at the moment?'

'I'm a teacher,' Santiago says.

This is useful, because Alice is then able to ask what subject, what type of school, where the school is, whether Santiago likes it and what the students are like. All this keeps them going for a while, but eventually the subject runs dry.

'So what do you do?' Santiago says.

'I work in HR,' Alice says.

'Oh right. For a big company?'

'For the council,' Alice says apologetically, aware of the crippling dullness of this answer. It has often seemed to have a chilling effect on conversations in the past.

But Santiago says gamely, 'Which council?'

'Lambeth.'

'Ooh, that's a good one,' Santiago says. There's a pause then, because there's not really much anyone can ask about a job in HR for the council, but after a few beats Santiago manages, 'So, do you enjoy it?'

'It's all right,' Alice says. There had been a time when she'd hoped for more. To be a teacher like Santiago perhaps, or even an archaeologist. Somehow instead she has got stuck, and she can think of no real reason for it now except her own character failings. It was a lack of confidence, she supposes. A lack of courage. She imagines for a moment being Hanna, being able to say, 'I work for the Foreign Office,' and watching interest bloom on the other person's face.

She adds, for Santiago's benefit, 'Sometimes I have to facilitate people getting fired, which isn't much fun. Though I suppose I facilitate hiring people too, so maybe it balances itself out.'

'The great circle of life,' Santiago says.

Over her shoulder, Alice sees Steve coming in through the door from the kitchen, his eyes moving blearily over the room. At the same time, she sees Vitoria, who is standing by the mantelpiece, put down her drink, dodge behind a couple of guests and disappear out of the door into the hall. Oh no, Alice thinks. This doesn't seem like the sort of situation that will improve with time.

Santiago says, 'It's amazing having Hanna back, isn't it? We've all missed her. Though we did manage to visit her in KL once, and that was a really cool trip. Did you get out there at all?'

'No,' Alice says. 'Work was very busy.'

'Lambeth Council needed you,' Santiago says sympathetically. Then she says she needs the loo, so Alice points out the door to her.

Left on her own, Alice heads into the kitchen to get more crisps for the depleted bowls. She finds Gabi in there, talking in fast, animated Portuguese to her friend Maria, whilst Hanna leans against the fridge drinking a beer.

'Hi,' Hanna says. 'Warn me if Michael's coming this way, will you? I had to pretend I was going to the loo to escape him.'

Alice hopes this is not what Santiago has just done. Everybody seems to be trying to escape everybody else. Perhaps she has accidentally thrown that kind of party. She goes to get three large packets of crisps from the cupboard.

'Then I hid in your bedroom for a bit,' Hanna adds. 'At least, I think it was your bedroom. The clothes in the drawers were quite colourful. And there were a number of cardigans.'

'Why were you going through my—' Alice begins, but Hanna continues, 'I don't know why he's got such a bee in his bonnet. I've only been back in England about five minutes, I'm not sure how I'm supposed to have leapt on to the property ladder already. And anyway,' she concludes, 'I don't even know how long I'm staying.'

Alice's heart drops. 'But your job . . .' she says.

'Yeah, I'll probably stay a couple of years. But after that, who knows? And anyway, there's no way I could afford to buy somewhere in London. No one can on their own, unless they're shockingly rich.'

'Michael never seems to take that into consideration.'

'I imagine he thinks we're just terrible with money, and are spending it all on fast living.'

Alice suddenly thinks, what if she and Hanna pooled their resources and bought somewhere together? She is momentarily gripped by excitement at the idea, before she realizes Hanna would never go for it. Or at least she wouldn't have done in the past. Maybe there's a chance now.

Gabi says, 'Alice, all the milk pudding is gone. It was a big success.' Then she says something to Maria in Portuguese, and Maria laughs. The two of them head out into the hall.

Hanna says, 'I wish I was bilingual. It sounds so cool, just casually switching between languages like that.'

'I sometimes worry they're discussing me,' Alice admits.

'Alice,' Hanna says sternly, 'that is very self-obsessed.'

Kemi comes in from the living room and says, 'There you are. One moment you were in the living room, the next you'd vanished.'

'You know me,' Hanna says. 'Wherever I am, I want to be elsewhere. You once said that was my motto.'

'Did I?' Kemi says. 'That seems rude of me.'

'It was. But it's better than your motto.'

'Which is?'

'*Eat, pray, eat.*'

Kemi snorts.

Hanna says, 'Or, *Have chlamydia; will travel.*'

'Jesus, it wasn't chlamydia!'

Alice looks from one to the other as they laugh. She can feel the invisible currents that move between them. Oh, she thinks unaccountably, that must be what it's like to have a twin.

'Alice,' Kemi says suddenly, 'you should have a drink.' She passes Alice the unopened can in her hand. 'I've been carrying this around for ages, ready to press upon you.'

'Thanks,' Alice says, receiving it. She is not a big drinker, but she doesn't want to seem boring.

'By the way, I like the "Welcome Home" banner,' Hanna says. 'Which of you drew all the Virgin Marys?'

'That was Vitoria,' Alice says.

'They're a nice touch.'

Alice cracks open the can and takes a small sip.

Kemi says to Hanna, 'Your mate Lola likes this guy she works with, but doesn't want to make a move because she's worried about ruining the friendship. You should come and talk some sense into her.'

'Yeah,' Hanna says. 'As the ruiner of many friendships, I'm well placed to advise.'

'She also thinks she might be too powerful for him,' Kemi says. 'Sexually speaking. These are her words, you understand, not mine.'

'Oh God,' Hanna says. 'I'm sorry.'

She and Kemi go out of the kitchen together, and Alice isn't sure whether or not she's supposed to follow. She hesitates a few moments, sipping her beer, and then decides she should have just gone with them, that it was stranger to stay in the kitchen on her own. But when she goes to stand in the doorway to the living room, there is no sign of Hanna and Kemi, and in fact Alice can't spot anyone she knows except Michael and Olivia, who are by the drinks table talking to Hanna's friend Lavinia, too far away to be easily reached. Alice notices that there is now a cluster of candles burning in one corner of the table, giving it the appearance of a shrine. She suspects Vitoria is responsible for this. The candles appear to be votive.

Probably what she should do, Alice thinks, is go and break into one of the small groups closer to her, introduce herself brightly and join in the conversation. That is surely what someone from the Foreign Office would do. But Lambeth Council hasn't provided the same social polish, and Alice is gripped by shyness. The longer she stands here alone, the more self-conscious she feels. She is halfway through her can of beer, and once that is gone she won't have anything to do with her hands.

Then she sees that Lavinia is coming towards her. Alice stands aside to let her pass on through to the kitchen, but it seems that Lavinia is not trying to get to the kitchen. She has come over to talk to Alice.

'This is a nice party,' she says.

'Thank you,' Alice says.

'I was just talking to your brother,' Lavinia says, glancing in the direction of Michael.

'Oh right.'

'He's got a real thing about home ownership,' Lavinia observes.

'Yes,' Alice says. She finds Lavinia's accent interesting. One moment she sounds American, and the next like an English aristocrat. Her eyes are interesting, too: wide apart and a shade of blue that is almost grey.

'He comes across as the sort of man,' Lavinia says thoughtfully, 'who, when asked what his favourite colour is, would say that he doesn't have one. Is he a nice brother?'

'On the whole, yes,' Alice says. She has always felt protective of Michael, though he has never wanted her protection.

She asks Lavinia, 'Do you spell colour with or without a u?'

'Depends on my mood,' Lavinia says. 'So, are you a home owner?'

'No,' Alice says. 'Are you?'

'No,' Lavinia says. She hesitates, then adds awkwardly, 'But . . . well, my parents are rich. So I can't pretend to be in the same position as most people. That would be fraudulent. Because I have a safety net.'

Surprised at her openness, Alice says, 'Oh. Well, that's handy.'

'They don't actually give me money,' Lavinia adds. 'I earn my own money, pay my own rent and so on. But the thing is, it's always there, in the background. I know that they could give me money. So I don't have that anxiety that most people have. Whatever happens, I'll always be OK.' She meets Alice's eye. 'So it's not the same as being truly independent.'

Strangely touched by Lavinia's confession, Alice blurts out, 'I went to a private school. Until sixth form, anyway.' *Our secret shame*, as Hanna used to call it.

'I know many people who went to private school,' Lavinia says. 'Having gone to one myself. Why did you leave? Hanna never mentioned it.'

'Our parents got divorced, and they couldn't afford the fees anymore.'

Lavinia considers Alice in that level way of hers. 'Were you sad to leave?'

'I thought I was. I was nervous about starting again somewhere new. But I think I was happier in the end. If you stay in the same place, you can sort of get stuck with that version of yourself. And . . . I think moving helped me become a bit more confident. Eventually.'

'You weren't confident when you were younger?'

'Not at all, no.' Unlike now, she thinks.

Lavinia says, 'Did you mind when your parents got divorced?'

'Yes. Are your parents still together?'

'Yes, but not happily. I don't remember ever seeing them laugh together, or touch each other. It's put me off the idea of marriage. It seems so arbitrary, their togetherness. Were your parents ever happy together, do you think?'

'I don't know,' Alice says. 'I don't know what that would even look like. Especially for my mother.'

She wants to say more, but they are interrupted the next moment by Steve, who looms up behind them.

'Has Vitoria come this way?' he says to Alice. He is standing much too close and his breath smells sour and beery.

'I think she might be in the loo,' Alice says. Out of the corner of her eye, she can see Vitoria climbing out of the window.

Steve nods, but then instead of leaving, he goes and stations himself by the mantelpiece, where he has a full view of the room.

Alice says quietly to Lavinia, 'Sorry, I'd better just go and let

Vitoria back in through the front door. She won't have her keys on her and she can't come back in through the window now.'

'I'm not sure what this game is,' Lavinia says, 'but it looks enjoyable.'

'I'll be back in a moment.'

Lavinia inclines her head gravely.

When Alice opens the front door, Vitoria is leaning against the wall outside, clearly confident that help would arrive soon.

'Everywhere I go, he appears,' she says, stepping past Alice into the hall.

'Where's Gabi?' Alice says.

'Probably she is looking for Steve. Is he still in the living room?'

Alice sticks her head round the door. To her disappointment, she sees Lavinia has been joined by Santiago and a couple of Hanna's friends from sixth-form college.

'Yes, he's still in there,' she says to Vitoria.

'Let's go to the kitchen and get a drink,' Vitoria says, taking her arm. 'By the way, I put out my candles in the living room. The atmosphere needed a little something.'

'They look nice,' Alice says.

In the kitchen, Vitoria gets two beers from the fridge, passing one to Alice, who hasn't quite finished her last one yet, though it has gone flat.

'I've never seen you drink beer before today,' Vitoria says. 'You like it, then?'

'Oh, I love it,' Alice says. In truth, the drinks she prefers are spirits with sweet mixers like Coke or pineapple juice so that you can hardly even taste the alcohol anymore. She always assumed her tastes would mature with age, but it has never happened. Cider is OK, at a push. She decides it's about time she got into beer, so she opens the new can, takes a large swig, and then splutters as some of it goes down the wrong way.

Vitoria is still hitting her on the back when James and Ye approach.

'Have you seen my ferret?' James says. 'We think he came this way.'

'Isn't he in his box?' Alice says.

'No, he was stretching his legs. But when I went to check on him, the door of your bedroom was open. Someone else opened it, I assume.'

'The ferret probably didn't open it himself,' Ye says.

Alice absorbs the information that there is a ferret on the loose at her party. She looks to Vitoria for help, but Vitoria, clearly feeling this is another of those strange English exchanges it is best to stay out of, says, 'I'm going to smoke.'

Well anyway, Alice reassures herself, ferrets are fine, aren't they? It's not like it's a rat. Nobody is scared of ferrets.

There is a shriek from the direction of the hall, making the three of them jump. They share a quick, alarmed glance and then head together towards the source of the noise. In the hall, they collide with Lola, who is emerging from the toilet.

'There was this huge squirrel watching me whilst I was peeing,' she says.

'Through the window?' James says.

'No, it was in the room with me. It suddenly appeared from behind the cistern.'

'It's very likely to be a ferret, not a squirrel,' Ye says.

James looks doubtful. 'It's not easy to mistake a ferret for a squirrel. They have a completely different build, and that's not even taking into account the tail.'

'Well, forgive me for not getting a decent look at it,' Lola snaps. 'I was taken by surprise.'

'I'm so sorry,' Alice says to Lola. 'It's just James's pet.'

'Is he still in there?' James says.

'How should I know?' Lola shakes her head in irritation and goes back into the living room.

Alice, James and Ye approach the toilet door cautiously, which Lola, with impressive presence of mind, has slammed shut behind her. But as soon as James opens the door a crack, a blur of dark fur streaks past them, shoots in and out of people's legs as it hurtles down the corridor, and disappears into the kitchen.

James hurries after it, calling, 'Sredni!'

Ye and Alice are left alone together.

'Don't worry,' Ye says. 'He doesn't bite, and he's used to people. He's very friendly. He'll go back to his box when he gets tired.'

'James or the ferret?' Alice says drolly, but Ye just gives her a puzzled look and says, 'The ferret.'

Alice goes back to the kitchen to retrieve her beer, and then heads to the living room. She wants to find Lavinia again, to tell her the story of the ferret, which she hopes will amuse her. But instead she runs into Lola in the doorway.

'So did you catch it?' Lola says.

'No,' Alice says. 'But apparently he's very friendly.'

'He didn't look very friendly to me.'

'No, well, I suppose you caught each other at a bad time,' Alice says.

'Yes. You know, my ex-boyfriend used to have a dog,' Lola continues conversationally, 'that would watch us having sex.'

Alice is taken aback, and can't think of an immediate reply. After a moment, she says, 'Couldn't you put it out of the room?'

'Then it would scratch at the door and whine, which was just as off-putting. It must be a kink,' Lola continues, 'for some people, to be watched by an animal while having sex. Everything's a kink for someone out there.'

'I suppose so,' Alice says.

'Voyeurism, but specifically involving an animal. But is that some kind of animal abuse, to involve one in your sex life, even passively?'

'I don't know,' Alice says. She is not sure how this conversation has befallen her.

Fortunately, Ye comes up then. 'I've sighted the ferret,' he says.

Alice and Lola look to where he's pointing. The ferret is crouched comfortably by the far leg of the drinks table, munching his way through what looks like a Dorito, which he holds neatly in his front paws. Alice says, 'I thought they were carnivores.'

'I think he eats everything.'

'Can you catch him?'

'It's probably best left to James. He doesn't always take to strangers.'

'But you said he was friendly,' Alice says.

'Yes, well, he is,' Ye says. 'Ish.'

Lola says, 'Excuse me. I'm going to make myself scarce. It seems to have a thing about me.'

She disappears, and Alice and Ye go in search of James again. They find him in the kitchen, leaning against the fridge chatting to Olivia, as if he had not a care in the world.

'We've located Sredni,' Ye tells him.

James, who was looking annoyed at being interrupted, perks up at this. 'Is he OK?'

'He's fine,' Ye says. 'He's next door eating Doritos.'

'Cool,' James says, and turns back to Olivia.

Ye gives Alice a small shrug, as if to say, *We tried*.

Alice is determined to pursue the matter, but at that moment Gabi storms in from the living room. 'Have you seen Steve?' she says to Alice.

'No. Why?'

'I heard he's coming on to Vitoria again.'

'Oh . . . Well, I don't think she wants him to.'

'Of course she doesn't! I'm going to kill him.'

Please, not at the party, Alice thinks. 'Perhaps you should just . . . break up with him,' she suggests.

Gabi rolls her eyes. 'Yes, Alice. Obviously I am going to break up with him. I am not literally going to kill him. But first I'm going to say to him all the things I want to say. I am going to *shout* them at him. I am going to show him up for what he is.'

Oh no, Alice thinks. 'Would it be better to wait until you've calmed down?' she says tentatively.

'No, it would not be better,' Gabi says, and stalks out.

Ye says, 'We should keep her away from the ferret. We don't want him getting agitated.' He follows James and Olivia, who are going through to the living room.

Alice is about to follow them, but then Hanna comes in through the back door, so Alice temporarily forgets about Gabi and the ferret.

Hanna leans against the fridge and says, 'Are you having fun?'

'Yes,' Alice says.

'Alice.' Hanna smiles at her (with unusual fondness, it seems to Alice. It occurs to her that Hanna is a little drunk). 'You've never liked parties.'

'I do like them,' Alice says. She wonders how she can more fully convey the idea that she is enjoying the party, so that Hanna doesn't think she is a drag.

Hanna goes and sits at the kitchen table, reaching for an open bag of crisps. She puts a handful into her mouth. After crunching for a few moments, she says, 'Did Olivia tell you she's pregnant?'

'Yes,' Alice says.

Hanna smiles. 'Yeah, she said it's a big secret, so I assumed that meant she was telling every single person she spoke to.'

'We'll be aunts.'

Hanna takes some more crisps, which she feeds into her mouth one by one, methodically. She says, 'You know, Michael likes to lecture me on my life choices, but he's made the poorest one of all.'

Alice doesn't know how to reply to this. She says, 'Well, she's not my cup of tea, but I suppose people have different tastes—'

Hanna laughs. 'Actually, none of us have a great track record when it comes to relationships,' she says. 'Michael married Olivia, who's a total fucking basket case, you're permanently single, and all my relationships have been disasters. Obviously something went wrong with all three of us.'

Alice is not enjoying this picture of them through Hanna's eyes. She says, 'We're fine. We're just like everybody else.'

'Do you ever think about our childhood?' Hanna says.

Alice is startled by this sudden change of direction. Warily, she says, 'From time to time.'

'Would you say it was a good one?'

'As good as most people's,' Alice says. 'Better than a lot of people's. It was fine.'

Hanna says, 'I'm not sure it was fine. What flavour are these crisps?' She inspects the bag. 'Oh, "cheddar and spring onion". Why can't they just say cheese and onion? Who do they think they are?'

She's definitely a bit drunk, Alice thinks. She says, 'Lots of people's parents get divorced. It wasn't unique to us.'

'I'm not talking about the divorce.'

They are interrupted at that moment by Steve's entrance through the door from the hall. He looks panic-stricken. 'Have you seen Gabi?' he says.

'I think she's looking for you,' Alice says.

'I know. God!' He exits through the back door to the garden.

Alice turns back to Hanna, but just then Gabi re-enters from the living room. 'Did he come this way?' she says. 'Vitoria says he was in the hall.'

'I think he might have left,' Alice says.

Gabi goes out into the hall.

Steve comes back in from the garden.

'This is all very exciting,' Hanna says.

'Can I hide in your bedroom?' Steve says to Alice.

'No.'

They hear Gabi's voice in the hall.

'Shit!' Steve bolts out of the back door again, and they see him pass by the window at the side of the house.

'Hopefully he'll just go home now,' Alice says to Hanna. 'He can climb the gate to get out. I don't know why he hasn't left already.'

'I hope he stays,' Hanna says.

Alice is relieved, at least, that Hanna's good mood seems to have returned, and that they have moved away from more dangerous conversational territory.

'Let's go and find Kemi,' Hanna says. 'She'll enjoy hearing about this.'

But in the hallway they are waylaid by Michael.

'Alice,' he says, 'did you know there's a large ferret roaming your flat?'

'He's a house ferret,' Alice says defensively.

Hanna has already disappeared into the living room, and Alice sees another opportunity with her sister lost.

'It's just ridiculous,' Michael says. 'And unhygienic.'

The doorbell rings. 'I'd better get that,' Alice says quickly.

But her relief is short-lived, because on the doorstep is Steve.

'All my stuff's still in Gabi's room,' he says. 'My wallet, my keys, my phone . . .'

'Fine,' Alice says. 'OK, yes.' She stands aside to let him in, and he slips quickly down the corridor and into Gabi's bedroom.

Alice goes into the living room. If she can't talk to Hanna, she is at least hoping to talk to Lavinia again.

And she is in luck, because there is Lavinia, standing with Santiago by the mantelpiece. Boldly, Alice approaches.

'Hello,' Santiago says, seeing her first. 'It seems there's a ferret on the loose.'

'He's very friendly—' Alice begins.

'I found him in my handbag a moment ago,' Lavinia says, smiling at her. 'I thought it might be a party favour you were giving out to all your guests.'

'And I was upset because I didn't get one,' Santiago says.

'I'm so sorry,' Alice says, but Lavinia only laughs.

'I'm afraid he ran off, or I would have tried to return him to his owner.'

Santiago says, 'We were just talking about this brunch place round the corner from here. It's called Jill's, we think. Or Julia's, maybe. Have you ever been?'

'No, I don't think so,' Alice says.

Lavinia says, 'Perhaps sometime we could—?'

They are interrupted by a huge crash and the sound of shouting coming from the kitchen. Around the room, heads turn.

Vitoria appears at Alice's side.

'Gabi has found Steve,' she says. 'He was in her room all along, taking a nap.'

'Oh God.'

Another crash, and the sound of breaking crockery.

'I think they're in the kitchen now,' Vitoria says.

And then Steve bursts through the door from the kitchen. 'She's crazy!' he tells the room. 'She's absolutely lost it.'

He dashes out into the hall just as Gabi rushes in from the kitchen looking murderous. But she is prevented from chasing Steve any further because at the same moment James enters through the hall door in pursuit of the ferret, who streaks through the legs of the guests, causing cries as he runs over people's feet.

James follows, pushing past people as he tries to catch the ferret.

The doorbell rings, but Alice barely registers it amidst the commotion.

The ferret has now climbed up on to a chair, then leapt on to the table, where it dives happily into the bowl of Doritos.

'Don't scare him!' James tells the assembled company.

Seeing Steve through the window – it seems he has made it out on to the street – Gabi bellows, 'Steve, I'm coming for you!' and hurls herself towards the open window.

This startles the ferret, who shoots up from the bowl of Doritos, dashes the full length of the table and makes a flying leap on to the sofa where Hanna and Kemi are sitting.

'Jesus Christ!' Kemi shouts, as the ferret lands in her lap. She jumps up (the ferret scrabbling to safety on the arm of the sofa), but knocks against the table in the process, upending Vitoria's display of votive candles.

James meanwhile has rushed over to the sofa and scooped the ferret up in his arms.

'There!' he says. 'Got him.'

But there is no time for anyone to express relief. They all seem to notice at the same time that the curtain is on fire.

'Shit!' Kemi says. 'Shit, shit, shit!'

'Someone get some water!' Hanna shouts.

Alice is paralysed by horror.

The next moment, Lavinia strides forward and forcibly wrenches down the flaming curtain. She bundles it up on the wooden floor and stamps out the flames with her thick-soled boots.

As they all stare at the singed remains of the curtain, Lola comes in from the hallway. James is holding his squirming ferret aloft. The air is heavy with smoke.

'Er, Alice and Hanna?' Lola says. 'There's a woman at the door who says she's your mother.'

BUT WHY ON EARTH, Alice will wonder later, did she come? Whatever her mother might claim, there was no possible way she could have believed herself to be invited. So why turn up like that? Why insert herself into every single situation, so that Alice is to have nothing to herself?

Of course, Hanna will never believe that Alice didn't invite her.

When their mother is announced, Hanna gets up without a word and goes out into the kitchen.

Alice is torn between following her, and dealing with the more immediate problem of her mother. But Kemi says, 'Go after her. I'll tell your mum I can't find you.'

So Alice goes into the kitchen, where Hanna rounds on her immediately.

'This is typical of you,' she says. 'I don't even know why I'm surprised.'

'I don't know why she's here!' Alice says. 'I really don't.'

'I should have realized this was your plan all along.'

It occurs to Alice that Hanna might not be reacting so forcefully if she were sober, but she knows better than to point this out. 'It wasn't my plan,' she says. 'Not at all. Honestly!' It's true that she mentioned the party to her mother, phrasing it as a small gathering she and Kemi were throwing. But Alice had definitely *not* invited her mother. She can't imagine how this misunderstanding arose.

'This is just a reminder that I can't trust you,' Hanna says. 'I never could. You can't do a single thing without Mum's involvement. You always go running to her. You just can't help yourself.'

'That's not true,' Alice says. Her eyes are stinging with the tears she's trying to hold back.

'Have you ever wondered why you've always been alone?' Hanna says. 'It's because you're so enmeshed with Mum that there's no room for anyone else.'

'I'm not enmeshed.'

'Yes you are. This family's so toxic I had to leave the country. I had to leave the *continent*.' When Alice opens her mouth to speak again, Hanna cuts across her. 'Oh yes, I'm being dramatic. That's what you all like to say, isn't it? Hanna's always so dramatic.'

There is a silence.

'I'm leaving,' Hanna says at last. 'This whole thing was a bad idea. I should have known.'

And she steps out of the back door. She will have to scale the gate to escape, but Hanna has always been an excellent climber.

Alice remains where she is, unable to hold back the tears any longer. She realizes after a moment that Kemi is standing in the doorway.

'OK, so I was wrong,' Kemi says. 'Turns out she isn't over it.'

ALICE DOESN'T SEE THE message from Hanna immediately, because she is in the library in Edinburgh with her phone on silent, reading a book about the Celts.

When she does check her phone, she assumes at first that the text is a joke. It says, *Alice, tell them the truth. Don't try to protect me. They'll make you pay.*

Alice wonders which of Hanna's friends has sent it. Very funny, she thinks.

Then she thinks, I don't get it.

She reads the message again, and realizes it must be a drunk text, not a joke text. Admittedly it doesn't look much like a drunk text, but then Alice has never sent one herself, so she isn't sure what they're supposed to look like. Also it is only the early afternoon, so a surprising time to be drunk. But perhaps Hanna is celebrating something.

All the same, Alice is unsettled. Standing outside the library with her jacket collar turned up against the cold, she rings Hanna. Hanna does not answer, though Alice had not really expected her to; Hanna has never been good at picking up her phone. Alice types out a reply to Hanna instead: *Hi Hanna! How's it going? Was that last message meant for me? Xx*

Then she stands there for a few minutes longer, frowning at her phone. No reply comes.

Alice is about to go back inside the library, but something makes her hesitate. As she usually does in times of uncertainty, she decides to ring her mother – who, unlike Hanna, answers immediately.

'Hello darling,' she says. 'I was wondering when you'd finally call.'

'Oh, but I called yesterday,' Alice says, amazed her mother doesn't remember. Does she now have to worry about her mother as well as Hanna?

'Yes, I know,' her mother says, 'but you hurried me off the phone so quickly we barely had a chance to chat.'

'We spoke for twenty minutes,' Alice says.

'How lovely to know you set a timer, and were actually counting down the minutes until you could get off the phone.'

'That wasn't what I meant,' Alice begins. 'You know I—'

'It's a pity you begrudge me even the occasional phone call. When I'm all on my own.'

'I don't begrudge you.'

'I could be lying here dead for all you know. I could be dead, with no one checking on me.'

'But you're not dead,' Alice says reassuringly. 'You're talking to me right now.'

'Oh Alice, must you always be so literal?'

Alice can see they are getting off track. She says, 'I'll ring you later for a proper chat, I promise. But I just wondered –' making her voice determinedly casual – 'if you'd heard from Hanna today.'

'When do I *ever* hear from Hanna?' her mother says. 'She never rings me. She never comes home. She's totally uninterested in her own family. I sometimes wonder what I did to deserve this.'

'OK, I just wondered,' Alice says.

'Should I have heard from her?' her mother says, sounding suspicious now.

Alice hesitates. But what can she say? That she got a weird text? She has absolutely no reason to think anything is wrong. Besides, if she does express concern to her mother, she knows from experience that her mother will react in one of two unhelpful ways: over or under. Either she will lose her head completely and insist on calling the police, an ambulance, the fire brigade, and perhaps the coastguard, or she will do the verbal equivalent of a shrug and say that Hanna is attention-seeking, that Alice should not fall for it. Alice knows that the latter reaction is far more likely, but it cannot be guaranteed. Every now and then her mother throws in a wild card.

She says to her mother, 'No, I don't think so.'

'Why are you suddenly chasing after Hanna?'

'No reason,' Alice says. 'I just fancied a chat.'

'I am free to chat,' her mother says forcefully.

Forty-five minutes later, when Alice has managed to extricate herself, she tries calling Hanna again. There is still no answer. Alice has almost convinced herself by now that everything is fine, that it is ridiculous to be getting anxious over a single, slightly cryptic, probably drunk message. But all the same, there is a strange nagging feeling that she can't shake.

She doesn't have Kemi's number, so after some careful thought she types out a Facebook message, trying not to think about how annoyed Hanna will be if she discovers Alice has been messaging her friends behind her back like a stalker.

Hi Kemi! How's it going? Have you heard from Hanna today?

Then Alice pauses, wondering how she can make the message seem less odd and out of the blue. After a moment, she adds cunningly, *I think her phone's broken. Can't get hold of her.*

She is just in the middle of telling herself again that everything's fine when Kemi's response arrives.

Oh my God, did you get one too?

THE TEXT KEMI HAS received runs along similar lines to Alice's, but is markedly less coherent.

'She sounds like she's taken something,' Kemi says.

'Taken what?' Alice says, for a confused moment thinking Hanna's committed theft.

'Drugs,' Kemi says patiently. 'It's worrying. We should make sure she's somewhere safe.'

On Kemi's instructions, Alice rings the porter's lodge at Hanna's college, and a porter goes to check Hanna's room. Hanna isn't there. Kemi, meanwhile, rings round a few of Hanna's other friends to see if anyone has spoken to her, but nobody has.

'I think you'd better call your mum,' Kemi says at last. 'She needs to know about this. And then we can all decide what to do next.'

Alice is appalled at the idea of explaining this situation to her mother, and of this vague, troubling 'next', but she knows Kemi is right. ('Though maybe don't mention the drug theory,' Kemi says. 'Just say she doesn't sound like herself.')

But in a sort of spooky synchronicity, Alice's mother rings just as Alice is picking up the phone to call her. Alice is only slightly surprised that her mother requires another chat so soon after the last one; this is not unprecedented. She gets ready to head her mother off before she launches into a further disquisition on her recipe for vegetarian moussaka, but before Alice can say anything, her mother says, 'Alice, I just had a phone call about Hanna.'

It is strange that even after her nervous discussions with Kemi, Alice's first assumption is that Hanna is in an ordinary kind of trouble, that she has thrown too wild a party or been caught smoking in her room or missed a few deadlines. But beneath this, Alice registers that her mother's voice sounds different: higher than usual, and taut, as though it has been stretched out too thinly.

'Well, is she OK?' Alice says. 'What's the matter?' She is suddenly cold, though she is in her room now, sitting with her back to the radiator.

'She's been taken to hospital,' her mother says.

Alice feels the world tip sideways. 'Is she hurt? What's happened?'

'No,' her mother says. The pegs are turned again, stretching her voice still more tightly. 'It's a psychiatric hospital. Alice, she's been sectioned.'

FOR MONTHS AFTERWARDS, ALICE has a recurring nightmare that involves all her teeth falling out. Sometimes in the dream she has come off her bike and knocked them violently out, but more often they drop out spontaneously while she is doing something unrelated, like working in the library or going round the supermarket. It is very strange. She has never worried about her teeth before now. She has always had excellent oral hygiene, and never needed fillings.

She and her mother spend the first week of Hanna's hospital stay in a Travelodge in Cambridge. Each night, they sleep across from each other in twin beds, though in fact neither of them sleeps much. Alice wonders how it is so easy to tell that someone else is awake with you in the darkness. It is almost as though the quality and weight of the air is different. Alice becomes self-conscious about making the smallest sound, even about turning over in bed, as if she must somehow avoid drawing attention to their shared state of wakefulness. And yet she ought to be used to sleeping in a room with someone else. In fact, it took her a while after she started at Edinburgh to get used to having a room to herself; it was strange to fall asleep without the sound of Hanna's even breathing. Each night now, she thinks of Hanna in her bedroom in the hospital, and wonders if she too is lying awake.

In the mornings, Alice is always ravenous, though in her normal life she doesn't have much appetite for breakfast. They eat in the small dining room of the Travelodge and Alice has the full English every time: eggs, sausages, bacon, hash brown, beans – she shovels it all down. Uncharacteristically her mother does not pass comment, though she sits across from Alice abstemiously sipping her coffee and eating a piece of fruit.

Then they will go back to their room, and Alice will sit at the small MDF desk in the corner and try to work on her coursework on the Celts, which is due in the following Monday (it has not occurred to her to ask for an extension; Alice has never asked for an extension in her life). During this time, her mother will go for a walk, or pace around the room pretending to tidy, which really just involves moving their few scant possessions from one part of the room to another. Both of them seem to be on edge all the time, jumping at the smallest noises, flooded with adrenalin. No wonder they don't sleep.

In the afternoons, they visit Hanna.

Not that Hanna – or rather this stranger who bears a passing resemblance to Hanna – is enthusiastic about their visits.

'You need to leave,' she tells them. 'They know you're here. They're in the walls.'

'It's all right,' Alice says. She's trying to keep her voice steady, not wanting to frighten Hanna with her own fear.

'I don't know why I'm here,' Hanna says.

'You're here because you're ill,' their mother says.

'Is that what they told you? I'm not ill.' But Hanna looks uncertain as she says this. 'It's only because they're watching me,' she adds. 'I'd be fine if they weren't watching me.' The hesitation again. 'I'm sure I'd be fine.'

'You'll feel better soon,' Alice says. 'You just need some rest.' She can hear how stupid she sounds. Hanna's behaviour paralyses her.

Hanna looks at her pityingly. 'You don't understand,' she says. Then glances over her shoulder again.

It is impossible, Alice knows rationally, to talk in any meaningful way to someone who is psychotic. You are always at cross purposes, and you cannot shake the unsettling detachment you feel throughout every conversation, the clinical, horrified fascination. She remembers this from her experience with Aunt Katy. That was disturbing enough, but it strikes Alice now that she has never seen Aunt Katy sane. She has no idea what the other Aunt Katy might have been like, the original one who vanished beneath the illness. Seeing Hanna like this is unbearable, because Alice keeps looking for her sister and finding instead a mad person.

The medication can take a while to work, Dr Walsh reminds Alice and her mother after their third visit (Alice is crying again, though the previous two days she had managed to hold the tears back until she and her mother were out in the car park). But Dr Walsh is hopeful that Hanna will start to respond within a few more days.

'Then she'll be all right again, won't she?' Alice says to her mother afterwards. 'Once the medication starts to work.'

'Is your aunt all right?' her mother says. She often seems to be angry at the moment.

Alice says, 'But there's no reason to think it's the same.'

Her mother says, 'What else does it look like to you?'

*

AFTER A WEEK IN the Travelodge, Alice's mother packs her off back to Edinburgh. Alice can't really argue since she has to hand in her coursework in person. But her mother also bans her from returning for a fortnight. Alice had planned to come back again the following weekend, but her mother says, 'It's six hours each way, Alice. It's simply not practical. And I don't want you making yourself unwell.' Alice wonders what kind of unwell her mother means. She doesn't have the money for the train fare anyway.

Their mother took a week off work after Hanna was first admitted, but her colleagues can't cover her classes any longer so she has to go back to London. Every afternoon she drives to Cambridge to see Hanna. It is a four-hour round trip. Alice knows she must be exhausted.

Back in Edinburgh, Alice tries to work but worries constantly about Hanna. Unusually, she speaks to her father on the phone every day. He wants to hear about Hanna, and Alice dutifully passes on any updates. He has been to see her in the hospital himself, but only once, at the beginning of the second week. Alice is aware that Hanna's behaviour doesn't offer much encouragement to visitors, but she still resents her father for not returning. Even Michael has been three times.

'Visits seem to upset her,' her father tells her.

Everything upsets her, Alice thinks. She's psychotic. But to her father, she only says, 'I'm sure she was glad you were there.'

ALICE RETURNS TO LONDON the day before Hanna is discharged, wanting to be there to welcome her home. It is almost the Easter holidays anyway, so she tries not to be anxious about skipping lectures. Her father pays for her train fare. Alice gathers her courage and asks him up front, and he says, 'Of course. Of *course*.' He transfers £200 to her account.

Their mother has decreed that Hanna will have Michael's old room. Alice wonders if Hanna will be amused at finally having secured this victory, or if she has lost her capacity for amusement. Their mother drives to Cambridge to collect Hanna, and in the meantime, Alice tries to make Hanna's new room as welcoming as possible. She cleans, and puts new sheets on the bed, and a brand new double-duvet cover she has bought from Debenhams with the remainder of her father's money. It is white, with blue and pink flowers on it, and Alice likes how fresh and cheerful it makes the room look. She puts real flowers in a vase on the bedside table too, a bunch of daffodils she got from Sainsbury's, then she arranges beside the vase a small stack of novels (a mixture of trashy and highbrow options, to cater for any mood) and a bar of fancy chocolate.

In the event, Hanna does not seem to notice these small touches. She stands in the doorway surveying the room, but makes no comment. Their mother puts down Hanna's rucksack in the corner and says, 'There, darling. Would you like a rest after the drive? I've made a lasagne for supper, but I can heat it up whenever you're hungry, so no rush.'

'And there's garlic bread to go with it!' Alice says. She suspects she's overdoing her cheery tone.

Wordlessly, Hanna pushes her trainers off without unlacing them and gets into bed, still wearing all her clothes. She draws the covers over her head.

Later that evening, their mother reheats some lasagne and takes it up to her.

'She's eating it in bed,' she tells Alice when she comes back down again. 'She'll be very tired for a while. It's the drugs.'

It is also, though Alice doesn't realize this at first, the depression that has engulfed her sister in the wake of the psychosis. For the next few weeks, Hanna seems able to do little more than sleep – for large chunks of each day as well as through the night – and, when she is awake, she is often crying. Alice has only rarely seen her sister cry before. Sometimes Hanna does not bother to wipe the tears away, but just stares ahead and lets them fall. Alice doesn't know how to help this version of Hanna any more than she knew how to help the mad one. Often she simply sits beside Hanna in silence, trying to keep her company, though if she ever reaches out to put her arm around her sister, Hanna pulls away.

Michael comes round every Saturday, bringing Hanna a magazine and some Fruit Pastilles every time. Some of his magazine choices seem to Alice quite surprising: one week he brings Hanna *Good Housekeeping*, another week *Woman & Home*, and one time *Country Life*. Still, Alice does see Hanna flicking through the magazines occasionally with an incredulous expression on her face, so at least they are offering her some distraction.

'You need to get her out of the house more,' Michael tells Alice.

'I've tried,' Alice says. 'I've suggested we go on walks and things, but she says she's too tired.' Or else does not reply at all.

'It's important to bring her out of herself,' Michael says. 'It's not good for her to dwell on things.'

'I know that.'

'I tell you what,' Michael says, 'I'll ask Olivia to come round and see her. She's very empathetic. She'll understand what Hanna's going through. I know she'll be able to help her.'

Alice thinks that this of all things is most likely to tip Hanna over the edge, but she does not say so, because she can see how frightened he is.

ALICE GOES BACK TO Edinburgh at the end of the Easter holidays to do her exams. It is a relief in some ways to be forced to focus on her work for a while. She rings Hanna every day, but doesn't have much luck with this; as usual, Hanna does not pick up her phone, and if Alice rings their mother to ask to speak to Hanna, Hanna is always too tired.

'Her brain needs to recover,' her mother says. 'Give her time.'

But Alice misses her sister. Hanna is always in her head, even when Alice is not directly thinking about her. It is strange how close Alice feels to Hanna during this time. It makes no sense, given Hanna is several hundred miles away and won't take Alice's calls. But Alice often feels an ache in her abdomen, just below her ribs, as if she has swallowed Hanna's misery whole and now she doesn't have space left to breathe.

BY THE TIME ALICE comes home for the summer, Hanna seems a little better. She is more alert and doesn't sleep so much during the day, though she still cries a lot. Everything seems to take her a lot of effort, from having a shower to going on short walks. Kemi is back home too and she and Hanna cloister themselves away in Hanna's bedroom for long afternoons to watch films. When Alice passes by the door one time, she is almost certain that she hears them laughing. She imagines for a moment going in to join them, but she has not been invited.

Hanna doesn't leave the house much during this time, but their dad and Susan do persuade her to come on a day trip to Whitstable with them. The change of scene and the sea air, their dad says, might do Hanna good. Alice finds all this quite a surprising turn of events, and clearly Hanna does too, because she says before leaving, 'I can see my ploy to get Dad's attention has finally paid off.'

Alice laughs at this, and can hear that she sounds slightly hysterical. But it is Hanna's first joke.

'How was it?' she says when Hanna is delivered back to them at the end of the day.

'Hard work,' Hanna says. She looks exhausted. It is only six o'clock, but she goes straight to bed.

DURING THE AFTERNOONS NOW, Hanna often sits out in their narrow back garden, reading or listening to music. Alice will sometimes go out to join her. She takes it as a hopeful sign that Hanna's concentration has improved enough for her to read again, and she likes sitting with her sister in the garden; it's the most time they've spent together in years. Alice knows she shouldn't be enjoying this so much given the circumstances.

Despite these hours together, they never discuss Hanna's illness directly, and after a while Alice starts to find this uncomfortable. She doesn't want Hanna to feel lonely, or like her illness is a source of awkwardness in the family; and she doesn't want them to be the kind of family that never discusses difficult things (though clearly they are). Alice decides eventually that she will have to be the one to change this, since no one else seems willing to broach the subject with Hanna.

'It's good to see you reading,' she begins one afternoon, as she and Hanna sit side by side in their garden chairs.

Hanna doesn't look up from her book, though she does raise an eyebrow. 'Thanks. I have actually been reading from quite a young age.'

'I mean, again. Now.' But Alice stops. Hanna knows what she means. Alice changes tack. 'It's nice to see you getting back to your old self.'

Hanna sighs at this, but does not respond.

Alice senses that she's already annoying her sister, though she's hardly even begun. But if she gives up now, she might never dare raise the subject again. She hesitates a moment longer, then says, 'You seem so much better now.'

'I am,' Hanna says. 'I had no choice but to recover. It was either that or receive repeated visits from Olivia.'

Alice laughs. 'It's so great that you're doing well,' she says. 'And you'll keep taking your medication, and you'll stay well.'

Hanna gives her a look. 'Yes, thank you, Nurse Ratched.'

There is a long pause, then Alice says in a rush, 'You know, you can still live a completely normal life.' She has done plenty of reading on this now. 'A lot of people do.'

Hanna turns to her. 'Alice, could you please fucking drop it? I don't need therapy from you. I've never asked for it. It was bad enough going through it all in the first place, I don't need to be reminded about it afterwards.'

Shaken by her tone, Alice says, 'I thought you might find it helpful to talk.'

'Well, I don't.'

'OK. Sorry.'

Hanna doesn't reply, but returns to her book.

'WELL, IT'S A HARD thing for her to talk about,' her mother says later, when Alice tells her about the failed conversation.

'But wouldn't it help her to talk about it?' Alice says.

'Clearly not.'

'Maybe if you tried as well . . .' Alice suggests.

'Let it lie, Alice,' her mother says firmly. 'She'll discuss it if she wants to, but she doesn't want to. Schizophrenia is a scary thing to talk about. What we must do is try our best to keep her steady, and prevent a relapse.'

'But she's already so much better now, isn't she?' Alice says. 'Another month or so and I really think she'll be OK again.'

Her mother gives her a look that seems to suggest Alice is an idiot. She says, 'She will never be OK.'

THE TROUBLE, HANNA THINKS later, was that their first meeting was too good. It had undone them. Far better to meet in an unstartling way that doesn't lend itself to mythologizing afterwards – through mutual friends, or online, or at a party you were both too drunk to remember. That way you might have a fighting chance of seeing each other clearly. The trouble for Hanna and Dan was that they thought their origin story was so good that it became a lens through which they viewed the rest of their relationship. The relationship became a tribute to the story.

Besides all this, since Hanna didn't realize she was lonely she also didn't realize she had to guard against the instincts of a lonely person. Pair up with me. Save me. Her illness, followed by the long, awful recovery, had made her susceptible, even three years later.

She meets Dan a few months after she returns to London following her graduation from Cambridge. Moving back proves more challenging than she had anticipated. Her mother, as it turns out, has taken it as a matter of course that Hanna will move back into the Morden house after graduating.

'I need to be more independent,' Hanna says.

'You can be independent from home,' her mother says.

'It's not the same.'

'It's good enough for Alice. Alice is back home again. It's a very normal thing to do.'

As if Alice is a reliable barometer for what's normal!

Hanna says, still trying to maintain her tact, 'I think it's important for me. After everything. To stand on my own two feet.'

'I just worry about you,' her mother says. 'Wouldn't you be better off here at home, where we can keep an eye on you?'

'I don't need an eye kept on me.'

'It hasn't been very long, Hanna. It's important that you . . .' But she stops.

What? Hanna thinks. Give up?

'Keep steady,' her mother says. 'Let me look after you.'

And isn't this what her mother has always wanted? To keep her children under lock and key? Those months when Hanna was back at home again, too ill to leave, must have been glorious for her. But Hanna hesitates now. She is being unfair. It was a harrowing time for her mother too. And of course Hanna is grateful for everything her mother has done, now that she is able to be. Deliberately, determinedly grateful. Still, she cannot help but wonder if there was a part of her mother that, whilst she would not have wished suffering on Hanna, nevertheless enjoyed having her in that weakened, dependent state. Perhaps part of the reason Hanna's so unwilling to discuss her illness with her family is that deep down she feels this sense of 'I told you so' coming from her mother, as if her mother knew all along that something was wrong with Hanna, and has finally been proven right.

Whatever the reason, Hanna knows it would be a dangerous surrender to return home now. It would be like being buried alive. (She is still prone to hyperbole, though even this hardly captures the aversion she feels to the idea of being shut up again in that bedroom, the scene of such terrible despair.) She will not relive those months of depression, the worst thing she has ever experienced. Hanna would have thought beforehand – if she'd ever given it any thought – that depression meant numbness, but it turned out that for her it meant feeling an overwhelming dread every moment she was awake. And the grief that crashed over and over her. She had been an open, bleeding wound. She cannot go back.

Both Alice and her mother are shocked when Hanna says she will look for a room online.

'What, with strangers?' Alice says.

'Strangers are just friends you haven't met yet,' Hanna says.

It will have to be strangers. Kemi is living at home to save money, Santiago has moved to Oxford to live with her boyfriend, and Lavinia has moved to Paris (because of course she has).

'With people you'll meet on the *internet*?' her mother says, her tone making it sound as if Hanna is planning to source flatmates from the dark web.

It is hard to stick to your guns in the face of such fierce and fearful resistance, but Hanna finds a room in a flat-share in Neasden where the rent is particularly cheap (explained by both the state of the house and the area; they are burgled within the first week of Hanna living there). Hanna can't afford anything else; she has found a job waitressing in a pizza restaurant, and it doesn't pay much. But all she needs is a bit of breathing space while she decides what to do next. She didn't apply for jobs in her final year of Cambridge as other people did, because it seemed almost inconceivable to her that she would actually graduate, that she would emerge from all of this with a degree and a future. It would have felt like a dangerous tempting of fate to think any further ahead than her final exams.

Then, with that strange sense of disorientation she experiences sometimes now, she finds herself with a 2:1 at the end of it all, and the world her oyster. But do you have to declare past major psychiatric illness on job application forms?

'Why would you?' Kemi says. 'It's nobody else's business.'

But it is hard for Hanna to believe it is all behind her, that she has somehow got away with it. 'What if they find out later and sack me?' she says.

'Then we'll take them to an employment tribunal,' Kemi says cheerfully. 'Anyway,' she adds, 'you're no more crazy than most people.'

'I suppose that's true,' Hanna says. She thinks of her mother.

So here is Hanna back in London, aged twenty-two, sharing a house with strangers, dividing her time between waitressing and filling out job applications, and above all trying to ensure that she doesn't go mad again.

The Dan thing begins with an invitation to a house party from Lola, the only one of Hanna's Cambridge friends currently living in London (Hanna had not considered her as a serious option for a flat-share because Lola is, well, Lola). Unfortunately, since Lola misses out the crucial detail of 'Close' when sending Hanna the address, Hanna ends up at a house on the wrong street: Clovelly Avenue instead of the nearby cul-de-sac Clovelly Close.

Hanna does think it strange that when she gets to the house, which is a Victorian period conversion like all the other houses on the street, she can't hear any sounds of a party coming from within. She wonders briefly if she is early, but she is never early. Perhaps the soundproofing is amazing, or else it's just not a good party. She presses the buzzer for Flat 2, and when the speaker crackles into life, a man's voice says, before Hanna can announce herself, 'Hey, come on up.'

The door buzzes and Hanna pushes it open. There is a narrow corridor with the door to Flat 1 on the left, and then some carpeted stairs up to Flat 2 on the first floor. The door opens just as Hanna reaches the top of the stairs. Standing there is a boy about Hanna's age, with rumpled sandy hair and a cheerful, open expression. He has pillow marks on one side of his face, suggesting he's just woken up from a nap. There is no music coming from the flat behind him, and Hanna can't see any other people.

The boy says, 'Hey, you're not Lauren.'

'And you're not Lola,' Hanna tells him.

It takes them a while to get to the bottom of this. By the time they do, they know each other's names, and Dan has heard about Hanna's unreliable friend Lola, and Hanna has discovered that Lauren is Dan's friend, who he was expecting around this time for their pizza and *Game of Thrones* night.

'We do get the post for Clovelly Close sometimes,' Dan says. 'I'm surprised we don't get more of their visitors too. This is actually the first time this has happened.'

'It must be annoying having to tramp around returning their post,' Hanna says.

'Oh, I don't,' he says. 'I keep it and read it.'

They smile at each other. Then Hanna says, 'I'd better be going. This party.'

'Second time lucky,' Dan says.

Hanna steps back and — she is not sure how it happens — misses her footing on the stairs. She might have fallen, but Dan jumps forward and grabs her just in time.

The door slams shut behind him.

'Shit,' he says.

Hanna, her heart beating fast from her near miss, steadies herself on the step. Dan quickly removes his hands from her.

'Are you locked out?' Hanna says.

'Yup.'

'I'm really sorry.'

'Not at all,' Dan says gallantly. 'I'm always getting locked out like this.'

'Exactly like this?'

'Yes, in exactly these circumstances.'

Hanna says, 'Does anyone you know have a key?'

'Yes, but I don't have my phone. It's in the flat. But it's OK,' he says, brightening. 'My flatmate should be back at some point soon, and he'll let me in.'

'Do you want to use my phone?' Hanna offers.

He shrugs. 'I don't know any numbers by heart except my mum's, and I'm not sure how much help she'd be. She lives in Norfolk.'

It suddenly occurs to Hanna that she could invite him to come with her to Lola's party. But that might seem weird. She hesitates.

'Look, it's fine,' Dan says. 'I really do get locked out all the time. Go to your party. Lauren and I can go round the corner to the pub whilst we wait for my flatmate.'

'Well, if you're sure,' Hanna says, seeing that the moment has passed to invite him to the party.

He comes to see her out, but at the main door they run into a new difficulty. Somehow, in the time they have been chatting at the top of the stairs, it has been deadlocked.

'Oh Christ,' Dan says. 'It's that tosser in Flat 1. He's always doing this.'

He goes to bang on the door of Flat 1, but there is no response.

'Yeah, he's gone out,' Dan says. 'He always deadlocks it on his way out, even if he knows other people are in the building. He's obsessed with burglaries.'

Hanna, reflecting on her own recent experiences, doesn't find this unreasonable. But she's dismayed by the situation. 'We're trapped here,' she says.

'Yes. In the nether zone. Sorry.'

Hanna sighs heavily. 'Has this happened to you before as well?'

He looks embarrassed. 'Only a couple of times. I really am sorry.'

'It's not your fault,' Hanna says through gritted teeth.

'If we want to go full *Peep Show*,' Dan says, 'we can get Lauren to feed us pizza through the letter box when she gets here.'

Hanna is not in the mood for jokes now. She's going to miss her party, or at least some of it, and this situation is starting to feel very awkward. But she reminds herself that Dan would not be stuck out here with her if she hadn't turned up at his door by mistake, so he's got just as much right to be annoyed as she has. However, he seems oddly relaxed about the situation. She is starting to get the impression that he is relaxed about most things.

'Will your flatmate definitely be back soon?' she says.

'Oh yes,' he says. 'Probably.'

'Probably isn't quite the same as definitely.'

She wonders about calling a locksmith, but doesn't have the money to pay for it, and doesn't feel she can suggest he pays given that it is at least partly her fault they are trapped out here. She sets herself a deadline: if the flatmate hasn't come back within an hour (an hour!), she will have no choice but to suggest the locksmith plan. She can't live here, in this corridor.

But for now she slides to the floor, leaning her back against the wall. After a moment, Dan eases himself down opposite.

'It's lucky,' Hanna remarks, 'that I don't yet need to pee.'

'That would be a challenge,' Dan says.

Also lucky that he's not a murderer or rapist, Hanna thinks (so far as she knows). She produces the bottle of wine from her bag – a five-pound rosé she got in the corner shop near her house – and says, 'Want some?'

She's started drinking again, having finally judged it safe to do so. Her sertraline dose is low these days, and the only effect of combining it with alcohol seems to be that she might get a bit sleepy.

They pass the bottle back and forth between them for a while.

'So how long have you lived here?' Hanna says.

'Two years,' he says. 'Since I graduated. I wanted to stay in London, and the rent was OK.'

He studied Product Design at Brunel, she discovers, and now he does computer-aided design for a visualization company in Lambeth (his office is near where Alice works, Hanna notes). Hanna has heard of some of the films he's worked on, and is impressed. His job sounds both creative and nerdy in a way she finds attractive.

Then Dan asks her about herself, and she tells him about the Neasden house, which leads to her mentioning that she graduated from university a year after her friends, and therefore had no one to live with. Dan proves the type to ask follow-up questions. So suddenly Hanna finds herself at the point where she can choose to retreat or go on and explain why she had to redo her first year of university. Of course, she will retreat, will say something vague about a family crisis, or claim she had glandular fever, or else pretend she flunked her exams and had to resit.

Except, just as she is deciding which lie to go for (she has tried out a few now, on various people, and has yet to pick her favourite), she hesitates. What if, just this once, she didn't veer away from the truth? She is half-aware that she is framing this as a kind of challenge to herself: tell this one person, since you are stuck here anyway, and since you will never see him again. This boy can act as the canary in a mine. She can examine how unnerved he is, and gauge from that what other people's reactions might be. If he responds with fear or disgust, she will never tell another person as long as she lives, but no one can say she didn't try to face up to it. No one can say she's a coward.

'Well, I got ill halfway through my first year at university,' she begins slowly. There is a touch of defiance in her voice too; she can hear it. She is daring him to judge her. 'Really ill, actually. First I stopped sleeping, and after that everything sort of unravelled.' She stops, regroups, forces herself to go on. 'Then, because I didn't realize I was ill, I got worse. And in the end, I sort of . . . lost the plot.'

'Lost the plot how?' Dan says. 'As in, got really stressed?'

'Yes, mainly that,' Hanna says. 'And also I got sectioned.'

'Christ!' Dan says. 'I didn't see that coming.'

'No,' Hanna says. 'It was quite the twist.'

'That must have been awful. I'm sorry.' He leans forward a little. 'What was it like?'

Hanna is moved, as well as surprised, by the simplicity of his response. People her age tend not to have learned yet how to respond with grace to painful topics. When Santiago told Hanna last year that her mother had been diagnosed with cancer, Hanna hadn't known what to say, had been more focused on not shaming herself by saying the wrong thing than on Santiago's feelings.

But Dan shows none of this self-consciousness. In his presence, Hanna feels a new, faint hope that she might not be marked forever by her illness.

She tries her best to describe for him what it was like to lose touch with reality, and he listens very carefully.

'You feel OK now?' he says eventually.

'Yes.' She hesitates. 'I was in hospital for a few weeks, then back at home for six months. Then I went back to university. But the thing is, it's never over. I'll always be worried now, waiting for the first flicker so I can catch it early.' Putting it into words for this stranger makes her realize how tiring the whole thing is. She has worked very hard to stay well, and still works hard. Although she doesn't need the olanzapine any longer, she still takes her sertraline every night, plus the occasional diazepam for anxiety. She monitors her moods carefully, cancels plans when she feels agitated or overtired, tries to get plenty of rest, calls her psychiatrist once a month to check in.

'It's basically a full-time job,' she says to Kemi one time, 'staying sane.'

'Except that nobody pays you for it,' Kemi says. 'So it's really more of a hobby.'

Now, Hanna tells Dan, 'Trying to guard against psychosis is a sort of paradox, because as soon as it's happening you've lost your insight, your ability to tell what's real and what isn't. So a part of me is always wondering if it's happening already, if it's too late and I simply can't tell.'

'That sounds frightening.'

'It is.'

When she first came out of hospital, she sometimes felt as if she'd woken up in a Salvador Dalí painting, everything in her landscape shifted or melted or distorted. Nothing was safe any longer, and whatever might have once been familiar, whatever she might have relied on, was changed or gone. For the first couple of months of her recovery, she would still see signs everywhere: a crow would fly overhead and for a brief moment Hanna would believe it was signalling to her – *a murder of crows, something is coming* – before she would remember that her brain was broken, and carefully, determinedly put the thought aside. So this was to be her life from now on: watching herself all the time, distrusting every thought, having to remind herself that the trees aren't sending her a message, that the birds aren't flying in a particular formation just for her. Nobody is following her, and nobody is listening to her thoughts.

Even now, more than three years since she was deemed well enough to return to university, everything feels precarious to her. It is like living without skin. But there is no one she can explain this to, because no one else could understand, not even Kemi, who understands everything about Hanna. Besides, Hanna has been enough of a burden already, enough of a downer to last everyone a lifetime.

But it has been shockingly easy to say all this to Dan, who looks at her so sympathetically, and is so unjudgemental in the questions he asks.

This is one of the first mistakes Hanna makes, being comforted by his reaction. She will not realize until much later on that she should have been wary. She is so busy feeling relieved that he isn't afraid of the psychosis that she doesn't see that it is more than this: in fact, he is drawn to it. There is still compassion in his response – Hanna is not wrong about that, and Dan is decent enough, as people go – but her mistake is in seeing only that, and not the prurience alongside it, how he savours her experience. How he is excited by it. There is an irony here, that Hanna, accused her whole life of seeking out drama, should so entirely fail to recognize this trait in someone else.

And they don't warn you, do they, exactly what to watch out for in lovers? The big things, yes, like outright cruelty or violence, but what about the subtler dangers? For instance, the risk of choosing someone who never really knows you, but knows only the version of you they have created in their own head. Later on, Hanna will learn to divide people into two groups based on their understanding of others. First, there are the people with no particular agenda, who will take their cue from you, who will wait quietly to learn who you are. Then there is the other group, the people who will not wait, but who conjure up a personality for you out of odds and ends of their own: some bits of you, certainly, but mixed liberally with scraps of their own needs and prejudices.

In Dan's defence, he is still young. He wants certain things from other people, and when he doesn't get them, he imagines them. He may later learn, as Hanna herself has to, to wait and listen.

DAN IS VERY INTERESTED in the fact that Hanna has a twin.

'Amazing!' he says, the first time the subject comes up. 'Are you identical?'

'No,' Hanna says.

'Well, are you similar in personality?'

'Not at all.'

'What's she like?'

'She's . . .' Hanna isn't sure she's ever consciously attempted to capture Alice's personality before. It's as difficult as trying to capture her own. 'She's nice. I think that's what most people would say. A nice person.'

'You're being very vague.'

'Well, I suppose she can be a bit *too* nice,' Hanna says. She looks for a succinct way to convey what she means. 'Alice is the sort of person,' she says, 'you can never watch sport with, because she always ruins it by over-empathizing with the losing team.'

Dan laughs. 'I think I see what you mean. Sort of.'

Dan had a sister once too, Hanna learns. She died in a car accident before he was born. His mother was driving, and Dan says his father never really forgave her. They had another child all the same – Dan – as a replacement, but it didn't make up for the loss, and they had divorced by the time Dan started school. Most of this information Dan has received from his aunt, his mother's sister, who has a drinking problem.

Dan says that although he didn't have any siblings growing up, he's never thought of himself as an only child: his whole life has unfolded in the shadow of his dead sister.

'It's a terrible story,' Hanna says. 'Your poor parents.'

'Yes.'

She can see how it still shocks him, even now, though there is something else in the way he tells and retells the story that she can't identify, something in the way he lingers over it.

The first time she meets Dan's mother, Hanna is surprised. Based on the tragic backstory, she had pictured Dan's mother as a fragile, wan-faced figure who rarely smiles. Dan hasn't said very much about her beforehand, always becoming evasive when Hanna asks questions.

As it turns out, his mother is a large, warm, robust presence, who hugs Hanna tightly when they first meet and keeps up a voluble flow of conversation throughout lunch. She wears her grey hair short and spiky, accessorized by large, colourful earrings, and asks Hanna a lot of questions about herself, responding with things like, 'Oh, wonderful!' and 'Well, I never!' as though Hanna is the most exciting person she has ever met. Hanna is utterly charmed by her.

'Sorry if she was a bit much,' Dan says afterwards.

'What? No, she was great,' Hanna says. 'I really liked her.'

'Yes, she's OK sometimes,' Dan says. 'It's my dad I really can't stand.'

'Parents can be tricky,' Hanna says, though she doesn't think there's anything tricky about Dan's mum. Imagine having a mother like that, who is so ready to be impressed by you, who doesn't pick apart every small thing you say or do. Imagine not having to take your mother's every remark and hold it up to the light to detect the sharp edge.

*

WITHIN A FEW MONTHS, Dan and Hanna have moved in together – a rented flat in Kilburn with large windows and beautiful light. By then, they have already started to argue. But they have their story, their quirky first meeting, and they have their laughter and the attraction that crackles between them. It doesn't occur to either of them to reassess.

They have done everything quickly, not just the moving in together – have gone almost immediately from being strangers to spending most of their time together. Hanna is in love with Dan, with his gentleness, his off-beat humour, his sandy hair that always looks freshly slept on. But above all, though she doesn't admit it to herself, what she feels is relief. Someone has accepted, even *chosen*, the maimed version of her, without knowing or caring that she used to be different – if he could only see how cool and confident she used to be! – and now she won't have to be alone anymore. And if the illness does come back (the terror that clutches her and stops her breath), there will be someone to help her, and she won't have to give up on everything and move back in with her mother. By being with Dan, she might be saved from becoming Aunt Katy.

Hanna feels chastened for the way she used to view her aunt. She knows now that Aunt Katy's illness was not a joke but a tragedy.

DAN SEEMS SURPRISED WHEN Hanna tells him she has been accepted on to the Civil Service Fast Stream.

'It's not what I imagined you doing,' he says.

Hanna shrugs. 'I have to do something.'

She can see that to him the civil service is a staid, unimaginative choice. Apparently he expects better of Hanna, assuming her to be wilder and more unpredictable. He hasn't realized, it seems, how Hanna craves stability and safety now. She wants a steady job, a reliable partner, a decent, affordable flat – all these sturdy foundations so that if the worst happens, if the earthquake comes, she will be shaken but not destroyed.

Dan says, 'You'll turn into your brother at this rate.' (He has had the pleasure.) 'Bustling around Whitehall and talking about the important memo you're working on.'

'Michael's not that bad,' Hanna says. She is surprised by her sudden urge to defend him. She adds, 'I'm doing the Diplomatic Service scheme, anyway. It might be quite glamorous. Think of the postings I could get.'

'Will you wear a pinstripe suit every day?'

'I might,' Hanna says. 'Unlike you, I don't see it as the zenith of human achievement to be allowed to wear jeans to work.'

Dan is silent for a moment. Then he says, 'I just don't want to see you wasting your potential.'

'What potential?' Hanna says. But she is nettled. She has started to notice this trait in him, his need to give her advice, to have views about her life as if he is better placed to judge than she is. He doesn't seem like this sort of person from the outside: there's a sweet diffidence in his manner when you first meet him, and those sudden flashes of boyish charm, as if he feels he is pushing his luck with you, and can't quite believe he's getting away with it. So it takes Hanna a while to notice how he also seems to distrust her, that he is unwilling to take her word for anything, that he believes she needs his guidance in all matters.

And he is never willing to concede. Nor, increasingly, is Hanna, and so arguments tend to rise up out of nowhere, from the most innocuous conversations, and escalate rapidly until they are enraged with one another and there is no way back to neutral ground. Hanna can see they are both at fault. She has never realized until now what an argumentative person she is. Maybe her mother was right all along; she is intolerable sometimes, even to herself. She can never let anything go, can never just ignore an irritating comment from him.

They argue about large and small subjects, from the death penalty (Hanna is against it; Dan, surprisingly, in favour) to TV programmes (Dan claims *The Sopranos* is hugely overrated, while Hanna loves it). One of their biggest arguments comes, totally unexpectedly, after Dan remarks that teacher training is a 'piece of piss'. It is unclear to Hanna – and remains unclear – what he is basing this on, since it is certainly not personal experience. Hanna protests that it isn't easy at all. Santiago has just completed it, and Hanna knows she's worked hard. The argument escalates, continuing for hours (how, Hanna isn't sure afterwards; it is as though their arguments are self-sustaining, carrying themselves along without much need for external participation). There is bad temper on both sides, and it ends with Dan refusing to come to bed with Hanna, insisting on sleeping on the sofa instead. Hanna is able to see afterwards that the argument was not really about teacher training, a subject she has barely thought about until that day; but she can't say precisely what it *was* about. Sometimes their relationship feels like a fight to the death, in which there is no space for their competing needs and opinions to coexist.

Perhaps part of the problem is not exactly that they are incompatible, but that they are too similar. Eventually, Hanna starts to see the same flaws in Dan as she sees in herself, and this is what makes it hardest to respect him. Sometimes she catches herself studying him with ruthless detachment, cataloguing his shortcomings; then it is disorientating, and a little frightening, to remember that Dan must do this too, that effectively she is looking into a mirror, judging harshly as she is judged harshly herself. Dan is quick to condemn other people, but is thin-skinned himself, and minds deeply what others think of him. He is impressed by people who Hanna feels are unkind, and yet hasn't she been dismissive of kindness in the past? Dan buys books by certain authors – Thomas Pynchon, David Foster Wallace, Herman Hesse – and displays them on his shelf, but although he probably intends to read them, he never does. He is always intending, but never doing. It is hard for Hanna not to tease him about this, though she can see how his face closes, how it makes him hate her. Why does she want to humiliate him, instead of helping him to cover up his weaknesses, as she tries to cover up her own?

One evening they go for a drink with her new friends from the civil service graduate scheme, and Hanna thinks they have a nice time. Dan is on his best, most charming form, making people laugh, asking them about themselves; Hanna is proud to have brought him along, proud to have him as her boyfriend.

But afterwards, when she says, 'Well? Did you like them?' he only says, 'They were OK.'

'Just OK?' It is impossible not to show how deflated she feels.

'Well, they were more or less what I expected. You know. Civil servant types.'

This again. 'How would you define,' Hanna says tightly, 'a "civil servant type"?'

'Just a bit . . . you know. Earnest.'

'They're not earnest. How can you say Ali's earnest? He's hilarious. He was making you laugh all night.'

'I was being polite.'

She sees he is not willing to give any credit to Ali, or any others in the group. But she is annoyed now. No one gets under her skin the way Dan does. When other people say stupid things, she is able to shrug and let it go, just quietly conclude they are being an idiot, so why can't she do this with Dan?

She says, 'Jen was a child actress, and was on a ton of BBC shows.

Then she moved to St Petersburg for two years after university, without knowing a single person or even, at the start, speaking any Russian. How can you say she's boring?'

'I didn't say boring. I said earnest.'

'There's nothing wrong with being earnest,' Hanna protests, before seeing she has lost her footing and conceded vital ground.

'I didn't say there was,' Dan says smugly.

BUT OFTEN, THEY ARE very happy together. When they are not arguing, they are exceptionally pleased with one another. Hanna seems to develop a kind of selective amnesia, so that during peace times she cannot remember the savagery of their arguments. Sometimes she imagines them being watched by an invisible audience, who will be impressed by how well they spark off each other, how much they make each other laugh, the obvious attraction between them. At other times, she wishes they had an audience because during some of their rows Dan will make horrible accusations – 'You're so arrogant! How can anyone bear to be around you?' or 'Maybe we should just break up,' or, worst of all, 'Do you think you might need to up your medication? You're sounding crazy' – that he will later completely deny having said.

'I would never say something like that,' he will claim. 'Don't invent stuff.'

It makes Hanna feel like she is losing her grip on reality again. She sometimes thinks about secretly recording him during their fights, but that too seems like the action of a mad person.

She tells her new friends at work their meeting story, and they say, 'Wow, that's so funny!' or, 'That's a great story for your kids.'

*

KEMI SAYS, WHEN HANNA asks if she can bring Dan along to the pub, 'Why not? You always do.'

'Would you rather I didn't?' Hanna is surprised. Kemi, usually so easy-going, sounds almost sulky.

'I wouldn't mind seeing you on your own,' Kemi says, 'every once in a while.'

'I thought you liked him.'

'I do. That's not the point.'

It is true that Hanna and Dan live together, so Hanna can see him whenever she wants. But she finds it reassuring to have him with her, and thought until now that she and Dan and Kemi made a good trio.

She says, 'OK, fine. I won't bring him.'

There is a silence on the other end of the phone.

'Are you annoyed?' Hanna says, incredulous.

Kemi says, 'I just don't see why everything has to change, just because you have a boyfriend. I don't see why we can't have our old friendship as well.'

'We do still have it!'

'No. It's not the same.'

Hanna is surprised at her. It is not like Kemi to be needy.

Kemi says, with the coolness of someone listing established facts, 'We don't see each other as much anymore, and when we do, Dan's there. And we used to speak on the phone every few days. Now it's once a fortnight at most, and not for long.'

'I'm sorry,' Hanna says. 'I've been busy with work, I guess. I'll try to make more time.'

'It isn't that,' Kemi says. 'It isn't that you're busy. We've both been busy before. It's just that I used to be the person you told about your day, and now Dan's that person instead. He gets all the pointless, funny

293

anecdotes each night, and then by the time you and I finally speak, you've forgotten them, and we just talk about general, vague stuff. He gets all the texture. I just get the outline.'

'I'm sorry,' Hanna says again.

'No, you don't have to be sorry,' Kemi says. 'I'm not explaining it well. It isn't that I blame you, even though it annoys me. Or maybe I do blame you a bit, but I can also see your side of things. I get that this happens when people get into serious relationships. Though to be honest, I didn't think it'd happen to us. So I need to adjust. I don't have anyone to tell *my* anecdotes to now.'

'You have Joe,' Hanna says. She likes Kemi's boyfriend very much, though Kemi still insists that they are not serious.

'But I don't want to tell them to Joe. I want to tell them to you.'

'You can still tell them to me.'

'No, by the time we speak, I've forgotten them, just like you've forgotten yours. Like, if something funny happens to me, I save it up to tell you. But then you're not free to speak for a week, and so by the time we talk, the moment's passed. Meanwhile if something funny happens to you, you just go home and tell Dan. So that's the imbalance. And it adds insult to injury if, when we're finally going to hang out, you bring Dan along.'

'Yes, I see,' Hanna says. She feels defensive, but she pushes the feeling down. Sounding more formal than she intends, she says, 'I'm sorry, Kemi. I didn't mean for things to change. I didn't notice that they had.'

'No,' Kemi says. 'It's always the person left behind who notices first.'

DAN SAYS, WHEN HANNA tells him about this exchange, 'Do you think maybe you and Kemi have outgrown each other?'

Hanna vehemently denies this. But she wonders all the same.

Perhaps because of Kemi's resentment towards Dan, Hanna finds that the only person she feels able to confide in about the volatility of her relationship is Alice.

Over coffee – they do this now, from time to time – she says, when Alice asks after Dan, 'He's fine. But . . . well, we had a huge fight last night.'

'Oh, I'm sorry,' Alice says, and really does look sorry. Most people would be leaning in to enjoy the story, ready to elicit all the juicy details (at least, Hanna feels that she herself would). Not Alice, who is allergic to any kind of conflict. She would rather everyone just pottered along quietly, being nice to each other. But what a boring world that would be, Hanna thinks.

When Alice doesn't ask, Hanna says, 'It was about whether white trainers look cool or stupid.'

To Alice's credit, she doesn't laugh. 'Have you made up now?' she says.

'Yes.' Hanna hesitates, then goes on uncertainly, 'The thing is, we fight quite a lot.'

Alice nods. 'But you do always make up?'

'Yes, of course.' She feels Alice has somehow missed the point, or perhaps she herself has not made the point clearly enough.

There is a moment's silence, then Alice says, 'Well, you're quite an exciting person. Fiery. I always imagined you'd have a fiery relationship.'

Alice makes it sound like a good thing. She makes instability sound glamorous. For a moment, Hanna finds relief in this vision of her relationship through Alice's eyes. But in truth, it doesn't feel glamorous to her. It feels tiring. She doesn't know how to say this to Alice. She is having the kind of relationship everyone expects her to have, perhaps the only kind she is capable of having, and Dan is handsome and funny and loves her, despite the fact that she was once sectioned and can't be relied upon not to get sectioned again in the future. So what is she complaining about?

HANNA HAD THOUGHT THAT old age, at least, might offer some protection against the kind of romantic upheavals she is experiencing. However, her father shocks them all one day by announcing that he has a new girlfriend.

'But he's almost *sixty*!' Hanna says to Dan in disgust. 'He's supposed to have settled down!'

'Do you think he dumped Susan, or Susan dumped him?' Dan says. 'No idea.'

Hanna, though she will not admit this even to Dan, and certainly not to Alice, is sad to see Susan go. She has grown fond of her over the years. It is true that Susan was never especially exciting, but she is a person who minds about other people's feelings, and Hanna appreciates this more now.

But Susan is out, and Christina is in. All Hanna has managed to glean so far is that Christina is originally from Denmark, though she has lived in England for years, and that they met at work. But this new relationship is apparently so significant that Hanna and Alice have been invited round for lunch at their father's house to be introduced. (Michael is in New York now, so is exempt from the whole thing, and might have refused, in any case, out of loyalty to their mother; he has remained, after more than a decade, little more than coolly civil to Susan.)

Alice also has some concerns about how their mother might view this meeting.

'Jesus, they've been divorced forever,' Hanna says. 'Don't be weird. And how is us meeting this new woman any different from us seeing Susan? Mum got used to that in the end.'

'I liked Susan,' Alice says mournfully.

Hanna only shrugs. Deep down, she is touched to discover their father still values them enough to want them to meet his new girlfriend. She will not admit this to Alice either.

ON THE DAY ITSELF, Hanna is surprised to find she is nervous. As a result, she takes Dan up on his suggestion of going for a pint in their local beforehand. Hanna had intended to stick to only one, but when they finish their first round and she asks for a Coke, Dan pulls a face.

'What?' Hanna says.

'Nothing.'

'I need to make a good impression,' Hanna says.

'Of course you do.' And he shrugs, as if it couldn't matter less to him what she drinks, or what she does at all.

Remembering all his comments about the civil service, Hanna wonders if he is taking this as further evidence of how tedious she is becoming. And perhaps he has a point. The old Hanna would never have worried about drinking too much before lunch. It's only this new Hanna who is so boring and careful, and who Dan is starting to dislike. Wounded by this idea, she says, 'Fine. Same again, please.'

By the time she gets to Barnes station, she is in much better spirits. She spots Alice immediately, standing just outside the station entrance, holding a cactus.

'It's for Dad,' Alice says, seeing Hanna noticing it. 'We can give it from both of us.'

'Does he have a particular thing for cactuses?' Hanna says. '*Cacti.*' She giggles at this.

'It's not a cactus,' Alice says. 'It's a succulent.'

This makes Hanna giggle again, so that Alice says, 'Are you all right?'

'Yes, fine. Sorry. A succulent.' She can feel the laughter rising up in her again, and accepts with dismay that the second pint on an empty stomach may have been a mistake. Trying to pull herself together, she says, 'It's very grown up of you to bring a plant for us to give him.'

'I don't feel grown up,' Alice says. 'When do you think that starts?'

'Not sure.'

They set off on the walk to their father's house.

'I hope it isn't awkward,' Alice says. 'I hope there aren't lots of silences.'

'There needn't be,' Hanna says. 'We just have to make sure we fill them. The Danish thing is useful, because it opens up lots of conversational vistas. Look –' she produces a crumpled piece of paper from her jacket pocket – 'I prepared a list of questions with Dan, to ensure we don't run out of conversation.' This was during the last ten minutes of their pub visit. They had been extremely pleased with their list.

Alice looks at her doubtfully. 'Are you sure that's necessary?'

'Yes. Now, I thought we could start with a series of questions on Copenhagen. I've heard it's a very clean city. Also, cycling in the capital – we'll get her take on it.'

'So long as we work the questions in naturally—'

'Of course.' Hanna scans the page. 'Also, are the Danes a religious people? Do they still think of themselves as Vikings?'

'I think we probably shouldn't overwhelm her,' Alice says. 'Not sure about the Viking thing.'

'The weather, too,' Hanna says. 'There's endless stuff we can ask about the weather. I think it gets really cold there. They might wear snow boots in winter. I've always wondered what snow boots actually *are*. We can ask her.'

'But let's not overdo it,' Alice says, sounding anxious now. 'She might not want to talk about snow boots.'

They have turned on to their father's street now, which is lined with grand semi-detached houses, the kind with stained glass in the panels of the front door.

'We're going to *charm* her,' Hanna says, though Alice still looks uncertain.

'Are you sure you're all right?' Alice says. 'You're not a bit . . . tipsy?'

'Only very slightly,' Hanna concedes. 'I'll be OK.'

They approach their father's door and Hanna gets to the brass knocker before Alice, banging it with more force than she intends.

'Hanna, this isn't a police raid!' Alice says.

'Sorry.'

Their father opens the door almost immediately, greeting them with an unexpectedly hearty, 'Girls! Welcome!'

He's lost weight, Hanna notices. She wonders if this is down to the new girlfriend. He's looking svelte. The word 'svelte' makes her want to laugh again, but she manages to control herself.

Alice proffers the plant, and he says, 'Oh, lovely. A cactus.' He kisses each of them awkwardly on the cheek.

'Actually, it's not a cactus,' Hanna says, stepping past him and taking off her jacket. 'It's a succulent.' Her speech, she is pleased to note, is clear and unslurred.

'They're not the same?'

'Well, cacti are a subgroup of the succulent family,' Alice says, sounding as if she has prepared a botanical lecture for the occasion.

'How interesting,' their father says, and he ushers them through to the kitchen, where he puts the succulent down on the side. 'And this,' he says, gesturing to the woman who steps forward as they enter, 'is Christina.'

Christina is a surprise. She is much younger than Hanna expected — around forty, Hanna thinks. She had assumed the new woman would be comfortable and motherly like Susan, hugging them and offering them chocolate pudding, but in fact Christina is all sharp edges and dark red lipstick, slender and elegant in a navy shift dress. She greets Hanna and Alice with disconcerting self-possession, coming forward to kiss them without ever making physical contact, like some kind of magic trick. She smells of something lightly floral and expensive. Hanna isn't prepared for such cool glamour.

She accepts a glass of prosecco from her father and takes a large swig to steady herself. Then, feeling she has to break the silence, which has settled upon them already, she says, 'Chilly today, isn't it?' A brief pause whilst she takes another sip of her drink, then she adds, 'Do *you* feel the cold much, Christina, being Danish?'

Christina looks surprised, then says, 'No, not especially.'

Alice, who has been watching Hanna with a wary expression, says quickly, 'It's so nice to meet you, Christina.'

'And you,' Christina says. 'I've heard so much about you.' Her accent is like the rest of her: subtle, measured, elegant. 'And twins, too. You must be very close.'

Since Alice doesn't seem to know what to say to this, Hanna fields it. 'We're sort of close,' she says. 'Not peas in a pod, but not chalk and cheese either. Though why chalk and cheese should be considered the two most dissimilar things anyone can imagine is beyond me.' She becomes aware that Christina is staring at her, and thinks that perhaps she has overdone the English idioms. She gulps down some more prosecco and then, to change the subject, says, 'What's the average winter temperature in Denmark, Christina?'

'I'm not sure,' Christina says, blinking. 'It can get quite cold. Maybe . . . minus fifteen?'

Hanna nods knowingly. Alice catches her eye, and seems to be trying to give her a repressive look. '*Snow boots*,' Hanna mouths at her.

Alice turns hastily to Christina and says, 'Dad says you've lived in England for fifteen years now? Have you always been based in London?' so Hanna can't get in any more questions for a while.

While Christina is talking to Alice, Hanna is able to study her more freely. She's very attractive, she thinks. And she wonders what Christina sees in her father, who's so much older than her. He does have money, she supposes. There's always that. He seems to have got richer over the past few years, while their mother has got poorer.

She tries to take another swig of her prosecco, and discovers the glass is empty. Her father discreetly takes it off her, and Hanna finds herself holding a glass of water instead.

'Been working hard recently?' he says to her under his breath. 'You seem a little . . . tired.'

'Yes,' Hanna says. 'I've been working very hard.'

'I'll get you some crisps,' he says. 'To tide you over until lunch.'

He can be a good father sometimes, Hanna thinks fondly.

HANNA HANDLES THE AWKWARD silences throughout the first part of lunch by making a series of increasingly specific queries about litter collection in Copenhagen, which Christina answers politely. Then Hanna's father takes over (rather abruptly, Hanna feels), and talks for a long time about the new line of interactive exercise toys his company is buying.

Hanna assumes Christina must find this interesting too, since she works for the same company. She wonders if her father was still with Susan when he and Christina first got together. On the phone, he'd told her offhandedly that he and Susan had split up, before informing her that he'd met someone new; but now Hanna thinks he may have reversed the order of events in the retelling. After all, he was still married to their mother when he began seeing Susan. Hanna watches him across the table as he smiles at Christina and reaches over to top up her wine. Hanna herself is sticking to water, and is already feeling a little better for it. The food is helping too. She thinks she's got away with it.

'It's a pity your brother couldn't join us,' Christina says.

'Yeah,' Hanna says, refocusing her attention. 'He's in New York, pretending to be important.'

'He is important, Hanna,' Alice says, because for some reason she is programmed to leap to Michael's defence. To Christina, she adds, 'He's an associate at a City law firm, and he's doing a secondment at their New York office.'

God, why don't you just marry him, Hanna thinks.

'That sounds very impressive,' Christina says. 'It's a shame Oscar couldn't be here either. He's at his acting class today.'

'Who's Oscar?' Hanna says.

'Christina's son, of course,' her father says, but not before Hanna has seen the quick glance Christina gives him.

'Oh! Great!' Hanna says, with excessive enthusiasm; she is trying to conceal her surprise. But this is so like her father, to have forgotten to mention this minor detail.

'How old is he?' Alice says.

Christina looks again at Hanna's father, more deliberately this time, and then turns to Alice and says, 'He is nine years old.'

'That's a lovely age,' Alice says, sounding like someone's grandmother. Then she asks some polite questions about Oscar's interests. Hanna has to admit at this point that Alice is doing quite well.

'He sounds very talented,' Hanna herself manages, as Christina tells them about Oscar's quickness in maths and the sciences.

'Oh yes! But you know, he enjoys drama most of all. He recently played Peter Pan in his school musical.'

'That's very impressive,' Alice says. 'The main part.'

'Everyone says he is a natural performer. He will do little performances when we are out, and even strangers are impressed.'

'He's an all-rounder,' their father says. 'Very talented. He has a lovely singing voice.'

Hanna realizes then that her father must know this child well, has presumably spent quite a bit of time with him. It gives her a strange feeling. She wonders if Oscar is neat and elegant like Christina. He sounds like an intimidating child.

He also, as it turns out, writes poetry.

'His poetry is very beautiful,' Christina says. 'He writes about animals a lot, but also about his feelings, and how he sees the world. He has a beautiful soul.'

'It sounds like he does,' Hanna says.

'And he is very attached to your father,' Christina adds. 'It's lovely to see them together.'

Hanna tries to smile at this.

Then her father stands up and says he is going to clear the plates so they can have dessert. Christina helps him, refusing offers of assistance from Hanna and Alice.

Whilst Christina and their father are out of the room, Hanna says to Alice, 'Did you know she had a kid?'

'No.'

'Why didn't Dad mention it? We looked like idiots.'

'It must have slipped his mind.'

'Absolutely typical of him.'

'This is quite hard work, isn't it?' Alice admits.

'It's like a Pinter play. Bet you're glad I prepared all those questions on Denmark now.'

'It was really strange when you kept asking her about recycling.'

'We haven't even started on Copenhagen's transport infrastructure yet.'

'*Please* let's stay off the subject of Denmark.' (Alice never knows when Hanna is winding her up.)

'But I want to hear about their cycle lanes—'

'*Hanna.*'

Christina and their father return then, bearing dessert plates and a lemon cheesecake.

'Cheesecake! Your favourite, girls,' their father says roguishly. (It is not.)

Once dessert has been served, the conversation turns briefly to Oscar again. Then, just as Hanna is gearing up to ask about Copenhagen's former tram system, mainly to annoy Alice, their father clears his throat.

'Well, this is very nice,' he says. 'It's very nice to see you both.'

Hanna thinks he's hinting for them to leave, which is weird because they've only just started dessert. She looks to Alice for guidance, but Alice is happily eating her cheesecake.

Their father goes on, 'There's something we'd like to tell you.' He pauses, awkward. 'Some good news,' he says. 'The thing is, Christina and I are getting married.'

Hanna stares at Christina, who is looking modestly down at her plate.

It is more of a shock than Hanna is willing to admit.

'Wow! Congratulations!' Alice says into the silence.

'Yes,' Hanna manages to add. 'That's great.' She smiles at her father and asks, 'Have you set a date?' which strikes her as an adult question. She watches her father look at Christina.

'In a couple of months, we thought,' Christina says.

'Wow!' Alice says again. 'How exciting.'

'What's the venue?' Hanna says.

'A hotel in Chiswick,' her father says.

'Oh, how nice,' Hanna says, rallying. 'Hey, I can get a new dress.'

Her father looks at Christina again, then says hesitantly, 'Actually, we're planning to keep it really small. Just us, really.'

And stupidly, Hanna still doesn't understand. 'So would you rather we all kept it a bit quiet, so people don't get offended?'

'I mean, it'll just be me and Christina,' he says.

For a few moments Hanna can't speak. Most of all it is a surprise to discover her father still has the capacity to wound her.

'What about witnesses?' Alice says.

'Well, Christina's friend and her husband are going to do that.'

'Right, yes,' Hanna says. A pause, then she says, 'Will Oscar be there?'

'Yes – but he's much smaller. We can't exactly leave him on his own, or dump him on a neighbour.'

You used to do that with us, Hanna thinks.

'Girls, you do understand, don't you?' her father says. 'It'll be easier this way. What with your mother, and everything.'

'Of course,' Alice says.

A silence, before Hanna remembers herself, and echoes, 'Of course.'

Another pause, then Alice says brightly, 'Well, how lovely. Congratulations again.' She raises her glass.

When they have all clinked glasses, Hanna pushes her chair back. 'Just nipping to the loo.'

Once she's locked the door behind her, she leans against the sink and tries to recover herself. But why is he remarrying at all, and why this new woman they'd never even heard of until recently? He was with Susan for over ten years (longer, for all they know), and never mentioned marrying her. But then it occurs to Hanna that the only difference might be that Susan never insisted on it. None of this would be driven by her father. So little ever was. As far as relationships are concerned, Hanna suspects that her father obeys Newton's first law: an inert object remains inert unless an external force acts upon it. It probably wasn't even down to him to exclude his children from the wedding. That was no more likely than it having occurred to him to argue. Even having known him her whole life, Hanna still has little idea of her father's personality. She is not convinced, in fact, that he has one of his own at all. A man with an indistinct outline, to be shaped by whoever he is with; standing water, ready to flow as directed.

What does it matter, anyway? Hanna turns on the tap and splashes her face. She is stone-cold sober now. She will go back and finish her cheesecake, and show them how little she cares.

You have such a coldness in you, Hanna, her mother has told her. *A real coldness. It frightens me.* Then she sighed and said, *Perhaps you'll learn to hide it better. Perhaps that's the best I can hope for.*

This was during a recent row, when Hanna was accused of not spending enough time with her family, but Hanna has heard the same from her mother in the past, about the coldness in her. She is cold, but she is also, at other times, overly emotional and dramatic. Hanna wishes her mother would make up her mind.

So there it is, Hanna thinks, turning off the tap. At least it might help her now, her natural coldness.

Back in the dining room, she reseats herself and takes a sip of her drink. Giving Christina her politest, most 'society' smile, she says, 'Christina, I've heard Copenhagen is an excellent city for cyclists. Is that right?'

Christina nods, looking slightly confused, and then slips away to use the loo herself. Hanna's dad goes to get another bottle of wine, which gives Alice time to say, 'Hanna, I'd literally *just* asked her the cyclist question. There was a long silence and I panicked. You've made us look mad.'

WALKING BACK TO THE station afterwards, Hanna and Alice don't speak much.

'I suppose we could always crash it,' Hanna says at last. 'Turn up in disguise.'

'He should have invited us,' Alice says.

'Well, they clearly don't want us there. And he was right that it would be awkward with Mum. At least we're saved from that.'

'But it's not right,' Alice says. 'It's not right that he didn't invite us.'

Hanna becomes aware suddenly that Alice is crying, silent tears that she wipes quickly away with the back of her hand.

'Hey, Al,' Hanna says. 'It doesn't matter. What do we care?'

'It's hurtful,' Alice says.

'All right. But it doesn't change anything. He's never wanted us around. Has he?'

She realizes when Alice doesn't reply that she was hoping Alice would contradict her. Which, of course, she does not.

'It doesn't matter,' Hanna says again.

They've reached the station now, and pause by the barriers to get out their cards.

'It's not even like I'd want to go,' Alice says, her voice thick. 'But I want him to have wanted us there.'

Beside her, Hanna is silent. At last she says, 'Hey, Oscar sounds like a right dickhead though, doesn't he?'

And Alice manages a weak smile.

IT COMES AS A surprise when Dan proposes, not only because they are too young, and none of their friends are anywhere near thinking about marriage yet, but also because they are going through a particularly rocky patch at the time.

'I don't care,' Dan says, when Hanna points this out. 'I don't want to lose you. I think we should get married.'

The source of their most recent trouble is Dan's new work friend, Jessica. She joins his company not long after Hanna meets Christina, and suddenly Hanna seems to be hearing her name all the time. Jessica and Dan have been working on a project together, and apparently Jessica is exceptionally quick and talented, as well as funny. She also, Dan tells Hanna, goes to the gym *every single day*. (Hanna is not entirely sure why she is being gifted with this particular piece of information. She feels vaguely accused.)

Hanna does her best to endure Dan's new enthusiasm. It is nice, she repeats to herself, that he gets on well with his colleague. It is nice. For a while, all of Dan's anecdotes seem to be about Jessica.

Then suddenly he stops mentioning her.

This, for some reason, is when Hanna really begins to worry. It doesn't help that now Dan goes out for drinks with his colleagues several evenings a week, which he never used to do previously.

'Maybe I could tag along sometime,' Hanna says. 'It sounds like fun.'

He shrugs. 'People don't really bring their partners along to work drinks,' he says. 'It would be boring for you.' But Hanna is sure she remembers him mentioning his colleague Nick's girlfriend having been there previously, and someone else's boyfriend; she is almost certain of it. Still, it is not like she can insist.

Dan also seems to have become more protective over his phone, or perhaps Hanna is just imagining that. He taps away on it quickly, and if she goes over to him, he turns the screen off. Hanna has never thought of herself as a jealous person, but it turns out that she is.

'But we had plans,' she'll say to him, hearing her own whininess. Christ, she sounds like her mother! And she and Dan didn't even have plans, not really. Just to have dinner at home together. Not surprising if he feels he's had a better offer.

'You said you'd be home by eight, and it's nine now,' she'll accuse him.

'One hour's difference!' Dan will protest. 'Does it really matter? It's Friday night, for God's sake! Look, I'm sorry, OK? I lost track of time. All the others were staying out way later than me. None of them had been given a *curfew*.'

Hanna will feel even angrier for knowing that Dan has a point; she shouldn't be berating him for being an hour late home on a Friday night. She is being pathetic. But she is maddened by it, as she waits for him at home, and the minutes go by, and it gets later and later. She pictures the fun he must be having, drinking with Jessica, laughing with her. Obviously by this point she has looked Jessica up on Facebook, and on the company website. She is not especially pretty, though she does have nice hair. Still, Hanna is not reassured. She also likes herself less for having looked her up.

Feeling herself losing him, Hanna makes a renewed effort. She starts to wear make-up again, and to choose her clothes more carefully. She even tries to get better at cooking. Yes, she can see how tragic all this is.

You've gone full Stepford, she imagines Kemi saying to her. But Hanna isn't confiding in Kemi much these days.

She is sick with fear at the idea that Dan is cheating on her, or that he is about to cheat on her. Over and over, she tries to talk herself down. It is not like he is going out on dates with Jessica. They are never one-on-one, from what Dan says. 'There were loads of us there,' he'll say offhandedly, when she asks who he was with. 'A really good group.'

And later, when Hanna makes the mistake of sharing her insecurities about Jessica: 'Come on, Hanna, we're just friends. I am allowed to have female friends, aren't I?'

Of course he is. Hanna doesn't know what's got into her. Dan has loads of female friends, and she's never minded. She likes them a lot, in fact, especially Lauren. So why is she suddenly obsessed with this Jessica person?

Finally, it occurs to her that this might be the beginning of paranoia again. Something's going wrong in her brain. The thought terrifies her. Dan seems to see it too. 'Are you *all right*, Hanna?' he'll say during some of their rows. 'Are you sure you're all right?'

Hanna resolves to resist the descent into psychosis at all costs. She will keep an iron grip on herself, and not ask him about Jessica ever again. But it is a hard battle. How depressing to realize that your boyfriend no longer wants to spend time with you. They don't laugh much together now. Presumably he does his laughing with other people. His arguing, with Hanna.

*

IT IS AFTER ONE of their bigger rows that Dan proposes. The row is about Jessica, though neither of them mentions her name. In fact, Hanna has kept her promise to herself and not brought up Jessica once since she made her resolution.

But on this occasion, she really does feel she is in the right. Because this time, they really did have plans. They were supposed to be going to the cinema together to see the nine p.m. showing of *Anna Karenina*, but at ten past nine Hanna is still waiting alone in their flat, Dan having not yet returned from his after-work drinks. Nor has he replied to any of the messages she has sent him. Hanna is starting to worry he is dead.

When he finally comes in through the door at quarter past nine, her relief lasts for only a split second before her anger obliterates it. It is immediately clear to her too, from the slight slackness in his face, the unfocused way he is looking at her, that he is drunk.

'What the fuck?' she says. 'The film started fifteen minutes ago! Where the fuck have you been?'

'Tube took ages to come,' he says.

'You didn't message me!'

'I was underground.' A pause. Then finally, 'Sorry, Han.'

'Well, brilliant. We've missed the film now. Thanks a lot.'

'We haven't missed it. It's only down the road, and it'll still be on trailers at the moment.'

'We'll miss the start. And I don't want to sprint there, buy tickets in a massive rush, then fumble about in the dark looking for seats while the film's already playing. I wanted to get there early, get some popcorn, pick good seats and enjoy the trailers.' At this description of what she wanted, tears of self-pity have started up in her eyes.

'Well, let's go tomorrow instead then.'

'I wanted to go tonight.'

'Well, let's go tonight then.'

Hanna takes a shaky, furious breath. 'We can't go tonight. It's too late.'

'It isn't too late if we hurry. Stop being so precious about your perfect cinema experience. It's a film, not your wedding day.'

'Fuck off, Dan.' She storms out, but it's a small flat, and there aren't many places to storm to, so she has to spend the next ten minutes pacing back and forth in their bedroom, too angry even to cry properly.

Later that night, when the anger has passed, and she feels mainly just tired and sad, she says to him, 'I don't want to do this anymore.'

'Great,' Dan says. He's sobered up now: the combined effect of Hanna's anger and several glasses of water. 'Let's stop all the arguing then, and just go back to how we used to be.'

'We can't,' Hanna says. 'I don't know how. That isn't what I meant.' With difficulty, she brings out, 'I think we should break up.'

A few beats, as Dan absorbs this. Then he says, 'No.' And more forcefully, '*No*, Hanna. That's not what you want.'

'I don't know what I want. I can't go on like this.' She begins to cry. 'I hate being like this. I didn't use to be like this. I don't understand what's happened.' She cries harder. His arms go round her, and for a moment she allows herself to lean against him, as if she can really be comforted, and by him.

'I'll change,' Dan says. 'We'll both change. Things will be different. I promise you, Hanna. We can't break up; we're meant to be together. We always were.' He is still slightly drunk, and above all still in love with the idea of them. He says, 'Relationships aren't always easy, are they? But we knew that going in. Surely what we have is important enough to fight for?' (This doesn't sound like a cliché to either of them at the time.)

And it's a little while after that, when Hanna has cried more, and Dan has cried too, that he says, 'I think we should get married.'

Hanna says, 'That's not a good idea.'

And Dan says, with that winning urgency she remembers from their early days, 'Yes it is. When you know, you know.'

'We're too young.'

'We're adults. We know what we want.'

'But you're only doing this because I said we should break up.'

'I'm doing it to show you how much you mean to me. Everything will be different if we commit to each other properly.'

And eventually, somehow, seeing an end to all their problems, Hanna says, 'Yes, all right.'

All great love stories involve conflict. Otherwise they might be nice to live, but they wouldn't be much good in the retelling.

HANNA HAS A SUSPICION that Kemi's reaction to the news of her engagement will not be one of pure, unadulterated joy, and she feels resentful about this. So the first person she tells is Alice, who can be relied upon for an uncomplicated response.

'Hanna, that's *wonderful*!' Alice says, as they have a drink in the pub the following evening. 'Do you have a ring?'

'No,' Hanna says. This is the first time it's occurred to her that she should have a ring. 'Not yet. It was quite spontaneous.' Then she adds, 'Anyway, engagement rings are a bit patriarchal, aren't they? A bit like a symbol of ownership. *This woman is taken*. Why don't men have them too?'

'Maybe you could both have one,' Alice suggests. 'Anyway, that's such happy news. Congratulations!' Then she goes to the bar and buys a whole bottle of prosecco for them to share, bringing it over in an ice bucket, with two flutes clutched against her body. Hanna is touched by this gesture. Alice doesn't earn much, and this is an expensive way to buy prosecco.

'To your engagement,' Alice says, raising her glass.

Hanna feels a rush of gratitude towards Alice, for her generosity and loyalty. She resolves not to take Alice for granted in future.

Her mother, too, is unexpectedly warm in her congratulations. Hanna had expected disapproval from her ('You're only twenty-six', 'Marriage isn't all it's cracked up to be', etc.), or at the very least some kind of insinuation that Hanna is doing it for attention. But instead her mother seems delighted.

'This is exactly what you need, Hanna,' she says. 'He's a very nice man, and he'll take good care of you.'

So, Hanna reflects, her mother thinks she requires care in the community. But at least she is being friendly for once.

Even Kemi doesn't launch into any of the objections Hanna had expected, meaning the counterarguments Hanna has rehearsed are not required. 'Well, that's great,' Kemi says. 'Congratulations.' But Kemi's reaction is far more muted than her mother's and Alice's, and Hanna is piqued by this, even though she'd expected it, perhaps because in truth she has doubts of her own.

WHEN HANNA TELLS HER father she is engaged, he rather surprisingly insists on taking her out for a celebratory lunch at an Italian restaurant in Islington. He himself is a newly married man now, so maybe he is more disposed to be excited about other people's engagements. Hanna is conscious of how flattered she is by his attention, and annoyed with herself for it.

Over pasta, he congratulates her, and over dessert – tiramisu for Hanna ('Not going for the cheesecake?' he asks her), a sorbet for him – he tells her Christina is pregnant.

Does he always save the big revelations for dessert, Hanna wonders, in case he needs to escape quickly afterwards?

'Really?' she says. 'How lovely.'

'She's four months along,' he says. 'It'll be a spring baby.'

But her father is too old to be having a baby. He looks especially old today: his cheeks are pouchy, as though they are sliding off his face, and his hair is thinning and grey. Most of all he looks tired. It is disconcerting for Hanna to realize how her parents are ageing. And one day they will be gone. It hardly seems possible.

'Darling, there's something I want you to have,' her father says. He hesitates, and Hanna watches him, curious. What does he have to offer that she wants these days?

But it is money. There's just a bit, he says, that he's been squirrelling away for a while. For a rainy day. He wants her to have it. For her wedding, and for her life with Dan afterwards.

Hanna looks down at her spoon, which she has been scraping around the little porcelain plate, trying to get the last residue of tiramisu.

He takes a folded cheque out of his wallet and passes it to her. When Hanna unfolds it, she sees the amount is £30,000. She cannot get her head around this much money.

'Put it in a savings account,' her father says. 'Keep it safe. Use it for the wedding, or as a deposit on your first home.'

Hanna is still staring at the cheque. 'Thank you,' she says eventually.

'The only thing,' he says, 'is that . . . well. Best not to mention it to the others.'

'The others?'

'Michael and Alice. I might be able to find something for them later on,' he says. 'But. Well, I want *you* to have this.'

Hanna does not ask why, does not ask anything at all, but he goes on anyway.

'I'm married now, of course. And the baby's on the way. The thing is, Christina worries so much for the baby, and for Oscar. He's never known his father. She's very protective of him, and of the baby. She hasn't had an easy life, and it makes her anxious about certain things.'

Hanna says nothing.

'I have to make sure they're properly provided for. She worries about it. And that's why, really, I want to make sure you have something now. Do you understand?'

She nods, though she does not really understand. 'Of course,' she says.

He orders more drinks then – amaretto for her and cognac for him – and tells her the baby will be called August if it's a boy (he pronounces it the Danish way, *Ow*-gust), and Alma if it's a girl.

'Your name looks a little Scandinavian too,' he tells Hanna. 'So you really will seem like siblings.'

But we will be siblings, Hanna thinks.

'I can't remember now why we decided to leave off the final h in your name,' her father adds. 'Maybe it was just an oversight.' Then he smiles at her – a strange, sad smile that she does not recognize – and says, 'You know, Hanna, you were always my favourite.'

Tears come to her eyes at this. It is not because she has finally heard what she wanted from him, but because now the moment has come, she finds it is too late, and she no longer cares. Most of all, she wonders why this feels so much like a goodbye. She doesn't know yet that she will not be invited to visit her baby brother when he is born, that every time she offers to come her father will make excuses, until Hanna finally gets the message that she is not welcome. She will only see her father a handful more times, all these occasions away from his house, in neutral settings, without Christina present. One time, he will bring August with him, but that is the only time Hanna will see her brother. She will never discover the reason for Christina's hostility, which will extend to Michael and Alice too. The woman is hateful, Hanna will eventually decide, and she will wonder how she didn't notice it during that first meeting.

Hanna has no way of knowing any of this yet, but somehow she senses a part of it. It makes her turn cold towards him, despite the sudden tenderness of his words, and she folds the cheque neatly and puts it in her wallet without meeting his eye. 'Thank you for the money,' she says.

As she walks back to the Tube, she thinks of when she was a child and he seemed like a god to her. For the imperfections of his love she had blamed herself. She cannot now remember the process of disillusionment, though she thinks it must have begun even before he left them. There is so much about her childhood she cannot recall, and many of her memories she does not trust. Nonetheless, she can articulate it now, almost, the feeling that her parents had owed her certain things, and that they have not paid.

'SO WILL YOU SPLIT it with Alice and Michael?' Dan asks her later that evening. His principles seem to rise to the surface sometimes, always at the most inconvenient moments.

'He might give them their own cheques,' Hanna says.

'Do you think he will?'

Hanna is silent. She had forgotten how Dan values certain kinds of fairness. After a moment, she says, 'Well, it's for our wedding, anyway.'

She already knows that she will not split the money. She feels it ought to be hers, that she has earned it, though through what process she cannot say. Plus Alice will tell their mother, of course, as she tells her everything. Hanna doesn't want her mother to know anything about this. She can imagine her mother's response – that Hanna is being bought – and hearing somebody else say it will make it true.

Dan is silent for a moment, and then says gently, 'It's up to you, obviously. But shouldn't a gift from your dad be shared between all three of you?'

Hanna shrugs. 'We're not that kind of family.'

LESS THAN A YEAR after his new son August (*Ow*-gust) is born, Paul is dead. A freak accident: a falling sign, which lands on him as he is walking between the Tube and his office one morning. The sign is red and yellow, metal, and has come loose from the front of a kebab shop. *Kebabulous!* it reads. It was (the inquest will eventually conclude) insecurely fitted to the wooden subframe on the shopfront, and had been improperly maintained.

In his last moments, Paul has paused briefly beneath the loosened sign to reply to a message from Christina. He saw her at home half an hour before, but this is irrelevant to Christina, who texts him at ten-minute intervals with updates about their son and questions about his current whereabouts. (He is not sure why; the answer is almost always 'at work' or 'on way to work' or 'on way back from work'.) But Christina does not take kindly to a delayed response.

It's a gusty day, and the metal sign is already tilting precipitously above Paul's head. He doesn't notice this as he types into his phone, but a workman putting up scaffolding a few doors down spots the danger and calls, 'Watch out, mate!' and then a man in a tweed overcoat crossing the road adds his voice as the sign pitches forwards: 'Hey, get out the way!'

The shouts come from different directions. Paul's head turns one way and then the other. Never in his life has he known what to do when receiving conflicting instructions. He hesitates, bewildered. There would not have been much time, in any case, for even the most decisive person to react. Within a couple of seconds, the sign has tilted all the way forwards and the final screws at the bottom have given way. Then it is falling, as the workman shouts a final, hopeless warning. Not many more seconds after that, Paul is dead. Passers-by manage to lift the hoarding off him, and the workman attempts CPR as they wait for an ambulance, but the head injury Paul has received is catastrophic, his death almost instantaneous. He is sixty-two years old.

Although the accident is reported in the national papers as well as in the *Evening Standard* and the *Metro*, Paul is initially not named in the reports, but simply referred to (inaccurately) as 'a man in his fifties'. Partly due to this, but mainly due to the fact that Christina decides to keep the information to herself in the immediate aftermath of the accident, Paul has been dead for almost a week by the time the children from his first marriage discover it.

WHEN ALICE TAKES THE call from Christina, she is lulled by Christina's calmness into a calmness of her own.

'Dead?' she hears herself saying. 'Are you sure?' Then, after a pause in which Christina outlines some of the details, 'Mm-hmm. OK. Well, thanks for letting me know.'

It is only after she has hung up the phone that she begins to tremble. The news seems impossible to absorb. And Christina has charged her with telling the rest of the family, so now she must call her mother, and Michael, and above all she must call Hanna. But she has not, she realizes, ascertained all the information she should have. Did Christina really say this happened on *Monday*, five days ago? Surely Alice, in her shock, misheard that part.

So when did it happen? And is the body still at the hospital? Can they see him?

She tries to call Christina back, but Christina, having discharged her duty so far as she sees it, does not answer. Nor does she answer any of Alice's calls over the following hour. Alice reminds herself that Christina is grief-stricken, that people behave strangely when they are in extreme emotional states. But she still feels it would be better if she had more information before breaking the news to her siblings and mother.

It is her mother she calls first, of course.

She can hear how steady her own voice is, despite how the rest of her body is shaking, and she hears her mother's sharp intake of breath. 'Oh, my poor darlings,' her mother says. But even at this unusual and unlooked-for tenderness, Alice does not cry.

'I can tell Michael and Hanna,' her mother says, but something makes Alice say, 'No, it's all right. I'll do it.' She doesn't know why, but she feels responsible for this appalling information, as though she herself summoned it into being when she took Christina's call. And for some reason her mother does not argue, for the first time in Alice's memory does not insist on her own involvement. Her mother sounds strangely depleted over the phone.

But Alice herself is filled with a terrible sense of purpose. It's Saturday morning, so it's likely Hanna will be at home. Alice gets on the Tube at Clapham North, changes at Waterloo. The strange calm is still present. It's like a chill at her core, though the trembling has eased. She is conscious, as the train hurtles along underground, of the cruelty of the blow she is about to deliver to Hanna, who has always loved their father the most. Alice does not want to arrive at the moment when it must be done. She imagines staying on the Tube instead, just riding up and down the Jubilee line forever, and never having to call their father's death into reality for Hanna. But how silly. The doors open at Kilburn and Alice gets off.

'OH. HI. DAN'S OUT at football,' Hanna says when she opens the door, as though it might be Dan who Alice has come to see. Then, 'What's wrong? Why are you here?'

A bit of an unfriendly greeting, Alice thinks, forgetting for a few seconds that something *is* wrong, and this isn't simply a social call. Then she recollects herself, and wonders how to begin. And now it occurs to her that this blow could be dangerously destabilizing for Hanna. It is true that Hanna has been well for years now, so that Alice has gradually learned to stop holding her breath. Still, she knows that this kind of illness does not ever really go away (she has her mother to remind her, were she in any doubt), regardless of Hanna's refusal to discuss it, or even acknowledge it.

But she is here now and the news has to be delivered. Should she make Hanna a cup of tea first? But this seems like an unforgivable delay. She tries to remember how she approached the task with her mother, and decides to follow the same pattern.

'I think you'd better sit down,' she says to Hanna.

'What, here?' Hanna says. 'In the hallway?'

'We should go to the living room.'

'You're being very strange, Alice.'

Alice can see Hanna is frightened now, so as soon as they're in the living room, she begins her piece. 'I'm afraid I have some bad news. Some very bad news.'

'What is it?' Hanna interrupts.

'It's Dad. Hanna, he died.' When Hanna doesn't speak, Alice gently outlines the few details she knows.

Then she waits for Hanna's reaction. But Hanna takes the news almost as quietly as Alice herself did, though her physical reaction is odd: she seems to pat herself down, briefly touching her arms and then her legs, as though checking for missing limbs, as though seeing whether she has made it through this announcement intact.

Then she says, 'A falling sign? What a stupid way to die.'

Alice wonders if there is something wrong with both of them.

Hanna says, 'What do you mean, five days ago?'

'I don't know if that's what she said. I might have misunderstood. I couldn't get through to her when I tried to ring back.'

'Well, try again now.'

Alice tries. Christina does not answer.

'Jesus Christ,' Hanna says.

They catch the bus together to Kentish Town to give Michael the news. What a way to spend a Saturday, Alice thinks: travelling around London telling people their father is dead.

Michael's response is a surprise too. Alice recites her script carefully – she's getting quite good at it, now she's on her third go – and then waits. She has by now come to expect people to appear underwhelmed by the news, so she is shocked by her brother's burst of grief. He has barely spoken to their father in years.

'He can't be *dead*,' Michael says. He is crying, and his words are indistinct. 'He can't be.'

Alice, sitting next to Hanna on the sofa, wonders when Olivia will be back. She feels that she and Hanna are ill-equipped to deal with this, that they need someone more emotional to step in. Michael keeps asking the same string of questions – when and how and was it quick and was it painful – none of which Alice has the answer to, but she realizes eventually that this doesn't matter, since Michael is not able to take in her

323

responses anyway. After a while Hanna gets up and goes to sit beside him. She puts her arms around him.

THEY GATHER AT THEIR mother's house that afternoon, the four of them, plus Dan, who sits beside Hanna holding her hand, and Olivia, who appears to be having the time of her life.

'It's just *dreadful*,' she keeps saying. '*Dreadful!* I can't get my head around it! Such a shock. My God, I almost fainted when I heard. Michael, didn't I almost faint?'

It's the first time in ages, Alice thinks, that they've all been together. Her mother looks like she's been crying, but since her mother does not acknowledge this, Alice doesn't feel that she can either.

Christina is still not answering the phone, so they remain unclear on many details.

'Weird to know your father's dead, but to know so little about it,' Hanna says.

'He might not be,' Michael says suddenly. 'What if this is just – Christina?'

Alice feels a brief stirring of hope. They do only have Christina's word for it, after all.

'Should we,' she begins, 'try calling Dad's phone?'

'I already did,' Hanna says shortly. 'It's off. And actually, now I think about it, I texted him earlier in the week, just to ask about the baby. I did think it was a bit weird that he didn't reply, because he usually does. Sort of makes sense now.' Alice looks at her, but Hanna won't meet her eye.

They look up the news reports then; it hasn't occurred to any of them to do this until now. This is how they at last fill in some of the gaps.

Pedestrian Killed By Falling Shop Sign, reads the headline in the *Evening Standard*. The reports from paper to paper are similar, usually giving the length and weight of the sign (Alice had no idea signs were so heavy), the time and location of the accident, the rough age of the victim and the fact that he was pronounced dead at the scene.

'It's so awful, seeing it in black and white like this,' Olivia says. 'I feel sick.'

'I remember reading about it at the time,' Michael says. 'On the Tube, on my way home from work. I remember thinking, Poor bastard. And then I didn't think about it again. I didn't realize it was Dad.' He sniffs and rubs his face. '*If* it was Dad,' he adds, with a touch of defiance.

'It seems likely that it was,' their mother says gently.

'Yeah,' Hanna says. 'He's dead all right.'

It seems likely to Alice too, despite Michael's resistance. The location is near their father's office, the age is more or less correct, and above all, Christina – though it is true that she has frozen them out since her baby was born – surely wouldn't invent a story like this. And why else would their father no longer be contactable by phone? Occam's razor, Alice thinks bleakly.

'But how are we meant to accept he's dead without seeing the body?' she wonders aloud.

Hanna says, 'I think we'll just have to use our imaginations.'

WHEN THE FOLLOWING DAY they have still made no progress with Christina, they call the hospital closest to their father's workplace, which turns out to be the right one. Michael makes the call in the living room at their mother's house, Hanna and Alice hovering behind him, their mother in the kitchen making tea for everyone. She did offer to ring the hospital on their behalf, but Michael seemed to feel it ought to be him.

'Thanks Mum, but I make a lot of important phone calls for work,' he said, causing Hanna to roll her eyes so hard that Alice was afraid they might fly out of her head.

They are eventually able to learn, after Michael has been transferred between several different people, that their father is indeed dead, that no amount of magical thinking can turn this into a grisly trick on Christina's part. Their father's body is no longer in the hospital mortuary, but has been released to the funeral director. Which funeral director? The person on the other end of the phone either doesn't know, or won't say.

They are anxious now in case Christina plans to hold the funeral without them, or has perhaps even held it already.

'But it's not possible,' Michael says. 'Nobody would behave like that.'

'Nobody *normal* would behave like that,' Hanna says. 'The woman's deranged.'

'But this all might be a huge misunderstanding,' Alice says. She has been thinking about this a lot. 'It might be that her phone isn't working properly so she isn't seeing our calls, and remember that she's just lost her husband. She might not be thinking straight.'

'Alice,' Hanna says. 'Don't be so—'

'So what?'

'So *Alice*-like. For once in your life, look at what's actually happening, not at what you'd prefer to be happening.'

Alice is stung. But they are all wounded at the moment.

'It's the will,' Hanna says suddenly. 'Don't you think it's about the will? She's getting everything and she doesn't want us to challenge it.'

'I doubt we'd have grounds to challenge it,' Michael says. 'Unless there's some technical invalidity.'

'Should we try calling the police?' Alice suggests.

Hanna raises her eyebrows. 'What are they going to do? Track Christina down and insist she invites us to the funeral?'

This was exactly what Alice hoped they'd do, but she doesn't dare admit this to Hanna.

'We can check the probate registry eventually,' Michael says.

They look at him.

'To see if Christina's executor of the will,' he says. 'And has applied for a grant of probate. To see if there *is* a will.'

'Shouldn't we focus on the funeral first?' Alice says.

'Well, we're not making a lot of progress with that, are we?' Michael snaps.

Alice feels like she might cry, but she forces the tears back and says, 'Maybe if we go and *see* her. Go to her house. It might be different in person. We can see if it was just a misunderstanding. And if it wasn't, then maybe we could sort of . . . appeal to her better nature.'

Hanna snorts.

Michael says, 'Do you really think she'll answer the door to us?'

'She might.'

'She won't,' Hanna says. 'It's no good. I don't think there's anything we can do.'

Alice doesn't remember ever seeing her sister look so defeated, except when she was at her most depressed, and she wasn't really herself then anyway.

Their mother comes back into the room at this point. Alice suspects she might have been listening at the door.

Their mother says, 'I think this has gone far enough.'

*

SO IT IS THEIR mother who goes round to see Christina the following day. Alice is the only witness to this, since Hanna and Michael can't easily take time off work, whereas Alice feels fairly confident that Lambeth County Council can manage without her for a while (or perhaps indefinitely). She takes a day of annual leave, claiming a family emergency. It feels like an evasion, even though it is true. She has told no one at work about her father's death.

Her mother has never seen the house in Barnes before, and Alice can tell, as they stand on the pavement outside, that she is taken aback by its size and grandeur. But her mother doesn't comment on this, simply adjusts her handbag on her shoulder and says, 'Right,' before striding down the path, Alice having to hurry to catch up with her.

At the front door, her mother doesn't immediately reach for the knocker, which surprises Alice, especially after their energetic approach. Instead they hover for a few moments, a couple of unwanted visitors readying themselves for the encounter – like bailiffs, Alice thinks. Or Jehovah's Witnesses. She wonders if Christina has seen them approach from the window, if she is watching them right now.

She says to her mother quietly, 'Do you think she'll be . . . ?'

'What?'

Nice, Alice had been going to say, but she knows how stupid that would sound. 'I don't know,' she says. 'I hope it isn't awkward.'

'We're only here for the funeral details,' her mother says with dignity, as if she is a person who has never behaved awkwardly in her life. 'It's no more complicated than that.'

She reaches out to bang the knocker.

Alice is bracing herself for the moment they must see Christina. It seems extraordinary to think her mother is about to come face to face for the first time with her father's second wife. And Alice, if she is truthful, has grown afraid of Christina, even though she hasn't seen her in person for a long time. Christina would not let them visit the baby, and in fact Alice has met her little brother only once, when she and Hanna went for a brief walk with their father on Wimbledon Common. August was only a couple of months old then, and had slept in his pram the entire time. The hurt of their exclusion still feels very fresh to Alice – and of course their father had gone along with it. It is strange to think there is someone out there who feels such an aversion towards Alice and her siblings. But they haven't done anything to Christina. It makes no sense for her to hate them. ('There are some really unpleasant people in the world,' Hanna has reassured Alice, unreassuringly. 'You can't always spot them at first glance.')

When some time has passed with no answer to the knock, Alice's mother bangs on the door again. This time, from somewhere within, they hear the sound of a baby's cry.

'She's definitely home,' Alice's mother says.

As they wait again, Alice finds she is holding her breath. She makes herself let it out slowly. Christina still does not come to the door. She must have seen them from the window, Alice thinks. Of course she will not let them in. She feels deflated, and foolish for believing her mother could solve their problems so easily, that somehow having a 'grown-up' involved would make a difference.

She is about to suggest they give up and go home when her mother raises her voice, startling Alice.

'Christina!' she calls. 'I know you're in there! We're not leaving, so there's no point ignoring us.'

'Mum!' Alice says, shocked.

'What?'

'I didn't think we were going to—' She breaks off, seeing her mother's face, and says lamely, 'I just hoped she'd answer the door.'

'Well, that was naïve of you,' her mother says. 'Clearly a more asser-tive approach is required.' She reaches out to bang the knocker again, and then calls, her voice even louder, 'Are you really going to stop my children attending their own father's funeral?'

'All the neighbours can hear you,' Alice says.

Her mother looks at her frowningly, as if to say, *That's the point*.

'Christina!' she calls again.

'I think we should go,' Alice says.

But now her mother is stepping off the path to peer through the front window. She raps on the glass, although Alice can see the front room is empty.

'We're not leaving,' her mother shouts, her face close to the glass.

'Mum,' Alice says pleadingly, 'I really don't think this is helping.' She can vividly imagine all the faces appearing in the windows of the sur-rounding houses now, but she is too mortified to look. How has this happened? They had not discussed the possibility of making a scene.

'This isn't going to work, Mum,' she says. 'She won't answer the door.'

'She will,' her mother says. She returns to the front door and bangs on the knocker again. 'I don't care how you behave after this,' she shouts. 'But you are not going to prevent my children from attending their father's funeral.'

Suddenly, the sash window above them is wrenched open, and Chris-tina's face appears. She looks furious, a far cry from the elegant composure Alice associates with her.

'I'm going to call the police,' Christina hisses, 'if you don't leave right now. You're upsetting my baby, and harassing me. It's *illegal*.'

Alice's mother doesn't seem phased by this threat. 'Feel free to call them,' she says. For a woman who had been shouting mere moments before, her voice is suddenly very calm. 'I'll be happy to tell them exactly why we're here.'

'I don't care what you tell them,' Christina says. 'You are trespassing and threatening me.'

'And I'm sure your neighbours will enjoy the show,' Alice's mother says.

'For God's sake!' Christina says. 'There's something wrong with you.' She withdraws her head and slams the window closed.

But a moment later, the door opens and they are face to face with Christina. She is paler than Alice remembers her, and holds August on her hip, a large, rounded baby with blond curls. He peers solemnly at the visitors. Alice stares back at him. He looks like their father, she thinks. It's more obvious now he's older. He has saliva dribbling from his mouth and as Alice watches, he blows it into a small bubble.

Alice's mother and Christina glare at each other.

Christina says, her voice low, 'You are harassing me and embarrassing yourselves. I'm grieving. What do you *want*?'

'You know what I want,' Alice's mother says. 'I want the details of the funeral so my children can say goodbye to their father.'

'They are not children,' Christina says. 'And I'm not stopping them attending. I've been very busy with all the arrangements. I'm *bereaved*, in case you have forgotten.'

'So are they.'

'They can come to the funeral,' Christina says. 'What do I care? I was going to invite them.'

'Good. Give me the details.'

Christina seems to hesitate for a moment. Then she shrugs. 'It's tomorrow. Mortlake Crematorium. Eleven a.m.'

'Thank you.'

Christina simply shakes her head in disgust and slams the door. Alice watches August's face disappear.

As they walk away down the path, Alice's mother says, 'She wasn't as attractive as I'd expected. I thought she looked rather gaunt, didn't you?'

THEY RING THE CREMATORIUM to confirm the details, not trusting Christina. It is a surprise to discover she is telling the truth.

'But can you imagine the repeat visit from Mum if she turned out to have been lying?' Hanna says. She seems to have found Alice's account of the morning's events amusing, which annoys Alice, because it was extremely stressful in person.

They are surprised to learn that their mother does not plan to attend the funeral with them. 'I don't feel the need to go,' she tells them. 'We've been divorced for a long time. Besides, I don't want to make things any more difficult than they already are.'

This seems like quite a sudden change of tack to Alice, but she does not argue.

ALICE ARRIVES EARLY IN Mortlake the next day. The crematorium is located just off the Thames path, so she takes a seat on a bench facing the river, her back to the car park, to wait for the others. It's a bright, lovely morning, and Alice is slightly dismayed to find herself feeling cheerful. She is looking forward to being with Hanna and Michael. Determinedly, she reminds herself that they are here for their father's funeral, and that they will soon have to face Christina. But a sense of unreality remains. It would have helped, she thinks, if they had seen their father's body – and if he'd been more of a vivid presence in their lives over the past few years. As it is, it is very difficult to grasp the fact that he is gone. My father is dead, she tells herself, experimentally. She does not seem to feel as much as she should.

Hanna and Dan arrive first, which is unexpected given Michael's famous punctuality. Dan hugs Alice and says, 'How are you feeling?'

'I'm OK,' Alice says, smiling at him. She likes Dan, who is charming and makes her laugh. His office is just a couple of streets away from hers, though she has only run into him once so far, whilst going to Pret to get a lunchtime sandwich (her Friday treat). But Dan had seemed genuinely pleased to see her when she tapped him nervously on the arm, and this had touched and flattered Alice. Dan makes her feel glamorous by association, and she wonders if Hanna feels the same. Though she supposes Hanna has always had enough glamour of her own.

Hanna is wearing her black parka with the hood up, though the sky is blue and clear. Under it, she wears black jeans and a black jumper. Dan is in dark grey jeans and a light grey shirt under his bomber jacket. Alice surveys them a little doubtfully. She herself is wearing a black cord pinafore dress over a cream roll neck. She is not sure if any of them looks smart enough. Briefly, she wishes that her mother were here too. But then Michael appears, coming along the Thames path in a dark suit and black woollen overcoat, and Alice decides he looks grown up enough to carry the rest of them. Olivia is not with him, which surprises Alice, though she decides not to mention it.

'Well,' Michael says abruptly, as if it is they who have been keeping him waiting. 'Ready?'

It's nice, Alice thinks, as they enter the crematorium grounds, to be arriving in a group like this. She feels less afraid of Christina now, although she does suddenly need to pee, which is usually a sign that she is nervous. She can probably go before the service, but she doesn't want to get separated from the others. Perhaps Hanna might come with her? But Alice can picture Hanna's expression if she asks to be accompanied to the toilet.

Then, as they approach the main building, and before Alice is ready for it, suddenly there is Christina. She is standing outside the entrance with another woman who looks a little older, both of them in black dresses and elegant heels. Christina turns as they approach, and her eyes fix on them. August is nowhere in sight. Alice would have liked to see him.

They draw level, but for a moment nobody speaks. The pause is excruciating. Alice wracks her brain for something to say, but comes up with nothing; all she can see, replaying in her head, is her mother hammering on Christina's door and Christina's angry face appearing at the window.

Michael handles the situation. Stiffly, he says, 'Christina. We're sorry for your loss.'

Christina inclines her head. She says, 'The chapel is straight ahead.'

And then, thank goodness, the encounter is over. But even once they're safely inside the building, Alice feels the chilling effect of Christina's stare. There is another uncomfortable memory stirring too, and as she follows Michael and Hanna and Dan down the corridor to the chapel, she tries to catch at the thread. Who does Christina remind her of? Then it comes to her: Milli Stephenson, all those years ago. Because Alice has been hated before, and it was just as difficult then as it is now to understand the reason behind it, unless it is due to some fundamental flaw in Alice's personality. She is relieved, guiltily, that Christina shows the same dislike for Michael and Hanna, so Alice doesn't have to view it as a personal failing this time.

Inside the chapel, Alice recognizes no one, though the room is already half full. She assumes the mourners are mostly friends of Christina's (perhaps of her father's too, but there's no way of knowing). There is no other family from her father's side; Alice's grandparents have been dead for years now. Her uncle, her father's brother, lives in Australia. Alice hopes Christina has told him what has happened. She makes a mental note to try to find him on LinkedIn that evening, perhaps contact him through his company email address.

She says to Hanna, 'Do you think I have time to go to the loo?'

Hanna rolls her eyes. 'Yes, of course. We'll save you a seat. Just try not to get caught up in the coffin procession when you come back.'

Alice finds the toilet, which fortunately is not far down the corridor from the chapel. She is very relieved not to run into Christina. As she washes her hands, she catches her own eye in the mirror. Your father is dead, she reminds her mirror self. The words still don't seem to carry much meaning.

When she returns to the chapel, she finds the other three sitting in the back row, a chair next to Hanna saved with Hanna's coat. Taking her seat, Alice says to her sister, 'What did you do to make Milli Stephenson leave me alone?'

'Milli who?' Hanna is squirming her way back into her coat. 'Freezing in here, isn't it?'

'Milli Stephenson. That girl who bullied me in Year 10.'

'Oh, her! Yes.' Hanna looks momentarily nostalgic. 'I said I'd tell everyone she was obsessed with you. I told her I'd bring in all the love letters she'd been sending to our house, and show them around.'

Alice takes this in. 'But she—'

Hanna sighs. 'Yes, Alice, obviously I made it all up. I was trying to play her at her own game. I would have gone through with it, probably. Forged some letters if necessary. I can be very convincing.'

Alice isn't sure what to say. 'Well. Thank you.'

Dan, who is sitting on the other side of Hanna, leans in. 'I can't believe I've never heard this story.'

'Well, I'm not actually all that proud of it,' Hanna says. 'With hindsight, I wish my whole plan hadn't revolved around our school's intense homophobia.' She gives Alice a sidelong glance.

Why is she giving me a sidelong glance? Alice thinks.

'I suppose you didn't know any better,' Michael says. He is sitting on Dan's other side at the end of the row, flicking through the order of service. 'This all looks pretty standard,' he says. 'The usual readings. That Dylan Thomas poem.'

'"Do Not Go Gentle Into That Good Night"?' Hanna says. 'That doesn't seem very suitable in the circumstances.'

'I suppose people often find it comforting. Especially since it's familiar,' Alice says. Despite her feelings towards Christina, it doesn't seem right to criticize the funeral readings.

'But he didn't have much opportunity to rage against the dying of the light, did he?' Hanna says. 'A bloody great sign fell on him.'

'And then there's "Do Not Stand at My Grave and Weep",' Michael says.

'Another classic,' Dan says. 'We had that at my grandma's funeral.'

'Ours, too,' Alice says. 'I really like it.'

Hanna doesn't reply. Alice suspects she would rather have a passage from an obscure Donne sermon; all this unoriginality bothers her. But there's nothing much original about grief.

The small chapel is filling up now. Alice thinks she recognizes a couple

336

of older men as colleagues of her father's, though she isn't sure. She tries to catch their eye to smile, but they don't look towards the back row as they enter. A woman in a large hat takes a seat in the row in front, and Alice's view is partially obscured. She didn't know people still wore hats to funerals. Briefly, she panics: should she and Hanna be wearing hats? But no, she reminds herself, even Christina isn't wearing a hat.

'Sherbet lemon?' Hanna says, reaching into the pocket of her parka.

'No thanks,' Alice says.

'Hanna,' Michael says, as Hanna rustles the wrapper and pops a sweet in her mouth, 'you're not behaving appropriately.'

'Forgive my social blunders,' Hanna says. 'I've never been to my father's funeral before.'

Dan laughs at this, and the woman in the hat turns round to look at them.

'She probably thinks we're funeral crashers,' Hanna mutters once the woman has turned away again.

Which we are, in a way, Alice thinks.

Then there is quiet, and music starts up, and the next moment the coffin is being carried in. Christina walks behind it, holding August. She is weeping. A small boy with dark hair walks alongside her, blank-faced; Alice assumes this must be Oscar. It gives Alice a visceral shock to see the coffin. She wasn't prepared, and suddenly she finds that she is crying too, messily, unexpectedly. Silently, Hanna hands her a tissue.

The pall-bearers place the coffin at the front and the officiant steps forward to welcome everyone. He is a bald man in a suit that looks slightly too small for him: one of those people Alice sees and immediately feels sorry for. But there is no reason to think he isn't happy with his life just because his suit doesn't fit, she reassures herself.

By the time he has finished his welcome, Alice has stopped crying. She pays attention to the readings as best she can, and to a piece of classical music she doesn't recognize. None of it seems to have much to do with her father. Nor does the brief eulogy, which is also delivered by the officiant. Listening to the words, Alice thinks they could be about anyone. They hear about his upbringing in Cornwall, his love of the sea (news to Alice), his passion for his work, his generosity and his sense of humour, all of it rendered, it seems to Alice, in rather general terms. She, Hanna and Michael are not mentioned at all, though Alice finds this doesn't upset her in the way she might have imagined. She wonders if it has hurt Hanna, but doesn't feel she can turn to look at her. There is substantial mention of August and Christina, and even Oscar.

'And now,' the officiant concludes, 'Christina would like to share with you a song that was particularly meaningful to Paul.'

'She isn't going to sing, is she?' Dan murmurs.

But no, they are going to be played the song through the sound system. The officiant fumbles with the remote for a moment, and then the opening piano chords pound out.

It takes Alice a moment to place the song, but only a moment. It's Journey's 'Don't Stop Believin''.

Now she does risk a glance at Hanna, whose expression of bewilderment must mirror Alice's own.

Was this song a favourite of their father's? Alice never heard him play it, nor even mention it.

Hanna says in her ear, 'Did he think of himself as the small-town girl, or the city boy?'

By the time the first verse begins, they are both shaking with silent laughter, despite Michael's disapproving glances.

*

THEY DON'T ATTEND THE wake afterwards. They have not been invited, and don't even know where it is. But Alice is relieved at this; it would be very awkward anyway, and they wouldn't know anyone except for Christina, who is hardly going to be keen to make small talk with them. Instead, Hanna, Alice and Dan go to a pub down the road. Michael says goodbye to them outside the crematorium, saying he needs to get some work done.

'Even today?' Hanna says.

'The work doesn't just do itself,' Michael says irritably.

'He's probably just distressed by the idea that *it could have been him*,' Hanna says after Michael has left, but she sounds half-hearted as she resurrects the old joke.

It is only lunchtime, but Alice finds herself *uncharacteristically* craving a drink. In the pub, she orders a lager shandy, and Hanna and Dan have beer.

After the first drink, Dan says he has to go. 'I said I'd be in for this afternoon's meetings,' he says. And to Hanna, 'You'll be OK, won't you?'

Alice watches Hanna's face close. 'Of course.'

He kisses her cheek – Alice is surprised Hanna doesn't turn towards him – and then pats Alice's shoulder, and is gone.

'It's a shame he has to work,' Alice says. 'But I suppose getting a full day off for your fiancée's father's funeral is trickier than getting the day off for your own father's funeral.' This seems to her like a convoluted sentence.

'He doesn't *need* to go in,' Hanna says. 'He *wants* to go in, wearing his dark clothes and a sombre expression, and tell Jessica it's been a difficult morning.'

Alice is shocked. 'Surely he——?' Then, 'Who's Jessica?'

'His work friend,' Hanna says.

'Oh, but if she's just a friend——' Alice begins.

'For now. If he's telling the truth. Anyway, he says it's all in my head, so I suppose it is. Not like me to be paranoid, right?' She laughs, without humour. 'No use worrying about it. Today should be about Dad. Another paragon of fidelity.'

Alice doesn't like it when Hanna talks like this. She thinks the alcohol might have been a mistake. Hanna's getting very morbid, as their mother would say.

Trying to ease Hanna's mood, Alice says, 'So which other eighties power ballads do you reckon Dad secretly loved?'

Hanna shrugs. She says, 'Guess we'll never know now.'

While Alice is still searching for a more cheerful conversational topic, Hanna says, 'Do you think Dad was pleased with how his life turned out?'

'I don't know,' Alice says. 'I wonder if anyone's life really turns out the way they hoped it would.'

Hanna is silent for a moment, and then says, 'Would you say life is a comedy or a tragedy?'

Alice is startled by this. Cautiously, she says, 'Neither, I suppose.'

'I think,' Hanna says, with the air of someone sharing a well-rehearsed world view, 'that there are two types of people in the world: those who view life as a comedy with a few tragic moments, and those who view it as a tragedy with a few funny moments.'

'OK. So which are you?' Alice says.

'The second, of course. All sensible people are in the second category.'

'I don't think my life is grand enough to be described as a tragedy,' Alice says. 'It's too small.'

Hanna doesn't reply to this, which makes Alice suspect she agrees. Instead, Hanna goes up to get them more drinks and some crisps.

'To our dead father,' she says, raising her glass when she comes back. 'I'm sure we've been cut out of his will.'

Alice says, 'Dad wouldn't do that. Wouldn't have done that.'

'Christina will have made sure of it.'

'What makes you say that?'

'Just a feeling,' Hanna says.

After that, Hanna gets increasingly drunk and, rather to her own surprise, Alice gets drunk with her.

THERE IS A WILL, but as Hanna predicted, they are left nothing in it. Alice wonders what miracle of foresight enabled Hanna to see in advance what most people could never have imagined. It turns out that their father made a new will shortly after August's birth, and it leaves everything to his second wife in the event of his death.

'We could challenge it,' Alice says. 'We could go to court.'

'It's not worth it,' Michael says. 'The legal fees, the complications. Trust me, it isn't worth it. Anyway, we don't really have grounds.'

'But it's *wrong*,' Alice says. She wonders if she is more upset about the will than she was about the death itself. If so, it doesn't reflect well on her. But of course it isn't really about the money.

'Do you think he didn't love us at all?' she says to Hanna.

'I don't know,' Hanna says. She has been unusually quiet since they learned about the will. 'I think he probably did. But it's sort of irrelevant what you feel if you don't act on it, isn't it?' She is frowning, looking away from Alice. 'His kind of love wasn't worth much in the end.'

AFTER THEIR FATHER'S DEATH, things seem to unravel very quickly. Correlation but not causation, Alice thinks later; it is not as though he had been some kind of linchpin in their lives. In fact, she is surprised at how little she misses him. The things that go wrong aren't related to his loss at all, or not in any obvious way. But Alice will always associate the beginning of the trouble with her father's funeral.

A week later, for instance: she is going to get the Tube home at the end of the day when she spots Dan and Hanna a little way ahead of her, standing outside the entrance of the station. They're kissing, and Alice quickens her step, thinking that now she and Hanna are getting on so much better, Hanna might actually be pleased to see her. But then Dan pulls back and says something to Hanna, who laughs and leans in to kiss him again, and of course it is not Hanna. Alice stops where she is, very abruptly, and the man walking behind her almost crashes into the back of her, has to swerve suddenly, mutters 'Fuck's sake' under his breath as he passes her.

Alice stands there, staring at Dan and the woman, feeling the blood pumping in her face as though it is she who has been caught doing something terrible. But they don't look round and notice her, which is probably for the best, because Alice has no idea what she would say or do. She imagines being like Hanna, storming over to confront them, oblivious to the scene she is making (or perhaps enjoying it). Alice isn't sure if her acute sense of humiliation is on Hanna's behalf, or down to her own failure to do anything other than stand rooted to the spot, gaping like a fish from a distance.

After a few moments more, Dan and the woman turn and head into the Tube station together. They are holding hands. So it must be serious, Alice thinks, if they are holding hands. It seems inconceivable to her, even having seen it for herself, that Dan could slight Hanna in this way. Why would he? What more could he want than Hanna? Alice isn't really aware of it, but she is experiencing a blow to her world view. If even this kind of love, between glamorous, charming people who have not had to settle just to avoid being alone, who have really and truly chosen each other, if even this kind of love isn't sacred, then surely no love is.

On the way home and all through that evening Alice broods on what she's seen. Of course she has to tell Hanna, but how? Somehow she feels more daunted now than she did when she had to break the news of their father's death, though that must have been because she was in shock then. Perhaps she is in shock now. Hanna and Dan are *engaged*. Alice feels a renewed fury against Dan, who has Hanna and still feels like he deserves more. And hasn't Hanna been through enough already? Her relationship with Dan had always seemed like a new beginning to Alice, a return to her old charmed life after her illness. Alice doesn't want to be the one to ruin this. And a small part of her is afraid too that if she is the one to tell Hanna, Hanna might blame her for it.

She wonders if the news might feel less devastating to Hanna if it came from Dan himself rather than an outsider. Because at least then Hanna would have the comfort of knowing Dan had decided to come clean, that he couldn't bear his betrayal of her after all. Alice tries to picture herself turning up at Dan's workplace, delivering lines like, 'If you don't tell her, I will,' and, 'I'll give you until the weekend, then that's it.' She cannot imagine saying things like this to anyone, let alone to Dan.

She is so distracted that Gabi frowns at her in the kitchen that evening and says, 'Alice, are you OK? Are you *sickening*?' And that night Alice can't sleep for going over and over it, and trying to work out what she should do, and how she could do it in a way that would cause the least pain to Hanna.

The next morning, feeling exhausted and wrung out, she does what's natural to her: phones her mother for advice. She tries to go through it all carefully and clearly, but she finds her voice wavering at the part where she says, 'And then I realized it wasn't Hanna. The woman wasn't Hanna.'

When she has finished, her mother remains silent. This surprises Alice, who had expected a torrent of outrage and disgust at Dan's behaviour; Alice had been looking forward to this, in fact, so they could both take some relief in condemning him, and expressing their own shock.

'What a shame,' her mother says eventually.

This feels rather inadequate to Alice, but she reminds herself that her mother has only just had this terrible revelation sprung on her, whilst Alice has had time to ruminate on it. Alice has no idea what she herself would have said if she'd had to pass comment immediately after seeing Dan and the other woman. Probably something much less coherent than 'What a shame'.

'But how shall I tell Hanna?' she asks her mother.

'Tell her?' her mother says. 'Of course you mustn't tell her.'

It takes Alice a moment to realize what her mother means. 'Yes, OK, it needs to come from Dan. But how do we make him tell her?' Again, she pictures confronting Dan at his office. The idea makes her cringe.

'No, that's not what I meant,' her mother says. 'I mean, Hanna needs to be protected from this information.'

Alice frowns. She has been pressing the phone too hard to her ear, and now becomes aware of this as her ear begins to throb. She switches the phone to the other side. 'I know we have to approach it carefully. But she needs to know.'

'Perhaps she does,' her mother says, 'but not right now. Not so soon after the funeral. Alice, she's just *lost her father*.' She sounds accusing, as if Alice might have had something to do with it.

'I know,' Alice says. 'It's awful timing. But — what else can we do?'

'Not tell her, of course,' her mother says.

'But we have to.' They seem to be going round in circles.

'And what if it triggers a relapse?' her mother says. 'Is that what you want?'

'Of course not.'

'Well, then.'

'We can't keep it from her,' Alice says. 'It's too big. And she's OK now. She coped with Dad's death.'

'This might be the straw that breaks the camel's back.'

This gives Alice pause, her old fears about Hanna resurfacing. What if Hanna has managed to stay well all this time, only for Alice to tip her over the edge with this news before she is strong enough to cope with it?

'It doesn't feel right to hide it from her,' she says. But she can hear the questioning note in her own voice.

'Why not,' her mother says, 'if it's for her own good? And besides, Dan might come to his senses. This could all blow over without Hanna ever needing to know.'

'But Mum —' Alice is newly aghast — 'she can't *stay* with him. Not after this!'

'Of course she can,' her mother snaps. 'Don't be so impractical. Dan's a nice man and he takes good care of her. She needs him. Don't ruin this for her just to clear your own conscience. That would be unforgivably selfish.'

Would it? Alice wonders if she has been presumptuous up until now in assuming she knows what's best for Hanna. Perhaps it's true that she's motivated more by a need to get this awful information off her chest than by a desire to help her sister. She tries to put herself in Hanna's shoes, to work out whether she would want someone to tell her. But she finds herself unable to imagine having a boyfriend like Dan in the first place, so her thought experiment doesn't get very far.

'Alice,' her mother says. 'You mustn't tell her. Promise me you won't.'

IT IS NOT THAT Alice is convinced by her mother's arguments. At the end of the phone call, she feels more confused than ever. But a day passes, and then another, and then a week, and although the issue of Dan and the Other Woman plagues her thoughts, somehow she does not manage to tell Hanna. And every day her mother will ask her, 'You haven't told her, have you?' and Alice will feel some measure of relief to be able to say honestly, 'No,' and at least remain safe from her mother's wrath.

It is only that she needs to take a bit of time to decide what to do, Alice thinks. So she hesitates, and stalls. But the more time passes, the more impossible it feels to broach the subject with Hanna. Because now, along with the difficulty of breaking the news in the first place, Alice will also have to admit to Hanna that she's concealed this news for a week (and then two).

After a fortnight, she messages Hanna to suggest they meet for a coffee. She has no idea yet of what her plan is, but she feels that things might become clearer when she sees Hanna in person. Unfortunately,

Hanna is unusually busy at work, and already has plans at the weekend. She suggests meeting the week after instead, and Alice finds she is relieved by this, as though she has been granted a last-minute reprieve.

By the time they finally meet, almost a month has passed. Hanna has suggested a post-work drink instead of a coffee, and whilst Alice would usually be delighted at the prospect of socializing with her sister, her anxiety builds as the day approaches. Now she is about to see Hanna in person, her previous decision to bide her time seems increasingly unjustifiable. The facts of the matter look bad: Alice has known for nearly a month that Dan has been unfaithful, and has repeatedly failed to tell her sister. Alice is appalled at herself. She doesn't understand how she has managed to justify this for so long, nor why she thought her path would become clearer over time. In fact, it is more muddled than ever.

THEY MEET ON A Thursday evening in a pub near Waterloo, at Hanna's suggestion. It is one of the grimier pubs along Union Street – the only pub in central London, Hanna says, that is never busy and where you never have to shout to make yourself heard. And she is right: unlike the heaving pubs along the Cut that Alice passes on her walk from the station, this pub is miraculously quiet when she arrives, the tables mostly empty. There are just a few small groups scattered throughout, plus a couple of old men who seem to be drinking together in total silence at the bar.

Hanna is at a table in the corner, two drinks already in front of her. She waves Alice over. 'I got you a pint of cider,' she says as Alice takes off her coat and sits down. 'I assumed that's what you'd want.'

Alice looks nervously at the pint. It took her two days to recover from the hangover after their father's funeral. 'Thanks,' she says. 'Have you been waiting long?'

'No, only a few minutes. I was quite startled to find I'd arrived early. Very unlike me.'

'How's work?' Alice says, deciding to warm up with a neutral topic.

'Oh, fine,' Hanna says. 'Well, good, actually. I realized recently that I'm one of those rare people who actually enjoys their job. How about you? How's the council?'

'Running like a well-oiled machine,' Alice says. The conversation feels stilted to her, so intense is her underlying anxiety. It is clear to her now – was immediately clear the second she saw Hanna – that she made the wrong decision, that she should have told Hanna straight away. She is shocked at the situation she's got herself into. She only did what her mother said, she suspects, because it gave her an easy way out.

'Are you all right?' Hanna says.

'Yes.' But how can she tell Hanna now? The moment for speaking up has not only passed, but passed so long ago that it must surely have lapped her several times by now.

'You know, I was thinking it's about time Dan and I set a date for the wedding,' Hanna says, when Alice doesn't speak. 'Everything's going better now. He's actually been really great recently. Feels like things have gone back to how they used to be.'

Alice is still silent, because to say something like 'Wonderful!' would only compound her betrayal.

'What's wrong?' Hanna says.

'Nothing,' Alice says, too quickly.

'Are you feeling all right?'

'Yes.'

'I thought maybe,' Hanna says, 'if you wanted to, you could be my bridesmaid. Along with Kemi, obviously.' She beams at Alice, waiting for her delighted reaction.

And in normal circumstances, this would be about the best thing Alice could imagine. Her teenage self would have been beside herself at the idea Hanna would ever like her enough to ask her to be a bridesmaid. But now it is like a cruel joke from the universe, a further reminder of what a terrible sister Alice has been.

'I can't,' she says, before she loses her courage again.

Hanna frowns. 'OK. No problem. Why not?'

For a brief, mad second Alice contemplates feigning an ideological objection to weddings. But it is no good.

Taking a breath, she says, 'I saw Dan.'

'OK,' Hanna says.

And although Alice hasn't provided any real information yet, she sees that Hanna has gone very still, as if she already knows what Alice is about to say. When Hanna doesn't speak again, Alice has to go on. 'I saw him with someone else.'

'When you say "with someone else",' Hanna says, deathly calm, 'what do you mean by that?'

'I saw him . . . kissing her. Outside Lambeth Tube station.'

'Who?'

'A woman. Some woman. I don't know.'

'Are you sure it was Dan?'

'Yes. I wasn't very far away, and they weren't kissing the whole time. They were also talking.'

'Right,' Hanna says. 'What did she look like?'

Alice tries to recall the woman's appearance as carefully as she can. 'Medium height, slim build. Shoulder-length brown hair. She was wearing a blue coat. And maybe white trainers, but I'm not one hundred per cent—'

'All right, I don't need the full police report,' Hanna snaps. More quietly, she adds, 'The bastard.'

'He is a bastard,' Alice says, enraged again on Hanna's behalf.

'I should have seen this coming,' Hanna says. Tears have come to her eyes, and she wipes them away quickly, furiously. 'Stupid of me. I thought things were getting better, but you see what you want to see, don't you?' She pauses, then adds, 'When was this?'

'When?'

'What day?'

'Friday,' Alice says.

'Last *Friday*?'

And now, of course, Alice is trapped. She had been starting to hope that there was no need even to reveal when it had happened; the important thing was that it *had* happened. But of course that was a ludicrous thing to hope for. Of course Hanna wants to know.

'Four weeks ago,' she says softly.

'*Four weeks?*' Hanna says, much less softly. The two old men at the bar turn their heads. 'Why are you only telling me now? Did you really say *four weeks*?'

'Yes,' Alice says.

'I can't believe this.' And Hanna really does look far more shocked at the delay than at the news itself. 'Alice, how could you do this to me?'

'I'm sorry!' Alice says. 'I'm so sorry. I didn't know what to do. I was worried about you.'

'God knows how long it's been going on.' Hanna rubs more tears from her eyes. 'Probably months. Or even longer. Shit, and there I was last night, asking him about setting a date for the wedding. Alice, you've made me look so stupid.'

'I'm sorry,' Alice says again.

'But why wouldn't you tell me?' Hanna says.

Alice had braced herself for her sister's anger, but she hadn't anticipated how hurt Hanna would be. This is much worse.

She says falteringly, 'I was afraid if you found out so soon after Dad's death it might be too much for you.'

'Why would it be too much for me?'

'I don't know.'

'What do you mean, "too much for me"?'

Alice stumbles on, 'I was worried it might make you ill again.'

'Why would it? I've been fine for years.'

'I know,' Alice says, feeling herself backed into a corner. 'But schizophrenia can be unpredictable, can't it?'

This silences Hanna for a few moments. When Alice dares to meet her eye, she sees that her sister is looking at her oddly.

'Alice,' Hanna says, 'what are you talking about?'

There is a long pause in which they simply stare at each other.

'I don't have schizophrenia,' Hanna says at last.

'But you . . .' Alice begins, only then doesn't know how to go on. Is Hanna deluding herself? Is denial of schizophrenia a sign of schizophrenia? But she can see she's getting her logic tangled here.

'That's Aunt Katy's illness, not mine,' Hanna says.

'But I thought—'

'That all mental illness is the same? One size fits all?'

'No, not at all,' Alice says, hopelessly out of her depth.

Hanna says, with forced patience, 'I was diagnosed with depression, which triggered the psychosis. That was the verdict of three different doctors.' She stops, then says in bewilderment, 'How can you not have known? Did you just assume it was schizophrenia because of Aunt Katy?'

'Yes, I . . .' Reluctantly, Alice adds, 'And also, Mum seemed to think that's what it was.'

'*Mum* told you?' Hanna seems stunned by this. 'But . . . why would she tell you I'm schizophrenic? She knows I'm not.'

'She must have been mistaken.'

'No. She was there at some of my appointments. They were very clear about it not being schizophrenia. They had to be, because Mum kept asking about it. Why would she lie?'

Alice doesn't know what to say. 'She wouldn't lie. Not about this. She must have believed that's what it was.'

Hanna says, 'Of course you're taking her side.'

'I'm not! I'm just trying to work out what's happened.'

'This is mad,' Hanna says. 'How have you spent all these years erroneously thinking I'm schizophrenic?' She starts to laugh, but breaks off again almost immediately. 'This is insane.'

'Well, we never used the word,' Alice says. 'The label. And you never wanted to talk about it. And . . . I suppose it *looked* a bit like schizophrenia.'

'It would only look like schizophrenia,' Hanna says sharply, 'to someone who's already decided it's schizophrenia.'

This silences Alice.

'This whole situation is absolutely bizarre,' Hanna says. 'How is *anyone* meant to cling on to their sanity in a family like ours? Does our mother just go around assigning mental disorders to people on a whim?'

'No,' Alice says. 'She must have misunderstood. Or I misunderstood.'

'I wonder what she's diagnosed you and Michael with,' Hanna says. 'I hope at the very least she's been telling people you have a personality disorder.' She stops, then says suddenly, her voice changed, 'How many other people has she told I have schizophrenia?'

'No one, I don't think,' Alice says, trying to keep pace with Hanna's anger and disbelief. She falters. 'Well, Michael, I suppose. And maybe Dad.'

'Dad went to his grave thinking I was schizophrenic?' Hanna says. 'Oh, terrific. Do you think that's why I was never allowed to go round there, or see the baby?'

'None of us were allowed to,' Alice says. 'And people with schizophrenia are very unlikely to be dangerous. That's a common misconception. Plenty of people with schizophrenia live a pretty normal—'

'Jesus fucking *Christ*, Alice! You don't need to be a cheerleader for schizophrenia anymore. Remember? Turns out I don't have it.' Hanna breathes out shakily. 'Why aren't you more shocked by all this?'

'I am. I just . . .' Alice's brain is struggling to keep up with this sudden rewriting of the last few years. How is it possible that she's spent so long thinking Hanna has the wrong illness? She says at last, 'I'm sure there's a reasonable explanation. I'm sure if you just talk to Mum—'

'I know she's unbalanced, but I don't understand why she'd be so invested in me having schizophrenia.' Hanna shakes her head in disgust. 'And I can't believe you just took her word for it and never asked me.'

'You never wanted to talk about it.' Besides, it isn't as though Alice has ever thought of Hanna as schizophrenic. She was always just Hanna. 'I don't think Mum meant to keep the idea going,' she says. 'It was a mistake.'

This is the wrong thing to say. Hanna's anger, barely under control before now, seems to peak. Her voice is cold as she says, 'You can't help yourself, can you? Whatever she does, you'll always defend her. Stupid of me to imagine anything might have changed.'

'I'm not defending her,' Alice says. 'I'm just trying to understand—'

'Well, maybe you should stop "trying to understand" and try facing up to things for once in your life. Everything has to be an accident or a misunderstanding, doesn't it? You can't handle the idea of anyone just being horrible, so you go into denial instead. You've done the same with Dan. You couldn't bear to acknowledge it, so you had to pretend it wasn't happening. You should have told me about him, Alice. You should have fucking told me.'

'I thought I was acting for the best,' Alice says, in tears now.

Hanna says, 'No, you're a coward.' She is on her feet, struggling into her coat.

'I'm so sorry,' Alice says.

'Of course you are,' Hanna says. 'You hate upsetting people. But in the end you just let people down.' Alice flinches at the contempt on her face. Hanna grabs her rucksack and slings it on to her shoulder. Then she is gone.

Alice becomes aware of the two old men at the bar looking over at her again. 'All right, love?' one of them says, and Alice wipes her sleeve across her face and says, 'Yes, fine,' which is obviously ridiculous given how much she is crying. 'I'm fine,' she says again, and tries to give them a watery smile.

She will never be fine, she thinks. Not now she has made Hanna hate her. She tries to gulp down the rest of her cider, which is flat and warm. There is a strange ringing in her ears, like the aftermath of an explosion. She gathers her coat and leaves.

CELIA HAS GROWN USED to being misunderstood. It has been the pattern of her life. But this is worse than anything she has experienced before, both because it is so outrageous, and because it is coming from her own child.

'I don't even know where to start,' Hanna says when Celia answers the door. 'You've really outdone yourself this time.'

'Perhaps you'd like to come in,' Celia says, trying to appraise the situation. 'Or would you prefer to harangue me from the doorstep?'

Hanna doesn't reply, but walks past her mother into the house. Celia follows her through to the kitchen.

'A cup of tea?' she says.

'No.'

'You really should have called ahead,' Celia says. 'I might have been out.'

'You're never out.'

This is hurtful and untrue, but Celia decides to let it go for now. 'Why don't you sit down?' she says, gracious even in the face of Hanna's rudeness. It is almost pleasant, in fact, to feel that she is the one in control of her emotions while Hanna is so out of control. Celia has a suspicion of what this is about: Alice must have let slip about Dan. She is determined to remain calm and imperturbable.

'I don't want to sit down,' Hanna says. 'Why have you been spreading lies about me?'

This throws Celia. 'Lies? What are you talking about?' And now her old fear is back: the illness has returned, despite their best efforts. Hanna is paranoid and accusatory. 'Just take a breath,' Celia says. 'It's all right.'

'It is *not* all right,' Hanna says. 'Why have you been telling people I have schizophrenia?'

This is so unexpected that Celia almost laughs. She says, 'I haven't been telling people that.'

'Yes you have. Alice. Michael. Dad. God knows who else.'

'Not for a long time. I don't know why they've clung on to the idea, if that is what's happened.'

'Probably because you *told* them and then never corrected it. Even though it was never true.'

Hanna has been pacing back and forth but Celia, trying to set an example of civility, takes a seat at the table. 'I may have mentioned it as a possibility, many years ago,' she says. 'It *was* a possibility. I felt we should be prepared.' It is true that Celia's worst fears have never been realized. It seems that the family curse has fallen on Hanna, but fallen slantwise: not Katy's illness after all, not exactly, but a related one. Certainly Celia would not say that she had been wrong in the beginning, even now; it was only that she didn't have all the information at the time.

She says to Hanna, 'Does it really matter what we call it?'

'Strangely enough, it matters to me.'

'None of us knew at the start what course your illness would take. The situation was very serious. We needed to face reality.'

'But it wasn't reality!' Hanna bursts out. 'You knew it wasn't. You were there at my appointments.'

'What do doctors know?' Celia says more sharply. 'They *think* they know everything, but they don't.'

'They see hundreds of patients with psychiatric disorders,' Hanna says. 'And you still thought you knew better than them. It's just so typical of you.'

'They may see plenty of patients passing through,' Celia says. 'But none of those doctors have lived with it. No one knows as much about that awful illness as I do. I've seen it up close. And it runs in families. You must know that. I was afraid for you. I was always afraid for you.' Her words seem to be running away from her now in her efforts to justify herself. 'I always knew this was coming.'

'Do you mean,' Hanna says, pausing in her pacing, 'that you've been waiting since I was a child for my latent madness to emerge? Well, that certainly explains a lot.'

That is not precisely what Celia had meant. If she were to try to puzzle it out now, she would say it was less conscious than that. But it is true that she's always watched Hanna with anxiety, her most volatile and difficult child. She thinks sometimes of when Alice and Hanna were toddlers playing with their shape sorter – Alice was so patient about rotating the shapes when they didn't fit, but Hanna was always quick to anger, would cry when she wasn't able to insert the shapes, and bash at the holes in frustration. Celia's heart would hurt for her daughter as she looked on, and she would hurry to help her.

She tried to tell the girls this story once, when they were teenagers, thinking it might amuse them to hear how early their different personalities had emerged. But Alice had said nothing and Hanna had said, 'I get it, you could see I was terrible even as a toddler.' This was not what Celia had meant at all, but of course Hanna would not give her the benefit of the doubt. Hanna will never know how every morning, even now,

Celia wakes with a falling sensation, the cold terror at what might become of her child.

'All I wanted,' she says to Hanna now, 'was for you to have an easy life.'

'Then why have you put so much effort into making it difficult?'

Celia is shocked into silence for a few moments. Then she says, trying to keep her own voice steady, 'Look, you're overwrought at the moment. You need to get all this back in perspective. I know you're upset about Dan, and that's making everything seem worse.'

There is a short pause. Then Hanna says, 'How do you know about Dan?'

And Celia is caught, because she can see immediately it would have been better not to have mentioned Dan. 'Alice told me,' she says, rather reluctantly. She has a feeling Hanna won't interpret this very charitably either, though she is nonetheless aware of a certain satisfaction in showing Hanna that not everyone in the family treats Celia with such total disdain.

'When?' Hanna says.

'Recently,' Celia says vaguely.

'Oh, sure,' Hanna says. 'This makes perfect sense. Alice saw Dan kissing someone else, and instead of telling me, I bet she went running straight to you.'

'She needed advice. It was very sensible of her.'

'Of course. That's why she didn't tell me for ages: you told her not to. I should have guessed.'

'It was for your own good. We acted in your best interests.'

Fiercely, Hanna says, 'You have never in your life had the first clue what my best interests are.'

'Of course I have,' Celia says. 'I'm your mother.'

'So what? As if being my mother counts for anything with you.'

Celia is speechless at the cruelty of this. She tries to remind herself that Hanna is in an emotional state; perhaps she doesn't mean what she's saying. After some thought, Celia says, 'We didn't want to upset you. And I knew you'd do something impulsive if we told you. I didn't want you throwing away a perfectly good relationship over something silly.'

'*Silly?* He's been cheating on me.'

Celia is relieved, at least, that she has managed to get Hanna on to a different tack. This feels a more profitable area of discussion than the question of who knew what about Dan and when, or who may or may not have schizophrenia. She says, 'Hanna, relationships are complicated. Dan's a decent man.'

'Perhaps he is. But not when he's with me.'

The next part, Celia will admit, doesn't come out quite as she intended it to. She says, 'What if you never find anyone else?'

'Jesus, Mum.'

'He will take care of you. There might not be another like him.'

'I don't need someone to take care of me,' Hanna says.

'You don't know that. You don't know you won't get ill again.' The lurch of fear is back. 'And then you'll need someone steady.'

'What, to help me cope with my fictional schizophrenia?' Hanna says.

'Well, whatever you choose to call it –'

'*Whatever I choose to call it?*'

'– you have a serious illness.'

'*Had*,' Hanna says.

'You need to take steps to protect your future, or you'll be sorry one day. You might wish you hadn't been so quick to dismiss Dan.'

'You really think I don't deserve a partner who'll be faithful to me?' Hanna says. 'I'm so damaged that I should just cling on to anyone who'll have me?'

'You're twisting my words. I just mean it's time you grew up and realized adult relationships are complicated. They take work.'

'Because you're such an expert,' Hanna says. 'Tell me, how successful have your relationships been? Dad left you, and there's been no one since. You don't even have any friends. Unless you count Alice, which seems pretty tragic to me.'

Celia feels a rage that frightens her. It takes all her willpower not to reach out and slap her daughter across the face. She says, 'If this is how you behave, is it really surprising Dan looked elsewhere?'

Hanna says, 'I don't know why I thought talking to you would help.'

EVER DRAMATIC, HANNA DOES not speak to her mother for a fortnight after their row over Dan and the schizophrenia misunderstanding. This is fine by Celia, because she is not speaking to Hanna either.

When Hanna does finally call, Celia assumes it is to apologize. But instead Hanna informs her — extraordinary, absurd — that she is leaving the country. She is taking up a job for the Foreign Office in Kuala Lumpur. She does not know, Hanna announces, if she will ever come back.

'So that's what you're going to do?' Celia says. There is a pitching, rolling sensation in her stomach that she identifies as anger (actually it is grief). 'Move all the way out there and pretend we don't exist?'

'I need to get away,' Hanna says. 'Have a fresh start.' She sounds cool and businesslike now, which Celia finds even more unsettling than anger.

'You need to get away from us? That's what you're saying?' Celia is almost crying, but the words keep coming. 'So everything's suddenly your family's fault, is it?'

'Not the family's fault,' Hanna says. 'Specifically, yours.'

'Don't be ridiculous.'

'You always loved me the least,' Hanna says. 'Just admit it. It doesn't matter now, so why not admit it?'

'Because it isn't true.'

'Of course it is. People think children don't notice these things. Of course they notice.'

'I loved you the same as the others!' Celia looks for a way to defend herself against these brutal accusations. 'If I was hard on you sometimes, it was only because you were a difficult child.'

Hanna says, 'A child will be what you tell them they are.'

'I wanted you to have an easy, safe life. That's all I ever wanted for you.'

'I'm a civil servant, for God's sake. My life only seems *unsafe* to you because I'm the one living it.'

'That's nonsense.'

'It isn't.'

'You're being selfish and unkind,' Celia says. 'But perhaps I shouldn't have expected anything else from you. You've always had a cruel streak.'

'Yes,' Hanna says. 'I know that. I've never liked myself much. But I think I might have been different with a different mother.'

Celia isn't able to reply to this, because the line has already gone dead.

WITHIN THREE WEEKS, HANNA has left the UK. It is the most dramatic flounce of her life.

Despite both Alice's and Michael's attempts to get in touch with her, she will not speak to either of them before she goes, not even with Kemi acting as intermediary.

'What if it's her illness again?' Celia says to Alice and Michael. They are sitting around the kitchen table in Morden. 'Why else would she behave like this?' She has seized on this idea, which both panics and reassures her.

'She's not ill,' Alice says. 'Kemi says she's fine. She's just really determined.'

'This is not a normal action,' Celia says. 'It's not the action of a sane person.'

'It certainly isn't,' Michael says. 'We should contact the authorities in Kuala Lumpur.'

'To do what?' Alice says. 'Have her committed for taking a new job abroad, which loads of people do all the time? Kemi says she's *fine*. She just doesn't want anything more to do with us.'

'Well,' Michael says, 'by the sound of it, you really did put your foot in it, Alice. Though I'm not sure why I'm being punished as well.'

'I should have told her about Dan straight away,' Alice says. She looks like she is going to cry again.

'You acted in her best interests,' Celia tells her.

Alice repays this attempt at reassurance by saying, 'But why didn't you ever correct us, Mum, when you realized it wasn't schizophrenia?'

'I didn't know what it was,' Celia says. 'Why should I? I'm not her doctor. Besides, it simply never came up.' She wonders why Alice is so determined to defend Hanna, despite the way Hanna has treated them all. 'I'm not sure why you're taking her side,' she says.

'I'm not . . .' Alice begins. And then, 'Well, somebody has to.'

Celia stares hard at Alice, who will not meet her eye.

'A few weeks seems a very fast turnaround to change jobs and move to an entirely new country,' Michael says. 'I think events must have been in motion for a while. I wonder if it was to do with Dad dying.'

'Well, if that's true, why on earth wouldn't she have told us?' Celia says.

'Perhaps she was waiting for the right moment,' Alice says.

Celia gives a short, rather hysterical laugh. 'How kind of her!'

CELIA IS CERTAIN, DURING the first months of Hanna's absence, that she will hear from her soon. But time passes, and Hanna does not get in touch. They know she is alive and well because they hear updates every now and then through Kemi, although Kemi is rather vague on the details. Yes, Hanna is enjoying her job. No, she doesn't know if Hanna has a boyfriend out there. No, Hanna doesn't seem to have any plans to come home.

Celia is deeply shocked by Hanna's behaviour. She could never, even during the most explosive of their past arguments, have foreseen this. But it is not as though Hanna showed much interest in her family even while she was in London, so Celia doesn't know why this new situation feels so unendurable. She is furious with Hanna, and she misses her. She thinks about her every day, knowing that Hanna most likely never thinks about her in return.

Every night, she finds herself saying what almost amounts to a prayer, though her views on God have not changed since she was a student: *Let her see how unreasonable she is being. Let her come home.*

They send Christmas and birthday presents. Celia knows that Alice emails Hanna too, though she does not ask what Alice says, and as far as she is aware, Hanna doesn't reply. There is some comfort, at least, in knowing that Hanna's coldness extends to Alice as well. That Celia is not alone in being shunned.

After the first year, Hanna does start to send cards in response to theirs, but her messages seem calculated in their curtness:

Dear Mum, Alice and Michael,
Happy Christmas.
Best wishes,
Hanna.

Best wishes? It would have been kinder not to have bothered at all.

CELIA HAS TRIED TO be thankful in the years since Hanna's departure for the two children left to her. But it is not enough. There is no recovery from a missing child. Hanna's absence feels like an amputation, the phantom limb still hurting every day.

Besides, Michael has offered little recently besides brief weekly phone calls (Celia suspects his wife is to blame), and even Alice has grown elusive. Sometimes Celia will have to ring repeatedly before Alice picks up the phone, and sometimes Alice will leave it hours before replying to her mother's text messages. Is Celia worth so little to her?

'I was at work, Mum,' Alice might say. Or, 'I hadn't looked at my phone.'

But everybody looks at their phone. And how long does it take to reply to a text message? Two minutes, that's all.

'You're all I have left,' Celia says.

And Alice says, 'That isn't true.'

But it is true. Celia's husband – ex-husband – is dead (and how like him to have died so frivolously), and so are her parents. Mark abandoned her and Hanna is lost to her. She has no contact with her sister beyond the occasional phone call in which Katy threatens to out her as a communist. But of course Celia won't burden Alice with any of this.

These days, she and Alice see each other twice a week: on a Sunday when they have lunch together and go for a walk, and then once for supper during the week. This seems to Celia about the least she can expect from her daughter. Some mothers see their children every day. Celia often feels that she is being squeezed in around the edges of all the things Alice views as more important. In these circumstances, it doesn't seem too much to ask that she and Alice will speak every day on the phone. It is not usually a particularly long call – often no longer than half an hour. Most daughters would be pleased to be close to their mother in this way. Celia would have been very glad if her own mother had wanted to speak to her on the phone every day. But there are still occasions – too many of them recently – when even this seems too much trouble for Alice.

It is not even as though Alice has many other people in her life. She has only ever had two boyfriends, and neither relationship lasted very long. Alice has never had a wide circle of friends either. Her mother has always been her main confidante. So if Alice doesn't answer the phone in the evenings, of course Celia worries something has happened to her. And if Alice does answer but says she can't speak for long, Celia can't fathom what else it is that Alice has to do. As far as she knows, Alice spends most of her evenings reading in her bedroom, or watching television with her flatmates.

If she can't rely on Alice, who can she rely on?

'You'll miss me when I'm gone,' Celia tells her, and Alice replies, 'Don't say that, Mum.'

Celia suspects her life would be easier if she felt a little less for her children.

SHE MIGHT HAVE BEEN forgiven for thinking that with Hanna's return, there would be a rapprochement. It is not that Celia has forgotten the things Hanna said to her, nor her appalling behaviour in cutting her family off for years. But all the same, Celia had felt a sudden, shocking lightness when she heard Hanna was coming home. And it would not have taken much from Hanna at all, just the smallest gesture of warmth towards her mother, some tiny indication that she wanted to put things right. There would be no need to discuss the past unpleasantness; they could have just picked up again as if nothing had happened.

However, at Katy's funeral Hanna was not exactly rude, but she was distant, formal, awkward. Like a stranger. Celia cried about it afterwards, once she was home. And that night, unable to sleep, she had sat up in bed hour after hour, thinking of Hanna. Most of all, she finds herself thinking of Hanna as a newborn baby: her beady little eyes like dark berries, her funny pursed mouth. The impossibly soft curls at the nape of her neck. It is one of nature's greatest cruelties that our children grow up and leave us.

A WEEK ON FROM the funeral, Celia forms a new plan to force a reconciliation with Hanna. The welcome-home party presents the perfect opportunity. It may only take a single, casual conversation, Celia imagines, in this kind of relaxed setting, for everything to be smoothed over. She has decided now that she is prepared to initiate things herself, since it has become painfully clear that Hanna will not.

Of course, it does not work out like this. Instead of accepting Celia's olive branch, Hanna storms out, leaving Celia standing humiliated amid an assortment of her daughter's peculiar friends. To be rejected so publicly compounds all of Celia's past grief, making it unbearable.

'Well, she didn't expect to see you,' Alice tells her the next day. 'She thought it was some kind of trap I'd laid for her.'

Celia is not sure if this is intended to be reassuring, but if so, Alice is not very good at reassurance. 'A *trap*? Is that what I am to you all? A *trap*?'

'No,' Alice says, 'of course not. It's just that she must have felt a bit ambushed.'

'I wouldn't have thought,' Celia says coldly, 'that a mother turning up at her own daughter's welcome-home party ought to count as an ambush.'

'She didn't expect you.'

'Well, why didn't you tell her I was coming?'

'I didn't know you were coming!' Alice says. 'I just mentioned that it was happening, I didn't know you were going to come. I didn't actually . . . invite you.'

Celia is too hurt to reply for a few moments. Then she says, 'You didn't want me there. I understand perfectly now.'

'It's not that. But it was a party for her friends. It was never supposed to be a family thing.'

'You were there, Hanna was there, Michael was there. Even Olivia was there. I fail to see how that wouldn't be considered a "family thing". But don't worry,' she goes on, before Alice can reply, 'I can take a hint. It's quite clear you don't want me around. I never thought,' she concludes, her voice shaking, 'that you would all go to such efforts to exclude me, that's all.'

'We weren't trying to exclude you,' Alice says. 'For God's sake, Mum. Not everything is about you.'

Celia is dismayed at the new sharpness in Alice's voice. Never in her life has Alice spoken to her in this way.

Alice is clearly as shocked as Celia is, because a short silence follows her outburst.

Eventually Alice says, not sounding as apologetic as Celia might have expected, 'It would have been better to have waited, that's all. Now Hanna's angry at me all over again.'

'Is that the only thing you care about?' Celia says. The cry of her childhood, of her whole life, rises up in her again: *What about me? What about my feelings?*

'Right now,' Alice says, 'yes.'

'Well, at least I know where I stand,' Celia says. 'Anyway, I have to go. I have things to do.' For the first time ever, she hangs up on Alice.

She tries to calm herself by making a cup of tea, which she sits at the kitchen table to drink. The room feels very quiet with only her in it, though she is always the only one in it. As the silence grows denser and heavier around her, she wonders about putting on the radio, but can't bring herself to get up. She is angry with Alice, of course, but much worse is the bleak realization that has come to her at last: there is to be no reunion with Hanna, not now, not ever.

She finds that her hands are trembling and stills them as best she can by wrapping them around the mug. There is a cold shiver within her that seems to go to her core, and cannot, it seems, be shifted by any amount of hot tea. Here she is, eight years old again. Unloved, unlovely.

2018

A WEEK ON FROM THE party, and Alice has heard nothing from Hanna. She has considered (several times each day) messaging her, apologizing again, asking if they can meet up. But as the days pass, Alice feels an increasing reluctance to do this. For the first time, she is experiencing strange stirrings of resentment against her sister. The feelings are so unfamiliar that it takes her a while to identify them. But hasn't she been here so many times before with Hanna, trying to mend things between them when Hanna isn't interested? Hasn't she run around after Hanna her whole life, always trying to please her, Hanna never pleased?

'Give her time,' Lavinia says, when they meet up for brunch the following weekend.

'But I have given her time,' Alice says. 'I've given her years already.'

'You're both older now,' Lavinia says. 'Things might be different.'

But things will never be different, Alice thinks. She has hoped for that long enough, and it's getting pathetic. Time to grow up (if only she knew how).

They don't talk about Hanna anymore after this; Alice feels, despite everything, that it would be disloyal.

She was surprised and delighted when Lavinia suggested meeting up. Often in the past she has felt a bit short of friends. Her colleagues at the council are mostly older than her, and although they are nice enough, no closer relationship has developed. Of Alice's three best friends from university, one stayed up in Edinburgh, another settled in Newcastle and the third moved to Vancouver, so it is rare for Alice to see them in person, though they do speak on the phone from time to time. Two are already married with young children, and the third is engaged. Alice is happy for them, but also disquieted sometimes at the way everyone else's lives seem to be moving forward, while hers stays the same year after year.

Of course, there is also Max, her university friend and ex-boyfriend, who she meets for walks occasionally. But their conversations remain curiously impersonal; they talk about work, and about current events, but Alice can't imagine confiding her feelings in him (this, she reflects, might be one of the reasons their romantic relationship faltered). Finally, there is Jess Moore from school, who unexpectedly found Alice on Facebook a couple of years back. Now Alice and Jess go for coffee sometimes, but if Alice is completely honest, she doesn't really enjoy Jess's company much more now than she did at school. Jess is single like Alice, and unhappy about it; she makes mordant remarks when they're together about how they will both die alone. Alice always leaves these meetings feeling faintly depressed.

So all in all, when Alice inventories her friendships, the catalogue seems disappointingly sparse. She sometimes fears that the judgement Hanna made when they were teenagers still holds true: Alice's best friend is her mother, if only by default.

Lavinia's invitation offers fresh hope, although Alice worried before the meeting that Lavinia might regret her impulse; Lavinia is so interesting and strange, and Alice is afraid of boring her. But to her great relief, the conversation has flowed remarkably easily between the two of them. Lavinia laughs often at things Alice says. Alice had not imagined her to be a person who laughs a lot, but it is pleasant to watch: Lavinia's face moves so quickly from grave to animated when something amuses her.

After they've finished eating and had a second coffee, they wander around Clapham for a while, still talking. Alice knows she should say she needs to go home now, that it is better to quit whilst she's ahead and before they reach the awful, crushing stage of running out of conversation. But she's finding it difficult to tear herself away. She feels a kind of excitement building within her as the time passes, and she wonders if Lavinia will want to see her again, and if so, when. She never, she thinks, felt this rising sense of hope with Max, nor on any of the dates she's been on since.

Then she catches herself suddenly: this is not a date.

'This is a date,' Lavinia says as they walk towards Clapham Common. She pauses and turns towards Alice. 'In my head, anyway, it's a date. Is it a date in your head?'

'Um,' Alice says.

Her moment's hesitation means that she never gets to answer at all.

Alice has always been a careful person. Most crucially, she always looks to her left and right before she steps out into the road. You might think she would be safe from accidents, but this of course would rely on other people being as careful as Alice, and other people are notoriously unreliable.

She does not see the boy coming, firstly because he is approaching from behind them, and secondly because they are on the pavement, where they might expect not to be mowed down. But she would have heard him coming, the telltale whir and rattle of wheels behind her, had she not been so entirely focused on Lavinia at that moment. The whole world had shrunk until it consisted only of Lavinia's face, her grey eyes.

So the first Alice knows of the young boy on the scooter is when he hits her, sending her flying forwards. She hears Lavinia's cry as she hurtles down towards the concrete. Although she tries to put her arm out to break her fall, there is not enough time, and she falls at an awkward angle, bending her wrist under her body and banging her head on the pavement.

Alice doesn't know it, but Lavinia responds quickly. 'You need to watch where you're going,' she snarls at the boy, as she crouches down by Alice who is now, terrifyingly, unconscious. She has a cut to her head which is bleeding profusely. A small crowd begins to form. Lavinia calls 999. The boy and his mother, who has finally caught up with him, have made themselves scarce.

Alice regains consciousness in the ambulance, and is initially confused about her whereabouts. She wonders if she is being kidnapped. Then she sees Lavinia sitting beside her, so either Lavinia is also being kidnapped, or they are travelling consensually. And for some reason Alice doesn't think of Lavinia as the sort of person who'd be likely to get herself kidnapped (unlike Alice herself, who would be a classic kidnap victim).

The paramedic says, 'You're all right. You had a fall.'

A fall? Alice thinks. Is she ninety years old? She remembers nothing of the accident, which the paramedics do not seem to regard as a promising sign.

In A & E, they clean the laceration to her scalp – it is fairly superficial, though head wounds always bleed a lot, the young doctor tells her – and put in three stitches. Her wrist is painfully swollen, but an X-ray reveals it to be a sprain, not a break, and it requires no treatment except rest and an ice pack. Then she is moved to a side ward, where she is to be kept in overnight for monitoring, in case of serious concussion.

*

IN THE SHORT-STAY WARD, there are twelve beds, most of them occupied. Alice is settled by a nurse into one of the free beds, the head board raised so she can sit up comfortably. It's strange to be treated like an invalid when really she's fine except for a bit of grogginess and a headache, plus the dull throbbing in her wrist. Alice feels like a fraud.

'Did you have plans for this evening?' the nurse says sympathetically, one young woman to another.

Alice briefly entertains the idea of saying, *Yes, just drinks with friends*, imagines being the sort of person who does reliably have plans for a Saturday night.

'No,' she says after a moment. 'Not really. I won't be missing out on much.' She had been intending to finish her book, and maybe have an early night.

Once the nurse has gone, Alice eyes her surroundings. The flooring is that cheap vinyl that she has only ever seen in hospitals – dull green and shiny in a way that makes her think of the surface of a lake. There is a small table and a blue plastic chair by the side of her bed, and a tray attached to the bed that can be pulled towards her. Some of the occupied beds have the curtain drawn around them, but in others she can see evidence of minor trauma: an arm in a cast, a recently stitched head wound, visible bruising to the face. A couple of patients seem to be asleep, or at least dozing, whilst others occupy themselves with their phones. Alice catches the eye of a few of them as she stares round the room, and tries to give them a cheery smile of greeting, but no one acknowledges her in return. She can't even make friends with her fellow comrades in disaster, she thinks.

Lavinia, who had squeamishly stepped outside whilst Alice was having her stitches put in, reappears now in the doorway of the ward.

'I briefly panicked when I couldn't find you,' she says. 'I was thinking of looking in the mortuary until a nurse directed me here.' Since Lavinia's expression and intonation remain as deadpan as ever, it is difficult for Alice to know if she is joking. Lavinia settles herself in the chair by the bed. 'Would you like me to go and fetch you anything from home? I could be back within an hour or so.'

Alice, slightly disorientated, thinks for a moment that Lavinia is referring to the old house in Wimbledon, her childhood home. She sees it so clearly in her mind's eye. Then she remembers that she hasn't lived there for eighteen years, that her home is one room of a flat-share in Clapham.

'Oh no, I'll be fine,' she says. 'Thanks. It's just one night.'

'OK.'

Still thinking of the Wimbledon house, Alice feels her mood dip. It is probably only that she is tired from all the afternoon's excitement. She lets her eyes drift around the ward again. In the bed in the far corner, she notices for the first time a girl who looks like she is only in her late teens. Her wrists are bandaged up to the elbows. There is nobody sitting with her. This makes Alice feel so miserable that she is actually afraid she might cry, which seems like an absurd overreaction to the sight of a stranger. But then, of course, she realizes that she is thinking of Hanna. So often it turns out she is thinking of Hanna, even when her mind seems to be on other things. In the days of her worst depression, Hanna said once, 'I want to die.' Once you've really feared for someone's life, you never stop fearing for it.

Lavinia says, 'You're thinking sad thoughts.'

'I'm all right,' Alice says. She seems to have gone down rather a morbid track. Perhaps it's the head injury. Making an effort to get control of herself, she says, 'Sorry this is how you're spending your Saturday. You really don't have to stay.'

'I'd like to,' Lavinia says, making Alice feel much better. 'Anyway, I've always been fond of hospitals,' Lavinia adds. 'They're a triumph of civilization.'

This makes Alice laugh, though again she isn't sure if Lavinia intends it seriously.

Then Alice sees Hanna appear in the door of the ward, which is startling; Alice wonders for an insane moment if she has summoned her sister with her recent thoughts. What is Hanna doing here otherwise?

'I called her,' Lavinia says, following the direction of Alice's gaze. 'I didn't tell you, because I didn't know if she'd come.'

'Of course I came,' Hanna says as she approaches. She sounds mildly offended.

'But I'm fine,' Alice says, torn between delight at seeing Hanna, and embarrassment at the fuss she's caused. 'I really am. They're only keeping me overnight out of an "abundance of caution", the doctor said.'

'Really, Alice,' Hanna says, standing by the bed. 'A scooter? I thought Lavinia meant a moped when she first told me, but no, a *children's scooter*. Christ, why can't our family ever have dignified accidents?'

'I'll get us all a coffee,' Lavinia says tactfully.

Alice watches her walk towards the door. The fluidity of Lavinia's movement, combined with her slenderness, gives her the appearance of melting away rather than leaving.

Hanna takes the seat Lavinia has just vacated. Neither of them seems to know what to say. Hanna is wearing jeans and an oversized red jumper, which Alice recognizes as one Hanna has had for years; it has holes at the wrists which Hanna used to push her thumbs through. Alice feels obscurely comforted by the jumper's presence.

'I called Mum, by the way,' Hanna begins. 'After Lavinia called me. I said you were fine, but she's coming in anyway. You know how she is.'

'You spoke to her?' Alice says.

'Yes,' Hanna says patiently, 'that's how I imparted the information.'

'Was she——?'

'She was fine. How's your head?'

'It's all right. Just a bit achey.'

They are quiet again. Alice reflects on the fact that all it has taken is a stupid accident to get Hanna to talk to her again. She wonders if she should have contrived to have one sooner, possibly years ago. Perhaps she could have faked her own death to lure Hanna back from Kuala Lumpur. If only she'd been more resourceful.

'How are they treating you here?' Hanna says, glancing around the ward. 'Have the doctors been OK?'

'Of course,' Alice says. 'And the nurses. Everyone's been great.'

'Good.'

Another silence. Alice can't think of a single thing to say.

Hanna says, offhandedly, 'So this kid on a scooter.'

'Yes.'

'Was it a hit and run?'

Alice tries to ignore the amusement on Hanna's face. She says, 'Well, Lavinia says he and his mum didn't stick around.'

'I wonder if he was over the limit,' Hanna says.

'It's not funny,' Alice says. 'If he'd hit an old lady or something he could have done real damage.'

'Yes, yes, I know. Sorry.' Hanna does look contrite for a moment, then adds, 'Though an old lady might have been quicker at getting out the way.'

'I was distracted,' Alice says.

'Yes,' Hanna says, seeming to imbue Alice's comment with more meaning than Alice intended. After a moment, she adds delicately, 'So, are you and Lavinia . . . ?'

This startles Alice. 'I don't know,' she says, feeling her face getting hot. 'We were only going out for brunch.'

'OK,' Hanna says. A pause. 'Have you always—?'

'I don't know,' Alice says again. She really doesn't. Everything has always felt like such a muddle. 'The person you're seeing,' she says diffidently, trying to change the subject. 'Is he nice?'

Hanna looks surprised. 'I'm not seeing anyone.'

'I thought you said when we had coffee—'

'Right – that. No, I was just winding Michael up.'

'Oh, OK,' Alice says, deflated. 'But did you meet anyone in KL?'

Hanna laughs. 'Yeah, I *met* quite a few people. But I want a boyfriend, now I'm home. A proper, serious boyfriend, who is nice and reliable, but not boring. That's not asking too much, is it?'

'No,' Alice says. 'That's not asking too much at all.'

'Kemi says she has someone in mind, though I have serious doubts about her judgement. Not that mine's infallible.' Hanna pauses, then says, 'Did you know that Dan actually *married* that Jessica woman he cheated on me with?'

'God!'

'Yeah, they have a baby now. I looked him up on Instagram. But I didn't really feel that much when I saw it. It was such a long time ago.'

'He was an idiot,' Alice says.

Hanna smiles at her. 'Well, it doesn't matter now. Water under the bridge.'

Alice wonders if this comment relates only to Dan, or to herself as well. She says, since now seems as good a time as any, 'You know, I didn't invite Mum to the party. I really didn't.'

Hanna nods. 'Yeah, OK. I may have overreacted. Somewhat.'

'I would have been annoyed too,' Alice says.

'It was a bit of a shock,' Hanna says. 'I felt like there was no escape from her.'

'I feel like that sometimes too,' Alice says disloyally.

Hanna gives her another of her sudden, delightful smiles. 'I know you do.' Then she adds, somewhat lessening the effect, 'Though you have to admit, you don't exactly help yourself there.'

'I know,' Alice says humbly.

'Anyway,' Hanna says, 'it was a nice party. I should've messaged you afterwards to say thanks. No manners.'

'You're welcome,' Alice says. She feels unreasonably pleased to have the party described as 'nice' by Hanna.

Hanna is silent for a few moments. She has grown thoughtful – awkward, even – and Alice tries not to feel alarmed.

'By the way,' Hanna says eventually. 'I have something for you.'

'What?' Alice says.

'Ten grand.'

'*What?*' Alice says again.

'Well, look,' Hanna says. 'I know you didn't *actually* have a brush with death, though I thought you had when I heard you'd been hit by a scooter, before I realized that meant a child's toy. But anyway, I wanted to get this off my chest. Dad gave me a bit of money. Before he died. A lot of money, actually. He wrote me a cheque for thirty thousand pounds, and I should have told you, and shared it with you and Michael, but I didn't, and I'm sorry.'

Hearing Hanna apologize is shockingly rare. Just as rare, in fact, as hearing their mother apologize. Generally, Alice thinks, neither one of them ever does apologize. The closest they will come is to say something like, 'I'm sorry you can't see when people are acting in your best interests' (their mother to Hanna), or, 'I'm sorry you feel I'm such a burden' (their mother to Alice), or, 'I'm sorry I'm not perfect, like Saint Alice' (Hanna to their mother). Or, their mother's favourite of all: simply, coldly, 'I'm sorry you feel that way.' Some of these statements might briefly sound like an apology, but they are of course Trojan Horses, non-apologies in the guise of almost-apologies.

'I'm really sorry,' Hanna says again.

'It's OK,' Alice says. 'I already knew about the money.'

This seems to throw Hanna. 'What? How?'

'You told me in the pub after Dad's funeral. You were pretty drunk. We both were.'

She watches the realization dawn on Hanna's face.

'I have no memory of that,' Hanna says. 'I assume you didn't tell Mum, since she's never thrown it in my face?'

'No, I never told her,' Alice says, pleased with herself for this. 'And anyway, I didn't mind. Not at the time, and not now. You were Dad's favourite. The money was meant for your wedding anyway, so it wasn't just a random gift. And I was glad to think you had it later, when you moved out to Malaysia.'

'But I never spent it,' Hanna says eagerly. 'I cashed the cheque – so it would be safe from evil Christina – but then I never touched the money. So we can split it now, between the three of us, which is what should have happened in the first place.'

'Dad wanted you to have it.'

'Who cares what he wanted?' Hanna says. 'He's dead. And he never had good judgement.'

'It's your money,' Alice says.

'It isn't. I don't know why I didn't just share it in the first place. It was stupid. I suppose I never saw us as much of a united front.'

Alice considers this. 'You weren't encouraged to,' she says. 'None of us were. I think Mum took more of a divide-and-conquer approach.'

Hanna nods ruefully. 'Exactly. Anyway, I'm not spending it, so you can receive your share or you can leave it sitting in my savings account forever, untouched.'

Alice hesitates only a moment longer before she says, 'OK. I'll take it.' She wonders what she'll do with the money. It's not enough for a deposit, but she can add it to her own savings, and maybe one day . . . Well, who knows. She could even leave London. There's no law that says she has to stay here. Though what would her mother say?

'Do you think you'll go and live abroad again?' she asks Hanna.

Hanna seems to mull it over. 'Probably not. I mean, it was fun. It was what I needed. But it wasn't real life. In KL, all my friends were other people who worked for the Foreign Office. We'd go out to restaurants in the evenings, travel round different parts of Asia when we had time off, you know. I had a really good time. None of us had any responsibilities outside of work. But I barely knew any Malaysian people. It wasn't like I really *lived* in the country. None of it was real in the end, and after a few years it started to feel wrong. Sort of like an evasion. So –' she shrugs – 'it was time to come home.'

'I'm glad you did.'

Hanna smiles at her – a little sadly, it seems to Alice. 'I know.'

'Mum's glad too,' Alice says. 'I know she doesn't always *show* it exactly, but she has missed you. A lot.'

Hanna smiles again, and this time she definitely looks sad. 'You don't always have to make excuses for her, Alice. It's not your job.'

Alice nods. She doesn't want to push her luck.

'I feel sorry for her really,' Hanna says. 'She'll always be lonely, and she'll always blame other people for it. There's something really wrong with her, I think. But she won't change. I've stopped hoping for it.'

'No,' Alice agrees, 'she probably won't change.'

'It's a shame for her,' Hanna says.

They are both quiet for a moment. Then Hanna says, 'So – do you think we're adults now?'

'Adults?' Alice says, confused by this change in direction. 'I don't know. I mean, we're in our thirties, so I suppose we must be.'

'I always thought I'd *feel* it somehow,' Hanna says musingly, 'becoming an adult. But I feel the same as I always did.'

'Me too.'

'Maybe it just sort of . . . creeps up on you,' Hanna says. She leans back in the chair and crosses her legs. 'Anyway, Alice, I'm glad you're not dead. I would have minded.'

'Thanks,' Alice says, touched.

Lavinia reappears then, carefully holding three cardboard cups.

'This is a fine gathering,' she says.

'We've been doing a proper deathbed scene,' Hanna tells her. 'Clearing our consciences and so on.'

She offers the chair to Lavinia, but Lavinia says, 'I'm happy standing. I prefer it. I'm one of life's standers, probably because I'm too tall. How's the headache, Alice?'

'It's fine,' Alice says. 'I don't think you're too tall. I like your height.' Then she becomes aware of Hanna glancing between them, and feels self-conscious. She is no good at these things.

(But four years and a pandemic later, she will be standing in Hackney Town Hall, in a simple blue dress, getting married. Life can be very surprising, as Hanna has often said. Hanna, eight months pregnant, though she has always said that she doesn't want children – yes, she has surprised them all again – will be their only bridesmaid, with Michael's three-year-old daughter as a flower girl. Michael, bursting with pride in his little girl, will do a reading, and their mother will hold Michael's son, still a baby, possessively on her lap throughout; Olivia misses the wedding, claiming a migraine at the last moment. Lavinia's wider family, several of whom have travelled over from various locations across continental Europe and North America, prove as wildly eccentric as might be imagined. Hanna's sweet, shy boyfriend is subjected to a lively account of the Ottoman–Habsburg wars by one of Lavinia's uncles, complete with re-enactments of crucial scenes.)

'I'm afraid I got you decaf,' Lavinia says now, handing Alice the coffee cup. 'I checked with a nurse and she said best avoid caffeine until tomorrow. And I got you a sandwich and a Mars bar from the shop, in case you get hungry later. Oh, and a bottle of water.' She produces them from her bag and places them on the tray.

'Thank you!' Alice says, moved by Lavinia's thoughtfulness.

Hanna raises her own cup and says, 'Cheers! This is starting to feel like a party. Anybody got a ferret?'

'Alice!' comes a voice from the doorway, and there is Alice's mother, looking pale and harassed. She is clutching her handbag and a cotton tote bag to her side as if she thinks she might get mugged any moment by one of the patients or nurses, and her grey hair is slightly dishevelled. She looks old, Alice thinks suddenly. When did she get so old?

'I'm fine, Mum,' she says, as her mother approaches her bed at speed. 'I'm honestly fine.'

'The bus took too long to come, so I tried to get a cab but I couldn't,' her mother says. She sounds shaky. 'It's these apps nowadays. You can't just get a cab like normal anymore, it all has to be through apps! And I was so frightened for you.'

'I'm completely fine,' Alice says again. 'They're only keeping me in to be extra careful.'

'I feared the worst!' her mother says. Then she seems to see Hanna for the first time. 'Oh,' she says. 'Hanna.'

'Hi,' Hanna says.

Lavinia gives Celia a gentle smile and says, 'Nice to see you again. I'm Lavinia. We met at Hanna's graduation.'

'Hello,' Celia says distractedly. Then, 'Oh yes, Lavinia. Of course I remember you. You lived with Hanna at university, didn't you?'

'That's right. She was very messy.'

'Oh, I'm sure she was!'

'I was not,' Hanna says.

'And I'd better be going,' Lavinia says, with an apologetic glance at Hanna. To Alice, she adds, 'I'll message you later.'

Alice beams at her.

With Lavinia gone, a new constraint seems to fall, as if the three of them are surprised to find themselves alone with one another. It is not the family reunion Alice might have hoped for. She had almost forgotten her surroundings whilst talking to Hanna and Lavinia, but now she feels acutely aware of the other patients on the ward, spectators at this awkward meeting between Hanna and her mother. Of course, they could pull the curtain around the bed, but Alice suspects this action would only draw more attention to them, and in any case those in the nearest beds would still be able to hear every word of their conversation.

Their mother is saying to Hanna, rather stiffly, 'Thank you for ringing me.'

'Of course,' Hanna says. She has got up to offer their mother the chair, and now comes to perch on the edge of the bed next to Alice.

Despite her self-consciousness, Alice is pleased to discover Hanna is staying. Surprised, too.

'What a horrible shock this has been,' their mother says.

'Yes, it must have been,' Alice says.

'Michael sends his love.'

'Oh, that's nice.'

'Now, I've brought you a few things.' Her mother pats the tote bag she's been gripping. 'A toothbrush and toothpaste, some pyjamas – just old ones of mine – and a couple of books. I wasn't sure what to pack, I was in such a state.' She places the bag on the small table by the bed.

'That's great, Mum,' Alice says. 'Thank you.'

'It's quite chilly in here,' her mother says. 'Are you warm enough? I should have brought you a jumper.'

'I'm fine,' Alice says, wishing her mother would speak more quietly. Then she feels guilty for being embarrassed when her mother is clearly upset.

'And they're going to let you out tomorrow morning?' her mother says.

'That's what they told me.'

'How's your head? Does it hurt?'

'Hardly at all.'

'And you're *sure* you're fine?'

'Yes.'

'You don't feel any confusion? Who's the Prime Minister?' her mother says with sudden urgency.

'Tony Blair,' Alice says, 'and things *can* only get better,' but although Hanna laughs, their mother does not.

'What year is it?' she says.

'Twenty eighteen,' Alice says patiently. 'Theresa May's Prime Minister.'

Her mother lets out a breath and seems to be making a conscious effort to relax. 'All right,' she says. 'Of course, I'll come and get you tomorrow morning, to make sure you get home OK. Just let me know when they discharge you.'

'There's no need, Mum,' Alice says. 'I'm fine, really. I'll just get the bus.'

'Get the bus on your own?' her mother says. 'When you're concussed? You might end up in Glasgow!'

Alice accidentally catches Hanna's eye at this point and has to look away quickly so as not to laugh at her expression of bemusement.

'I really dislike those children's scooters,' her mother says. 'I think they're so inconsiderate, the parents who let their children speed along the pavement like that. It was an accident waiting to happen. Perhaps people will finally take note,' she concludes darkly, as if Alice's injury was a painful but necessary sacrifice to the cause of pavement safety. 'And did the child even apologize?'

'I don't know,' Alice says. 'I was unconscious.'

'Well, thank goodness you weren't killed.' For a moment, despite her bluster, she looks like she might start weeping.

'I really am fine,' Alice says, for what feels like the millionth time.

'I wonder if they'll bring you some supper,' her mother says, quickly dashing a tear from her face. She glances around as though she expects waiting staff to appear at any moment.

'Lavinia got me a sandwich,' Alice says.

'That's good. Hospital food isn't very nice. I remember when I was in hospital after having you girls, I used to dread the meals. But they'd be so insistent that I eat.'

'Oh, I don't know,' Hanna says, in her first contribution to the conversation. 'I quite like hospital food.'

There is a short pause, as they are all forced to remember Hanna's stay in hospital.

Alice says quickly, 'But you always enjoyed school lunches too.'

Hanna shrugs. 'What can I say? I prefer my food stodgy and beige. I find it comforting.'

'You liked stodgy food when you were little too,' their mother says. It sounds like an accusation, but Alice suspects that their mother is simply looking for something to say to Hanna.

'Don't all children enjoy stodgy food?' Hanna says neutrally. 'It's not like Alice and Michael were feasting on prosciutto and olives.'

Alice is anxious, because already the conversation seems to be going wrong, and Hanna, whether or not their mother has noticed, is becoming defensive.

'Your favourite food was mashed potato,' their mother tells Hanna, with that strange abruptness that has become more noticeable in her as she gets older. 'And yours, Alice, was macaroni cheese.' Alice has no idea where she's going with this. To Hanna again, their mother continues, 'You used to like having your mashed potato with peas, and you'd mash the peas into the potato and call it a potato cake. And Alice would complain because she didn't like how you squashed the peas and it made your mashed potato look green.'

'It made me feel sick,' Alice says.

'You were lovely children,' their mother says. 'I'll never forget how lovely you were when you were little.'

Alice has heard all this before, of course, her mother's regular refrain. She knows her mother wishes sometimes that they were still young children.

'Well, life was easier then,' Hanna says shortly.

'I don't know if it was though,' Alice says, because she feels she must intervene; she is afraid this might be one of those conversations that lead to an argument out of nowhere. 'I think we just forget when we're older all the hard things about being a child. I remember feeling anxious a lot of the time. It's not always true that children are happier than adults. Even if you had a nice childhood,' she adds hurriedly.

'You were an anxious child,' her mother says. 'You used to worry a lot about other people's feelings. You've always been kind, even when you were very young.'

'That's true,' Hanna says. 'Credit where credit's due.'

'And you, Hanna,' their mother says. Hanna glances up, surprised. '*You* have always been spirited. Since you were little.' Their mother sounds almost angry about it. 'I used to think that if you'd lived in a different time you might have led a revolution.'

Hanna doesn't speak for a few moments. Then she seems to rally and says lightly, 'Troublesome. You mean I was troublesome.'

'Yes,' their mother says. 'You were.'

Hanna smiles slightly and nods, satisfied.

Their mother says, 'But being spirited is not –' she hesitates, then finishes awkwardly – 'is not always a bad quality.'

Hanna is wearing a strange expression, Alice thinks: a mixture of amusement and bewilderment, and something else Alice can't identify. 'Well,' she says after a moment. 'Thanks very much.'

It is evening now; the sky outside the windows at the end of the ward has grown dark.

Their mother says, 'I think it's time I went. Now I know you're all right. I don't want to disturb the others.'

Too late, Alice thinks, reflecting that the rest of the ward now knows all about her overbearing mother and her penchant for macaroni cheese.

'And you're sure you *are* all right, Alice?' her mother says.

'I'm completely fine.'

'Will you text me before you go to sleep?'

'Yes, if I remember.'

'And when you wake up in the morning, and to tell me when to come and meet you?'

'Yes.'

'And in the night, if you can't sleep?'

'Well,' Alice says. 'Maybe.' Definitely not, she thinks.

Their mother nods, still looking unsatisfied. She hoists her handbag up on to her arm.

Hanna gets up off the bed. 'I'd better go as well. Alice, message me tomorrow too. But not before you go to sleep, or during the night. I don't want to be inundated with nuisance messages from you.'

Then her mother kisses her, and Hanna pats her shoulder like Alice is an elderly relative or a sick dog, and Alice watches them walk away. It's nice, she thinks, that Hanna and her mother are leaving together. Though perhaps this simply means they will walk in silence towards the hospital exit, separating as soon as they reach it, pretending not to know each other once Alice is no longer there as a unifying presence. Alice sighs and settles back on her pillows, deciding that she can't worry about this just now.

But when they are nearly at the ward door, she hears her mother say to Hanna, with a formality that sounds rehearsed, 'I haven't had supper yet. Would you like to get a bite to eat somewhere?'

And then Alice can't quite catch the rest because now they are almost out of earshot, but what she thinks Hanna says is, 'Yes, all right.'

ACKNOWLEDGEMENTS

THANK YOU FIRST OF ALL to Caroline Hardman, my agent of many years, for her clear-sighted intelligence, her tenacity, and her integrity. Thank you to Jon Riley, Jasmine Palmer, Elizabeth Masters, Ana McLaughlin, Chris Keith-Wright and the whole team at riverrun for their enthusiasm and general brilliance. It's a pleasure to be published by them. Thank you to Penny Price (once again) for her forensic copy-editing; any errors or inconsistencies were all reintroduced, joyfully, by me.

Thank you to my university friends, who weighed in with great zeal on questions large and small, leading to the Great Headphone Debate of 2021. Thank you to Topes, for patiently answering my questions about toy buying. Thank you to Issy Sudbury, who lived in Kuala Lumpur for three years for the sole purpose of scouting novel locations on my behalf. Thank you to John Maloney for detailed and thoughtful comments on the opening chapter; you are a sensitive and tactful reader, as well as a wonderful friend.

Thank you to my mum and dad for enabling me to complete the edits on this book whilst grappling with a newborn. In recompense for you having to endure my nonsense for more than three decades, I based the parents in this novel on you. Just joking.

Finally, thank you to my husband for meeting chaos with good humour and the necessary levels of resignation. Sorry Chris, but I am the tide, and you are but a feeble Canute. And thank you as well to our baby, who didn't actually lend much practical assistance, but is admittedly very cute. I was going to say that her only contribution was bashing at my keyboard and spilling my tea, but then that could also describe my own work process, so people in glass houses, etc.